Elaina walks the reader through the long life of a woman wounded as a child, betrayed as a young woman, and matured through reconciliation, her faith restored through love.

Kary Oberbrunner,
author of *Your Secret Name*,
The Deeper Path, and *Day Job to Dream Job*

Elaina

Other Books by Faye Bryant

Novels
Grandma, Mom, and Me Saga
Louise
Elaina
Beth (2020)

Non-Fiction
Ramblings from the Shower |
Integrity, Faith, and Other Simple Yet Slippery Issues

Coffee, Bible, Journal:
Musings from the Comfy Chair with a View

Elaina

FAYE BRYANT

Powell, Ohio

Printed in the United States of America

Published by Author Academy Elite
P.O. Box 43, Powell, OH 43035

www.AuthorAcademyElite.com

Paperback ISBN-13: 978-1-64085-749-0
Hardcover ISBN-13: 978-1-64085-750-6
Ebook ISBN-13: 978-1-64085-751-3

Library of Congress Control Number: 2019908359

Chapter 1

"Daddy!" the chubby, raven-haired girl squealed as Dutch Drew walked through the back door of the wooden clapboard house.

He thought to himself, *I'll never get tired of hearing that little girl's voice calling me that. I love my boys, but my little girl is somethin' extra special.*

Scooping his daughter up from the floor amid her giggles, he walked to the stove where his pregnant wife was stirring something in a large cast iron pot. He leaned in and planted a kiss on her flushed cheek.

"How's the prettiest woman in all of Arkansas doin' this afternoon?"

"I don't know about her, but this woman is tired and hot." Louise sat down on the bench at the kitchen table.

Looking at his daughter Dutch said, "I think your mama is the prettiest girl ever; what about you, Sis?" calling Elaina by his pet name for her.

"Mama pretty," the almost-three-year-old stated, nodding her head.

"There you have it, Mrs. Drew. You are definitely the prettiest woman in all the world, not just Arkansas." Dutch sat in the chair at the end of the table, bouncing Elaina on his knee.

Dutch and Louise had three sons. Alec was fifteen now, smart as a whip and always tinkering with things. Harland Clement, Dutch's namesake, was thirteen and a quiet, compassionate soul. He was just a boy but he would listen to anyone, whether child or adult, share their dreams and feelings all day long. Seth, at nine years old, was the baby boy. He was never still. Always playing and running, it never mattered if he had a playmate or not.

They'd lost a little boy two years ago. He'd only lived one day. That liked to have broken Louise's heart. The three boys they had were good boys, kind and helpful and mostly obedient. Then along came Elaina. When she arrived, Dutch lost his heart to the hazel-eyed girl. Not quite three, she was already trying to keep up with her brothers. She had a doll but was just as happy chasing after Seth, even trying to climb up in the barn loft after him. It was a sight to see her try to scramble up the ladder.

Now, Louise was pregnant again. She swore up and down that it felt like she was carrying another girl, but he would have to just wait and let the doctor show him. He knew that, whether it was another little honey like Sis or another rough-and-tumble boy, they would love this one as much as all the others.

It was a typically hot August day in Northeast Arkansas. Louise was staying close to the house, choosing to enjoy whatever breezes would blow through her simple home. She was sitting in her favorite rocking chair as Elaina played on the floor.

Being large in pregnancy in August was rough. She felt the grip of another contraction.

"Mama? You 'kay?" Though not quite three, Elaina had noticed the pain flash across her mother's face.

"I'm fine, sweet girl. I'm just fine." She patted her daughter's head. "It might be a good idea if you'd holler for your daddy, though. I think we're gon' have a baby today."

"Yay, Mama!" The little girl skipped merrily through the house to the back porch, where she started yelling for her father. "Daddy! Daddy! Mama says come!"

Louise chuckled hearing the singsong. After the loss of her last son, she remained worried about this one. She knew that Dutch was keeping his ear attuned to the house, awaiting the sounds of this moment. It didn't take long before she heard his boots thudding on the back porch. She leaned back in her chair, gently rubbing her belly.

"Daddy's here, Mama!" cried the little girl, riding in her father's arms. "I brung him!"

Louise laughed, and nodded at her husband. "You might want to get Mother here, Dutch. I think we're about to have this baby."

"Do you want me to get Doc Lancaster?"

"No, I don' think so. Mother will be able to handle anything that comes along. She's about as good as any midwife comin' and goin'."

"All right. I'll head on over right now. Don' you be givin' birth till we get back, hear me? Miss Elaina?" He sat his daughter on the floor.

"Yes, Daddy?" She looked up at him solemnly, her hands clasped in front of her.

"I want you to stay right here by your mama and do whatever she tells you to. One of your brothers should be here from school soon. You just hold Mama's hand and love on her. Okay?"

"Yes, Daddy! I do that!"

Dutch leaned over and kissed his wife then raced out the back, the screen door's slap signaling his rapid departure. Louise heard him slapping reins on the mule's back. Riding over the hills was much faster than around the roads. Her father would drive Mother here with all the necessary midwife tools. She leaned her head back as another contraction took hold.

The next day Elaina was standing beside the bed, looking at the new baby girl lying there. Agnes Ann was so tiny, with jet-black hair and ivory skin.

"I hold her, Mama?" Elaina asked.

"Well, I don't know, Miss 'Laina. You're mighty small yet."

"I careful, Mama!"

"How about you come up here and sit with me, and you can hold her on your lap."

The words were barely out of Louise's mouth before the toddler had scrambled onto the bed.

"Whoa there, Sis! Be careful. Your sister is ..." Louise searched for a word Elaina would understand. "... breakable."

The little girl's eyes grew wide. Louise was sure she was thinking about the canning jar she had dropped a few weeks before. Dutch had lifted her high up away from the shattered glass, but not before she had seen how the container was broken beyond use.

"Break-a-ble?" Elaina sounded out the word. "Like jar I drop-ded?"

"Sorta like, dear. Here, let me show you how to hold her."

Louise cradled the baby as Elaina settled in next to her on the bed. The child's legs were straight out in front of her.

"Now hold your arms out like you're gonna carry wood in."

Elaina held her arms out like she did when Daddy was going to put a piece of wood on them for her to carry inside. "Like this, Mama?"

"Yes, ma'am. Now I'll lay Agnes Ann across your arms and you cradle her like I do. Do you see?"

"Yes, Mama."

Once Louise was satisfied with how her daughter was holding her new sister she leaned back and relaxed, watching and listening as Elaina cooed and talked to her new sister.

"Agnes! You so pretty! Your hair is black as mine." The baby smiled slightly and Elaina squealed. "Mama! She smiled at me!"

"She sure did, 'Laina. She already knows your voice and loves you."

"She does?" The little girl's eyes went wide.

"Sure she does. She's heard you talking the whole time I was carryin' her. Remember all those times you'd be sitting on the stool, watching me cook, and we'd talk?"

"Yes, Mama."

"She heard you then. And those times when I would read you a storybook?"

"Yes'm."

"She heard you then. She recognizes you and her smile says so."

"Wow, Mama!"

Elaina went on to talk to her sister, explaining who everyone in their family was.

"You love Daddy, Agnes, he the best. Alec is so smart, cain't fool him at all." She shook her head for emphasis. "Clement so nice. Him help Mama and Daddy, him help you." Elaina looked at her mother, noting her eyes were closed. "Don't tell, but Brother Seth is my favorite. Him fun!"

Louise smiled, keeping her eyes closed as Elaina chatted with Agnes, imparting her vast nearly-three-year-old wisdom with her baby sister.

5

Two years later, in mid-December, the scene repeated itself. Except Agnes was the little girl on the bed next to Louise, while five-year-old Elaina flitted around them.

"Agnes, be careful! Cherilyn can break! And don' push on her head, it will go right through to her brain. Be careful!" the bustling little mama fussed.

Louise grabbed her oldest daughter's hand. "It's all right, Elaina. I'll watch her close. Would you go and get me a glass of water? I'd sure love that."

"Yes, Mama!" she cried, and she raced across the wood floors on bare feet to get a glass of water for her mother.

Four years passed before Varina Kate was born. Elaina was now nine years old, and a great help around the house. When Louise went into labor this time, Elaina knew just what to do. As soon as her oldest brother had headed off over the hill to get their grandmother, she began the preparations for supper. Louise could hear her drawing water and the familiar splashes as potatoes were dropped in it. Before long the smells of ham and green beans, potatoes, and cornbread filled the little house. Louise knew her family would be well taken care of as she delivered this little one.

Holding her newborn, Louise looked at the expectant face of Cherilyn. Agnes was explaining to the little girl how she had held her when she was a newborn, sitting on the bed next to Mama.

"Can I do that, Mama?" Cherilyn asked.

"Of course you can." Louise patted the bed beside her as she cradled Kate.

"You have to be careful, Cherilyn. Kate can break. And don' be pushin' on that dent in her head, you can hurt her brain!" Agnes said as she helped her sister onto the bed.

Louise stifled the laugh that bubbled forth, recalling how the two older girls had discussed these very things, each in their own turn.

Chapter 2

Elaina could barely remember life without her sisters. She didn't really remember when Agnes was born since she wasn't even three when that happened, but she was five when Cherilyn showed up. Since Mama and Daddy had waited another four years after that, she was nine when Kate came along.

The other girls were more girlie. Oh, they played rough with the boys sometimes, but they seemed to prefer to play house and make pies and nurse their baby dolls more than climbing trees and fishing. Elaina preferred going with her brothers to have fun with them. Those days when Daddy would let her help him were the best of all.

She loved it when he would hitch up a team and lay blankets across the drag harrow. She always knew that meant she could go with him. She would get right on top of the blankets and ride over the clods of dirt, helping to break them up.

Daddy taught her how to use the hoe right so she didn't cut down the delicate cotton seedlings. It was their cash crop, so every plant was important. She had learned how to pick cotton when she was just four, dragging a cotton poke Daddy had made specially for her. She didn't like the hot and dusty work, but as long as Daddy said she could do it she would work till he said stop.

In her eyes, Dutch Drew hung the moon; no one could tell her any different and she knew he loved her extra special, too. Her brother Seth ran a close second to Daddy. He always watched out for her, keeping her from stepping in yellow jacket nests and from sassing her parents. Seth would take her to the creek to fish, using rolled up bits of biscuits from the breakfast table as bait. Some days they would bring home a bounty for supper. Other days, it was just a grand time sitting and talking. Elaina loved that her brother took time with her.

Once the cotton was in the ground and growing was her favorite time because the whole family took a big fishing trip. She loved hearing the words, "We're going to White Bluff tomorrow." That meant that by daybreak the wagons would be packed, the fishing poles readied, the canvas gathered, and the fun would begin. The ride over to White Bluff was the hardest part of the day, because three hours was so long to wait when one was excited.

She loved how everyone worked together to set up the wagons and make camp. The women set up the kitchen area, while the men made sure the horses and mules were tied off with long ropes in a grassy patch. They brought a half barrel into which they poured water from the river so the animals could drink.

Everyone kept an eye on the little children and each other. Elaina never went deep in the water because she didn't know how to swim, but she enjoyed putting her feet in to cool off.

She and her brothers would splash each other, trying to see who would get the wettest.

Ever since she could remember, Elaina had been amazed at how they would get their fishing worms. In all the stories in the books at school, they were always digging them up from the ground. Not the Drews and Raffertys. They shook trees. Her mama, grandma, and aunts would hold their aprons open while the men and older boys would shake the big branches on the Catawba trees. The black and pale yellow segmented worms that were clinging to the bottom of the large heart-shaped leaves of the trees that shaded their camping area would fall into the waiting cloth. Before long the aprons were full of the caterpillar-type creatures. Daddy had a special box in which to store their bait. He'd add a few leaves from the tree in there, and they'd have all the worms they needed. Sometimes the worms were so big they could cut them into several pieces to lure the catfish, bream, and crappie that loved them.

The men and boys, and sometimes the girls, would bait hooks and fish through the morning while the women sat in their rocking chairs, talking and watching after the babies. Lunch was always a picnic of bread, cured ham, and cheese brought from home. The thick and hearty sandwiches filled everyone up.

Early in the afternoon, just as the temperature was getting really hot and the younger children started to complain, Dutch called off the fishing. Their catch had been slid down stringers and tied off to a tree. Each stringer was long enough to lead out into the water so that the fish remained fresh for the afternoon.

"Swimmin' time!" Dutch called.

It took mere moments for britches to be rolled up. Every child had worn their play clothes to fish in and to wear when they got into the water. Their mothers had also made sure each had an extra set of clothes. Most of the time, though, on these trips everyone just stayed in the clothes they came in.

Washin' up in the river or a pan of water was good enough for camping.

Everyone, even Grandpa Jerry, got in the water. The little girls giggled at the way he pretended to fall, and how he hollered like he was going to get them all soaking wet. The day was full of laughter and fun, and for those few days life seemed so easy.

After a while, the mothers called their children out of the water for naps. Quilts were spread across the grass under the shade of the tall oaks and maples, and children laid out; some not wanting to take a nap, but every one of them doing so. Even the young men leaned against wagons or trees and dozed. Mamas rocked and smiled at their brood, enjoying the time off from regular life before they too drifted off to doze as soft breezes kept the summer heat at bay.

Later, as the sun dipped toward the horizon, the menfolk pulled the fish up out of the water and worked together to clean them in preparation for frying. They used the tailgate of Grandpa Jerry's wagon as a table to clean them on. Soon, the aroma of potatoes and fish frying on an open fire wafted on the breeze. Every child and adult could feel a tummy rumble begin. It wasn't long before everyone was gathered around the fire, plates piled high with fish and potatoes and hush puppies.

"Hoo-wee, Louise. That was some mighty fine eatin'!" Dutch proclaimed, patting his belly.

"Yep," Grandpa Jerry agreed.

"Mama, you and Grandma did extra good!" Clement stated.

In turn, everyone declared their gratitude for the ladies who had prepared their meal. The girls set about cleaning up. Seth and Clement went to the river and brought up buckets filled with water, pouring it into metal dish pans they set next to the fire. Once it was heated, the pans were set off the fire and the girls went to work washing plates and silverware. Elaina washed, Alec's wife Jodie rinsed, and Agnes dried. Louise oversaw the process, making sure the dishes were stacked up, covered, and ready for the next meal.

The evening was a time Elaina dearly loved, when everyone sat around the fire telling stories. Some of the stories she'd heard a hundred times, but they were the stories of her family and she loved every one.

Like usual Grandpa told about the trip from Illinois to Arkansas, and how his beloved Shana had been snake-bit. Elaina saw her mother's eyes fill with tears for the only mother she'd ever known growing up. Her own mother had died when she was just a year old.

The funny thing about Grandpa's tale of the trip from up north was, there were monsters everywhere and trolls under bridges and all sorts of adventure. Elaina noticed he would wink at her mother when he told about those things, and she began to understand he was telling the stories to entertain the children. *It works*, she thought.

Then Grandpa launched into the story of how he met Grandma Freda, and how he courted her until she caved in and married him and started having more children. Some of their aunts and uncles seemed more like cousins because they grew up together.

After almost a week of living like pioneers without homes the family packed up and left their camp at White Bluff and made their way back to Hilltop, and regular farm life resumed.

Chapter 3

"Elaina, get me my Bible," Dutch said, wiping his face as Agnes carried his plate to the sink.

"Yes, Daddy" Elaina replied as she walked into the living room. She knew Daddy's Bible sat on the little table between his and Mama's chairs. She carried it back to him, then helped clear the rest of the dishes from the table.

"I saw somethin' in here this morning when I was readin' that kinda made me chuckle. It's like God knew what farmin' in the hills of the Ozarks was like. Let me see if I can find it." He thumbed through the pages, then ran his finger down the page until he got to the verse he was talking about. "Here we go. It's Psalms 65, verse 9 and followin'.

"'*Thou visitest the earth, and waterest it: thou greatly enrichest it with the river of God, which is full of water: thou preparest them corn, when thou has so provided for it. Thou waterest the ridges thereof abundantly: thou settlest the furrows thereof: thou makest it soft with showers: thou blessed the springing thereof. Thou crownest the year with thy goodness; and thy paths drop fatness. They drop upon the pastures of the wilderness: and the little hills rejoice on every side. The pastures are clothed with flocks; the valleys also are covered over with corn; they shout for joy, they also sing.'*

"Now, ain't that just a picture of how the Lord takes care of our farms?"

Louise nodded. "It sure 'nough does. I wonder why I haven't ever noticed that!"

"I hadn't really paid attention before. The words really just raised up off the page to me today. I figure the Good Lord is tryin' to show me somethin', I jus' don't know what it is."

"I think God just shows us stuff like that at the right time we're gon' need it, Daddy. Least that's what the preacher said a few weeks ago," Seth replied thoughtfully.

"You're probably right, Seth" his father said. "I think we're gon' pray that all this is true for the Drew farm this year—that we have the rain we need at the right time, that our harvest is plentiful, and that we're all healthy enough to pick when it's all ready."

"I think that's a fine idea, Daddy," Clem replied. "I reckon we should start now, shouldn't we?"

"I think you're right, son. Do you want to lead us tonight? We can take turns every night after supper."

"Yes, sir. I'll pray."

The family bowed their heads, though Louise had to snap her fingers a couple of times to keep Agnes and Cherilyn from wiggling. When the prayer was finished, she said, "All right, girls. Go wash those faces and get your nightgowns on. It's almost time for bed."

"Aw, Mama!" the girls whined in unison.

"Scoot!" she said as she pointed toward their room.

Elaina sat down on the floor next to her father's chair and leaned her head on his knee. "Daddy, I love our family! I want us to always be like this."

Dutch patted her head. "Me too, Sis. Me too."

That next Sunday, when the preacher finished his sermon he asked if anyone wanted to know how to get to Heaven to please come to the altar. Elaina made her way to the altar. The preacher waved to his wife, who knelt beside the girl.

"Elaina, do you want to go to Heaven?" the lady asked quietly.

"Yes, ma'am. I do."

"Good. Let's go over what it takes to get there."

Elaina nodded, and listened as the pastor's wife explained how Jesus was God's only Son, that He had come to the world as a baby, and grew up never committing a sin. She said that even though He had never done wrong, He was crucified like a criminal.

"Oh, my! That's horrible!" the girl whispered back. She had heard the Bible story about Easter and knew it came out all right, but she let this godly woman further explain so she would fully understand the way to Heaven.

"When Jesus hung on the cross, He was carrying all the sins of everyone on earth forever. Even though we were thousands of years into the future, all our sins were on Him, too."

Elaina's eyes grew wide. "You mean when I've smarted off to Mama, He carried that?"

"Yes, dear. He did."

"Okay," she said thoughtfully, "how does that get me to Heaven?"

"Well His crucifixion, burial, and resurrection for our salvation is a gift from God to us. But a gift is no good to us until we accept it and unwrap it, right?"

"Right."

"All you have to do to be saved, Elaina, is accept this gift of Jesus' sacrifice for you. Once you've opened it, you start living for Him."

"That's all?"

"That's all. You choose to change your path from the sinful one you're on now, to following Jesus and begin to live for Him."

"I don't think I'm really all that sinful, though."

"I understand, but God says that we're born sinful. And you know, if He said it it's truth."

"Yes, ma'am." Elaina's face reddened as she remembered times she had been harsh to her sisters and had told a fib or two. "I want to accept His gift."

The pastor's wife explained that she needed to decide about changing her path of sinfulness and to choose to follow Jesus in word and deed. Once she decided that, she needed to pray and tell God that.

"Can I do that now?" Elaina asked.

"You certainly can."

The girl plunged right in. "Dear God. I guess I'm a sinner. You said so. I know that Jesus died for my sins and He rose again for my salvation. I want to be different, God. I want to follow Jesus. I want to go to Heaven. Save me, please. Amen."

The preacher's wife looked up at her husband and smiled. He led the congregation through the last bars of 'Just as I Am' then stopped the song.

His wife and Elaina stood from the altar as he said, "Folks, we have a new sister in Christ! Miss Elaina Drew has accepted Jesus as her Savior!"

Louise and Dutch walked to their daughter and hugged her tight. When the closing prayer was said, everyone lined up to welcome the pretty dark-haired girl into the family of God.

Chapter 4

A little more than two weeks after her tenth birthday, Elaina's world changed forever. She was at school that Monday afternoon. It was a sunny day for a January, and even though the ground was dusted with snow and the air was crisp Teacher had let all the children go outside for recess. Elaina was jumping rope with her friends. She could see her brother, Seth, playing catch with some of the boys.

Her arm was arched upward, looping the jump rope up for the girl who was jumping, when she saw Seth drop to the ground. He didn't move. Elaina screamed, and dropped the rope. Running to Seth she fell to her knees and gathered him up in her arms, drawing him against her.

"Seth! Seth!" she repeated, willing him to open his eyes and talk to her. "Help me! Someone! Help!" she cried, laying her hand on his chest, hoping to feel the strong heart inside beating.

There was no strong heartbeat like she knew he should have. She could barely feel a flutter. By now her sister Agnes stood beside her, her finger pressed at the corner of her mouth, her dark eyes wide with fear.

"What's wrong, 'Laina?" Agnes asked.

"I don't know, Agnes. Where's Teacher?" She looked around frantically.

"She's gettin' some boys to go get Mama and Daddy." Agnes whimpered.

Elaina rocked back and forth, softly humming hymns she and her brother would sing at church. She looked up at Agnes and said, "Go on inside, Agnes. Get warm. Daddy will be here soon enough. He'll make everything right. You just go on inside, your teeth are chattering."

"Yours are, too, 'Laina!" the little girl whined.

"I know. I'm just gon' stay here with Seth. You go on in." Agnes leaned to hug her and they held each other tight for the briefest moment, then the younger girl went inside the schoolhouse.

Elaina's heart was breaking. She knew her brother was gone. She just couldn't believe it. He was playing and having fun one minute, and the next he was just gone.

When Dutch ran across the schoolyard she was sitting with her head bowed over her brother's, whispering to him even though she knew he couldn't hear her.

"'Laina?" Her father's voice. "'Laina?" She felt his hands strong on her shoulders.

"Daddy, I-I couldn't help him," she stammered. "He was gone so quick."

Several of Seth's friends were gathered around, and Dutch said softly to his daughter, "Come on, 'Laina. We're gon' let these strong young men put Seth in Papa's pickup truck so's we can take him to see the doctor." Her eyes drifted to see her father's father standing beside his truck.

"But, Daddy, he's—" Her voice faltered.

"Shh, Sis. I know. We need to take him to the doctor right away."

It didn't make sense to her, this taking her brother to the doctor when he was clearly not sick, but she lay his head back on the ground and stood up beside her father. Hand in hand they watched the boys carefully lift Seth and carry him to the pickup truck, where the teacher had laid a blanket. Elaina ran to the schoolroom and called for Agnes to come on, they had to go.

"You girls go on. I'll keep your school books and papers for you. Go on. Your family needs you now," the teacher said soothingly as she hugged each girl.

The girls climbed into the seat of the truck between their father and Papa, while the boys sat in the bed of the truck with their friend—not a single one of them unwilling to go with the Drew family.

Agnes wept softly and Elaina stared silently out the window as Dutch drove the six miles to the hospital at Stafford. The teens in the back didn't seem to notice the cold, though they did turn their backs to the wind.

As soon as the truck stopped at the hospital, the boys jumped out of the bed of the old truck and carefully lifted their friend from it. They carried him inside, where they placed him on a rolling stretcher and nurses took him away. They all stood in the lobby, faces ashen, their lives changed in that sudden, startling blink of an eye. Shifting from one foot to the next, sliding their hands into and out of their pockets, they waited alongside Seth's sisters and grandfather.

Dutch had followed the stretcher through the swinging doors leading to the doctoring area of the little county hospital. He had told Elaina to take care of her little sister, and the boys had, one and all, taken it upon themselves to stay there to watch over the girls and their Papa.

The minutes crept by with little noise in the tiny lobby. The boys talked quietly, the girls wept some. The sense of loss hung heavy, like an unyielding entity in the room. Papa paced from window to window, staring outside, sadness etched on his kind face.

The creak of the door slowly swinging open filled the room like a firecracker. Dutch walked through, his shoulders slumped, his head hung low. The boys encircled him as his daughters ran to embrace him.

"Mr. Drew, it just don't make sense," one boy said.

"You're right, son. It don't make a lick of sense, but it's what is. Our Seth has gone on to Heaven." Dutch patted the boy on the back.

Each young man shared a word with the grieving father, shook the grandfather's hand, and gave a hug to the two girls.

"Let's go, boys and girls. Mr. Lloyd is coming to pick Seth up to take him on to Russell's. The doctors and nurses will take care of him until then. Dad will drive you boys on back to the school before we go home."

"No, sir, Mr. Drew. We want - if it's all right with you, we want to go to your house. We had Teacher to send word to our folks that we would be going there. Me and the boys have talked, and we want to help y'all best we can."

Dutch spoke sadly, "That's mighty nice of you boys. I don't want y'all gettin' in any trouble."

"No, sir. We won't," another boy spoke up. "I told my sister to tell our mama and daddy. That means everyone in the county knows I won't be home for a while." Muffled chuckles hung in the still air.

"All right, then. You boys pile up in the back and pull that blanket up over you to block the wind. We'll go slow to keep from freezin' your noses off. Girls, y'all get back in with me and Papa. Here, here, wipe your noses before we go. Your mama is goin' to be mighty sorrowful, we don't need for her to have to wipe runny noses, too, now do we?" He handed his handkerchief to Agnes who then shared it with her big sister, both girls striving to put on a smile. "There we go. Let's get on home, now."

Dutch led the way to the truck, getting his girls settled in the seat. Elaina watched him step away from the truck for a moment and take a deep breath before he got in. She thought that the way he sat down seemed like the very life had been taken out of him.

When Dutch pulled the truck into the driveway at their little wooden house, he turned it off and admonished the girls to stay put for a few minutes. He nodded at his father, both men understanding this horrible task. "I want to tell your mama before y'all come in. I'm thinkin' she already knows, but let's make it a little easier on her hearin' this bad news, okay?"

"Yes, Daddy," the girls chimed.

Elaina watched him walk up the steps to the house, his shoulders sagging. She took Agnes' hand in hers.

"We've gotta be strong for Mama and Daddy," she said.

"I don't know how to do that, 'Laina," Agnes replied.

"Me neither, Agnes. I guess we have to be extra good. You know, not pick on each other or Cherilyn. That might make it easier on them." Elaina smiled wanly.

Agnes nodded. The two girls and their grandfather sat silently for a few more minutes until their brother Clement drove into the yard. They watched him dash through the front door.

"I reckon we can go on in," Elaina said. Papa nodded and got out of the truck.

"I imagine it's all right." Agnes' voice was thin and fragile. Elaina slipped her arm around her sister and held her close. The dams behind which their tears had been held burst. Both girls wept great gulping tears, their bodies shaking at the enormity of their grief.

"Oh, 'Laina! What are we going to do?"

"I don't know, Agnes. I think we need to go on in, though." Elaina looked at her younger sister and used her sweater sleeve to wipe away the vestiges of little-girl grief. "Now, wave your fingers in front of your eyes when we get out so's they don't seem so red when we go in," she admonished, beginning to do the same.

Having waited for his granddaughters' tears to subside, knowing they needed the respite alone, Lane Drew opened the door of the truck and ushered the two grief-stricken girls to the front door.

Elaina and Agnes slipped quietly into the front room, hearing their parents explaining to Clement what had happened. Clement, the strong, quiet brother, erupted in cries of anguish. His deep sorrow was evident.

Chapter 5

Elaina sat on the little chair near the front door, the one she would always toss her sweater on when she arrived home from school. The one her mother fussed at her often for doing so. It was the chair saved for guests, but she felt like a guest in the house today—like she didn't belong. Not because she wasn't being seen to, but because home was different now. Her Seth wasn't going to be here anymore.

Seth had been the one who held her hand when she first went to school. He was the one who had made sure she had a good place to sit. He was the one who made sure the other kids didn't pick on her. He was the one who looked out for her, helped her pick cotton and corn and soybeans. He was the one person, other than Daddy, whom she felt really loved her. And he wasn't going to ever be there for her again.

Elaina's eyes filled with tears again until she heard sounds outside. She quickly realized it was the boys, the friends of Seth who had come with them to the hospital. They were chopping wood and feeding the animals. They were doing what they knew the family wasn't thinking about getting done now. She saw one of them, Seth's best friend Joe, step in from the back porch and speak quietly to Daddy. Daddy spoke with him a bit, and then the boy bounded back outside. She heard Papa's truck start up and she stepped out onto the front porch.

He's moving Papa's truck, she realized. *And now they're moving Clement's car. I reckon we're gon' have more folks comin' and needin' a place to park.*

In moments the boys had cleared the driveway and the front yard. There was no longer any snow to be seen in the Drew yard. Now people who came would be able to see where they could safely park their cars and trucks. The boys came back up on the front porch, giving Elaina a little pat on her arm.

Joe stopped, "'Laina, I'm so sorry. I loved him like he was my brother."

"He thought you were pretty special, Joe. You boys were like twins."

He laughed. "Sometimes our mamas thought we were. Hey, you okay?"

"I reckon I will be," the ten-year-old replied.

"Listen, I know how Seth looked out for you. Don't tell nobody, but I knew you were his favorite sister. He liked the other girls fine, but you were extra special to him."

"Oh!" Elaina gasped, her eyes sparkling with fresh, unshed tears.

"I'll keep an eye out for you from now on, 'Laina. I can't be Seth, but I'll do my best to take up the slack. If you have any problems you holler for ol' Joe, you hear?"

"Thank you, Joe. I will," Elaina replied dully as they walked into the living room.

It wasn't long before the boys went to their homes, having done all they could for the Drews. Elaina found her mother in the kitchen and hugged her tightly.

"Mama, I couldn't do..." Her voice caught.

"Shh, child. Of course you couldn't. The Good Lord called and our Seth had to go on. We don't understand. I don't know how we *could* understand." Her own voice faltered and she kissed her daughter's black hair.

"Let's get these counters cleared, 'Laina. People will be bringing stuff in soon and we want to have room for it."

Elaina sniffled, "Yes, Mama" and they set to work making sure all the dishes were put away in the cabinets and all things that might trip somebody up were stowed away under shelves. Louise stood in the middle of the room, turning slowly, looking high and low to be sure she was ready for other women to come in and take over her kitchen.

"I think that will do, Sis. Now, when ladies come in with food you bring them right in here. Let's be sure and put any drinks over here by the sink, that way if tea or lemonade gets spilled it won't make everything sticky." She wrinkled her nose and Elaina giggled in spite of herself. "Have them put any pots of soup on the stove, but be sure to leave this one burner for the coffee pot. We'll have to keep that goin' for folks." She whirled around to the cabinet above the stove. "Do we have coffee? Oh, dear. We may have to get some more."

"Mama, we can get Clem to go to the store," Elaina said, hating the frantic look on her mother's face.

"Yes, yes. We'll do that."

"Mama, why don't you go on and sit down. When folks come, they're gon' want to see you and Daddy. I can stay in here and make sure everything is done. I reckon if Jodie comes she'll be able to take over, but until she does I'll do it." Elaina suddenly seemed old beyond her years.

Lightly kissing her daughter's forehead, Louise answered, "You're growing up too fast on me, Elaina. I never wanted this. I know what it's like to have to be a grownup too young, and I wanted you to be a little girl until you had to become a woman. This will only be for a little bit, though. We'll get through these next few days together and you'll be able to just be the little girl you are. I love you, Sis." She then turned and walked into the living room to greet her parents as they came in the door.

Grandma Freda walked into the kitchen, her eyes quickly taking in the cleared counters ready for visitors, and boomed, "Well, Miz Elaina, do we have a pot of coffee cookin' yet?" Turning back to the door, she called, "Jerry! Bring that pot of soup on in here! I want to get it on the stove." She winked at her granddaughter.

Elaina bustled to get water pumped into the coffee pot, added the grounds, and stoked up the fire to get it cooking. Her grandmother easily took the reins of taking in food and drink, brought to help the grieving family in true Southern fashion. Alec and his wife Jodie arrived soon after. Alec had left work as soon as he'd gotten word about his brother. Seeing Freda had control of the kitchen Jodie slipped into the girls' room and closed the door, turning it into a play world to occupy the little girls.

Neighbors came and went till well after dark, some sitting with the family for a time, others just stopping by to drop off food and share their sorrow. Elaina acted as Grandma's assistant, wearing one of her mother's aprons and guiding friends to place their offerings on table or counter.

Grandma declared it was time for Dutch and Louise to have some supper, and she insisted that they come into the kitchen to do so. No one argued with Grandma Freda much, not even Grandpa, so they moved into the kitchen, sitting around the family table. No one sat in Seth's usual spot. It just didn't seem right. It was a sorrowful night to be sure, but the family was together. And that in itself lent strength and peace.

Elaina stayed at home the next day, taking care of her sisters while her brothers went to work and her parents went to talk to the undertaker. It was cold outside, but she and Agnes bundled up Cherilyn and Kate and went for a walk. Being outside seemed to help lighten everyone's mood. Elaina thought to herself, *Poor Kate, she won't ever know Seth. She's not even old enough to notice he's gone.*

When they returned to the house Elaina made some hot cocoa and the girls had a tea party with it, enjoying some cookies their teacher had dropped off the evening before.

"Okay, Miss Cherilyn, I think it's time for your nap, isn't it?" Elaina announced.

"No, is not," Cherilyn retorted, her hands sassily propped on her hips.

"But I need for you to lie down with Kate," Elaina admonished, pouting. "Kate needs her nap, she's so little."

Cherilyn relented, and slipped under the covers in the bed she shared with Agnes as Elaina placed Kate in the crib.

"Agnes, do you want to take a nap, too? I thought I saw you rubbing your eyes a minute ago."

"No, 'Laina. I'm not sleepy." This was said even as she yawned.

"Agnes lay down with me!" Cherilyn cajoled.

"See there? Cherilyn wants you to lie down with her." Leaning in to whisper, she encouraged, "Maybe if you lie down with her, she'll actually take a nap."

Sighing, Agnes looked at Cherilyn. "Well, scoot over. I can't get in if you're in the way!"

Soon all three girls were asleep, and Elaina waited on the couch for her parents. When she heard the truck pull into the driveway, she put on her sweater and slipped quietly out the front door and down the steps.

"Hey, Mama. Hey, Daddy," she greeted softly.

"Where are the girls?" her mother asked.

"They're lyin' down, takin' naps," she replied.

"All of them?"

"Yes, ma'am. Agnes was tired, too, and I told her that if she would lie down Cherilyn would go to sleep. And I told Cherilyn that Kate needed her to take a nap now so she laid down, too."

"My smart girl!" Dutch declared, beaming.

"When are we going to—" Elaina choked, unable to finish her question.

"Day after tomorrow, Sis," her father replied. "Thursday afternoon. We'll meet out at the Sunnyvale church where the preacher will say a few words, then we'll bury him there in the plot we bought." Shaking his head, he lamented, "Sis, it's just not right to be buryin' our boy out there before we go in the ground." His voice was gruff with unshed tears.

Louise wept softly at his words and he draped his arm across her shoulders. "Come on, girls, let's go inside and get out of the cold. I might need me a cup of coffee and some of that cake Grandma Freda made."

Chapter 6

Thursday was a dreary day. It was as if the heavens wept for Seth along with the family. The family sat in the front pew of the church on the hill. The pastor of Sunnyvale said a few words, then let their preacher from Pilgrim's Rest speak. He had known Seth since he was a baby and told about that one particular Sunday when he had gone to the altar and gave his life to Jesus. He mentioned seeing him courtin' several different girls the last few years, though none of them seemed really serious. He recalled how it didn't matter what anyone needed, they had only to ask and Seth was right there to pitch in and help. He said that Seth was a born leader and had made his mama and daddy proud.

Six of Seth's friends lined up around his coffin and carried him down the gravel road, deep into the cemetery where they'd helped dig the grave. They placed the pine box on the boards across the hole. The preacher spoke a few more words as family and friends gathered around. Elaina looked at the people around her, family who had known Seth all his life, friends he'd grown up with, church folks and neighbors. It seemed like everyone from the Hilltop community had come out to honor the laying to rest of her brother.

After the preacher finished, four of the boys each grabbed an end of the ropes that had been laid across the grave with the boards. They lifted the coffin and the other two boys pulled the boards out of the way. Slowly the four began lowering the coffin bearing their friend's body, working to keep it level.

Elaina kept her tears in check until she heard the sound of the dirt clods her mother dropped hitting the wooden lid of the coffin. She knew that everyone circled around that grave heard her gasp and saw her tears, but she couldn't help it. She felt Agnes' arm slip around her waist and dropped hers to Agnes' shoulders. Her parents urged her and the other children to walk back up to the road where they waited while their friends filled in the grave, saying their final good-byes to the boy they'd all loved.

"Mama, I'm gonna miss him so much," Elaina gulped.

"Oh, I know, Sis. I'm going to miss his smile—you know the one, when he looked like he was up to somethin'?"

Elaina giggled. "Yes'm, I know that one. You always knew he was gettin' ready to do or say somethin' funny."

"Seth had the prettiest eyes," Agnes said softly. "Pretty as a girl's."

Clement chimed in, "Yeah, that got him some ribbin' from some of the boys."

Once the work of the burying was finished and the boys had headed to the Drew house for supper, the family stood by the grave, holding hands and weeping. Tears flowed freely for all; even the older brothers, men fully grown.

Finally, Dutch urged his family back to the road. They walked up the hill to the churchyard where they'd parked. They drove slowly across the hills back home, as if the sorrow of the day was too heavy for the vehicles to haul quickly.

When they arrived at home they found Jerry and Freda holding court, making sure everyone had food and drink. The house was filled with the people who loved them, who worked with them, who went to school with them.

Elaina watched the people part, like the Red Sea when God parted it. She had learned about that in Sunday School. They were letting Mama and Daddy get into the house. She watched them walk in and Grandma called them to come into the kitchen and get some supper. She knew Grandma had been making sure they were eating, because she knew that neither one of them felt like doing so. She'd just heard her mother telling her father last night that it hurt to breathe. Elaina understood that. Ever since she'd seen Seth fall to the ground, she'd felt like she couldn't get a full breath. Every time she closed her eyes she saw his beautiful lashes closed against his face, knowing they would never open again.

Just this morning, when Mama's friend Lexie stopped by, she heard her mother say, "The doctor said his heart was enlarged." She had seemed to stumble on the word. "He had some big word he used, but that's what it meant. He said it made it to where his heart didn't pump right and something about when he was playing, it just gave out. It just quit." Lexie had hugged Mama and said some soothing words, but Elaina hadn't heard those.

Now she wandered through the house best as she could, listening to stories told about her brother. She had to smile at some of the things Alec and Clement told. She'd never heard those before. Mama and Daddy must not have either, because Mama looked plumb shocked by some of them.

"Mama?" Elaina said after everyone had gone home. Mama and Daddy were sitting in their rocking chairs, while she and Clem sat on the couch.

"Yes, 'Laina? What is it?" Her mother's voice sounded tired.

"It's just so quiet now," the girl said softly. "It seems strange after everyone bein' here the past few days."

"I was jus' thinkin' the same thing," Louise replied.

"I kinda like it, but it kinda seems like the knowin' about Seth is heavier now," Elaina tried to explain.

Clem nodded his head. "I feel that, too, Sis. It's like now we have to carry the whole weight of his—" He choked on the words. "—his death all by ourselves now."

Daddy spoke up. "Y'all are right. For the past few days, we've had family and friends and neighbors come and carry the burden with us in those first days when the pain was too hard to bear. They helped us so much. Now that the weight is a little less they've gone on, and we're able to carry it."

Elaina shook her head. "I don't think I can carry it, Daddy." Her eyes brimmed with tears. Clement handed her his handkerchief.

"You're stronger than you think, Sis. Just like your mama and me and Clem. It's gon' hurt, rightly so. Seth was our boy. Your brother. And he's gone and left a big ol' hole in our hearts and in our home. That's gon' hurt for some time to come."

"I reckon so, Daddy."

"It's gettin' late, 'Laina. Why don't you go on to bed. Grandma Freda made sure everything was spic and span before she left, so we can all just go to bed and sleep till mornin'."

Clem stood and walked toward the back of the house where his bedroom was. "I'm gon' on, Mama, Daddy, 'Laina." He stopped short of the door and turned back. "It just don' feel right goin' in here and not tusslin' with Seth."

Elaina rose and ran to her brother and hugged him tightly. "I love you, Clem."

"Love you, Sis. See you in the mornin'."

"Goodnight, Mama," Elaina said as she leaned in to kiss her mother's cheek. "Goodnight, Daddy." He had stood and she hugged him tightly, her arms encircling his waist.

"There, there, my girl. You sleep tight. Your mama and I will still be here come mornin', don't you worry." He kissed the top of her head and turned her toward the bedroom she shared with the three younger girls.

Chapter 7

Spring came and went. As much as Elaina loved flowers, seeing them sprouting up this year didn't faze her. All she could think about was missing her brother. True to his word, Joe had made it known that she wasn't to be bothered by boy or girl, nor was her little sister. Clement had made an extra effort to spend time with her, trying to fill the deep hole of grief left by Seth's passing.

The seasons were completely uneventful to her; cotton was planted like usual and cultivated like usual. It grew, the bolls erupting out of the plants, making the fields look like they were covered with snow just like every year. The family toiled together with other sharecroppers to pick the cotton and get it to the gin in time to get the best prices.

Elaina never liked the picking but would stick right to it when her daddy was in the field, she wanted to be with him that much. She would do anything to make him proud of her. School had barely started a month ago but, like many of her classmates, she got an excuse to stay out during the harvest because the family needed her help getting in the cotton.

When December arrived, there was bad news on the radio that was being talked about all over the community. It was something about airplanes from Japan had flown all the way across the ocean and bombed a place in the territory of Hawaii. There had been a bunch of United States ships in the place called Pearl Harbor and a whole lot of them were destroyed, and a lot of sailors and soldiers were killed. Elaina even heard the president speak about it.

"Daddy, what does it mean that we're at war with Japan?" she asked when the president's speech ended.

"Well, you know how we've been hearing about the bombings and all the fighting in Germany and France and Italy and England?"

"Yes, sir."

"Well, Japan decided to do that to us, out of the clear blue sky, Sis. So now Mr. Roosevelt just said that we're not taking that lying down. We're going to go after the ones that did that to us. There's gon' be a lot of our boys have to head off to fight."

The students at the Hilltop School studied the maps to understand where Japan was and where the islands of Hawaii were. They measured the distance and talked about what had happened. Elaina listened and participated, but it didn't mean much to her. Japan was so far away from Northeast Arkansas that she figured the war would never touch them there.

Unfortunately, that hope was dashed when two of her cousins and several young men from Stafford were called up for service. It became a habit to visit weekly with Grandma and Grandpa to hear the letters from her cousins to learn how they were doing. Elaina didn't always understand what they were saying, talking about trenches and places she had only heard of on the radio. The family gathered around the radio each evening to hear the war report and Elaina listened intently to hear any news of her family.

The next July, the crops were in the ground and the temperatures were getting hotter. Soon it would be time to go on their yearly fishing trip. Elaina slipped into the barn where her father was feeding their mules.

"Daddy, I wanna learn how to swim."

"Well, Sis, you jus' have to get in the water and let go."

"I get scared, Daddy. I can't jus' let go. My head goes under the water."

"That's when you gotta kick, girl. Kick your feet like a bird flappin' her wings."

Shaking her head stubbornly, Elaina replied, "I don't know how, Daddy. I get so scared I can't do it."

"Well, Sis," Dutch stated, "I reckon we need to help you learn."

Elaina's smile lit up the gloomy shade of the barn, and her voice was light. "When, Daddy? When can we go? Where will we go?"

"There now, Sis. Don't go gettin' all het up! Let me think on this a bit," he laughed as he finished the task at hand. "I'm thinkin' we can start out over in the pond on Jerry's place. It ain't big, but it's big enough to get you started, and if it ain't rained it will be clear, too."

Elaina's crinkled nose told him she knew how muddy that pond got, but she said happily, "Okay, Daddy. When are we goin'?"

"I reckon we could go over there this afternoon. You go in and get your chores done, and long about three o'clock we'll head over to get you wet. You be sure and let your mama know, but don't let the other girls hear."

"Yes, Daddy!" the girl yelled back over her shoulder as she ran the short distance to the house, determined to help her mother. She stepped into the bedroom that she shared with her sisters and made the beds, not minding that Agnes and

Cherilyn were supposed to help. Then she took the broom and swept all the floors through the whole house.

When she started sweeping in the kitchen, her mother turned from the counter and asked, "Child, what's got into you?"

"I'm helping you, Mama," Elaina sang, the broom keeping a rhythm as she moved it across the floor.

"I see that, but this isn't like you, 'Laina. I usually have to drag you in here to get somethin' done. What's goin' on?"

Walking close to her mother, Elaina shared softly, "Daddy said he would start teachin' me how to swim this afternoon. He said we'd go over the hill to Grandpa's place and start in that pond out in the field. You know the one, don't you?"

Nodding thoughtfully, her mother replied, "I do know that pond. It always had some angry snappers in it. Maybe you and your daddy should go down to the creek instead. I'll have a word with him, see what he thinks."

"Jus' don't let Agnes and Cherilyn hear, Mama. They'd want to come, and then Daddy would have to watch over them and I'd never get to learn!" the girl groused, pouting.

"I won't let them hear me. If y'all will go about three o'clock, the little girls will be down for their naps. I'll keep Agnes here doin' somethin'. You and your daddy will have your lesson time."

Elaina wrapped her arms around her mother's waist, squeezing her in a tight hug. "Thank you, Mama! Thank you!"

"What are you thankin' Mama for?" Agnes' voice interrupted.

"Oh nothin' really, Agnes Ann. I just wanted to thank her for being our mama." Her smile lit the room and Louise smiled with her, nodding to Agnes.

"Your sister is being right sweet today, young lady. She's done made your bed and hers, she's swept every floor in the place, and here she is asking what else she can do."

Agnes sullenly intoned, "I was gon' make my bed, Mama."

Elaina ran over and hugged her sister. "Now you don't have to! I made it for you. You get to play some more!" Seeing her mother's approving look, she went on, "I just have to finish sweeping in here and all our indoor chores are done!"

Agnes brightened and said, "Really? Me and Cherilyn can just play?"

"Yes, ma'am! What are y'all gon' play?" Louise asked.

"We're playin' school. Cherilyn don't know what it's like, though, but we can still play. I guess later on we'll play house, and she can be my neighbor and come visit at my house. She'll bring her baby and all."

Elaina had an idea. "Mama, can we make them a couple houses?"

"What do you have in mind, 'Laina?"

"We could take three or four of the chairs out in the yard and a couple quilts and lean up against the fence and make a couple little houses!" Her eyes sparkled.

"I reckon that would be all right, but you girls better have my chairs and my quilts back in this house before supper and before the dew falls." Louise laughed as the girls scurried to carry the kitchen chairs outside.

Elaina directed her sisters in how to set the chairs out from the fence several feet, two per girl, then they lifted a quilt and lowered it to cover the fence made of wooden slats that ran around their yard. They then tugged the other side of each quilt to drape over the tops of the tall ladder-back chairs. Instantly, the construction was transformed into the most wonderful houses. Each girl had one all her own, and each girl made their little home special for them. They each made a room for their dolls, stocked their kitchens, and sat in their living rooms. Their imaginations would carry them throughout the whole day.

Returning to the kitchen, Elaina took up the broom to finish her sweeping.

"That was mighty nice of you, Sis," her mother said quietly.

36

"Thank you, Mama. I reckon it don't hurt to be nice to the girls once in a while."

"No, it don't hurt at all."

Chapter 8

That afternoon, her sisters all washed up and tucked in for naps, Elaina slipped out the back door to meet her father. She'd put on the old clothes that she wore working in the fields and her mother had tied her hair up off her shoulders.

She walked hand in hand with her father down the red dirt road and across another, until they came to the creek her mother had suggested in place of the pond.

"Daddy?" she began.

"Yes'm?"

"I'm kinda glad we're goin' to the creek instead of Grandpa's pond."

"Why's that, Sis?" her father queried, grinning at her.

"'Cause I don' want no snappers biting at my toes for invadin' 'em!"

Daddy laughed heartily and they continued walking toward the slowly moving stream.

Elaina and Dutch talked about all sorts of things on their walk, even broaching the subject of Seth's death, a subject that made both of them teary-eyed. They talked about the war that was going on over in Europe; her Uncle Jay was going in the Army and would soon be over there. They talked about the cotton and the upcoming fishing trip. They talked about the moon shining in the daytime and clouds gathering. Dutch listened to his daughter's hopes and dreams with rapt attention. She told him of wanting to graduate school and work in an office somewhere.

"I really don' want to pick cotton all my life, Daddy."

"I understand that, 'Laina. Ain't nothing wrong with havin' dreams of better times. Farmin' is what I know. I love it. You don't love it like I do, and that's all right. You just buckle down at school. You'll soon be workin' in some big city office and I'll be so proud of you."

"So, you won't be mad if I don't stay here in Stafford?"

"Well, I won't be real happy to have you move off, but I reckon one day you'll marry and you'll be moved out of the house then anyway."

"Shew, Daddy. I don' want to marry nobody!"

Dutch laughed aloud. "Well, you might be a little young to be gettin' hitched, so we won't worry about that for a while."

Soon they were at the water's edge, and Elaina wavered on her resolve to learn to swim. She stepped into the water until it came to her knees, then stopped.

"Come on, Sis. You can't swim there; you've got to come on out where it's a little deeper."

"I'm scared, Daddy."

"I know. I'm right here. I'll be right here for you. You ain't gon' drown."

Elaina stepped slowly closer to him, gasping as the cool water reached her belly. Dutch showed her how to lay out and float.

"Just pick your feet up, Sis! I'll hold you."

Elaina leaned back against her father's hands and lifted her feet from the bottom. She cried out as she left the control of standing and began to float, repeating over and over, "Don't let me go, Daddy!"

They stayed and played in the water a while, letting the girl get used to being in the deeper water, testing her floating skills again and again.

Dutch patted her on the head and said, "I reckon those little sisters of yours will be gettin' up from their naps soon, if they're not already up. Let's head on home."

Elaina whined, "Oh, Daddy! I was havin' so much fun! Do we have to?"

"Yes, ma'am. We do. I told your mama that we'd be home so that the little girls don't wonder so much about what you and I were doing."

"Oh. Okay, Daddy. I reckon it wouldn't be good for them to be all upset about not gettin' to come swimmin'."

"No, it wouldn't. It would hurt their feelings."

"Good thing we'll be all dry when we get home, huh, Daddy?" she quipped.

"A very good thing!" Dutch replied, sliding his arm across her shoulders.

The swimming lessons went on for two weeks. The next week was the family fishing trip. Elaina would walk out to her father, knowing he would be right there for her and not let anything happen to her.

After the fun of the fishing trip had come and gone, where Elaina had been able to wade out into the water a little deeper than before, garnering quite a bit of cheering on from Clement, Dutch took his daughter back to the creek, determined to get her swimming this summer.

They were in the creek, and Dutch had just gotten Elaina to put her face in the water and keep it there for a few seconds, when he cried out.

Elaina stood straight up quickly, "Daddy! What's wrong?" she cried.

"Oh, oh, oh, Sis. I had a terrible pain. I couldn't keep from hollerin'!"

"What do I need to do, Daddy?" the girl asked fearfully. She'd never seen her strong daddy exhibit any sort of pain or weakness. Now he stood there in the water, grasping onto her to remain upright. He pressed his fist into his stomach and tried to take a step.

Faltering, he said through clenched teeth, "Get me to the bank, Sis."

Elaina lifted his arm and placed it over her shoulders. Bracing him up, she walked slowly to the bank, the water shedding from their skin and clothes as it became more and more shallow. She helped her father sit down on the grass at the side of the creek.

"Do I need to go get Mama, Daddy?" she asked nervously.

"I don't think so. Let me just rest here a bit and then we'll see."

They sat on the side of the creek for almost half an hour. Dutch lay back against a maple tree while Elaina watched him carefully, plucking a blade of grass every few minutes and tearing it into little pieces.

"You're gon' make this a bald spot on the bank, Sis," Dutch stated weakly.

"I'm sorry, Daddy. I'm just scared. I want you to be all right. Are you sure I don't need to go get Mama?" she said, desperately wishing Seth was here. He'd know what to do.

"No, no. I'm about ready to get up and head home. How about you?"

Elaina popped up and helped her father stand. He seemed like he was back to normal and they walked back home, talking about everything as they usually did. It seemed like Daddy was always able to move her mind off the troubling things. When they got home, Elaina helped her daddy up the steps into the house and into the kitchen. She told her mother in hushed tones what had happened.

Mama said, "That's somethin' else, Dutch Drew. Why don't you sit down," and she pulled out a chair. "'Laina, you go get cleaned up and changed. Check on the girls for me, too; they've been playin' house for some time and they've gotten a little quiet. I'm wonderin' what they might be up to."

Elaina slipped away to do as she was told. In her room, she poured out a little water and washed her face and hands and put on her regular day dress. She untied her luxuriant black hair and brushed it, slowly pulling each stroke through. The hazel eyes looking back at her in the mirror showed worry. She took a deep breath and finished brushing her locks, then turned to go outside. Looking back in the mirror, she pasted a smile on her face so as to not scare the little girls.

Elaina stepped quietly out the front door, wincing at the sound of the screen door's creak. She walked off the porch to the side yard, where her sisters had set up their houses of chairs and quilts.

"Knock, knock!" she said, walking up to the one where Agnes played.

"Who's there?" the bright reply came.

"Just your favorite big sister!" Elaina teased.

"I only have one big sister," Agnes' voice returned.

"Then I must be her. Can I come in?"

"Sure, just be sure to wipe your feet!" Agnes said, sounding more like an older citified lady than a little country girl.

Elaina wiped her feet on the grass patch outside the makeshift door then stepped into Agnes' pretend home. Agnes offered her tea and cookies and then called out for their sisters to join them. Soon the little quilt house was full of Drew girls, sharing afternoon tea.

As they played, Elaina heard the sounds of the car starting. *It must really be bad if Clement's goin' to get the doctor,* she thought.

"'Laina!" Louise's voice called from the back door.

"Comin', Mama!" Elaina called back. "I'll be right back, ladies," she said to her sisters before scampering from the tea party.

In a hushed tone, Louise said, "Elaina, we're takin' your daddy to the hospital. He's got somethin' wrong with his tummy. I need you to watch after the girls. Can you do that?"

"Mama, what's wrong with Daddy? Is he bad sick? Did the swimmin' make this happen?"

"I don't know what's wrong, child, but I know he needs to see the doctor. We'll go see Dr. Lancaster and he'll fix your daddy right up, you'll see. Now, I've put some beans on for supper already, but you'll need to make some cornbread and maybe fry some taters later on. Keep an eye on the time, 'cause I want those little girls fed before six this evening. You hear me?"

"Yes, Mama. I'll do it. Can I hug Daddy before y'all go?"

"Of course, Sis. Go on in."

Elaina rushed into the kitchen, falling to her knees next to the chair where her father still sat. Flinging her arms around him, she said, "Daddy, I don't want you to be sick!"

Dutch patted her head and replied, "Oh, Sis. I'm not really too bad sick, I don't think. Just had a pain. I'll go see ol' Doc Lancaster and get some kind of medicine and I'll soon be right as rain."

"I'll take care of the girls for you and Mama, Daddy. I'll do a real good job."

"I know you will, 'Laina. I'm proud of you. We'll be home before you know it. Now, if the girls ask any questions you just tell them I said everything will be okay."

"Yes, Daddy," she said softly.

"Now, go on. They'll be missin' you. Keep them busy till we get gone."

Chapter 9

Elaina wiped her tears and stepped back outside into the hot Arkansas sun. Turning her face to the sky she whispered, "Please God, let my Daddy be okay." She went back to the tea party where the girls, in their queenly manners, asked if everything was okay. To which she replied that they were indeed and that she simply had to take care of a certain matter. They all lifted their cups with their pinkies extended and sipped the water, making believe it was tea.

Elaina played with the girls as they had tea then visited Cherilyn's house, little Kate just happy to be in the middle. They told stories as they pretended. Finally Elaina excused herself, saying, "Ladies, I must go in and prepare a meal. I do hope you'll join me for supper in a bit." Her sisters agreed and two-year-old Kate clapped happily.

The quiet of the kitchen was foreboding as Elaina peeled potatoes and sliced an onion and set them to frying. Mixing up the cornbread batter she then poured into her mother's big cast iron skillet, she wondered what was taking the grown-ups so very long.

The girls had eaten and were washed up and in their nightgowns when their parents and brother pulled into the driveway. Elaina quickly shushed the younger girls, reminding them that their daddy was sick and didn't need them hollering and fussing.

Clement helped Dutch through the front door and led him to the padded rocking chair where he sat down carefully. Louise followed, and after setting her pocketbook in the bedroom walked to the couch and sat down. She beckoned her daughters to her and gathered them up close.

"You girls smell so good!" she murmured into Cherilyn's soft, dark hair. "And you're all ready for bed, too. What good girls you all are."

"Mama, 'Laina fed us beans and taters and she made cornbread. It was good. Then she made us get all washed up and stuff," Cherilyn shared.

"Very good, that's what I told her to do," Louise replied. "And you girls minded her, didn't you?" Even Kate bobbed her head in agreement.

"They were really good, Mama," Elaina stated. "No one fussed or nothing."

"That's so good, girls. Now, Daddy's gon' have to go to bed shortly, so y'all go over and give him hugs and kisses and scoot off to bed, too."

The younger girls hopped up to obey but Louise held Elaina's hand, keeping her on the couch with her. The three little girls went to their father and hugged him carefully, each receiving words of love and encouragement along with his brilliant smile.

"My, you girls have been so good this evenin'!" he exclaimed. "I reckon there ain't any better girls in all of Kreg County!" His daughters beamed. "Now, you girls go climb in bed and say your prayers. I will see you in the mornin',” he said as he kissed each one.

“Nighty-night, Daddy,” Kate gurgled as she waddled back to her mother for a hug and kiss. Louise carried the toddler to her bed to tuck her in for the night.

“'Night, Daddy,” Cherilyn intoned. “Sleep tight.” She followed her mother and baby sister to the shared bedroom.

“Goodnight, Daddy. But Daddy, why does Elaina get to stay up?” Agnes complained.

“Because your mama and I need to talk with her and Clement, that's why, Miss Nosey.” Dutch gently swatted her backside as she turned to walk to her bedroom, a tiny giggle escaping her lips.

The moments ticked by agonizingly slowly as they waited for the girls to drift off to sleep. Louise had come out and waved the others into the kitchen, farther away from the girls. There she saw the pot of beans still sitting on the stove and the skillet with cornbread in it beside.

“Oh, my girl! You held some for us, didn't you?” She smiled at her oldest daughter.

“Yes, Mama. I figured y'all would be hungry. Do you want some? Daddy? Clem?” She reached to the shelf and retrieved three bowls and three small plates which she carried to the stove. She ladled beans into each bowl and a chunk of cornbread onto each plate and set them before her parents and brother.

“Do y'all want coffee or water?” she asked.

“No coffee, Sis. We'll have water,” Dutch replied.

The soft clink of spoons in bowls nearly drove Elaina mad as she tried to wait patiently for the news of what was wrong with her precious daddy. She slipped quietly to the front room, listening for the soft, even breathing of sleeping little sisters. When she heard it she walked back into the kitchen, where the table was now cleared and the three adults sat sullenly.

“Mama? Daddy? What's goin' on?” she asked.

"Well, Sis, it seems I'm pretty sick."

"No, Daddy! Did you get sick because of the creek? Is it because we went swimmin'?" Tears ran down Elaina's rosy adolescent cheeks.

"Shush, child! Let your daddy talk," Louise chided.

Looking down at his folded hands, Dutch continued, "Dr. Lancaster thinks I've got a tumor in my belly here. Cancer." Elaina gasped. "He said it don' look too good. He thinks I need some rest in the bed for a while. He give me some medicine to take. Hopefully it will make me all better." Dutch's brown eyes looked tired yet hopeful as he lifted them to Elaina's.

The girl shook her head, fear and disbelief filling her heart. What on earth would she do, would their family do, if something happened to Daddy?

She voiced the question. "We've got cotton in the ground, and garden coming in. What do you want me to do, Mama?"

"Well," Louise started, turning to their son, "Clement, you're gon' have to take over the man-of-the-house chores. You handle the crops and the stock. Your daddy will help with decisions you don't know how to make, but mostly we need to let him rest."

"Of course, Mama," Clement declared. "I'll do whatever I need to, even if I have to take off from work or even quit. I'll be here."

Louise patted her son's hand. "I know, son. I know. We couldn't ask for any better help. Now, Elaina, you're gon' have to fill in for me. I'm gon' be takin' care of your daddy, and I will need for you to take care of the laundry and the cleanin' and the cookin'. We'll set Agnes Ann to takin' care of the younger girls. She can read 'em stories and play with them. That should keep her and the little girls busy. We'll even see if sometimes Jodie can come and get them and take them places. This will be hard for them, not understanding this sickness and what it does."

"Yes, Mama. I'll do whatever I have to. You can count on me," Elaina promised, her eyes brimming with tears.

"I know you two will do just right," their father stated. "You're both good children and you're both smart and strong. I'm gon' have to depend on you to help me and your Mama and then to help her when I'm gone."

Elaina's tears erupted and her body was wracked with sobs. Louise scooted close to her and slid her arm around her. The girl leaned into her mother, weeping against her.

"There, there, child. Yes, get it out. Your sorrow is mighty powerful right now. Let it out. Tomorrow we'll have to be strong. Tonight, we'll just be weak and worn."

The family remained there around the table, quietly discussing how things were to work in this time when Dutch couldn't do his usual work. Finally, Clement helped Daddy to the edge of his bed. Leaning over, he whispered to his father, "I love you, Daddy."

"I know, Clem. I love you, too. We'll get through this. Now, you go on to bed. Your mama will help me get on in here."

Elaina stood in the middle of the living room as her mother gently closed the bedroom door. She looked at her brother, who nodded solemnly to her. Blinking back bright tears, she turned and went into the bedroom she shared with her sisters.

Chapter 10

Elaina quickly learned how to get up early and get the coffee brewed before the others awoke. She cooked breakfast for the family and called them to it like she'd heard her mother do for all of her twelve years. Louise helped her in figuring what to prepare for each meal. She improved in making biscuits, and her gravy was delicious. She learned how to make a pot roast tender and how long to cook fresh green beans. She made getting the garden produce in fun for the little girls to help with, even breaking beans.

Sitting on the floor of the front porch, she said to her sisters, "Let's do a roundabout story."

"What's a roundabout story, 'Laina?" Agnes had asked.

"It's a story we all tell," Elaina replied.

"How can we all tell a story?" Cherilyn questioned.

"Well, we make it up as we go along. It's just like pretendin' when y'all make your little houses, but we're telling the story."

"We need some way to take turns," Cherilyn observed.

"Why don't we…" Elaina thought before continuing. Placing the bucket of fresh-picked green beans in the middle of the porch, she lifted a handful and showed the other girls. "We each take a handful of beans. When we've broken that handful, it's our turn until someone else finishes their handful. What do you think?"

The little girls, except Kate, who just watched the girls while holding her baby doll, grabbed up a handful of beans and got started. As she saw the first handful Agnes had grabbed almost done, Elaina said, "Once upon a time…" and waited for Agnes to go on.

By the time the story was finished, the beans were all broken. The girls were amazed that the usually tedious chore had been done without the usual boredom, complaints, and bickering.

The family learned how to get along with this new way of doing things. Alec and Jodie dropped by more often. As Louise had predicted, Jodie would pick up the little girls and take them for a ride a couple times each week. Their daughter Adele, just a few months older than Kate, fit right in with them, so the excursions worked out happily.

Kate and Cherilyn didn't realize what was going on. Agnes, though, was old enough to understand, but she contained her sorrow when taking care of her younger sisters. When they were napping, sometimes she would visit with Elaina and the two would talk.

"'Laina, he's gon' die, ain't he?" she asked her big sister, watching her rubbing little girl dresses on the washboard in the backyard.

"The doctor don't think he's got much chance of livin', Agnes." Elaina breathed out, her hands never slowing.

"I don't want him to die, 'Laina. I don't!" Tears of anguish spilled down the cheeks of the nine-year-old girl as she scuffed her bare feet on the grass.

"I know. I don't either. I don't know what we'll do if he does." Elaina sniffed, wiping her cheeks with the back of her wet hand. "He's our rock, Agnes. He's—" her voice broke and Agnes nodded her understanding.

The family would visit Dutch in his room. Clement and Alec had set up a couple chairs so that visitors could sit nearby and talk with him. On a few occasions, they helped him outside to sit on the front porch. He enjoyed the gentle swinging as he and his wife sat there watching their family; little girls playing house, older daughter sewing or breaking beans or playing with her sisters. They could hear Clement out back, calling to the mules as they drew the cultivator through the cotton.

One of those outdoor excursions was for Agnes' birthday. The whole family gathered around. Jodie had come over and helped Elaina prepare a special meal. Clement and Alec set up a table in the front yard and the little girls picked flowers to decorate it. Alec and Clem carried Dutch in his rocking chair out to sit in the shade, making it easier for him to join in. His wide eyes made his daughters laugh.

"Y'all come on! Get those hands washed and yourselves in these chairs. 'Laina and I are bringing out the dinner and y'all better be ready!" Jodie called as she carried plates and silverware to the table, her shrill voice sounding like it would invite the neighbors from the next three farms.

Soon the table was overflowing with fried chicken, mashed potatoes, fresh vegetables, gravy, and rolls. The family surrounded the table and held hands as Dutch quietly offered thanks.

When everyone was sated, Elaina excused herself and slipped off to the kitchen. She lifted a cake from the counter and carried it outside. When Jodie saw her at the door, she started singing, "Happy Birthday to you..." and the whole family chimed in.

Agnes clapped her hands and Clement declared it was time for her birthday spankings. Her wide eyes and squeals made everyone laugh.

Later that evening, after the day was done and the family was settled in, Dutch declared it had been a good day. Sitting on his lap, Agnes declared it was the best day ever. Seeing her father so happy, Elaina had to agree with her sister. *The best day ever.*

"Elaina! Can you come help me?" Clement called from just outside the back door.

"I have beans cooking on the stove, Clem. I need to keep an eye on them."

Louise's voice drifted in from the living room, "Go on, Elaina. I'll keep an eye on the beans. Clem needs your help, so go on and help."

"Yes, ma'am," Elaina said, wiping her hands on her apron before lifting it over her head. "I'll be right there, Clem."

Her brother was waiting in the backyard, shuffling his feet back and forth.

"What can I do?" she asked.

"I need you to take a ride with me." He nodded toward the barn where she saw the mule blanketed and ready to ride.

"Where we goin'? What's up?"

"C'mon. I'll help you up." Clement put his hands together, making a step to help his sister up onto the blanket before swinging himself up behind her. Taking the reins, he clucked to the mule and they rode off in the direction of the cotton field.

"What's goin' on, Clem? We didn't bring hoes or nothin', so we can't work the field. What are you up to?"

She heard the smile in his voice as he replied, "Our grandmother requested our presence at her house this afternoon, and we've got to be gettin' on." He slapped the reins on the mules neck, urging him to step a little faster.

"Grandma wants us... Clem, doesn't she know we have work to do? We can't be lollygaggin' around all day."

"I know we've got work to do, Sis, but you know we can't say no to Grandma Freda."

Giggling, Elaina replied, "You're right about that. I think the last person that said no to her hasn't been seen in the county for years! Grandpa won't even say no to her!"

Grandma's stubbornness was a long-running family joke that never lost its fun. The two rode over the hills until they came to the gate of the Rafferty place. Elaina slid down and opened the gate, then closed it again behind them. She ran ahead of the mule, calling for her grandmother as she approached the house.

"Grandma! Grandma! Me and Clem are here!"

"Well you don't have to holler, Miss Priss. You're sure 'nough gon' wake the dead if you keep on!" Freda laughed as she gathered her granddaughter into her arms in a great hug. "C'mon, Clem. You come on down here. Tie that animal off where he can get some water and get on in here."

"Yes, ma'am!" Clem declared, winking at his sister.

The Drew children followed their grandmother into the wooden house on the hill. As soon as they entered, they both noticed the smell of Grandma's delicious pies drifting on the breeze. They were surprised, because Grandma didn't usually bake pies in the summer. She always said it was too hot.

"Y'all come on in here and sit down. As I recall you both like a good apple pie, so I've got some already sliced for you and a glass of milk to go with it. Sit! Sit!"

Both Clement and Elaina sat down and began eating their pie. It was a treat because, while Elaina could cook the meals, she wasn't up to adding on desserts yet.

"Thank you, Grandma!" Elaina said, washing a bite of pie down with a big gulp of milk.

"You're right welcome, Sis. I wanted to give you two somethin' special for all the hard work you're doin'." She nodded as though hearing a reply. "You two have been asked to take on bein' all grown up when you're not and that's hard on a little one."

"Grandma, I'm not little," Clement said. "I'm 21 years old now."

"Well, that's right and all, but to me you're still little. It's a blessing that you're still at home for your mama and daddy."

"Yes'm," he replied, his tanned skin tinged pink.

"I wanted to spend some time with you two, talkin' and such. I know this is hard on both of you. Alec feels the pain, but he's got a wife and child, and the little girls are so young."

"Agnes is hurtin', Grandma," Elaina piped up.

"Sure she is, but it's as a little girl, sweetie. You're hurtin' as the favored daughter, the first girl, the one who thinks her daddy hung the moon." Freda patted Elaina's hand. "Your heart is breakin' different than your sister's."

Elaina wiped away a tear that slid down her face as their grandmother went on. "When y'all finish your pie, you head on over to the creek on the far side of the field. Your grand-daddy has some bait and fishin' poles ready for y'all. I reckon he's expectin' a piece of pie, too, so we'll wrap up a piece for you to take to him."

Elaina looked at Clem. "Can we?" she asked.

"I-I— Grandma, we really should get back home."

"Your mama said it would be fine. The crop is in the ground. Clem, you've been keepin' it clear and clean and it's lookin' good. There's nothing to be done in the fields. Your mama can watch over the cookin' for the afternoon. Agnes is doin' a fine job watchin' over your sisters, so y'all can take an afternoon off. Now, let me cut a piece of pie for Jerry and y'all can head on over. And when you get done, you stop back by here; I've got a couple pies you can take on home with you."

Elaina clapped excitedly as Clem wiped the last crumbs from his mouth. "I reckon we're goin' fishin', 'Laina," he said. Elaina saw a smile tilting the corners of his mouth, the first she'd seen since they'd found out about Daddy's sickness.

In moments the two left the house and climbed back aboard their mule to ride across Grandpa's acres to the creek.

Elaina carried the pie to him. "Grandpa, Grandma said you'd want this. It's mighty good."

"Well, well! That smells like Grandma's apple pie, but I know she don' bake like that in the heat of summer."

"She did it, Grandpa. She baked not just one, but three or four!"

Jerry Rafferty laughed heartily. "Oh, these women! When they don' know what to do, they cook. Ain't nothin' wrong with that. Matter of fact," he said, patting his belly covered by his overalls, "I kinda like it." He tousled Elaina's hair and nodded toward the bank of the creek. "I've got y'all some poles strung up and ready. Just put some bait on 'em and set a spell."

Jerry dug into his apple pie and Clem baited two hooks and handed one pole to his sister. Once their lines were in the water, the two sat back. Elaina felt some of the tension of the past weeks drain away from her as she acted like a normal twelve-year-old.

"It's pretty rough at your house right now, ain't it?" their grandfather said.

"Yessir," they intoned together.

"Tell me what's goin' on. Your mama don't always share everything with me. I'd like to hear it from y'all."

Elaina looked at her brother, unsure if she should share. His nod told her to go on.

"Daddy is in a lot of pain, but he tries really hard to hide it from us. He don't eat a whole lot, so he's gettin' really skinny. He kinda looks like a bag of bones, Grandpa!"

"I see," he murmured. "What else?"

"He's gettin' weaker," Clem added. "When I help him from the bedroom to the chair, he leans on me a lot harder than ever before. I reckon it's a good thing he lets me help him."

"And your mama? How is she holdin' up?" His concern for his daughter was etched on his face. "She lost her boy just two years ago, now this. How's she holdin' up?"

Elaina sniffled, her own heart still broken over her brother Seth's death. "She's so sad, Grandpa, but she puts on a brave face for all of us. She takes good care of Daddy, makin' sure he's had a bath, that he eats as much as he can, that he takes his medicine even when he don't want to. I don't know how much sleep she's gettin'. It seems like she's up all night tendin' to him."

Clem continued, "But every time we see her she puts a smile on, especially around the little girls. She don't want them to worry about Daddy. I might need to do a better job of gettin' her to eat. She's been skippin' some meals."

"Uh-huh," Jerry grunted. "You might tell her the little girls want her to eat with them. You know she'll eat more with them, because she'll be wantin' them to eat well."

Elaina nodded. "That's a good idea, Grandpa. Mama loves us kids. If she thinks we're doin' poorly, she'll move heaven and earth to make it better for us."

"That's right. That's just how she is. Reckon there's any need for me to call Harriet to come? She's still got a passel of kids at home, but the older ones can take care of the younger ones. Do you think your mama would want that?"

Clem shook his head. "I don't think so, Grandpa. Mama don't want no one else takin' care of Daddy. The only reason she lets me help move him is because she just don't have the strength."

"Uh-huh. Your mama is one strong woman. That she is. Hey, 'Laina! You've got a bite! Don't lose that!"

Elaina squealed as she snatched the pole, snagging the hook into the jaw of the crappie. Soon Clem and Grandpa were pulling their own fish in, and before long the discussion was tucked away into the back of their minds as they relaxed and enjoyed the afternoon together.

Chapter 11

Two weeks later, Dutch took a turn for the worse. The pain had grown more intense and the medicine given to help it had been increased. When he wasn't thrashing and moaning in pain, he was asleep in a morphine stupor. Louise had made the decision to only let the little girls see him when he was asleep. She could tell them he was resting and dreaming happy dreams. Holding them close, she would describe happy dreams of little girls and big cotton crops and new shoes and fishing trips. The smiles on their little faces lit up the room.

Elaina would spell her mother from time to time, staying by her father's bedside. Soothing him when the pain overrode the medicine, speaking to him as though he were awake.

It was the end of August when he left them forever. Louise watched the life leave her beloved, with Clem and Elaina standing by. They tried to console her, Elaina offering her a corner of her apron to wipe her tears much as Louise had done her when she was little. Tears finally subsiding, Louise stood and walked to the mirror over her dresser. She patted her hair into place and, using a damp cloth, wiped her face.

Turning to her two children, she said, "Okay, let's go tell your sisters."

The three walked into the living room where Agnes was reading fairy tales to Cherilyn and Kate as though she were the teacher in the schoolroom. Louise sat down hard in the rocking chair, her shoulders sagging.

"Mama?" Agnes' voice was thin and fearful.

"Babies, your daddy's gone on. He's with Jesus and Seth and my mama now." Louise's words were barely above a whisper. She cleared her throat and looked at Clement. "Son, would you go tell your brother and y'all go get Mr. Lloyd?"

"Yes, Mama," Clement said, turning to leave to do her bidding.

Elaina sat on the floor at Louise's feet, unwilling to move far from her mother. Cherilyn started crying and ran over to sit on her sister's lap. Kate mimicked her big sister and ran over, almost knocking the other two over. Louise giggled in spite of her grief, then Elaina joined her and in moments their laughter filled the house.

Short-lived though it was, the laughter helped mother and daughters. They sat quietly in and around that rocking chair until the two sons arrived, followed closely by the undertaker. Jodie had stayed home, choosing to tell their daughter about her grandfather's death there.

The funeral would be held on Tuesday evening, giving time for word to get around and friends and family to make their own arrangements. Louise set the time to allow for folks to get their daily work done before coming out.

Once again Elaina greeted people at the door, leading them into the kitchen to deposit their gifts of food on the counters. She remarked to her grandmother, once again present to help, that there was even more than when Seth had died.

"Folks loved your daddy, 'Laina. He was a good man."
Freda seemed to have a hard time getting her words out.

"He was the best, Grandma," Elaina choked out.

The woman and the girl nodded their understanding of
the other's tears as they shifted desserts that had been placed
on the table to give room for someone to sit and eat.

*Was it just two and a half years ago that we sat right here for
Seth?* Elaina thought that Tuesday afternoon as the preacher
talked about her daddy. Her mind wandered through her memories—riding the harrow, fishing trips, driving on Daddy's lap,
learning to plow with him behind her, the lessons he taught
her, even the times he called her down for being a little smart
with her mama. Hot tears slid down her cheeks, seeming like
they would never stop.

Instead of teens carrying a coffin down the hill it was a
group of farmers, with Dutch's two boys leading at the front.
Clement and Alec each lifted the box that held their father's
body, and tried to watch the path through their tears. Just
off the gravel road through the Sunnyvale Cemetery, on a
curve near the back, they led the way to the open grave just
up the hill from his son's. Louise followed the coffin, leaning
on her eldest daughter, both struggling to keep the tears at
bay. The three other daughters followed, Agnes carrying Kate
as Cherilyn held her hand. Jodie came along, carrying her
daughter Adele.

Friends, neighbors and other family gathered around to
hear the preacher's final words, then stepped over to offer
words of condolence to the widow and her children. Elaina
had stepped to the head of the grave and watched the process
of lowering the coffin into the ground. Her breath caught in
her chest as the box dropped below the level of the ground she
stood on. Her tears flowed unabated, and she used one of her

father's handkerchiefs to wipe them. She barely noticed that Agnes and Jodie had shepherded the younger girls back up the hill so they could move around without disturbing the adults.

She looked up as she felt an arm slip around her waist. It was her mother.

"I don't know what we're gon' do, 'Laina. I sure don't. But I know the Good Lord has always taken good care of us and I don't think He's gon' stop now."

"I reckon He will, Mama. I just wish He'd left Daddy here to help Him," she said.

"Me, too, Sis. Me, too." Mama's use of Daddy's nickname for her this time brought fresh tears to Elaina's eyes. "There, there. I didn't mean to make you cry more! I'm just so used to hearin' your daddy say that..." Louise's voice faltered.

"It's all right, Mama."

The men who had filled in the grave were tamping down the last bit of dirt, mounded up over the place where Dutch Drew's body lay. Elaina lay the August wildflowers she had gathered around the church yard yesterday on the fresh dirt.

"Do you want me to bring the girls back down here, Mama?" she asked.

"Maybe Agnes and Cherilyn. I don't think Kate understands at all—" Her mother thought a moment. "No. Bring all three of them. They all need to say good-bye to their daddy. You go on up there and get them, and I'll have a moment by myself with him."

"Yes, Mama," Elaina replied, turning to walk up the hill behind her brothers and the men who had helped them bury their father. The sun was setting and the sky had taken on beautiful hues of orange and purple, though the girl barely noticed.

She hugged Clement, Alec, and Jodie, then said, "Mama says we all need to go and say our good-byes to Daddy."

"Us, too?" Agnes asked.

"Yes, all of us. Even Kate. Mama said." Elaina took a deep breath, wiped her eyes one more time, and took her baby sister from Agnes. "Come on, Sweet Pea. Let's go down the hill and say goodbye to Daddy. Mama's waiting."

Those friends and neighbors who had gathered watched as the heartbroken family slowly made their way down the hill.

Chapter 12

"I don't want to go to the field, Mama!" Elaina whined. "My fingers are raw now from pickin' cotton!" She lifted her hands to show her mother.

"Mine are, too, 'Laina. We can't stop just because we hurt. We have to get this crop in or we're not gon' be able to live through this winter. Now get up and get a move on."

The arguments had become the most frequent means of communication between mother and daughter. The younger girls usually hid when their voices rose, not knowing how to help or whether they should try. Agnes and Cherilyn worked together to keep the baby happy.

"I never had to do this kind of thing when Daddy was alive," Elaina muttered, tossing her head, making the deeply black hair swish across her shoulders.

"Nor did I, Missy," Louise nearly snarled. "But Daddy's not here now and we've got a cotton crop to get in. We have to get it in soon in order to keep our house. Now, do you want to just sit here and live in a ditch when the cold hits, or do you want to get out to the field and have a roof over yours and your sisters' heads?"

Sighing, Elaina rose from the wooden chair at the kitchen table, knowing as she had when her mother had first called her out of bed that she would eat a bite, drink some milk, then take her poke to the field to pick cotton. She just couldn't seem to say "Yes, Mama" anymore.

She stomped a few steps toward the bedroom. "I'll be ready in a couple minutes, Mama."

"All right," Mama said. "I'll meet you in the barn."

If only Clement didn't have a stinkin' job, she thought as she pulled on a pair of pants and a long-sleeved shirt. She knew that, even with the heat, she needed the protection from the cotton or she'd be covered in scratches and welts. She added her high-top shoes to protect against any snake bites. "Agnes Ann! Mama says you're to feed the girls and watch them. Y'all be good, you hear?"

"You're not good!" Agnes barked.

"You're not me!" Elaina retorted. "We've got to help Mama now. I know that, too. It's just so hard! She expects me to do everything! I have to cook and clean *and* help in the fields. I can't wait till I'm all grown up and can get married!"

As she turned the knob on the back door, Elaina grabbed her wide-brimmed straw hat to shade her through the day. She walked to the barn where her mother had gathered two long cotton pokes, the long sacks no wider than the space between rows made to follow the picker by the strap crossing over one shoulder and under the other arm. The two trudged across the grassy field to the crop, carrying the sacks. Once in the rows to be picked, they began pulling the ripe white cotton off the opened bolls. After many years of picking the crop, the two had learned how those petals of the bolls could prick one's fingers. They had to be careful, because they didn't want to send cotton with blood on it through to the gin.

Mother worked beside daughter throughout the day, both filling their pokes, pushing each handful down against the first so as to fill the entire length of the poke.

"For each handful to be so light, this cotton gets awful heavy in the bag," Elaina said.

"That's a fact. That *is* a fact," her mother replied, wiping sweat from her brow.

"I wish the girls were big enough to help out here, Mama."

"I know. They's some families that have their kids out in the fields from the time they can walk. I don't want them to have to do that, 'Laina."

"But it wouldn't hurt 'em, Mama. Agnes could pull a good-sized poke, and Cherilyn could do halves. And what about Jodie? If you're gon' leave Agnes watchin' Kate, she could leave Adele there and come out and help us."

Standing and looking to the edge of the field where three tall trees shaded a patch of ground as big as a house, Louise said, "You know, maybe we could get Jodie to bring Adele over and we could set Cherilyn to watchin' over Kate and Adele over there under the trees. Then we could have Jodie and Agnes helping out here."

Elaina shrugged. "Maybe so. It would be awful nice to have the help."

"I'll speak to Alec about it. He and Clement should be here long about three o'clock or so. He's comin' right out after he gets off work. When he gets here we'll work till you finish your poke, then you can take his car on back to the house and get supper goin'."

"Yes, Mama," Elaina drawled, too hot and tired to argue or complain.

"'Laina, I know it's hard. I know what it's like to be a little girl and have to take on the job of mama. I was eight years old when Harriet went off and married Andrew, and I had to take on all the house duties. And I didn't have no mama around to teach me how to do everything. I know what it's like," she emphasized. "Now, let's see which one of us can get to the end of this row first!" Pulling the cotton faster she saw her daughter pick up speed, too.

At the end of the row waited the wagon with a barrel of water and a bit of shade. The two sat in the shade, enjoying the cool drink while the ginners shook the cotton out of the pokes into the wagon. All too soon, their break was over and they walked to the other end of the field. It was easier for them to pull the poke toward the wagons instead of having to turn and pull a full one back up the rows. They leaned into their work, pulling cotton and stuffing it into the bag over and over, their backs aching, their skin hot, their hair matted under their hats. They talked a little, but mostly just picked and kept moving.

True to her word Mama talked to Alec, and the next day Jodie came to the field. She laid out a big quilt and told Cherilyn to keep Kate and Adele on it or very close. Then she joined Louise, Elaina, and Agnes in the rows to gather in the crop. The women talked, sometimes they sang hymns. The girls went right along, somehow feeling like they belonged to the womanhood, though they were still children. In the middle of each afternoon the brothers came in from work, bringing snacks for all of them and picking almost double what the women did. Elaina was grateful to see them coming each day.

The family managed to get the cotton crop in before the price dropped and received enough money that, even when split with their landlord, would be enough to get shoes for each one of them along with not just one but two new dresses as well. They would have to watch their money carefully when they went to the store for staples, but they had plenty of vegetables put up from the summer garden.

Elaina realized that, just like her mother had said, the Good Lord was taking care of them.

Chapter 13

The next summer the little family of woman and girls worked together with their landlord to plant the cotton, and their neighbors helped with getting their garden planted. Sometimes Louise and her two oldest girls would work for neighbors who had other crops planted, picking beans and cabbage and whatever else was ready. Sometimes they were paid with money plus a bit of the produce, which made life much easier on the family.

The sweltering days of summer had finally cooled slightly, the daily high temperatures finally dipping back into double digits. School started and each of the girls was excited about having a new summer dress and a winter dress. Elaina hated it when they had to start school wearing the heavier material. She understood that Mama would buy those so they would last longer for them. This year each girl also had a new pair of shoes that fit them, relegating their old shoes to be worn in the fields and for play.

Just after Mama's birthday, the cotton was ripe and ready for harvest. It had to be picked, so Elaina stayed out of school to help with the picking that would go on for a full two months. She had other friends who had to miss school, too. It was just the life of a farm family.

One morning when Agnes and Cherilyn were getting ready for school, Elaina complained that her stomach hurt. She and Mama were getting ready to go to the field to pick.

"'Laina, we go through this every time I ask you to go to the fields. I tol' you I know what it's like. I know you don't like it but we've got to eat, don't we?"

"Yes, Mama, but it hurts really bad!" She was rubbing her belly with her hand, round and round right at her belly button.

Thinking it was yet another ploy to avoid going to the field, Louise shook her head. "Come on, girl. We've got work to do. You'll be jus' fine."

When they walked into the field, Louise's sister-in-law Mellie greeted them.

"Oh Mellie, I'm so glad to see you!" Louise hugged her tightly.

"Me and Wiatt decided I'd come help with your harvest and let you and the girls have the money."

"Oh, Mellie! That's so kind of you, but I can't let you work so hard and get nothin' out of it."

"I'll get somethin' out of it. I'll have the joy of being able to help my sister and her family. Family sticks together, Louise; you know that."

Louise brushed tears from her eyes and lifted the strap of her poke over her head. She nodded at Mellie and they moved into a row to start picking.

Elaina slipped the strap of her poke around her neck and across her shoulder. She had only worked about half a row when Mellie noticed the girl had stopped and was standing bent over, both arms holding her belly.

"Louise! What's wrong with your girl?" she called.

"My belly hurts, Aunt Mellie," Elaina replied in a groan.

Walking to the girl, Mellie placed her hand to Elaina's forehead. "Lord, Louise! This girl's burnin' up with fever! Here, 'Laina, you drop that poke. Let's get you over here to the shade."

"Mellie, are you sure she's not puttin' on? She was whinin' about comin' out here this mornin'."

"Feel her face, Louise. She's got a fever. And she's hurtin' next to her belly button here. She needs to see the doctor right fast." Mellie's expression brooked no argument.

Her face flushed, her skin clammy yet dry, Elaina whimpered. She was awake but not really awake even as she walked beside her aunt. Her mother touched her face then jumped back, shocked that she hadn't seen the fix her daughter was in.

Looking around, she saw her son running toward them. "Clement, you need to take 'Laina to the doctor. You need to go fast!" She murmured, "I don't know what I'd do if I lost another..." Mellie slipped an arm around her.

"We ain't gon' lose her, Louise. Now Clem, you get on. Drive fast, but drive careful."

Clement picked his sister up and ran to the car. He lay her limp body across the back seat and slammed the door. Once seated he closed his door and raced out of the field to the road, red dust rising from the tires as he went. Turning onto the highway, he raced to Stafford as fast as he could go.

Elaina lay still as she could, every movement causing pain. She heard her brother's voice softly speaking, "Oh, Lord. Please don't take my sister. We can't lose her. Please let my sister live." He pulled the car right up to the door of the doctor's office. He lifted Elaina then raced through the doors, calling for Dr. Lancaster.

"Here now, what's all the hullabaloo?" the doctor asked calmly as he walked out of an examination room, wiping his hands on a towel.

"Doc, it's 'Laina! She's bad off. She's all feverish and hurtin' somethin' fierce. You gotta help her!"

The doctor snapped to attention. "Follow me, young man. Let's bring her right in here." He walked into the last examination room, brightly lit with a bed ready for a patient.

Clement lay his sister down and the doctor began his examination, pressing here and there, watching the girl to see if there was any reaction. When he pressed below her belly button and slightly to the left, she winced. He moved his hand to the right a little bit more and pressed again. Elaina cried out, rising slightly. She rolled to her side and vomited.

Nodding his head, the doctor looked at Clement. "It looks like appendicitis, and it looks like it's pretty bad. We need to do surgery on her right now."

Lying back, Elaina saw her brother's eyes wide and frightened, and she felt fearful of what the doctor was saying.

"Clem?" she said weakly.

"No, no, Clem, Elaina, this is not what took your daddy. This is not cancer." He looked at his patient. "Your appendix is infected and it's swollen up, and it's going to keep making you hurt and can make you very, very sick if we don't get it out of you." He patted her shoulder. "You lie back and get some sleep. I'll take care of this, get it out of you and get you healthy again."

Elaina collapsed onto the bed, still feeling fearful. She felt so tired and her body ached all over. She tried to focus on what the doctor was saying.

Dr. Lancaster called for his nurse then turned back to Clement and said, "I'm going to have to do surgery on her here, Clement. There's no time to move her to the hospital. It's that important. Her appendix is swollen up really bad and I'm afraid it could burst. If it does, it will spread poison all through her body. Now, you go on and get your mama. Tell her what's going on and bring her back here."

The nurse entered the room and with the doctor began wheeling the bed out of the room toward the small surgical suite at the back of the office.

As they walked, Clem followed them. "You're sure 'Laina's gon' be okay, Doc? I can't—" His voice broke as he thought about losing another loved one.

The doctor called over his shoulder, "I'm sure, son. You get on your way and bring your mama. By the time you get back, I'll most likely be all done and your sister will be on the mend."

Clement quickly drove back to the field. Once there, he walked through the rows to reach his mother and aunt. Out of breath, he stopped to catch his breath as both women waited, not quite patiently.

"Well?" Louise finally asked.

"She's got appendicitis, Mama. Dr. Lancaster said it was close to burstin'. He's operatin' on her right now." Louise's eyes filled with fear and tears and Clement hugged her close. "Mama, he said it wasn't nothin' like what happened to Daddy. He said this would be jus' fine, but that I need to get you there so you'll be there when 'Laina wakes up."

Louise dropped her poke and raced toward the car, calling out to Mellie that she would be back as soon as possible.

Chapter 14

Elaina felt awake, but her eyes were closed. She still felt pain in her belly, but it was different now. She didn't feel so hot that her eyes burned, and she didn't feel like she was going to throw up. She moved her hands back and forth, feeling soft linen under her. She heard her mother's voice, soft and urgent. What was that she was saying? Elaina listened hard. Mama was praying. She was telling God she'd messed up by thinking her daughter was foolin'. She begged God to let her be all right.

"Mama," Elaina croaked, her throat dry as a bone.

"'Laina!" her mother cried aloud. "Oh, Sis. I'm so sorry! I should have listened to you. How are you feelin'?"

Her voice still weak, Elaina said, "Thirsty."

"Oh! Yes, let me get you some water," her mother declared. She stepped to the door of the room. "Nurse! Can I get her a glass of water?"

The nurse walked in, her starched, snowy white uniform rustling as she walked. Checking on her patient she determined that a bit of water would be fine, and she left to get some.

"Mama?" Elaina queried. "Where am I?" Her last memory was falling down in the field near her house. She knew this white room wasn't home or school or church.

"You're at the Stafford Hospital, Sis. You had your appendix almost burst. That's why you had such a fever and all that pain. Dr. Lancaster operated on you and took it out. Then the ambulance wagon brought you here. Now you'll be okay."

"Mrs. Drew? Here you go." The nurse handed her a glass filled with water. "Don't allow her to drink too much at one time."

"Thank you," Louise said as she took the glass from the nurse and carried it to the bed. Placing her hand behind her daughter's head, she helped her take a sip.

"Ow, Mama!" Elaina whimpered. "That hurts!"

"Uh-oh. We raised you up too much. Let me raise the bed some so's you don't have to bend you up." Louise moved to the foot of the bed and leaned over to turn the hand crank that caused the head of the bed to lift up. When she saw Elaina frown, she backed it back down a tiny bit then stopped.

Soon Clement peeked around the doorjamb. "Anyone in here need a visit?" Elaina noticed how the dark curl so like Seth's dropped over his deeply tanned forehead. Then she heard little-girl giggles.

"Are the little girls with you?" she asked.

"Little girls? What little girls? I came to see you!" The whispers and giggles filled the hallway. "Oh! Do you mean these little girls?" He led their three sisters into the room, reminding them to be quiet as could be or the nurse would get them.

All three girls raced over and piled onto Elaina's bed even as their mother admonished them to be careful to not hurt their sister. They asked question after question.

"What's it feel like to be operated on?" Agnes asked.

"What did they do with your 'pendix?" Cherilyn queried.

Kate was teary-eyed and asked quietly, "You okay, Sissy?"

Elaina tried to answer all their questions but after only a few minutes became sleepy again, the effects of the anesthesia and pain medicines taking over.

"All right, girls. Let's go on home and let our Elaina rest. She's had a big day and she needs to heal up so she can come home to us."

Louise kissed her daughter's forehead then shepherded her family out the door, closing it softly. Clement led them to the car and they were soon on their way home.

Elaina remained in the hospital for ten days, the doctor wanting her to heal up completely from the surgery. The hospital volunteers brought her books that she devoured, being able to read for hours on end, uninterrupted by sisters or chores. It might have been a hospital, and she was in some pain, but it was like heaven on earth to the teen. She didn't have to work, she got to eat meals she had no hand in preparing, she didn't have to take care of anyone else, and she was the center of attention.

That last day of her hospital stay, the doctor talked with her mother.

"Louise, you're gon' have to let her off from the fields for at least another month and a half." Elaina's eyes sparkled with delight as she heard those words. "And you, young lady, I want you to take care of yourself. You'll be able to do most of your normal home chores. Don't be lifting the big heavy pots and don't lift your baby sister, but you can cook and such. Y'all have a washer, right?"

Mama nodded. "A fine wringer washer, Doc. Dutch got it for me about a year before he passed."

The doctor replied, "Fine, fine! 'Laina, you can help with laundry, just don't be carrying a whole basket full. After you wring out a few pieces, you can throw them over your shoulder to carry them to the line like I've seen some of you ladies do. I don't want you lifting heavy things, but there's plenty you can get back to doing." He chuckled. "I'll be sure and tell your teacher she needs to send your schoolwork home so you can keep up."

Elaina groaned, "Thank you, Dr. Lancaster."

Once he'd left them alone, Louise gathered up the gifts and flowers that had been brought to cheer Elaina. "Let's get you packed up, Sis, and get you home. Clement will be here shortly to drive us. I'm gon' make your favorite Sunday dinner tonight, even though it's not Sunday."

"Thank you, Mama. I reckon it's been hard on you havin' me in here."

"It's been different, it has. But we've worked things out and we'll keep on workin' them out. You can be a big help to me by takin' care of the house while I'm workin'. You tendin' the washin' and cookin' will mean I don't have to worry about it. You're a good cook, my girl, and you do a very good job with the clothes. You pay good attention to what needs done." She lifted her daughter's new school dress from the bag she had brought and turned to show her. Smiling, she said, "We'll get through this, 'Laina. We will, and we'll be just fine. Now, let's get you up and dressed before your brother get here."

The action of sitting up was still somewhat painful, but Elaina rose and scooted to the edge of the bed. Her mother helped her out of the hospital gown, then slid the navy blue dress over her uplifted arms. She stood to smooth the skirt down while her mother retrieved her shoes and socks from the bag in the chair.

"Sit down there, Sis. I'll help you get these on," Mama said.

"I feel like a little girl again, Mama."

Keeping her head low, Louise declared softly, "I thought I was gon' lose you, little girl." Her eyes were bright when she looked up at her daughter. She encircled Elaina in a sudden and fierce hug and held her tight. The knock on the door startled them both and Louise stood quickly. "Here's Clement now."

"Your chariot awaits, madam." He bowed low like the fancy chauffeur they'd seen in a movie, and Elaina giggled.

Once home Elaina was escorted into the house where she was welcomed by her sisters, her niece, and her sister-in-law Jodie.

Jodie boomed, "Well, it's about time you got back home to us, Elaina!" She shooed the little girls out of the room and helped Elaina get settled on the couch. "Now, you just set right there. I'm going to help your mama get some supper on. Alec will be here shortly and we'll have a party to welcome you home!"

The teen leaned back against the cushions and closed her eyes, listening to the sounds of life in her cozy home. Being pampered in the hospital was nice, but it didn't smell of Mama's fried chicken and mashed taters, and there weren't pretty curtains on the windows. She hadn't heard little girl voices, either. She sighed deeply. It was good to be home.

With another five or six weeks to go in the harvest season, the family began a new rhythm. Louise went to the fields when Agnes and Cherilyn headed to school. When the school day ended, the girls walked home to change clothes then joined her. They were little, but they could pick cotton. They might not pick as much as her or Elaina, and certainly not as much as their brothers, but at this point every little bit helped.

While they were gone, Elaina kept Kate occupied as she tended the house. She was mindful of the doctor's instructions to not lift anything very heavy, including her baby sister. She and Kate worked out a system. When Kate wanted to sit on Elaina's lap, she would call her to the couch. Once her sister was seated, she would scoot over to sit on her lap and enjoy the attention. Elaina would sing to her and talk to her. When it was time for her nap, Elaina would sit on the side of the bed and tell her a story until she fell asleep.

Elaina figured out a schedule for getting up early to cook breakfast and when to start supper. Clem would help her washing the pots, then put them back on top of the stove so she wouldn't have to lift them from cabinet or hook. She learned how to get potatoes in from the cellar without lifting too much, and managed the laundry like the doctor had suggested. It seemed like a good way to do the laundry, since it broke things up more. She would run the washer, wring out several pieces, then step off the back porch and across the yard to the clothesline in the sunshine and hang them. She would go back to the tub and wring out a few more pieces and repeat her trek. The process kept Kate occupied, too, because she had to take every step her big sister did.

By mid-November, the cotton was all in and delivered to the gin over in Byrd. Mama was back in the house and things seemed more normal. She and Elaina shared the task of planning supper, and began having Agnes and Cherilyn help. They even let newly four-year-old Kate help set the table.

Thanksgiving found Louise, Elaina, Jodie, and Clement's bride, Christine, in the kitchen cooking for the whole family. Louise's father and stepmother would be going over to their daughter Rose's house for the meal. She and her husband Andrew had the room for everyone to come over and they only had one child, so the family would gather there. Harriet and Louise's brothers all had their families to share the holiday with, so the Drews stayed home.

The aromas filling the house had everyone's mouths watering by noon. Turkey roasting, pies cooling, sweet potatoes cooking, and vegetables simmering made the house seem big as a mansion and cozy as a bedroom. The men sat in the living room, discussing work at the shoe factory, and the war in Europe and the Pacific while Kate and Adele played on the floor.

Elaina walked into the living room and said, "One of you needs to get the leaf from under the couch so we can get everyone around the table."

Alec said, "We don't have to do that, some of us can—"

Elaina interrupted, "Mama said."

She and Clement laughed as Alec rose from the couch and knelt to reach under it, pulling the spacer for the kitchen table that would allow extra people to gather around it.

"We're gon' let the little girls have their own table, but all us grownups are supposed to be around the table," she told her brothers.

Clement tousled her dark hair. "Since when are you a grownup?"

Turning back to the kitchen, carrying the table leaf, Elaina huffed, "Mama said."

The men guffawed, which set the little girls to giggling.

Soon Louise called out, "Kate! Adele! Cherilyn! Y'all come on in here and wash up, then we'll fix your plates. The rest of y'all get ready, too."

The little girls jumped up and ran to the kitchen. Elaina and Agnes drew water into a large bowl and helped them wash and dry their hands, then filled their plates with turkey and dressing, potatoes and gravy, yams and vegetables, and all that the women had prepared. They carried the plates to the living room to find that their mother had prepared a little table for them, complete with a tablecloth and chairs. She motioned for the girls to come and sit down and quietly told them to wait just a minute, that they were going to pray, then they could eat.

The rest of the family gathered around the table, where Louise had them all hold hands.

"Lord, I reckon You've taken good care of us again. You've give us a place to lay our heads that's dry and warm, You've give us a good crop this year, and You've give us our 'Laina back. Now we're sitting here with our whole family before a table full of food that You've given us. We're mighty thankful for all this and Your Son Jesus, too. Amen."

And upon her "amen" the sound of chairs scooting on the hardwood floors filled the house. As the food was passed around, the conversations began.

"'Laina?" Clement asked, "who's that fella that you've been talkin' to after church the last few weeks?"

"Hmm?" Elaina quickly popped a bit of turkey into her mouth.

Agnes giggled. "It's Grant Kerr! She's all moon-eyed over him!"

Louise's brows arched as she listened to the good-natured banter and watched Elaina's cheeks redden. She decided she'd have to learn a little more about this Grant fellow.

Chapter 15

"Laina! You're not s'posed to be touchin'!" Agnes taunted. "Hush, Agnes Ann Drew! You're with us, you can see nothin' is goin' on. Just hush." Elaina's cheeks flushed deeply even as her pale hand was dwarfed by the large tanned one of Grant Kerr.

The spring day was warm as they walked the dirt road together, Agnes having been sent by their mother to chaperone the couple.

Grant was a transplant. He was born in Memphis and his family hadn't lived in Kreg County long. His dark good looks had sparked the imagination of many of the local girls. Elaina loved his dark wavy hair and deep chestnut brown eyes. She even liked his widow's peak. He was older; he'd just turned nineteen last November, but Elaina was now fourteen. A curvy, dark-haired beauty much older than her years.

Grant laughed and, reaching back, grabbed Agnes by the hand and drew her up to walk with them. "There. Does that make it better? I'm not just holding 'Laina's hand—I'm holding yours, too!"

Now it was Agnes' cheeks that turned red. She stammered, "Uh, well, I guess it's okay." She left her hand in his, and glanced past him to her sister. Elaina's hazel eyes danced with merriment at Agnes' new predicament.

"Hey!" Grant stopped.

"What is it?" Elaina asked.

"I think I hear something down there, past the thicket," he said, pointing just off the road to their right. The brush was thick, but there was a tiny path where game and children had made their way through.

"Should we go see what it is?" Elaina asked innocently.

"I'll go," Grant replied, "but you might want to follow me so if something gets me you can get help." The mischief in his eyes was plain to see.

"What am I s'posed to do?" Agnes whined.

"You stay up here, Agnes. Watch for anything that comes up outta here and you holler if you see someone coming."

Having a good idea what the two were up to, Agnes huffed and sat down on an old tree stump.

Grant guided Elaina down the hill and through the thicket. There Elaina saw a quilt laid out in a small clearing. She stopped and looked up at Grant.

"What is all this?" she inquired.

"This is a place where we can sit and talk without your little sister hearing everything we say."

"Oh," she replied. Blinking, she added, "Oh! Oh my!"

Elaina followed the handsome man to the quilt where he pulled her into his arms and kissed her. He brushed her black hair off her shoulders and cupped her cheek.

"I've wanted to do that forever, but there's always someone with us."

Flustered, Elaina sat down on the quilt, her heart racing and her cheeks flushed bright red.

"You wanted to kiss me?"

"Sure 'nough. You're the prettiest girl in all Hilltop community and I want you to be my girl." He sat down beside her.

The fourteen-year-old smiled at him, unsure what she should do or say.

"What do you say? Will you be my girl?"

"I think you're the most handsome boy—man—I've ever seen, Grant. And you're fun to be around, too. I think I'd like to be your girl."

His eyes danced as he leaned in to give her another kiss, his lips lingering on hers a moment. She thought of the kisses she'd seen in the movies and tilted her head like she'd seen the pretty actresses do.

"'Laina! Grant!" they heard Agnes yell.

"I reckon we'd better get back up there or she'll run and get Mama," Elaina grumbled. "I wish we could stay right here and talk and…" Her voice trailed off.

"I know, Princess. I wish it, too. But you're my girl and that's just fine. We'll have our time to talk. And now I can talk to your mama about courting you. She needs to know I've got some plans about you."

Her eyebrows arching, Elaina was about to ask what he meant by that, when they heard Agnes call out again, "'Laina! I'm gon' go get Mama!"

"Oh hush, you silly girl!" she yelled back. "We didn't find anything, but we were tired and took a break for a minute. We'll be back up there real quick."

Grant stood and took Elaina's hand. Pulling her up, he pulled her tightly to his chest and lifted her chin. "My girl," he whispered just before kissing her again. "Now let's go before your sister gets brave enough to come out here."

They left the quilt, knowing that Agnes' sharp mind would think even more happened than did. Grant made up a great tale of finding monster footprints and broken trees and being scared to go further than the thicket.

Agnes rolled her eyes. "I know you're pullin' my leg, Grant Kerr."

He stopped walking. "Do you want to go back? I'll show you, then you can go find whatever made those tracks."

"Uhh, no. No. That's okay. We need to get back home." She skipped ahead of the couple, who sauntered behind her, hands clasped.

Elaina could still feel the heat of Grant's kiss on her lips and cast many sideways glances at this handsome man, because he really was a grown man, who wanted her to be his girl. He wanted her! Her heart skipped more than one beat as they walked along. She wondered what he meant about having plans for her.

As they neared her home Grant lifted her hand to his lips and kissed it, then let it go. There was no sense in raising her mother's ire. He would talk with her about courting Elaina and then he'd be allowed to hold her hand in public.

Elaina worked beside her mother, cleaning up after supper. "Mama?" she asked.

"Hmm?" her mother returned.

"Mama? How come you were so quick to let Grant start courtin' me? You usually have to wait and think and stuff."

"Well, Sis. Back at Thanksgiving when the kids were teasing you about Grant, I thought then I'd better take a look at this fella. I saw the look in your eyes and the blush on your face and I realized that you were plenty taken with him. So, I talked with Alec later and had him ask around some at the plant."

Eyes wide in wonder, Elaina said, "You did that?" Shaking her head she inquired, "What did Alec find out?"

"Well, you know he's not from around here. I knew that right off. We don't know a whole lot about him other than at work. He works hard and does what he's s'posed to. He don't shirk any, it seems. He just digs in and gets the job done. Alec said that the folks that work right with him like him. They say he's got a quick wit and a kind heart. I figured that even with not knowing his family much, I could let him court you."

Elaina smiled excitedly, but her mother intoned, "That don't mean you act any less the lady, Missy." Pointing the wooden spoon she'd been washing, Louise went on, "You may hold his hand between you two when seated. You may walk with him and hold his arm. You are not to be alone with him at any time, do you hear me?"

Elaina felt both disappointment and anger rising up in her. "You don't trust me, Mama? I ain't gon' do nothin'!" she sputtered.

"Child, I don't trust two kids who think they're in love being alone and lettin' nature take its course. Right now y'all need to spend time together, talkin' about life, about what you like and what he likes. You need to learn some of each other's quirks and crazies. That way, if'n he asks you to marry him, you'll know better what you're gettin' into."

And so the courtship began. They were allowed to sit separate from the family, but not out of sight of them. When they walked home from church, Agnes had to walk with them. They tried the thicket ploy a couple more times until Agnes caught on that they were in the bushes kissing. Her "I'm gon' tell Mama!" soon ended that.

When the planting began, Grant was right there helping. He brought Louise gifts of coffee and flour and sugar. He brought the girls little trinkets and candy. When the family got together for meals, he talked and laughed with the brothers as though he'd known them all his life.

Chapter 16

In July, the time for the Rafferty family reunion came along and Grant was once again helping however he could. He brought his truck to the Drew home and loaded all the girls and the food into it. Then he walked Louise to the passenger door and helped her in. He lifted Elaina to ride in the back with her sisters, then climbed in behind the wheel.

Elaina felt a little put out that he hadn't let her sit in the middle up front, but figured it might not be polite since the shifter was right there and her mama riding up there, too.

Once at the picnic grounds Grant gave each girl a package to carry to the serving tables, making it a fun little parade to carry the food. He had the little girls giggling and happy to be helping. Louise shooed him and the little girls away, but kept Elaina close.

"'Laina, tell me about you and Grant," she said quietly.

"What, Mama? Me and Grant what?"

She stirred a pot filled with beans, then looked at her daughter. "Are you in love with him, 'Laina?"

Elaina blinked several times, trying to put her words together.

"I am, Mama. I love how his eyes sparkle when he talks to me. I love how he helps you and the girls. I love that little smile he has that makes him look like he's got somethin' up his sleeve. I love his hair…"

Laughing, Louise said, "Oh, my girl. You've got it bad, all right." She looked around at the gathering relatives. "Let's take a walk for a bit," she directed her eldest daughter.

"But Mama, we need to—" Elaina started, then hushed and followed her mother.

Once they were out of earshot of everyone, Louise spoke. "Elaina, Grant asked me today for permission to ask you to marry him. I'm just not sure—"

Elaina squealed and flung her arms around her mother's neck. She whispered excitedly, "Mama! He's gon' ask me?"

"Shush, Sis. I said he asked if he could. I ain't told him yes or no yet. I wanted to talk to you and find out what your thinkin' is."

"Oh, Mama! I do want to marry him! He's so handsome and so kind!" Elaina gushed.

"But, Elaina." Her mother hardly ever used her real name. "You're only fourteen. You're just a child and he's a man fully grown. I jus' don't know." Her doubts were etched on her face.

"But you were young when you married Daddy!" Elaina declared.

"I was seventeen, ma'am," Louise snapped. "I was three years older than you are right now, and before you say anything about running a house remember that, at the time I married your daddy, I'd been keeping house all by myself for nine years. You haven't had to do that."

Elaina sighed. "I'm sorry, Mama. I'm jus' so in love!"

Shaking her head, Louise said, "I will talk with your brothers and see what they think."

"Can you do that today, Mama? Please?" her daughter begged.

"I'll see what I can do. Now, let's go over and help get the food on the tables." Her attention shifted to the reunion. "I wonder if Et will be here. Oh, look! There she is. And there's Wiatt and Mellie. It's so good to see everyone. Daddy will be so happy."

The picnic grounds overflowed with food and laughter as the descendants of Jerrold Sherman Rafferty gathered. Many stories of the old days were told. Grant sat with the men and listened intently while Elaina helped her mother and aunts. The children played tag and hopscotch until they were called by their mothers to come and eat.

Once Harriet's husband, Andrew, the preacher in the family, returned thanks, the elders of the crowd went through, filling their plates with food. Elaina watched her grandparents as they looked over each pot and pan to determine if they liked what was in it. Tapping her foot, she silently urged them on. Right behind them were her mother's brothers and sister. Just like when they were children, the jostling and joshing ran rampant. It seemed to Elaina to take hours before it was her turn to go through and choose her meal. Grant walked with her, and when their plates were piled high with food he drew her to the table farthest from the rest of the family. Agnes and Cherilyn started in their direction until a glare from Elaina stopped them in their tracks.

"Girls, come over here!" their mother called, making a fuss over them.

"Yes, Mama," they chimed as they plodded over.

"What's up with Grant and Elaina, Mama?" Agnes asked bluntly.

"Nothin' I don't reckon, Agnes Ann. Now eat your lunch. Your grandpa's about ready to head to the desserts." Little Kate squealed, hearing the word desserts, her favorite thing ever, and everybody laughed.

Grant and Elaina sat across from each other at the painted wooden table. She kept her eyes focused on her plate as they ate. Her excitement was hard to control; she was sure if she looked him in the eyes right now, she would explode with pure joy.

"'Laina?" Grant said softly.

"Yes, Grant?" she replied.

"Do you want some tea? I'll go get us some." Her heart sank. Maybe he wasn't going to ask her today. Mama had said he had asked her for permission to ask. Maybe he thought he had to wait until he had that permission.

"I'll go get some for us," she stated flatly. She stood then lifted her right leg out from under the table and turned to walk to the table laden with tea and lemonade and ice water. Taking two of the glasses from her mother's kitchen, she filled them with the sweetened tea her mother had made. She knew the other jars of tea were made by her aunts and cousins, but she liked her mama's the best.

It's a good thing I know how to make it like Mama, she thought as she carried the glasses back to the table where Grant sat. She noticed the food on his plate was nearly gone.

"My, my!" she cried. "You've done eat 'most all your food!"

"I have!" he declared. "Your folks are some of the best cooks in the whole wide world!" Grant waved at her mother as he spoke the words just a bit louder than necessary.

Elaina sat down and began to push her food around on her plate. She took a bite or two, but she was too nervous to really eat.

"If you're not gon' eat, do you want to go for a walk?" Grant asked her.

Brightening, she jumped up. "Yes, I'd love to." She carried their plates to the big washtub filled with soapy water. She tipped her plate, allowing the scraps to fall into the slop bucket nearby and used her fork to urge the last bits off. She slid her plate into the sudsy water, then scraped Grant's plate. After

Elaina washed the plates and silverware, Grant dried them and stacked them with their mates. He placed the teen's hand in the crook of his arm and walked to her mother.

"Ms. Drew, I'd like to take Elaina for a walk if that's all right with you."

Louise looked at the table where the younger girls sat.

"We won't go far, ma'am," Grant intoned. "We're just gon' walk around the picnic grounds so's I can make room for some of your delicious desserts."

"All right, Grant," Louise replied, giving her daughter the look that told her to most certainly behave herself.

With her hand on his arm the two sauntered toward the street at the back of the picnic grounds, just past the pavilion. Grant told stories about working in the shoe factory, making Elaina laugh. They turned right on the lane that ran up to the highway and continued their stroll. Elaina could feel the eyes of everyone on her.

Unable to stand it any longer, she asked, "Is there something you want to talk about, Grant?"

"Not yet," he replied.

"Not yet?" she said. "Why not?"

"Because I don't have the permission of your mama to," he declared, his dark eyes dancing with merriment at his girl's bewilderment. Leaning down to whisper in her ear, he said, "You know what I'm gon' ask, so what are you gon' say?"

She looked up at him, batting her eyes, and laid on her Southern accent to sound like that Scarlett O'Hara in the movie she'd seen. "Why, Mr. Kerr, however on earth would I know what you're gon' ask me?" She giggled.

Grant laughed. "Well, I reckon I might not have anything to ask after all."

"What?" Elaina exclaimed.

Grant roared with laughter, drawing looks from the family still gathered around the tables.

"Pretty girl, as soon as your mama gives me permission I'm gon' ask you to marry me. I want you to be Mrs. Kerr."

Before she could squeal, he pressed his finger to her lips. "Shh. I don't want your mama or your brothers knowin' I told you."

"Oh, Grant! Mama told me you'd asked her. She said she's got to talk to Alec and Clem before she'll say. I don't know if she'll get to talk to them today. Christine may want to go on home, and with the little ones Jodie may want to get home, too. We may have to wait till tomorrow for her to even see them, and then they may not come to church!" Her words tumbled over one another like newborn calves tripping over their own legs.

"Shush, 'Laina. We'll find out when it's time. Until then, you know I love you enough to want you to be my wife."

The fourteen-year-old girl felt so strange hearing those words. It seemed that just yesterday she'd been playing with dolls and playing school with the other girls. Now she had a beau and was maybe going to become a wife. Hovering between girlhood and womanhood she slipped her hand back onto his arm, her cheeks slightly flushed, and they finished their walk.

As the family sat around visiting that afternoon, Elaina's brother Alec caught up with her. "I hear you've turned a fella's head."

"What?" she replied innocently.

"Mama asked me what I thought about Grant Kerr."

"Oh, I see."

"'Laina, do you love him? Really love him? I mean, you're just a girl—"

"I'm very nearly a woman!" the girl cried, then ducked, realizing several had heard her outburst. "I ain't no little girl, Alec."

"I reckon not, Sis. I'm not sure you're old enough to get married yet, but I've seen Grant at work. He seems like a good sort. I've seen him helping you and Mama and I suppose I could see y'all gettin' married."

Elaina swung her arms around her brother's neck, thanking him over and over. Just then, her brother Clement walked up and the same conversation began again.

Clement's reaction was different, Elaina noticed. He seemed reserved. While his mouth offered her congratulations, his eyes seemed sad. She didn't ask him about that, and years later would wish she had, but for now she was happy to have the blessings of her family.

Chapter 17

Just over a month later, when the August heat was really making itself known, Grant and Elaina wed. She wore her best Sunday dress with one of her mother's kerchiefs pinned across her shoulder-length black tresses. Her groom wore a simple suit borrowed from a friend, a white shirt buttoned to the collar, and a tie.

As Elaina started down the aisle of the same church her parents were married in, she thought Grant was the most handsome man ever created and marveled that he was hers.

Just as Mama and Daddy did Elaina and Grant met their guests outside the church, under the shade trees. The men of the church had set boards across saw horses to make long tables and the ladies of the church had prepared a delicious meal for the newlyweds and their guests—with everything from fried chicken and mashed potatoes, to meatloaf, roast beef, fresh-from-the-garden vegetables, and plenty of blue-ribbon desserts.

When the party was over, the churchyard all cleaned up and put back to rights, Grant drove them to their home. He had rented a little place about a mile from Elaina's mother and sisters. It wasn't quite in town, but not quite in the country either.

They walked to the door hand-in-hand and Grant stopped.

"What's wrong?" Elaina asked.

"Oh, nothing. Nothing at all," he replied. Scooping her up in his arms, he carried her across their threshold just like she'd seen Cary Grant do in the movies. She wrapped her arms around his neck and kissed her new husband on the cheek.

"Welcome home, Mrs. Kerr!" he said, setting her back on her feet.

Elaina twirled slowly, examining her new home. She had known he had found them a house, but this was her first time inside it. Her mother hadn't felt it proper for her to visit there before she was married.

"Oh, Grant! It's so pretty!" she cried.

"And it's all ours, baby."

She turned into his arms, bubbling about fixing this and that, curtains here and there, dishes and pots and pans.

"Can that wait a bit?" he asked his new wife.

"Well, of course it can." She smiled, her face tilted to his.

Kissing her softly on the lips, he stated simply, "This is our wedding night."

Elaina nodded, and followed him into their bedroom. Mama had told her about men and women joining and making babies, but she had never explained the how of it. The child-bride determined to learn as she went.

Later that evening the couple sat at their kitchen table, finishing their supper. They talked about the dreams they had for a family and a nice house and growing old together.

"Grant?"

"Hmm?"

"Do you reckon somebody'll do a Chivaree for us?"

"Oh, I don't know. Some of the guys from work might."

Her eyes widened and her cheeks flushed deep red. "Oh, I hope not!" she declared, covering her face with her hands.

Laughing, her husband said, "What's wrong with a little Chivaree, 'Laina?"

"I don't want the men you work with seeing me in my-in my..."

"In your honeymoon all-together?" he supplied.

"I won't be sleeping in my all-together, Mr. Kerr! Not if there's the least chance someone's coming for a Chivaree!"

Grant roared with laughter, taking her hand and pulling her over to his lap. "Don't worry, 'Laina. You put on your nightgown and your duster and you can get into bed. If someone comes, you'll be all ready for them."

Tears filled the young bride's eyes, knowing that she didn't want to be made a spectacle of. If her brothers had arranged a Chivaree it wouldn't be so hard to take, but Grant's friends? She didn't know them, and she didn't know how they would react to her. She turned out the lamp by their bed and curled up next to her husband, resting there but determined not to fall asleep.

Suddenly, the couple was awakened by the sound of someone beating on their doors. The noise came from the front and back. Sounds of laughter rang above the rattle of pots and pans when somebody set off a bunch of firecrackers.

Grant slid from under the covers and grabbed his pants and shoes. Elaina sat on her pillow, the covers pulled up to her chin.

"Chivaree!" the revelers at the front door hollered.

"Chivaree!" the partiers at the back door called back.

Grant stepped through the bedroom door, pulling it closed behind him. Elaina heard him open the front door and walk onto the porch. She heard his smooth, deep voice as he talked to the people out there. The sound of the pots and pans began again and Elaina squeaked and pulled the covers over her head.

Her heart started racing when she heard the front door open and the noise seemed to pour into the house. She pulled the light robe she wore closer around her and looked around, wondering how she could hide and where. Finally her gaze fell upon the window. It seemed her only option.

As she turned the lock on the window, she prayed that it would move easily and silently. She slid her fingers down to the handle at the bottom of the lower sash and lifted. Her heart felt like it would pound out of her chest. The sash slid up easily and, best of all, quietly.

Elaina stuck her head through the window and looked down. The drop to the ground wasn't too far; she worked her right leg through the opening, then her left. With her toes pointed toward the ground, she hung just a moment on the window sill before dropping to the ground. She hadn't even noticed the bush that was there until now. As she ran into their back yard toward the trees, she could hear the revelers shouting and calling for her.

The teen found a large oak standing sentry among the others at the tree line and she took refuge behind it, pulling the tail of her nightgown close so it wouldn't be seen.

"Elaina!" she heard voices call.

"Oh, Missus Kerr!" another voice rang out.

She shook her head. Even if she stepped out now, she would be laughed at and mocked for not allowing the celebration of the Chivaree to envelop her.

Why, oh why didn't I just walk into the living room when Grant did? she asked herself. *Then I wouldn't be hidin' out here in the dark not knowin' what's going on in my own house.*

Leaning against the tree she shivered, even though the night was warm. She wondered if Grant would come out to get her or just let her wonder if it was safe. Within moments of that thought, she heard footsteps nearing her hiding place.

"'Laina?" a voice whispered.

She remained still, though she was certain whoever it was could hear the incessant drumbeat of her heart.

"'Laina, it's me." her husband said quietly. "They're all gone now. You can come back in."

"Are you sure? I'm so embarrassed!"

Grant gathered her into his arms and kissed the top of her head. "I'm sure. Everyone's gone and they aren't mad or nothin'. I made sure they knew that you were mighty tired after all the wedding stuff. It was mostly the guys from work. Your brothers didn't even show up."

The couple walked back to the house. Inside, Grant lowered the bedroom window then turned to his child bride. He ran his fingers through his thick black hair. "Ready for bed, Mrs. Kerr?" he asked, a twinkle in his dark eyes.

Elaina slipped under the sheet and the bedspread her mother had given them and patted the bed beside her. "Yes, Mr. Kerr; I'm ready."

Chapter 18

Elaina easily slipped into the role of wife as far as the cooking and cleaning went. She'd been doing that at home ever since her father had died. She sometimes thought Grant wanted to make love more than was proper, but she had no idea what "proper" was. When she'd asked her mother, she was told to pleasure her husband whenever he wanted.

Their first Valentine's Day as husband and wife approached and Elaina went all out to make Grant's favorite meal. She had joined with her sisters to cut hearts out of red paper for school and kept a couple for herself. Shortly after he left for work that morning she decorated their kitchen table, and began cooking right after lunch.

When Grant opened the front door he heard her singing, and smiled. He had stopped by the general store in town and picked up a candy-filled heart. He stepped into the kitchen with it behind his back.

"Hey, 'Laina. I'm home!"

"Grant!" She ran to him, throwing her arms around his neck. She kissed him then smiled up at him. "I'm glad you're home. I missed you."

"Missed me? I was just here this morning!" he joked.

"Well, with it bein' a special day and all, I…" Her voice trailed off.

"Special day? I thought you turned fifteen last month. And Christmas was before that. What special day could this be?"

Huffing slightly, she dropped her arms and started to turn.

"Now, now, young lady. I know what today is, and I got you something."

"You did? Somethin' for me?"

"For you," He stated, holding the big heart out to her.

Her hazel eyes filling with surprise, Elaina cried out, "Grant! That had to be so expensive!"

"And what if it was? I got a right to spoil my best girl, don't I?"

"Well, I reckon. As long as I'm your best girl."

Chuckling, he patted her backside and asked how long till supper was ready.

Elaina set the heart on the table between their plates and said, "Long enough for you to clean up, dear." She laughed as he snorted about having to wash up for dinner. He sounded like her brothers used to when she was little. Were all boys like that?

After they'd eaten their meal, Elaina opened the box of candy and offered it to her husband. He took a piece and held it to her lips. She took a bite then offered him one. After they'd eaten a couple chocolates each, she said softly, "I have a gift for you, too, Grant."

"Really? What is it? I didn't see nothin'"

"Well, you can't see it yet—not really."

Grant frowned, looking at her across the table. Elaina stood and walked around the table to him. She lifted his hand from the table and put it on her belly.

"Your gift is right here," she said shyly.

"What? You're—we're—a baby?!?" He jumped up, the chair falling over behind him as he scooped his wife up and swung her around excitedly.

He carried her into the living room and sat down in the chair with her on his lap. "When did you find out?"

"Just yesterday. Mama took me, so she knows. I swore her to a secret. I wanted it to be a surprise for you."

"Oh, 'Laina! I'm so happy!" he exclaimed, hugging her close. "I can't believe it, I'm gon' be a daddy."

"And I'm gon' be a mama," Elaina whispered.

"What's wrong, Little Mama?" he murmured against her hair.

"I'm kinda scared, Grant. I ain't never done nothin' like this before."

"Aw, now, you got your mama and Jodie and Christine," he said, naming her sisters-in-law. "They'll help you. And I'll be here for you. Sweetheart, we're gon' have a baby. I bet we'll have a little girl and she'll be the spittin' image of her beautiful mama."

In September, Doreen was born. With her parents' dark hair and dark eyes and her mother's creamy skin, she looked like a China doll.

Elaina watched as Louise held her little girl there in the hospital and smiled as her mother declared that she looked just like her mama had when she was born. Grant was so excited to be a father that he handed out cigars at work and even at church, whether they smoked or not.

Agnes held her niece carefully and showed her off to her sisters. "Look, Cherilyn, she looks just like Kate did when she was born." Cherilyn nodded her agreement.

"Me? I looked like Doreen?" six-year-old Kate asked.

"You sure did," Cherilyn replied. "Your hair was black and curly like hers and your eyes so dark. Her smile is even like yours."

"Huh. What do you know." Kate took a closer look at her niece.

"Grant, we need to go to Grandpa and Grandma's house so they can see Doreen," Elaina stated as they left the hospital.

Grant was driving very carefully, keeping an eye on his wife as she cuddled their baby in her arms. "Are you sure? Are you too tired? I don't want you to overdo. And besides, is it good for Doreen to be out like this?"

Elaina giggled. "You haven't been around babies much, have you?"

Red tinged his tanned face as he shook his head.

"It's okay, Grant. Grandma Freda has helped bring half this county into the world. When my little sisters were born, Mama kept them home about a week before she'd take them to church. That was goin' out in public. Goin' to family is different. It will make Grandma and Grandpa really happy to see our girl."

"All right, then," he replied. "Lean back and relax. I'll head over to the Rafferty place."

Elaina did lean back and rest her head on the back of the seat. She kept her daughter cuddled close, making sure the bumps of the old gravel roads didn't disturb her. When they drove into the yard of her grandparents' home, her grandmother rushed out onto the front porch.

"Oh, my! Elaina! Grant! Did you bring that precious baby by for me to see?"

"Well, of course they did, Freda! Why else would they be here. Do you reckon they've even been home from the hospital yet?" Jerry laughed as he joined his wife on the porch.

Grant trotted around the car and opened the door for his wife and helped her out. Closing the door, he then helped her up the rock steps to greet her grandparents.

"Grandma, Grandpa, this is Doreen—your great-granddaughter." Elaina pulled the blanket away from her daughter's face to show her off.

Freda clasped her hands, beaming with pride. Jerry nodded, and slapped Grant on the back.

"Do you want to hold her, Grandma?"

"Well now, am I breathin', Missy? Of course I want to hold that baby! C'mon, let's go inside. Jerrold, would you heat up that coffee pot and share a little with Grant? And maybe 'Laina would want some lemonade."

The family moved into the living room, Freda helping her granddaughter navigate without bumping or tripping on anything. They sat together on the couch and Elaina handed her baby girl over to her grandmother.

"Oh my," Freda kept repeating. "'Laina, she looks just like you did when you came into this world. But I see her daddy in here, too." She ran her finger along the baby's widow's peak and under her chin. "Yes'm, I see Grant here, too. She's beautiful. Just beautiful."

Jerrold returned from the kitchen with Grant on his heels. Elaina giggled seeing the tip of a cigar peeking from the pocket of her grandfather's overalls.

Chapter 19

Halfway through October, Grant brought up the subject that the auto plants up in Detroit were hiring. He explained to Elaina that the money he could make up there was more than double what he was making at the shoe factory.

"We could stay with my aunt and uncle until we found a place," he told her.

"I don't know, Grant. You grew up in Memphis but the furthest I've ever been from home is Ward Creek, and Detroit is a whole lot bigger than that."

"Yeah, it's big, but it's got a lot for young couples like us. Your brother is up there, you know. Have you heard any complaints from Jodie? No. She's enjoyin' it up there. Come on. Let's do it. We'll get out of this little town and make a name for ourselves."

"Well, I reckon we can give it a try. Will we get a place soon after we get there? I don't want to have to live with your aunt and uncle for too long. I don't want to put them out."

"Just for a little bit. We'll start looking for a place of our own as soon as I get my first paycheck."

Grant seemed like he had thought of everything and had the plans for their move all worked out, so Elaina said, "Well, I reckon we need to go talk to Mama and let her know. When are we gon' move?"

Grant thought a moment. "Well, I should work out the rest of this week. Can you get the house packed up by Saturday?"

"Saturday?" she cried. "*This* Saturday?"

"Yeah, this Saturday. We could leave out early Saturday morning and get there by lunch time Sunday. We can do it."

"Except that I'm the one who has to take care of a baby and wash clothes then pack them and pack up the furniture and the dishes and…"

He wrapped his arms around her. "Hush, 'Laina. I'm gon' help. You get the clothes done and packed. Maybe your mama and your sisters can help you pack them and the dishes. I'll get a couple guys from work to come and help me load up the furniture Friday after work."

She sighed heavily, the thought of moving so far from home both frightening and exciting. She knew Stafford, knew the people, knew the town, and she was known. How would she get around in Detroit? What were the people like there?

"I reckon that would work. If we're gon' do this, we need to go tell Mama now." She gathered up the baby and headed outside.

It was Grant's turn to sigh. He muttered to the empty house, "I had hoped this move to the city would help untie those apron strings and make Elaina stand on her own two feet." He walked to the truck and drove them to Louise's house, where they told her the news.

"Oh my goodness!" she exclaimed. "Now I'll have two of my children living up there with my grandbabies. I reckon you know what's best, Grant. Elaina, I've got some errands to run first thing in the mornin', but I should be able to be at your house before lunch. We'll work on getting all the clothes washed up and packed. At least I can keep an eye on this beautiful granddaughter of mine while you do that." She cooed at the dark-haired baby on her lap.

"That would be really nice, Mama. I don't know what-all I need to do or even how to do it."

"Well, the furthest I've ever moved was from Grandpa's house to here, but we'll get it all figured out."

The next three days were a blur to Elaina, filled with washing clothes, nursing her baby, cooking, and cleaning their house top to bottom. Her mother was a great help, watching the baby while she put their meager but treasured belongings into boxes and tied them with string to make the journey to Michigan.

Friday evening, Grant brought home a group of men from work to help him load the truck. Most of the furniture belonged to the house, except for the baby's crib and bassinet and all her things. The men made quick work of carrying boxes stuffed with clothing and towels and tablecloths and loading them into the truck. Grant tied a canvas tarpaulin over everything.

"Is there a way to get to the diapers while we're on the way?" Elaina asked.

"Yes, ma'am! I even tied everything in so's that you can use the tailgate as a table to change her on. We'll be able to use that as our picnic table, too."

"That's wonderful," the young mother stated with little enthusiasm. Her heart was still heavy at the thought of leaving her mother and sisters.

"Now, 'Laina, you know we're gon' be better off up there. We'll have the money we need to have a good life. We'll be able to raise our children up where they won't be pickin' cotton to get by. And we can send your mama some money to help her and the girls if you want to."

His wife's eyes brightened. "We can send them some money?"

He nodded. Elaina flung her arms around her husband's neck, thanking him over and over between kisses on his cheeks.

"I reckon that made you happy," he chuckled.

"It did! Oh, Grant! If Mama didn't have to work so hard, that would be wonderful. And it might mean that the girls could stay in school instead of leaving early because of having to work the fields." She kissed him once more, then turned to pick up her pocketbook. "Speakin' of Mama, she's got supper ready for us over there since all our pots and pans are packed up on the back of that truck."

"Ha. I hadn't thought of that." He pecked her on the cheek. "I reckon that's why I have you to take care of the little things."

Louise had invited all her family to dinner to send Elaina and Grant off. They ate and talked and laughed long into the evening. The couple wound their way back to their little house and quickly fell asleep on the pallet of blankets Elaina had kept out of the truck. She knew she would be able to roll that up and slide it in between other things in the morning.

Chapter 20

The trip to Michigan was long, hot, and tiring. Though the fall temperatures were comfortable outside the truck, the temperature inside was miserable. Elaina would try to open her window, but her tiny daughter couldn't handle the wind. She recalled Grandma Freda's words that letting the wind blow in Doreen's face would steal her breath, and she didn't want anything to happen to her precious baby.

Doreen would get grumpy at being held, then when Elaina laid her on the seat she would cry to be held. Elaina spent most of the hours gazing out the window, looking over harvested corn and wheat fields. She would crinkle her nose when they passed a hog or chicken farm.

The couple talked of their plans, their dreams, and how they would go about getting their own place.

When Grant drove onto the ferry at Cairo, Illinois to cross the Mississippi River, Elaina felt her heart pounding in her chest. She feared the water of the constantly rolling river because her swimming lessons had died with her father. She didn't say anything, choosing to avoid ridicule by taking deep breaths and sitting in the truck to hold the baby instead of joining her husband at the rail. Once they were back on land she rode quietly, her eyes glued to the broad waters of the Ohio River flowing alongside them as they drove further north.

The family had been on the road for just over eight hours when they found a travel court. Grant said they could afford the night there since he wouldn't have to pay his uncle for board until after he got his first pay from the plant.

"It's a clean place," Elaina said as they enjoyed the hot meal at the motel's restaurant.

"It sure is. Clean as your mama's house," Grant replied.

"This food is good, too." Elaina returned, taking another forkful of mashed potatoes and gravy.

"Not as good as yours, Mrs. Kerr."

His wife blushed and he laughed heartily. "You sure do embarrass easily, 'Laina."

"It ain't something to laugh at!" she retorted hotly.

"I ain't laughing at you! I think your cheeks with that rosy color are right pretty. Reminds me of the first day I saw you in the churchyard. You were chasin' after your baby sister and your niece."

It was Elaina's turn to laugh. "I did that a lot at home."

Lightly rubbing the soft hair of their daughter, Grant said, "And now you'll do it for your very own babies."

They finished their meal and walked to their room. Grant carried the baby and held Elaina's hand.

"I sorta feel like a rich lady, stayin' at a hotel and eatin' in the restaurant," Elaina said.

"Honey, this is just the beginning. We're gon' stay in the finest places and eat the richest food. We'll be well off in no time!"

Wide-eyed, the young woman listened as her husband dreamed aloud.

The next morning they ate at the restaurant again, enjoying a hearty breakfast. Elaina saved some for their time on the road, unsure when they would come across a place for their lunch.

Eight long hours of driving brought them to Uncle Cal's apartment near the center of the city. Elaina had spent the last hour with her head leaning out of the truck window, looking up at the tall buildings that made up the city.

"Grant, would you just look? There's buildings to the sky! And look, there's people livin' in them, too!" she cried. "And look at all the people on the street! Cars galore and people walkin', too. Where is everybody goin'?"

"I reckon they're either goin' shoppin' or goin' to work or comin' home from work or somethin'. There's a lot of folks livin' in this city, 'Laina. And now we're some of 'em."

"You mean we'll be living here? Right here?" she asked, awestruck.

"I mean we're almost to Uncle Cal's place." He told her the building number and the street name, showing her how to look for each.

Elaina called out as soon as she saw the street name and Grant made the turn onto the avenue. He drove past the tall buildings slowly, keeping an eye out for the right number. They both saw the building they were looking for on the right-hand side, the numbers painted gold on the arched window above the front door.

Looking around, Elaina said, "Where do we park?"

"Uncle Cal said to go to the next street and turn right and there's a parking area in the alley back there. He said it's marked. It's a good thing we only have one truck."

"Why is that?" Elaina gaped as they turned, looking up at the arched windows so far above her head. The only other windows she'd seen like that were in the fancy church back home.

"They only allow two automobiles per apartment. Uncle Cal has one and we have one. Otherwise we'd have to pay to park anywhere near."

"Pay to park?" Elaina exclaimed. "Why, back home we've got a whole field to park in!"

"And a whole lot less people and a whole lot fewer jobs," Grant replied, as though instructing a child.

He turned in to a dirt and gravel square filled with automobiles of every style and found a place to park their truck. He climbed out and walked around to Elaina's side. She handed the baby to him and stepped out of the truck.

"Do I need to bring stuff in now?" she asked, looking at the brick building before them. There were doors with steps along the bottom part of the building, spaced out evenly, while the upper doors opened onto balconies.

"No, let's go in and make sure they're home, then me and Uncle Cal will take care of all our stuff. We're not gon' need most of it, so we'll have to store some of it until we have our own place."

The young couple found their way to a door into the building and went in. They discovered it was on the bottom floor. Finding the door, Grant rang the bell for his uncle's apartment. The door flew open—Elaina was almost certain Aunt Evie had been listening at the door.

"Grant! Come in, come in! Is this your lovely bride? Oh! And your beautiful baby girl. She's so pretty! Look at all that dark hair!" The older woman reached to take the tiny baby from her nephew's arms and cuddled her close.

"Yes, Aunt Evie, this is Elaina and you're holdin' Doreen."

"Doreen. What a pretty name." She gave a nod to the child's mother and turned to walk into the living room.

"Cal! Come here. The children are here!" she called out.

"They're here? Already? I thought it would be after dark!" He grabbed Grant's hand and shook it heartily. "You made good time. It's good to see you, son! How's your daddy?"

Evie motioned for the couple to sit on the sofa as she held the little girl. Elaina heard her cooing and quietly talking to Doreen.

The men talked about family, Cal being the brother of Grant's father.

"I still don't understand what got into my brother to move from Memphis to a little hick town like Stafford."

"He and Mama are happy there, Uncle Cal. It's a nice place."

"Yeah, but it's no Memphis!" Cal replied, his disdain for rural life clear.

Evie drew Elaina into the kitchen where she directed the young mother to pots and pans and dishes.

"No better time than the present to get started, I reckon," she said.

"Get started?" Elaina asked.

"Grant said you'd be happy to do the cooking around here. He said you're a good cook. I reckon it's time we find that out. I've got a chicken laid out. Let's see what you can do with it."

Speechless, Elaina walked to her husband's aunt and lifted her daughter from the older woman's arms.

"I'll be back in a few minutes." She walked out of the kitchen and out the door. She kept walking until she reached their truck, seething with anger.

"What are you doing?" she heard Grant's familiar voice.

"What am I doing? What are you doing, telling your aunt that I'm going to be the new cook for her?" Angry tears filled the young woman's eyes.

Guffawing, Grant said, "Oh, she's pickin' at you, 'Laina! She's happy to have us stay till we find our own place."

"I'm sure she is, thinkin' she's gon' have a cook and probably a maid, too. What did you tell her, that I'd be the house slave? If that's the way it's gon' be, buy me a bus ticket. I'm goin' home." She climbed into the truck and slammed the door.

She saw Grant's dark features grow darker before he walked around the truck to the driver's door. Sliding into the seat, he said, "'Laina, it's just for a little bit. Just till we get our own place. Aunt Evie needs help. I figured since you're gon' be there, you could help out with the cookin' and cleanin'. That's all. No one thinks you're gon' be a slave or nothin'!"

Elaina huffed and said nothing, holding her daughter close. The newborn, sensing the tension, was fussy and wriggled in her mother's arms. Elaina kissed her softly on the head and hummed a favorite hymn to calm herself and her baby.

"Oh, for Pete's sake, Elaina!" Grant exploded. "We just got here. Do you have to be so difficult?"

Elaina gaped, slack jawed, then she bit out, "I am not being difficult. I was just told by a complete stranger that I'm her new cook. I agreed to help. To help, Grant," she emphasized. "Not to be the one and only. I could have kept doin' that at Mama's."

"Wouldn't you be that if we had our own place?" he asked quietly, his anger evident in every syllable.

"Well," she sputtered, "I guess. It just was just a surprise the way she said it."

"All right. I understand. Aunt Evie has always had a vinegar tongue. She's just that way. Now come on. Let's go back in and maybe you and her can get started different."

Sighing, Elaina said, "Okay. But I'm helping, Grant. That means that she has to do the main stuff." She hopped out of the truck and said, "We need to take Doreen's crib in. She's getting tired and fussy and needs a place of her own."

"You couldn't lay her on a blanket?" he asked sullenly.

"No. I can't. I already seen a bug crawlin' and I'm not putting my baby down on that. If you want me to help your aunt fix the supper, then you'd better get our baby's crib in there."

The couple bickered a few minutes longer then Grant lifted the crib down from where he'd lashed it, thankful he'd tied the parts together. Elaina reached into the truck and brought out the baby's diaper bag.

Once inside, Cal and Grant worked to put the crib together while the two women talked in the kitchen. Elaina let Evie hold the baby and began cutting up the chicken to fry. She peeled potatoes and opened a can of green beans.

She turned to the other woman. "Will this be okay? Fried chicken, mashed potatoes—I can make some gravy—and some green beans?"

Evie smacked her lips. "That sounds just fine. I can't fry chicken to beat the band. Cal will be real appreciative of that. He hasn't had any good fried chicken since we left Memphis." Her tone had changed and Elaina began to warm up to her.

After dinner Cal pushed his plate away, leaned back in his chair, and patted his belly. "That was the best fried chicken I've ever had! Bar none. Even those diner gals in Memphis didn't make it that good."

Elaina blushed as Grant heaped on the praise. "'Laina's a very good cook. I think she could make shoe leather taste good!"

Chapter 21

That first Christmas in Detroit was hard on Elaina. She missed the gatherings and parties with friends and family. She missed hearing her mother singing carols as she baked her pies and cakes. She had wanted Doreen's first Christmas to be at home and special. Instead she had to make do in the apartment with Grant and his family. The Christmas tree stood in the tiny space between the sofa bed she and Grant shared and where the dining room table sat. Elaina figured someone might call it cozy. She remembered that the house she grew up in was small, but there were at least seven people living in it all the time. It had never felt this crowded. Her heart ached for her country home.

I suppose I could write Mama a letter, but what would I tell her? If I told her how sad and homesick I am, she'd worry for me. I'll just send her a Christmas card and tell her we're doin' fine, Elaina thought as she pushed Doreen's stroller down the sidewalk toward the Five and Dime. *Grant has already had one paycheck. We should be able to start lookin' for our own place soon.*

January brought Elaina's sixteenth birthday and unexpected anguish. Grant was working the graveyard shift at the plant, which meant he was leaving about bedtime, then he would get home when she was rising and sleep through the day. With Cal working day shift, the schedule was very hard for everyone in the little apartment. Four adults and a baby in barely over 600 square feet was often maddening. Elaina took the baby for walks while Grant slept in order to keep her from waking him up. The last time Doreen's happy squeals had woken him, his rage had frightened her so badly it took Elaina an hour to calm her. She was afraid what might happen if the baby were to cry.

The weather had turned extremely cold in the city. Snow blanketed everything and Elaina was reminded of home. The city was relatively quiet until midmorning when traffic began moving again. As she prepared breakfast, Elaina fretted about what she would do to keep herself and her daughter busy and out of the apartment while Grant was asleep that day. Once he was asleep and Evie was ensconced in her bedroom, reading her magazines, Elaina bundled Doreen up and placed her in the stroller. She placed a blanket over her daughter and bounced the stroller out the back door and down the two steps to the alley pavement.

Taking off at a brisk pace she rounded the corner and was ready to cross the street when the traffic light changed, when she felt a hand roughly grab her arm.

"Where do you think you're going?" she heard her husband growl in her ear.

"Grant, I'm just taking Doreen for a walk so that we won't be wakin' you up. I was gon' down here to the Five and Dime to wander around. She likes to look at the gewgaws, and that way the apartment is quiet for you." Elaina's voice quivered as she struggled to release her arm from his grip.

"Got yourself a boyfriend workin' the counter down there at the Five and Dime?" His voice mocked hers.

People walked past the couple, little noting them or the fussy baby in the stroller. Elaina snatched her arm from Grant's grip and gathered herself up. Her hazel eyes flashed fire as she replied to him through clenched teeth.

"I have no boyfriend, Grant Kerr. I am a married woman. I don't flirt with men. I have you. I was tryin' to do you a kindness, but if you'd rather the baby play patty cakes while you're tryin' to sleep so be it. She's about ready to get out of the buggy anyway." She turned back toward the alley.

"Aw, 'Laina!" Grant cried, rubbing his face and running his fingers through his hair. "Why do you do me this way?"

Calling back over her shoulder, Elaina walked toward the apartment. "Whatever do you mean, Grant? Be kind to you? I really have no idea." She could feel her curls swishing across her shoulders with every step, her anger punishing each heel against the pavement.

"'Laina!" Grant called as he ran toward her. "Wait! Stop! Wait, girl!"

Elaina stopped, refusing to turn and look at her husband, making him come around the stroller to look her in the face, happy for the distance between them, however slight.

"I woke up and you weren't there, 'Laina. I didn't know where you'd gone. When I looked out the door I saw you turning the corner, bouncing all happy like, and I just knew you had to be on your way to meet someone."

"Oh!" the teen snarled. "Sometimes you can be such an idiot! I was bouncin' because it makes our daughter happy. I was caring for her." She pushed the stroller and he jumped out of the way then grabbed hold of her arm.

"I'm sorry, 'Laina. I shouldn't have…"

"Shouldn't have what, Grant? What shouldn't you have done?" She stood with her hand on her hips, her anger of the past months flowing unfettered. "You shouldn't have come running out here like a fool without a coat? You shouldn't have grabbed me? You shouldn't have had the thought that I'd be meeting another man just because I wasn't there when you opened your eyes? What shouldn't you have done?"

"Oh go on, 'Laina. You don't understand. Go on to the store." Pulling his wallet out, he continued, "Here. Buy you and Doreen something pretty and have lunch at the counter. I'm sorry."

Elaina watched him walk down the alley, rubbing her arm. She knew it would be bruised, but what could she do? She looked at the money in her hand and saw a twenty dollar bill. Her eyes widened. Twenty dollars? When she could get her and Doreen both a dress for five? What was going on with her husband? She lifted her handbag from the stroller and turned the brass-colored clasp, releasing the strap that held the bag closed. She tucked the money into an interior pocket, pushing it deep so that it couldn't be reached by someone trying to steal from her.

Doreen's sweet babbles reached her mother's ears and Elaina returned the pocketbook to the space by her daughter's feet and turned back toward the traffic light.

When Elaina returned to the apartment, it was almost four o'clock in the afternoon. She had bought a meal at the lunch counter in the Woolworth's store. It wasn't Thanksgiving or Christmas, but she was able to have turkey and dressing with mashed potatoes and gravy. She'd also gotten green beans, because Doreen loved them. She had held the baby on her lap as they ate the meal, laughing as her baby smacked on the green beans with great pleasure. She had also found two of the prettiest dresses for the baby, one all ruffles and bows and the other less frilly, having simple lines and a matching collar. She had also found a dress for herself on sale. It was black with little hearts like polka dots all over it. The collar was white and it came with a narrow black belt. She couldn't wait to model it for Grant.

Elaina lifted her baby from the stroller along with the bag of clothes and her pocketbook. She walked up the steps and opened the door quietly, checking to see if Grant was awake. Seeing the sofa bed was in the sofa position, she opened the door wider and stepped inside. She bounced the baby on her hip as she walked over to her husband. He raised his hands to take the baby, who giggled happily as she dove into her daddy's arms.

"Whatcha got there, Mrs. Kerr?" Grant nodded at the bag hanging on his wife's arm.

"I found Doreen two of the cutest dresses! Oh, Grant, I'm so thankful you gave me the money to get them!" She set the bag down, scurried back to the door to pull the stroller inside, then opened the bag and pulled out the clothing. Holding the frilly baby dress, she showed him and said, "This one can be her dressy dress, for if we go to church or somethin'. It's a bit big, but that means she'll have some time to wear it before she's grow'd out of it."

Grant touched the light pink fabric and ran his fingers over the lace and smiled. "Our princess will look beautiful in this!" he declared.

"Uh-huh. And this one," she said, pulling out the simple frock, "is for every day. Whenever we go anyplace, she'll look adorable in this!" She watched her husband's face for his approval.

He gave it, saying, "This is a pretty purple, 'Laina. I think it will look good on our girl. You did good. Now, what else do you have there?"

She lifted her dress from the bag, holding it folded until she stood, then let it drop as she held it against herself for him to see. "It's so soft, Grant! And I can wear it to church or to the store or anywhere. It should last me a good long time."

"As long as you don't go gettin' fat, it should," he muttered.

"Hmm?" she asked, twirling as she held the dress to her body.

"Nothin'," he said. "It's pretty, honey. It should look right nice on you. Now, when are we gon' eat? I'm so hungry I could eat a bear!" He said this last bit as he held their daughter aloft and wiggled her side to side. Her squeals of delight filled the room.

"I'm not sure what Aunt Evie has set out, but I'll see about getting supper started. Do you have to work tonight?" Elaina stood, folding her dress and laying it in the box that held their clothing, then lay her daughter's new dresses on top.

Walking into the kitchen, Elaina found a roast sitting on the wooden cutting board. She washed her hands and set about searing the meat before adding potatoes and carrots and onions. She hummed until Grant turned on the radio. As dinner cooked, she washed up the breakfast and lunch dishes, wondering to herself what Evie actually did around this house. She took a deep breath and exhaled slowly, determined not to say anything—unwilling to face the older woman's ire or that of her own husband.

Chapter 22

After supper, the family watched *On Stage, Everybody* on television while Elaina washed the dishes and cleaned the kitchen. As she wiped the table, she noted Evie holding Doreen. She wished the woman would let her baby rest in her crib.

Later Elaina kissed Grant as he left for work, waving until she could no longer see their truck's tail- lights in the alley. She went back inside and changed Doreen's diaper and snuggled her in a warm, thick sleeping gown. She sat on the sofa, nursing the baby. Gazing at her daughter's face, she dreamed of having her own home where she would be putting her baby down to sleep in her crib and then going to her own bed to sleep.

Elaina woke from dozing, still holding her little girl. She looked around to see if Cal and Evie were still up, but she saw neither. She sighed, realizing she would have no help to set up the bed tonight. She lay Doreen down in the crib, careful not to wake her. She then flipped the sofa cushions up and grabbed hold of the strap under them. Tugging hard, the framework of a bed lifted and unfolded from the sofa. She set the feet of the bed down as quietly as she could and smoothed the sheets and blankets.

Elaina lifted her sleeping baby from her crib and placed her in the bed. She loved hearing her daughter's soft breathing through the night, and having her close made it easier to keep her from waking Cal and Evie. She lay one of the sofa cushions near the edge of the bed to prevent her daughter from rolling onto the floor. As she did, she noticed her new clothes lying in the box. She slid off the dress she'd worn all day, rolling it up for the laundry, and slid the new dress over her head. The sleeves reached to her elbows and the hem was below her knees. She smoothed the skirt, and buckled the belt. She held up her hand mirror to look at herself in her new dress. She had just returned it to the box and was sitting on the side of the bed rolling her stockings down when she heard a floorboard creak.

"What do you think you're doing, Missy?" Aunt Evie's voice was loud and shrill, causing Elaina to jump and nearly drop her mirror. She glanced at her sleeping daughter, hoping the woman hadn't scared the baby.

"I'm getting' ready for bed. I was tryin' on the dress Grant bought me today, if you must know," she hissed at the old woman.

"I see what you're doin'!" Evie snarled. "You're gettin' ready to go steppin' out! I told Grant weeks ago that you're no good!" Elaina's jaw slackened in shock.

"You told him what?" she choked.

"I told him I could tell by looking, the way you're always sneakin' out when he goes to bed and stayin' gone all day. You ain't nothing but a cheap whore!"

Elaina blinked back tears, feeling bruised by the words and the vile evil they were spoken with. Cal appeared in the bedroom door.

"You get those stockings off, Missy," he demanded. "You ain't goin' out tonight."

Taking a deep breath, Elaina tried to calm herself and the older couple. "Aunt Evie—"

"Don't you call me that. I ain't an aunt to the likes of you!" the older woman nearly screamed.

Elaina gaped at the woman whose gray hair waved wildly around her head like a strange halo.

"I said you take those stockings off right now!" Cal stepped toward Elaina, rage filling his dark eyes.

Elaina rose and quickly stepped into the dining area, almost falling into one of the chairs in her attempt to escape the angry man. She kicked off the stockings she had rolled down and stood there wearing only her underthings, blushing madly. She had never been seen in her undies by anyone other than her mother and husband, and the doctor of course. She glanced at the dress she had placed n the box of their clothing. Suddenly, the dress was snatched from her hands.

"I'll just take this," Cal growled, reaching into the box and ripping the dress from its resting place. "You ain't gon' need it to go steppin' out in. I'll give it to your husband in the mornin'!" He emphasized the word husband, as though Elaina had forgotten Grant was hers.

"Cal, Evie, that's my dress. Grant bought it for me today. Just let me fold it and put it away again." Elaina's conciliatory tone seemed to anger the two even more than the fact that she didn't deny the charges being laid against her. "I was just trying it on. I wanted to see it on me before I modeled it for Grant."

"I bet you did. You wanted to see it on you in some other man's arms! You whore!" Evie spat as her husband pressed toward their nephew's wife.

Elaina had stepped away from the onslaught, keeping her daughter in her sight until she felt the doorknob against her back. Cal kept pushing toward her, spewing hatred and anger with every step.

"Cal! Evie! Stop! I'm not doing anything wrong!" Elaina cried, stepping away from the door, her back now against the wall.

"Not in my house you ain't, you worthless whore!" Cal snarled, grabbing Elaina by the wrist. And in one swift movement he opened the back door and pushed the younger woman through it. "You get out and you stay out! Whatever Grant decides to do with you is up to him, but you ain't comin' in my house again."

Elaina fell onto the snow-covered top step, her slip twisted around her thighs. She shivered as she tried to stand, her body feeling every scrape of hard-packed snow, concrete, and brick. She knocked on the door, to no avail. Angrily she pounded harder, yelling at Cal and Evie to let her back in, stomping her bare feet with each syllable to keep them from freezing to the stoop.

After several minutes of pounding and freezing, Elaina walked down the steps and to the next door. She was freezing and scared to death. Those mad people had her daughter in there and she had no idea what they might do to Doreen.

Elaina made her way up the steps and knocked on the door, seeing lights on deep inside the apartment. Her teeth had begun to chatter as she saw a shadow moving toward the door.

"Lord, child! What are you doing out here nearly naked in the snow? Come in here right now!" the kindly woman said.

"I'm Elaina, ma'am. I live next door with Cal and Evie. My husband and daughter, too."

"I've seen you coming and going. You're pretty regular in taking that sweet baby for a walk. Is your man working graveyard?"

"Yes, ma'am. I take her out so he can sleep in the daytime."

"I used to do the same thing. Elaina, did you say? I'm Cora." She placed a blanket around her guest. "I thought I heard Evie having one of her tantrums. What's she—"

Elaina started to weep. This woman's kindness was too much after months of berating and hatred at the hands of Grant's aunt and uncle.

"There, there, sweetheart. Where's your baby?"

"With them, Miz Cora. With Cal and Evie." She started crying in earnest, fearing what the hateful pair next door might do to her child.

"Oh, she's a wicked one, I know, Elaina. She's so full of hatred it just spills out sometimes, and Cal goes right along with it. You just happen to be the one it's pouring out on right now. She should be better in the morning after some sleep."

"She called me a worthless whore, Miz Cora." Elaina was barely able to whisper the words.

"Oh, child. I'm so sorry. It sounds like they're on a real tear tonight. How long are you and your little family going to stay there?" she asked kindly.

"Well, Grant said we'd only be there a month, maybe two. But that was last October." She sniffled. "I was ready the first night."

Chuckling, Cora said, "I saw you light out across the alley that evening. You hopped in that truck like one thing." Her gray eyes danced at the memory. "You're a spunky little thing. Why haven't you pushed to get your own place?"

"I'm not sure. Every time I bring it up, Grant says we don't have enough money."

"Oh, hogwash!" Cora said, waving her hand in the air dismissively. "If he's been working at the plant since October, he's made enough money to get you a nice place. Unless Cal is charging him a war pension for rent."

"I don't think we're paying any rent. We help with the groceries some, though."

"Yes, ma'am. Your husband should have a nice little nest egg to be able to rent you a house, not just an old apartment. You push for that. You get you and your baby a nice little house with a yard for her to play in."

"Oh, that sounds so beautiful, Miz Cora."

"I'm sure it does, Elaina. Babies need a yard as they grow into children. For now, we'll make a nice little bed for you on my couch and you'll sleep right here. When morning comes, we'll go talk to Cal and Evie and get all this straightened out." She walked into her bedroom and came out with blankets and pillows. Elaina felt like she'd died and gone to heaven to have someone doing something for her instead of demanding she do for them.

Cora led her to the bathroom to get cleaned up, bandaging a large scrape on the young woman's knee. "Now, you finish washing up and get under those covers."

"Yes, ma'am. Thank you, Miz Cora. I truly appreciate this."

As Elaina lay there on the couch, curled up in a tense ball under blankets warm and smelling of fresh sunshine, her tears flowed freely. The Kerrs' words had cut her to the core. She knew she had never done the thing the woman had accused her of, but remembering back to that morning on the street she began to realize that Grant thought that way, too.

"Lord, what on earth is goin' on?" she prayed softly as her eyes grew heavy, finally closing in sleep.

Elaina was jolted from her slumber by the soft touch of her rescuer.

"Here, child; put this on and we'll have some coffee before we go see Evie." Cora handed Elaina a warm chenille robe that zipped up the front and floated down to her toes.

"Thank you, Miz Cora. This is so soft!" Elaina said, zipping the robe closed.

"And here's some shoes of mine I haven't worn in ages. They aren't the best, but they'll be something on your feet when we walk outside. No need for you to freeze yourself."

"Thank you, Miz Cora." Elaina blushed, then asked, "May I use the powder room?"

"Of course you may!" she chuckled. "I have to get up and go once or twice a night nowadays. That's why I heard you so easy last night. If I'd been asleep, the Japanese could have bombed Detroit and I would have missed it."

Rejoining the elderly woman, Elaina saw she'd already folded up the blankets and lay them on the pillows.

"Now, you do drink coffee, don't you?" Cora asked her guest.

"Yes, ma'am."

"Do you like cream and sugar in it?"

"Yes, ma'am, if it's not too much to ask."

"Of course not! That's how I like mine, but not everyone is like me. Here you go. Sit down right here and drink that down. Here's some toast, too. You might need a bit of strength before we get you home."

The sixteen-year-old exhaled a long, sad sigh. "I'm almost afraid to go home, Miz Cora. I don't think they would hurt Doreen, but then I didn't think they'd throw me out of the apartment, either."

"Shush now, Elaina. We'll cross that bridge when we walk next door. Cal and Evie sometimes go a bit wild. I'll go with you and we'll have a little talk with her. Cal has already gone to work. I'll make sure you and your baby are all right before I leave you there."

Elaina felt the soft warm hand of the woman fold hers in. It felt like when Daddy would hold her hand as they walked the fields. She felt safe here.

Chapter 23

Cora walked up the steps to her neighbors' door and knocked lightly. Elaina had told her that Grant would likely be asleep, and she didn't want to wake him.

The door opened a scant inch or two and Evie's face peeked through the space.

"Oh, Cora, it's you. I didn't know who on earth would be knocking on my door this hour. Who do you have with you?" She squinted, but didn't seem to recognize Elaina.

"Do you mind if we come in, Evie? It's a mite cold out here." Cora smiled pleasantly.

"Oh dear. Well, our boy Grant is sleepin' right now. I suppose you can come in, but we've got to keep it quiet." She opened the door further, admitting the two women.

Instantly Doreen spotted her mother and cried out for her, her arms lifting toward her. Elaina quickly crossed the floor and pulled her daughter into her arms. Hugging the baby close, Elaina murmured softly against the child's dark curls. She walked back into the dining area and sat at the table where the older women were talking softly.

"Oh, Elaina, there you are! I was wondering where you'd slipped off to. Doreen needed a clean diaper when I got up, but she's all better now." Evie clucked at the baby, nodding at her. "Aren't we all better, Miss Doreen?"

The baby gurgled happily, her tiny fingers wrapped tightly around her mother's.

As Elaina weighed her response to Evie, Cora spoke up, "She was visiting me, Evie. We had the most delightful time together! This young woman is such a darling. I'm so glad she came over."

Evie looked surprised, as though she had believed that Elaina was in the apartment the whole night. Elaina frowned, wondering if she was losing her mind.

"Well, I had no idea you two knew each other," Evie said haltingly.

"Of course we do, Evie!" Cora chided. "How could I live next door to such a treasure as Elaina and not know her?"

"I guess you couldn't." Evie's voice trailed off, a look of confusion on her face. Her manners took over and she asked her guest, "Would you like some coffee, Cora? I've got some cookin'."

"That would be real nice, Evie, thank you." The old woman watched as Evie rose to pour coffee. Leaning to Elaina she said, "She has these spells, child. She has no more idea that she said or did those things to you than a bird."

"But, Miz Cora! She and Cal kicked me out. I was nearly naked!" Elaina replied in a hoarse whisper. "I would have froze to death if it weren't for you!"

"I know, I know. But the woman has no recollection."

"What am I going to tell Grant when he wakes up?"

"I believe I'd be telling him that you're moving. You've been here long enough for him to have saved up enough to get your own place. I think it's time." Cora smiled at the returning Evie to end the conversation.

After chatting over coffee and cinnamon rolls, Elaina walked to the living room and retrieved a pair of wool slacks and a long-sleeved sweater. She carried them and Doreen into the bathroom, where she unzipped the chenille robe and stepped out of it. She folded it carefully, then removed the slip she'd slept in and dropped it to the floor. She slipped Cora's shoes from her feet and placed the robe on top of them. Once dressed again, she slid into a pair of her own shoes and carried her baby on her hip and the shoes and robe in her hand.

"Oh, Elaina! Thank you so much for loaning me those! That will be just perfect! I can't tell you how much I appreciate your doing this," Cora declared, smiling at the girl.

Evie watched the two women talk, her blank expression showed she hadn't noticed Elaina's attire previously.

Far too soon for Elaina's taste, Cora was gone. Evie excused herself and lay down for the nap she said she needed. Elaina lay a blanket on the floor and sat on it with her daughter, trying to keep her as quiet as possible while her husband slept.

Doreen began rubbing her eyes and Elaina stretched out on the blanket with her. As her daughter began to doze, she thought about all that had happened the night before and all that Miz Cora had told her. This wasn't the first time Cal and Evie had done something like this. When would it happen again? Had they caused Grant to believe them? Did he carry the same sickness in him? She determined in her heart that she would talk to Grant about moving, and if he didn't agree she would somehow get a bus ticket home to Stafford and she and her daughter would live with her mother and sisters.

As she nursed Doreen, Elaina felt his eyes on her and turned to find Grant watching her and the baby.

"Good morning," he said flatly.

"Good afternoon," she replied.

"Where were you last night?" he asked quietly.

"Next door."

"Why were you next door?"

"Your aunt and uncle kicked me out." Elaina kept her replies simple and without editorial.

"What do you mean they kicked you out?" Grant scooted up in the bed, sitting back against the pillow.

"I mean they accused me of steppin' out on you, almost ripped my new dress off me, then kicked me out of the back door wearing nothin' but my slip and underthings! If it wasn't for Miz Cora, I'd have froze to death."

"Uncle Cal and Aunt Evie?" Grant questioned incredulously.

"Yes, your aunt and uncle. And now Evie doesn't remember a thing about it. Miz Cora heard the fussin' and opened her door to me. She said Evie does this sort of thing every so often. She called it a 'spell'."

Nodding, Grant said, "Uncle Cal has said something about Aunt Evie's spells before. I didn't have any idea what he meant, though."

Gathering up her nerve, Elaina said calmly, "I want to move, Grant. I want to move now."

"Oh, 'Laina! We need to—"

"Don't 'Laina' me, Grant Kerr! Either we move or I'm goin' home and I'm takin' our baby with me!" Her words were spoken firmly as she looked her husband in the eye.

"Well," he said, swinging his legs off the bed, "I reckon we need to go house huntin', 'cause I ain't havin' you and my baby off in another state without me."

Elaina squealed and jumped from the floor to fling her arms around his neck. "When can we start?"

"Right after we have some lunch," he replied.

Elaina kissed Grant softly then whispered, "Thank you, Grant."

He patted her on the bottom as she walked to the kitchen and she swayed her hips extra wide as she walked.

Within the week, the little family had moved their meager belongings to a house of their own. It was a frame house with gray asphalt siding, and was closer to the plant. It had a little yard that was fenced in, just perfect for a little girl to play in. The front door opened into a modest living room, big enough for a sofa and two comfortable chairs. The kitchen and dining room melded together, which suited Elaina just fine. It allowed her to keep an eye on her family as she worked to prepare meals and clean up. She could imagine Doreen doing her homework at the table while she cooked. She could help her figure out words and spellings as they went, despite having left school in the eighth grade. The bathroom had a tub with a tube sticking out of the wall. Grant told her it was a shower they would stand under like a waterfall instead of sitting in the tub. Elaina had never seen one, but she quickly grew to enjoy it. The house boasted two bedrooms, one slightly larger than the other. They placed the crib in the smaller bedroom and Doreen quickly learned to enjoy her own space to sleep and play in.

Not long after they'd moved in Elaina's brother Alec and his family came to visit, and Elaina took great joy in preparing a meal for them all. She fried two chickens and mashed enough potatoes to feed an army.

"'Laina, who-all are you feeding?" Jodie asked, laughing.

"I'm just gon' be sure no one is hungry!" Elaina joined in the laughter.

"I'll be takin' some of that chicken in my lunch box tomorrow night," Grant declared, rubbing his stomach.

"If there's enough," Alec rejoined, "I'll sneak some for mine, too."

Elaina smiled as she stirred the gravy, her heart filled with a happiness she hadn't known since arriving in Michigan.

Four years after Doreen arrived, Grant and Elaina had a son. They named him Aaron, using Grant's middle name and making his middle name Seth after Elaina's brother. The family made a trip back to Arkansas to introduce Seth to his grandmother. Doreen took great pride in watching over her little brother. That was until her aunts and cousins wanted to play. That was when she would holler at her mother to take him, making everyone laugh.

Louise made several trips to Michigan, visiting with Elaina and Alec, getting to know her grandchildren. She brought her younger daughters along, showing them the big city along with visiting their brother and sister.

Just after Seth's second birthday, a tension began in Elaina's home. It was almost like having a living being in their house. She didn't understand what it was, but she feared it. Grant was working more and hanging out at the pool hall after work. He would get home late, then go right to bed. He had finally made it to day shift, so he was up early the next morning and off to work.

Elaina wrote to her mother often but never included her fears about her marriage, even though she thought she saw some of Evie's spells showing up in Grant. His swings from loving husband to raging tyrant were frightening, but she couldn't worry her mother with that news.

Chapter 24

Elaina loved her little house with the asphalt siding that looked like brick. There wasn't much of a front yard, barely room to park two cars, but the back yard was plenty enough room for her two kids to run around in. Doreen had a tricycle just like her cousin Adele's and she rode it every time she was outside, the ringing of the little bell filling the air.

The young wife adored making the little house a home, with little decorative touches here and there. She had found some pretty pink fabric, nearly sheer, with little white dots lined up across it. She set to work sewing curtains to hang at each multi-paned window, allowing light in while keeping prying eyes out.

It became a ritual for the Drews and Kerrs to have dinner together on Saturdays. They alternated weeks for hosting the dinners. Elaina loved going to Alec's house out in Flint. The girls and Seth had a gigantic yard to play in. Peals of laughter would fill the air as the daddies kept an eye on the children while the mommies prepared the meal.

Tomorrow would be the Saturday that she and Grant would load up their children and drive to Flint. They would leave around noon and spend the afternoon with the family, enjoy dinner together, then head home before the hour became too late. Elaina hummed as she prepared her Friday supper, placing pork chops in the skillet. She couldn't wait for Grant to get home so she could tell him the news. She rubbed her hands over her belly, remembering when she'd made this announcement the first time almost seven years before. Had she really only been fifteen then? That seemed a lifetime ago. Now that little girl was finishing up first grade, her luminous dark eyes so expressive despite being half-hidden by the glasses she required.

Elaina looked through the kitchen window and saw her children were playing in the back yard. Seth was pushing a giant dump truck her mother and Clem had brought him last fall for his birthday, and Doreen was giving her doll a ride on her tricycle.

She turned when she heard the front door close. She called out, "Hey, Grant. I'm in the kitchen fixin' your second favorite meal."

"My second favorite?" Grant replied, setting his lunch box on the counter. He leaned over and gave his wife a peck on the cheek then sat down at the table.

"Uh-huh. Pork chops, fried taters, corn, and biscuits. How's that sound?"

"Sounds good," he said absently.

Elaina made sure all the burners were on low, then stepped to the table to sit with Grant. She took his hand in hers.

"I have something to tell you, honey," she said softly.

He rubbed his hand over his face, rasping across the brief bit of day's growth on his chin. "What's that, 'Laina?"

Her excitement filled each word. "You're gon' be a daddy again!"

"I what?" he asked.

"I'm pregnant, Grant. I saw the doctor last week and his nurse called me today. We're gon' have another baby!" Her words tumbled over each other in their haste to be heard.

"Whose is it?" he asked flatly.

Surprise etched Elaina's face. "Whose is it? It's yours, of course!" she cried.

"Not likely," he stated.

"I don't know what you're talkin' about! Of course this baby is yours, just like Doreen and Seth are yours!" She could feel the flush of anger and shame rising in her cheeks.

"I know you've been runnin' around on me, Elaina. I've seen where you've traipsed out of here, going God knows where. Me and Alec have been talking about it for a while now. Even Jodie thinks there's somethin' goin' on."

Elaina's jaw dropped. She couldn't think. How could she be runnin' around on him when she never left the house without two little children in tow? Her brother and sister-in-law believed this? What about Mother? Had they told her this lie?

"Grant Kerr, when on earth would I have had time to be runnin' around? Would it be when I'm sitting with our children in the park? Maybe it's at Doreen's school? Oh, no, it's probably at the grocery store. I don't go anywhere alone. I'm not runnin' around on you!"

"Lies. All that comes out of your mouth is lies." His anger was rising. "I don't know who and I don't know when. All I know is, if you're pregnant it's not my baby, and before long you won't be my wife."

With that he stomped from the house, slamming the front door in his wake. Elaina sat stunned, her tears falling freely. She felt as though a truck had just run over her. Her entire world was shaken. She stood and turned the pork chops in the pan, stirred the potatoes and corn, then walked to the window again. She hoped the children hadn't heard the words their father had said to her.

"Doreen! Seth!" she called. "Y'all can play for about fifteen more minutes, then we'll have supper!"

"But Mama, Daddy's not home yet," Doreen replied, riding the tricycle up to her mother.

"He came home, honey, but he had to go out again. We'll make a plate for him and leave it in the oven." She choked the words past the lump of fear lodged in her throat. "For now you and your brother play a little longer, then we'll get washed up and eat." She brushed a lock of hair back from her daughter's face, then kissed her on the forehead.

"Okay, Mama." The little girl rode away, calling to her brother.

Back inside, Elaina went through the motions of finishing up the meal and setting the table. She longed to call her brother, but Grant had said he believed these lies about her. "What on earth am I gon' do, Lord?" she prayed.

After the children were fed and bathed, and the kitchen cleaned, Elaina sat with them on the sofa. "Hey Doreen, how about you read Seth and me a story book?"

"Yay!" the three-year-old clapped his joy. He jumped down and ran to their bedroom and grabbed his favorite book, *A Year on the Farm,* then ran back to his mother and sister. "Dis one, Sissy! Dis one!"

The three got comfortable as Doreen began to read. Seth would point out the pictures that matched what she read. Elaina smiled despite the pain and confusion in her heart. She loved these two so much and she would love the little one growing in her belly, too.

Chapter 25

The next morning, Elaina woke to find that Grant hadn't returned home. His lunch box sat on the kitchen counter where she had left it after emptying it the night before. She had dutifully prepared a sandwich and added cookies and a pickle as she did most nights, and left them together with a napkin in the refrigerator. They were still there. Seeing them there she sighed, and wondered where he had spent the night.

She reached past the prepared lunch and lifted a package of sausage and the carton of eggs from the shelf and set about preparing breakfast for her babies. She had to wipe tears from her eyes several times, finally using the tail of her apron to wipe them dry. Once the meal was prepared, she woke the children and ushered them to the table. She worked to make this day seem like any other day.

Once Elaina had walked Doreen to school, she and Seth walked through the park. She pushed him on the swing and helped him climb the ladder to the slide. She watched as he gathered up other children to play tag among the equipment. Her heart was full of love and heartache.

While her son took a nap Elaina cleaned the house, starting with the bathroom. She scrubbed every surface and laundered everything. She had every inch of clothesline filled with clothes in the early spring sunshine. Once she'd done all she could, she sat in the chair at the dining room table and wept.

Finally she picked up the receiver of the telephone, their one luxury, and dialed her sister-in-law. She had to know what was going on.

"Hello?" the familiar nasal tone.

"Jodie? It's me, Elaina," she said quietly.

"Oh," was the only reply.

"Jodie, what's goin' on?" The silence on the other end was deafening.

"Elaina, I don't know that I need to be talkin' to you right now."

"Why not? I'm sitting here without any idea what is happening. My husband accused me of runnin' around on him and I'm just as confused as a calf at a new gate!"

"Elaina, you can't fault Grant. He's done all he can, what with your behavior. I can't believe you've done him this way!" the older woman intoned.

"Done him what way, Jodie? I've had his children, I've cooked his meals, I've cleaned his house, I've suffered with his aunt and uncle. What more can I do?"

"I reckon you could keep from sleepin' around, 'Laina! Pretty much all a man wants is for his wife to be true to him."

Elaina yelled into the phone, "I *have* been true to him! Are you not listening to me?"

"You don't have to take that tone with me, Elaina Kerr. I didn't do nothin' wrong. I just feel so sorry for those babies."

"What babies?"

Elaina heard her sister-in-law's audible sigh. "Your babies, of course."

"There's nothing wrong with my babies. They're just as healthy as can be. Doreen has a little trouble with her eyes, but the glasses are helping right well."

"When the divorce happens, you ninny. Those babies are gon' be hurt, pure and simple, and it's all your fault."

"Jodie, please, what has Grant told you and Alec?"

"He's told us about you gettin' up in the middle of the night to go meet this man you've been seeing. He said you met him when y'all lived downtown. Said you used to go to the Woolworth to meet up with him. He talked about how you get up and leave him and the babies all alone while you carouse around, flaunting yourself like a streetwalker." She hiccuped a cry. "Oh, Elaina, how could you?"

"I-I—" Elaina stuttered. She took a deep breath and said, "Jodie, those are all lies. When I drop into bed at night, there's no goin' anywhere. I don't want another man. I have Grant." Her voice trailed off as she considered how late he had been staying at work, how often he had been going to hang out with his friends, the light of truth starting to peek under a corner of the memories. "Jodie, it's lies. All lies. I have been true to Grant. Always."

"Now Elaina, it don't matter how much you say so, you remember the Bible says your sins will find you out. Now yours have. You just better be makin' plans for where you're gon' go and what you're gon' do."

"Where I'm gon' go? Jodie, I'm not goin' anywhere. I haven't done anything!" she cried.

"Look, 'Laina, I have to go. Adele's makin' a mess; I have to get her before it gets worse. You might be best off if you'd just own up to what you've done and ask Grant to forgive you. He might just do that." Elaina heard the phone click dead.

She couldn't understand this. Her brother knew her, had known her all her life. He knew she wasn't some trollop runnin' around on her husband. He knew she loved her kids beyond measure. Now he was believing a man who was lying about her?

Elaina opened the front door and collected the mail from the box. She was happy to see a letter there from her mother and opened it quickly. Her joy at seeing the letter soon faded to dismay as she read the words.

Dear Daughter,

I am writing after hearing about your behavior for several months from your brother and your husband. I am shocked by you. You were raised better than this. You spoke vows before God to love your husband and be true to him till death parts you. How dare you to go to another man? What are you thinking?

Now I hear that you're pregnant by this other man. Oh, Elaina! Where is your mind? What have you done? You know Grant now has every right to divorce you, then what will you do? Where will you go? You won't be coming here. I won't have you come in here, an adulteress, staying with my two young and impressionable girls.

Stop this affair. Don't see this other man again!

Love,
Mother

Seth had woken from his nap and was happily playing in the sunshine of the backyard when the phone rang. Elaina left her perch on the back step to walk into the kitchen to answer it.

"Hello?" she said, keeping an eye on her son through the window.

"Elaina?" Her mother's voice seemed weary coming through the line.

"Mama! Oh, Mama! It's horrible!" Her tears were already flowing.

"You stop that crying right now, Missy. You brought all this on yourself. I can't imagine what you've been thinking.

You were raised better than that. I'm so glad your daddy's not here to see this. It would just kill him!"

Elaina gasped at the angry tirade coming through the phone. Her own mother really believed she was sleeping with another man. She sank into a chair and leaned her elbows on the table, keeping the receiver pressed to her ear as though any space would allow the vile words to gain life in the air around her.

"Mama, I ain't done those things Grant has said. I wouldn't do those things. Not ever."

"Well, apparently you would!" her mother vented. "Grant has shown Alec proof!"

"What proof could he show him, Mama? I don't leave the house except when Grant or the children are with me. I don't go anywhere but to Doreen's school, the park, and the grocery store."

"You don't go to church?" Mama seized on the omission.

"No, Mama, we don't. Grant don't want to and I don't want to leave him on his day off from work." Elaina thought how if she had been going to church he would be saying now that she was steppin' out on him on Sunday mornin's, too.

"Well, of course you wouldn't go to church! You know God is mad at you. You know He don't like this kind of thing. He says don't commit adultery, 'Laina, and now you have. He says don't lie, and that's what you're doin'!"

Elaina sighed. "Mama, I have not committed adultery, and I am not lying."

"There you go again. Girl, you are breaking my heart. I just can't believe—" Her voice caught. "I can't believe you'd do this. My poor grandbabies."

"Well, I can see that you're not gon' believe the truth, so I'm gon' go on out and do what I do every day. I'm gon' walk with your grandson to your granddaughter's school to get her and then we're gon' stop at the park so they can play on the slide and swings and monkey bars. Then after about thirty minutes or so, we're gon' walk on back here to the house, and while they play I'm gon' cook dinner for them and their father." She emphasized her next words, "Just like I always do, Mama."

Her mother's voice grew quiet. "Are you meeting *him* at the playground?"

"Mother!" Elaina cried into the phone.

"Well? Are you?"

"Mama, I will not even dignify that—yes, I will. I *am* meeting someone at the park, yes. It's a lady whose children play with mine. Her name is Jeannette. She's from Missouri, but not the bootheel. We talk pretty much every day. But she sure ain't a man. Maybe you should sneak up here and watch me and see where I go and what I do." Then she hung up the phone, lay her head on her arms, and wept.

"Mama?" Her son's sweet little voice wafted through the window.

"Yes, baby, I'm comin'." She wiped her eyes and walked out the back door. She lifted Seth in her arms, gave him a hug, and asked, "What can I do for you, my love?"

Her afternoon was spent just as she'd told her mother, and she tried to go through the motions without this cloud of ugliness bothering her, but she couldn't shake the fear that her entire world was falling apart. Everything she had known yesterday was now gone.

She prepared dinner and set the table, where she and the children ate. They asked about their father's absence, and she told them she thought he must still be at work.

Elaina sat on the couch. The children were long in bed, dreaming dreams about who knew what. She had read to them from *King of the Wind*. The children loved hearing about the thrill of the horses racing in far-off Arabia. The only horses they had ever seen were the ones the policemen rode. Elaina talked about the horses their grandparents had had and what it was like to ride them and plow with them.

They had begged her to read more, but it had been several minutes past their bedtime. Now all was quiet. She sat there in the near darkness, trying to figure out where Grant could have come up with the notion she was stepping out and why her brother and mother believed him.

Elaina jumped when she heard the screen door at the back open. When she heard the key in the lock, she knew it must be her husband. She sat still, waiting for the battle she just knew was coming.

Grant stepped into the house, quietly closing the door. An aura of stealth was in his every move.

She watched him slip into the kitchen, then she said softly, "Your dinner is in the oven."

Grant started, knocking a glass into the sink. "'Laina! You scared the life out of me!"

"Uh-huh." She was so tired of talking when all she was hearing was lies.

Her husband pulled the plate from the oven, frowning over the state of the food. "It's all dried out," he complained.

"It wasn't at supper time," she replied tersely.

"Yeah, well, I was—" he faltered.

"Where were you, Grant? I'm the one accused of runnin' around, but you're the one who's never here. Where were you?"

"Aw, Elaina, why do you have to bring that up? Here I am tryin' to eat my supper and get ready for bed. It's late and I got to be able to get up early to go to work in the morning."

"Never mind," she replied, walking to the bedroom door, "I'm going to bed." She turned to look back at him as he stood framed in the kitchen's light. "Right where I will be all night long." She closed the bedroom door behind her and walked to her dresser. She looked down at her hands, seeing how badly they shook. She didn't know if she was afraid or angry. Maybe a little of both. She couldn't trust herself to talk to him more right now so she undressed, put on her nightgown, and slid into the bed. She heard him enter the room and kept her eyes closed as though she were already asleep. In moments she felt him lay beside her, even laying his arm over her like they had every night since their marriage.

It was as though nothing had happened. It was as though she hadn't been raked over the coals by her sister-in-law and her mother. It was as though her heart hadn't been trampled like an old newspaper on the street. She wept silently until she fell into a fitful sleep.

Chapter 26

That spring, as her belly began to pooch out with pregnancy, Elaina took note that Grant was coming home late more nights than not. His shift ended at two in the afternoon, but he was rarely home before midnight. She made excuses when the children asked about his repeated absences. Doreen was old enough to understand that something ominous was going on, but her mother could see that she hid her fears in the taking care of her dolls and her brother.

The summer was hot and Elaina spent a lot of time at the park, as did many of the other young mothers. The trees made for much better shade than most of their yards, and the children could play together. Most days Elaina packed a picnic lunch for them, laying out a tablecloth for them to sit down on like they'd seen in their picture books.

She and Grant argued more. She complained of his late nights, and he continued to say she was having an affair. He claimed to be hurt and dismayed, while she remained confused.

She was unable to wear sleeveless shirts because she wanted to hide the numerous layered bruises on her upper arms.

They had tried to keep the weekly meals with her brother and his family going, but once her pregnancy began to show the disdain her brother turned on her was unbearable. A few times she stayed home alone, watching as Grant and the children climbed into the truck and drove away. She loved the cheery stories her daughter told her when they returned home. Before long, though, Grant stopped going, too. He made various excuses about having someone make repairs to the truck, about talking to someone about repairs for the house, and many others. His supply of them seemed to grow each week. Once, when she was doing his laundry, Elaina caught a whiff of perfume that wasn't hers. She assumed that it had come from hugging Jodie or maybe his aunt, but that didn't make sense because it was one of his work shirts.

One day in the middle of August, Grant came home early. It was early afternoon, and when he came in the children were taking their naps. He motioned for Elaina to join him in the kitchen. Concerned, she rushed to him.

"What's wrong?" she asked.

"I have something to give you," he stated.

She looked at him expectantly. He motioned for her to sit down at the table, joining her.

"Now, Elaina, I don't want you gettin' all upset and wakin' the children."

"What is it, Grant?" Her voice sounded flat even to her.

He handed her a packet of folded pages. She took the papers and spread them open on the table. Just as her eyes fell on the words, he said, "I want a divorce, Elaina."

Her mouth agape she read the words, though much of the document was in a language she didn't understand. It was English, for sure, but the words made no sense to her. Therewith and thereto and party of the first part were scattered about on the heavy white paper. Finally she focused and realized it was saying that Aaron Grant Kerr was seeking to dissolve his marriage with Elaina Drew Kerr. She read further and saw that he was claiming adultery as the reason, and that he wanted full custody of both their children. The papers made no mention of their baby she carried. She looked up at her husband.

"Why, Grant?"

"It says right there, 'Laina. Adultery. I can't go on knowing you're sleepin' with another man. I just can't do it."

"I see." She said the words, though she didn't see at all.

"I'm takin' the children, Elaina. I won't have you ruinin' their lives. They deserve a good mama."

"I am a good mama, Grant. Your lies don't make that any different." Elaina rose and began making a snack for the children, who would soon be waking.

"You're not a good mama, 'Laina. You've done betrayed their daddy and you betrayed them. You've betrayed your good upbringin' and your family. I can't believe you still hold your head up."

Holding herself in check, she replied, "I hold my head up because I have done *nothing* wrong."

"Fine," he said. "You can tell the judge all about how you've been faithful and true; we'll see if he believes you. Even if he does he won't give you the children—you've got no job, no way to raise them. And I'll fight payin' you any alimony. I ain't payin' for you to take up with every Tom, Dick, and Harry. I had to bring you the papers. Now you've got 'em. I'll be at Alec's." He rose, grabbed a paper sack and strode into their bedroom, grabbing his clothes from the closet and dresser. He stopped in the bathroom to get his comb and razor, and then he was gone.

Elaina sat at the table in stunned silence. She had no one to talk to. Her husband had poisoned everyone against her, even her own mother. She looked at the clock and decided to get Doreen and Seth up from their nap. Once they had eaten their snack, she sent them outside to play.

She picked up the phone and told the operator the number in Arkansas she wanted. The clicks and hums of a long-distance connection filled her ear, and she hoped she would get a good response.

"Hello?"

"Grandma?"

"Elaina? Is that you? Oh, child, is that really you?"

Elaina's tears flowed freely. "Yes, Grandma, it's me."

"Oh, my baby. Your mama told me what's goin' on."

Elaina's heart dropped. Grant had even poisoned her grandmother.

"I can't believe your mama believes what that man is sayin' about you. Why, that's the silliest thing I ever heard!" Freda's voice was clear and sharp as she went on. "Your grandpa and I never did like that man you married, but we held our tongues. He always had that look about him. Shifty. And he's so much older than you, Elaina."

"He's not so much older, Grandma," Elaina intoned, her heart soaring with the realization that someone believed her, believed *in* her.

"When you met and married he was a man of nineteen and you were a child of fourteen. You hadn't even courted anyone else, so you didn't have nothin' to compare him to." Elaina could almost hear her shaking her head in that way that brooked no argument. "I wished time and again that Jerry had stepped up and said somethin' when you wanted to marry him. God knows Louise didn't see nothin' 'cept having one less mouth to feed."

Elaina started to object, but her grandmother cut her off.

"Oh, hush. You're old enough to know now what's what. Your mama was lost as a goose when your daddy passed. She was strugglin' day in and day out to put food on the table and keep the roof over your heads. When Grant came along and wanted to marry you, she jumped at the chance. I reckon she figured he'd be good to you, though."

"He's done all right, Grandma. He's not hit me or nothin'."

"My goodness, he'd better not have hit you! I'd take a bus up there right quick and spit in his eye!" Elaina had a picture of her grandmother with that birch stick covered with snuff tucked into her cheek. If she spit in someone's eye, it was going to be pretty bad. She giggled in spite of herself.

"Grandma, you don't have to worry about gettin' on the bus. He's not hurt me like that. He's broken my heart, though." Elaina crossed her fingers, refusing to admit to her grandmother about the bruises that even now speckled her arms.

"Then he's broken mine," Freda said.

"He's filed for divorce, Grandma. I've got the papers right here. He's—" Her voice broke. "—he's gon' take my babies away from me, Grandma!"

"He *what*? How on earth is he gon' do that? Anyone who knows you knows you're a good mama to those babies."

"Alec and Jodie don't. They've been around us the whole time we've lived up here and they think I'm horrible."

"Oh, poo. That Alec sometimes don't see past his own nose. I bet him and that husband of yours are in the same Masonic lodge, ain't they?"

Elaina hadn't thought about that. They were indeed both in the same lodge. Alec had invited Grant in shortly after they'd arrived in town.

"Yes'm, they are."

"Well, there you go. It's no wonder."

"You mean Alec would believe him over me because they're brothers in the Lodge?"

"I'm thinkin' that's perfectly likely. Them Masons are somethin', 'Laina. It ain't right how they choose each other over family, but sometimes they do."

Elaina knew that her grandmother had brothers who were members of the Masons, but she didn't know much more than that. She figured it was up to Grandma to explain any further.

"'Laina, I want you to come home."

"Grandma, I can't. I don't have money and I can't stay with Mama; she wouldn't have me."

"You come here. To me. You come and bring those babies."

"Oh, Grandma! I'm big as a house pregnant, too."

"I know you're expectin'. Your mama told me that. She swears up and down it's this mystery man's baby, but I know it's your husband's. Good night in the mornin'! What that Louise will believe!

"I'm gon' wire you the money to get yourself some tickets. You pack up for you and the children and you come here. We've got plenty of folk who can deliver that baby when it comes. Now, you go to packin'. I'm gon' call Harriet and get her to take some money to the bus station. I'll call you when she gets back. You should be able to get on the bus by this time tomorrow afternoon."

Elaina sniffled, her tears flowing freely. This love her grandmother was showing felt so warm and complete. "Yes, ma'am."

When she'd hung up the phone, she checked on the children. They were both still playing happily, so she stepped into her bedroom and pulled the battered suitcase from under the bed. Seeing it brought memories of the trip from home to this city. What a trip that was! She recalled the innocent girl who had watched the river and gaped at the tall buildings, and shook her head. Now she was a woman with two children, one on the way, and a husband who was divorcing her.

As she gathered her underthings, she wondered how long she would be in Arkansas. Grandma had mentioned being there when the baby came, but that was at least six weeks away. Doreen would be starting second grade right after Labor Day. Would she be back home then? She shook her head, not knowing but trusting that God and Grandma did.

She unbuckled the leather straps around the suitcase and opened it, lifting out the smaller one. She would put the children's clothes in the big one. The extra room would make it easier to pack for the two of them. She opened the smaller case and began the process of packing her own clothes.

"Mama?" Her daughter's voice was soft.

"Yes, dear?" Elaina turned to the door.

"What are you doing?"

"I'm packing, Doreen. We're goin' on a trip. We're gon' go see my Grandma and stay with her for a little while. Do you remember Grandma Freda?"

Doreen's face brightened as she recalled the little frame house and the big barn. "I do, Mama. She's nice, except..."

Elaina laughed, "I know. Except that she dips snuff! I wish she'd stop that, but it makes her happy I guess. Is your brother inside?"

"No, ma'am. He's still outside playing."

"That's fine. Let's see what all we need to get together for this trip. We're gon' be ridin' a bus to Stafford!"

"A bus? You mean like the buses we see going through town?"

"Yes'm. We'll get on one of those buses and we'll ride through the night till we get to Stafford. Someone will meet us at the station and drive us to Grandma Freda's house."

"Oh, Mama! We're going on an adventure!"

"Yes, we are. Now, how about you go pick out some clothes to take with us. Get plenty of play and school clothes, and we'll need one of your pretty dresses for goin' to church."

"Church, Mama? We don't go to church."

"We will when we're stayin' with Grandma. She won't have folks under her roof not goin' to church."

"Okay, Mama."

"Once you bring those in, we'll see about your underthings and socks and shoes."

Elaina's heart felt lighter just making the preparations.

Chapter 27

The bus pulled into the station, and even as Elaina ushered her children onboard she reviewed how she had left the house. She had given her neighbor the last of the quart of milk and the eggs she had. She told the lady she would be gone for a while and asked her to keep an eye on the place. The woman had hugged her and agreed, telling Elaina to be safe. She'd pressed a slip of paper with her phone number and a ten-dollar bill into Elaina's hand. When Elaina had protested the older lady had clucked, reminding her that the walls weren't all that thick and the houses weren't all that far apart. Elaina's cheeks burned bright red again as she remembered these words. Her last act had been to write Grant a note to tell him where she and the children were. She supposed that once she arrived in Stafford her mother would call Alec, so the note wasn't really necessary, but she had decided to be nice.

She settled Seth in the seat by the window just behind the driver so he could look out. She sat beside her son and her daughter slid into the seat on the other side of the bus. Leaning her head back against the seat, she sighed deeply.

The driver of the bus noticed the little family and asked Seth if he was the man of the family. The little boy grinned up at his mother and told the man he was. Big Sister Doreen rolled her eyes at his answer, but said nothing. The driver kept both children engaged almost the whole trip from Detroit to Indianapolis, while Elaina took several cat naps.

They changed buses in Indianapolis, St. Louis, and again in Memphis before making it to their last stop in Stafford. They had been traveling almost 18 hours, but the children had slept through some of it. Once inside the station she dragged the suitcases to the bathroom, where they all used the facilities and washed up in the sinks. The cold water on her face felt so refreshing. She remembered the heat of an Arkansas August very well.

"Okay little ones, let's go see who's here to pick us up." Doreen led her brother by the hand as their mother carried the two suitcases.

"There's my Lanie!" a booming voice echoed through the bus station.

Elaina turned to see her cousin, Andy Keys. She squealed at the sight of his broad grin and open arms.

"Mother said I'd better not be late, so here I am!" he said as he enveloped Elaina in a bear hug. He winked over her shoulder at the two children, which made Seth giggle.

"I'm so glad it's you, Andy. It's good to see you. How is Aunt Harriet?"

"Oh, she's fine." He lowered his voice. "She's kinda torn up about all that's goin' on with you. You know she loves Aunt Louise a lot, and she's all upset about what's goin' on with you." He released her from the hug and leaned down to look at the little boy and girl.

"Now, who's this?" he asked.

"I'm Doreen and this is Seth. That's our mama," Doreen said, pointing at Elaina.

"Well, I guess that makes me your cousin!" He stuck out his hand to shake hers. "I'm Andrew Keys, but most folks just call me Andy."

He gently shook her hand then seriously shook Seth's. "Did you help drive the bus, young man?" Seth's eyes grew wide and Andy laughed. "Maybe next time you will."

Andy lifted the suitcases and led the way out of the station to his car. The children watched closely as he deposited the bags in the enormous trunk, then climbed into the back seat when he opened the door. Elaina scooted into the passenger seat, and when Andy slid behind the wheel he started the motor and drove straight through town to their grandmother's home in the country.

As they passed through the city, Elaina couldn't help but look down the street her mother lived on. She saw the little white house, saw the front porch swing, and recalled the last time they sat on it together, shortly after Seth was born. She wiped away the tears that crept unbidden down her cheeks and joined the banter between Andy and her children.

"Mama!" Doreen cried as they turned down the gravel road. "We're really out in the country!"

Elaina smiled. "Yes, we sure are. Grandma lives on the same place she and Grandpa bought years and years ago. I played at their house a lot when I was your size."

Both children stood, holding the back of the front seat, watching through the windows as they observed great fields of corn and cotton. Elaina regaled them with stories of picking the white bolls when she was a little girl, telling how her father had let her help with the plowing.

"Wow, Mama! I didn't know you grew up a farmer," Doreen said in awe.

Andy chuckled. "Your mama was a fine farmer, too. She got right out there with your grandpa and made every step he did. When he went on, your mama was a huge help to your grandma. Did you know she drove the car when she was just twelve years old?"

"Did you really, Mama? You were just a girl? How could that be? Only grownups drive cars." The little girl popped off question after question.

"Yes, I drove when I was twelve. Your grandma didn't drive back then and your grandpa had already taught me. Grandma talked to the policemen and got me a special license so I wouldn't get in trouble."

"Have you told 'em about drivin' into the gravel pit?" Andy asked, mirth filling his voice.

"I have not, and you don't have to bring that up!" Elaina replied quickly.

"What, Mama?" her daughter asked.

Hitting her cousin with a brutal stare, Elaina answered, "I was driving the car one day. Your grandma, Aunt Cherilyn, Aunt Agnes, and Aunt Kate were in the car, too. I went around a curve a little too close to the edge and we went right down into the pit where they made gravel for the roads. I switched the gears and pushed on the gas pedal and *whoosh!* out we came." She looked at her daughter whose mouth hung slack, her eyes wide as she seemed to try to picture that adventure.

Andy turned the car off the road onto a hard-packed red dirt driveway, and followed it up to the Rafferty farm. They could see the little wooden shotgun house past the gate. Elaina smiled as she looked at the old barn sitting so near to the house, remembering how when she was little Grandpa would brag about how he could pee off the corner of the front porch and hit the roof of his barn.

Andy pulled up to the gate and Elaina climbed out of the car to open it. Once he pulled the car through she closed the gate, unsure if there were any cattle in this field, but old habits were hard to break.

Suddenly, there on the porch stood Freda Henderson Rafferty, her grandmother. Elaina's heart leapt with joy and her mind flooded with so many memories. She ran past the car where Andy was parking it and up the steps, into her grandmother's waiting arms.

"There, there, child. You're home now," Freda said. Elaina wept as she felt the love enveloping her in that warm, hard embrace.

"Oh, Grandma!" she sobbed. "I don't know what to do! I don't know what to do!"

"Shush now, here come your babies." Freda handed her the dishtowel to wipe her cheeks. She called out to the children, "My goodness! Look at these two! Come on up here, Miss Doreen, and let me look at you." She opened her arms and welcomed the child.

"It's good to see you, Great Grandma," Doreen said politely.

"Well, it's mighty fine to see you, Miss Prissy!" The older woman kissed the child on the cheek. "If you'll go right inside there through to the kitchen, you'll find a treat just for you two kids."

Elaina nodded when her daughter sought permission. "Bring your brother some, sweetie." She didn't know what her grandmother had prepared, but she knew it would be good.

Meanwhile, Andy and Seth had made their way onto the porch. "Well, well, well," Freda said. "Who is this fine young gentleman here?"

"Grandma Freda," Andy said, as though introducing a king, "may I present to you Master Aaron Seth Kerr, late of Detroit, Michigan." Turning to Seth, he said, "Master Seth, your great-grandmother, Grandma Freda." He bowed low and moved the little boy closer to Freda.

Seth stepped forward shyly and held out his hand. His three-year-old voice small, he intoned, "Hello, Gramma Freda."

Freda's smile was radiant as she gathered the child into her arms and hugged him fiercely. "Well now, it's mighty good to meet you, young Seth. Your sister is getting a special treat for you. Oh, here she is now."

The screen door slapped the frame as Doreen stepped through. She was chewing and handed her brother a sugar cookie bigger than her hand. His eyes grew wide as he looked for assent from his mother. She nodded and the little boy began devouring the golden delight. Freda set him down and motioned toward the door.

"Andy, you bring their suitcases inside. I'm gon' put them in the rooms at the back, where the children usually stay." She looked over her shoulder. "You children can play right out here, just stay this side of the fence and out of the barn. You hear me?"

"Yes, ma'am!" Doreen called.

Elaina followed her grandmother, breathing in the sweet smells of times past, memories marching through her mind, capturing her heart. They reached the two bedrooms where her mother and uncles had grown up.

"Here you go, 'Laina. You take this one; it's got the bigger bed and the children can have this other room. They each get a bed."

"I don't remember you havin' these rooms like this, Grandma."

"Well, I reckon you don't. I figured when my grandbabies started having babies I needed to have rooms made for them to come visit me or I might never get to see 'em."

"Oh, Grandma!" Elaina hugged her. "This is wonderful. Thank you so much!"

Freda walked back to the living room, saying over her shoulder, "I'll give you time to unpack, Sis. When you're ready, we'll see about some supper."

"Yes, ma'am."

Chapter 28

Elaina told Andy where to put the two suitcases. Each room had a dresser, where she unpacked clothing and placed it neatly. She placed the smaller suitcase into the larger and closed the cover. Once she had buckled the straps, she slid it underneath her bed. She sat down on the bed, her body tired from traveling, from dragging suitcases, from carrying this baby and leading two others. Sighing heavily, she pushed her shoes from her feet and rolled the stockings from them. Lifting the traveling dress over her head, she hung it carefully on the hook near the dresser and pulled a cotton shift on in its place. She walked barefoot into the living room where her grandmother sat, her snuff-covered birch stick snug in her jaw.

"Whew, Grandma, I didn't realize how tired I was!" she said as she sank onto the couch. She heard war whoops and shouting as her children ran and played in the yard.

"I reckon we can rest a bit before we start supper. Andy's gone on home. You sit right there and tell me what's goin' on."

Elaina launched into the story, sharing about her daily routine, the things she had endured while living with Grant's aunt and uncle, and finally what Grant was saying about her now. She told of the conversation with Jodie, and how Alec wouldn't even talk to her now. She shared about the letter and phone call from her mother, and cried as the weight of the story overcame her.

When she'd finished, Freda sat quietly rocking for a few minutes. Elaina could see she was thinking out each part of the story, weighing this and that, turning each puzzle piece round and round until she saw how they fit together.

"Yes'm," she said. "I'm thinkin' them two bein' Masons is part of it. I think your brother won't look past the nose on his face and Jodie will say whatever he says. You know she likes to keep trouble stirred up. He thinks his so-called Masonic brother is honorable but he's not." She waved as Elaina started to defend Alec and Grant. "He's not, 'Laina. You've got to just see that."

The weight of the truth saddened Elaina. "I guess you're right, Grandma."

"Well, have you done anything this man is saying you did?"

"No, ma'am! Not one!"

"Then I reckon an honorable man wouldn't say such things, would he?"

"No, ma'am. I reckon an honorable man wouldn't."

"Fine. And an honorable man who knows you wouldn't believe them either," Freda stated firmly.

Elaina only blinked at her, these thoughts foreign to her broken heart.

"And I hate to say it about my own girl," she said, "but your mama ain't actin' very honorable either."

Elaina's eyes grew wide in amazement.

Noticing her wonder, Freda said, "What? You don't think I can see when my children choose wrong? I'm old, child, but I'm not blind."

Elaina giggled nervously. She could remember hearing the preacher talk about honoring your parents and wasn't sure if saying her mama was wrong would be right.

"I don't know what's got into Louise. She knows better, but I reckon Alec's got her convinced. Here's what I'm thinking, Sis. You said your man has been staying late to work and visitin' with his friends a lot?"

"Yes, ma'am. Most evenings he's not been coming home till long after supper."

"Uh-huh," Freda said.

"What do you mean, Grandma?" Elaina queried.

"It's a mite suspicious, Sis. Now, I ain't lived in no city like Detroit, but I reckon people are people no matter where they live. Your man was stayin' away from your house, not comin' home, and makin' up stories about where he's goin' and what he's doin'? And he says you're the one steppin' out? I don't want to hurt you, Sis, but I'm thinkin' he's got himself a girlfriend."

Elaina sat stunned. She looked at her grandmother, then at her hands. She tried to remember recent months when Grant would come home later and later. She studied on when she'd done his laundry and smelled that faint perfume. Finally, she shook her head and stood.

"I can't think about this right now, Grandma. What do you want to do for supper?"

"I've got a chicken already ready for the pot. I was hopin' you might make your chicken and dumplin's. You know how well I like those. Oh, your grandpa sure loved 'em."

Elaina smiled, and knelt beside her grandmother's rocking chair. "Grandma, I'll make you whatever you'd like. I can't thank you enough for taking me and the kids in right now. I know Mama is gon' be mad as a wet hen, but you did it anyway." She kissed the old woman on the cheek, wiped the tears that had slipped from her eyes, and rose. "Would you keep an eye on Doreen and Seth for me? They're not used to having a whole park to call their own."

"I'll do just that, Sis." Freda lifted her heavy frame from the rocking chair and padded to the door. She watched the two city children as they rolled down the hill then ran to the top again. "Doesn't matter which children they are, rollin' down a hill is the most fun that can be had."

The next day, Clem came to visit. Elaina was hesitant as she walked out onto the porch, but Doreen raced out to meet her favorite uncle.

"Clem," she greeted him quietly.

He opened his embrace of Doreen to include his sister and she walked into it tearfully.

They heard Grandma Freda calling to Doreen to come to the kitchen. The child rambled off, leaving the brother and sister alone.

Elaina stepped off the porch onto the first step then, using the pole holding the porch roof up for balance, sat down on the porch. Clem moved to the other side of the pole and dropped down there, letting his lanky legs swing from the porch like when they were children.

"You'll probably be in all sorts of trouble bein' here, Clem. Mama will be so mad at you."

"Mama has been mad at me before and she'll be mad at me again, Sis. It's all right. I don't believe it," he said quietly.

"Don't believe what, Clem? That I'm a whore, a harlot?"

"No. I don't believe what-all Grant and Alec have said. That's not you. You're as good a girl as there ever was."

Tears flowing, she choked out, "Thank you, Clem. I was beginning to think that everyone I know believes the lies. I haven't had an affair, and this baby is as much Grant's as Doreen and Seth."

"You're just gon' have to give Mama some time, 'Laina. She'll realize she's done you wrong, Sis." His soft voice reminded her of Daddy's. "Until she realizes the truth, you'll have me, and I'll do anything I can for you."

"Oh Clem, thank you. That makes me so happy. I almost don't want to go to church, 'cause I know Mama will be there."

"Well then, don't go to church," he answered simply. Elaina's eyes opened wide and he laughed. "See? There's worse things. You go and you hold your head up, Elaina. You ain't done a thing wrong, so you don't go hangin' your head. If someone don't want to believe you, they'll find out at some point how wrong they are."

They talked a while longer until Doreen and Seth came out. Her brother hugged them both and told them to go look inside his truck. There they found a ball they could kick and throw. It was big enough that Seth could take part in fun and games.

Just as the sun was setting, Grandma Freda called to them, "Are y'all gon' come in and eat or am I gon' throw it out?"

Elaina giggled. "How many times did we hear that same thing when we were little?"

Clement laughed heartily. "I remember Mama would holler that across the fields at us."

"All the time!" Elaina groaned as she pushed herself up from the porch step. "I've still got a good six weeks before this baby gets here, but I swear I'm ready now."

Clement held out his hand, helping his sister up the steps and into the house. The children were tagging along right behind them, Seth proudly carrying their new ball in his arms.

Chapter 29

Elaina stayed at her grandmother's farm, only going to town when Freda did. She was unwilling to face the stares and judgment of her mother and her mother's friends alone. She was certain Mama had discussed her wayward daughter with them, likely in detail, but she knew that no one would say or do anything as long as she was with Grandma Freda.

Doreen had taken to exploring in the trees near Grandma's house, finding shady places where she could play with her dolls. She often set up picnics and invited her brother.

That first Sunday Elaina walked into Pilgrim's Rest Baptist Church right behind her grandmother, her head held high, holding her children by the hands. Grandma Freda had agreed with Clem, telling her to not let her head hang, that she had nothing to be ashamed of. She nodded briefly to her mother and two youngest sisters as she walked by, astonished to hear her mother shush them from saying anything to her. When she and the children were arranged in the pew next to her grandmother, she felt that callused old hand wrap around hers.

Looking at her grandmother she heard the whisper, "Look up, Sis. You've got nothin' to be ashamed of."

Once the service was finished, Elaina walked up to her mother and told her children to say hello to their grandmother. They excitedly gave hugs and kisses. Her sisters hugged both children and Kate hugged her sister before her mother noticed and pulled her away.

"Louise, I'll have a word with you," Freda said, and walked away toward a bench under the trees. Louise dutifully followed the stepmother, the only mother she had really known.

While the two older women talked, Elaina's sisters fawned over Doreen and Seth. Cherilyn couldn't resist rubbing her sister's pregnant belly, asking when she expected to have her baby.

Elaina kept sneaking looks over at her mother and grandmother and saw that the discussion was heated. Her mama looked fit to be tied, but Grandma Freda was cool as a cucumber. Elaina thought there must be something special about being the oldest member of the family.

All too soon, mother and daughter rose from the bench. Freda waved for Elaina to come along. She gathered up the two children and joined her grandmother. They started walking toward the farm, which was only about a mile away across the fields.

"Well, I talked with Louise," Grandma said. "She's not very happy that you're here. I explained to her that it didn't matter if she was happy, that you were gon' be here amongst family while this matter is goin' on. I told her I believe you, and that I would stand by you no matter what that husband of yours says."

"What did she say, Grandma?" Elaina asked.

"Huh. Not much good, Sis. Not much good." She drew Doreen's attention to a patch of daisies in the field and told her and Seth they could pick them to take home. Both children squealed with joy and ran to gather their prize. "She said she just can't support you, Sis. She says she believes what Grant said. I tried to get her to see the truth, but she's bound and determined to disagree. She's hard-headed, that one."

"I figured as much, Grandma. She's always been pretty tough with me. Thank you for tryin' though." She caught Seth as he sped to her with a bunch of flowers grasped tightly in his little hands. "Here, young man! Be careful you don't roll right away from here!" Her son laughed as he tromped merrily back to Grandma Freda's house.

Almost three weeks later Louise relented, allowing Agnes, Cherilyn, and Kate to visit their sister at their grandmother's house.

"Grandma! Elaina!" Cherilyn's lyrical voice spilled in from the front porch.

"We're in the kitchen!" Freda called back, and the girls walked past the screen door into the cooler shadows of the house.

Elaina smiled at her grandmother as they heard the padding of bare feet on wood floors. Soon she was engulfed in hugs as her sisters wrapped their arms around her, never letting her rise from her chair.

"You girls aren't gonna get in trouble for bein' here, are you?" she asked.

"Nope," Kate said simply as she looked around for her niece and nephew. "Where's Doreen and Seth?"

"They're in their bedroom. They're supposed to be napping, but I bet they're playing."

"Can I go see?"

"Of course you can. If y'all want to go outside it's okay, too."

Kate hugged Elaina and ran down the hall to spend her time with the children.

"Well, girls," Freda began, "just how did y'all happen to be here today? Did your mama have a change of heart?" She placed

FAYE BRYANT

a bowl of black-eyed peas on the table in front of each girl so they could join in the task of preparing them for canning.

Agnes spoke up. "No, Grandma. Not really. We just kept after her about being able to see you and our sister." She smiled at Elaina. "You might say we nagged her into letting us come."

Freda chuckled. "I guess having you three fussin' would wear her down. I won't often tell you three to do such, but in this case I'm proud of you for doin' it."

Cherilyn worked at stripping the peas from the moist pods, her eyes returning to her sister's swollen belly often. "'Laina, does that hurt?"

Cherilyn had been just a toddler when Louise was pregnant with Kate, and didn't really remember it. Now, at seventeen, she was curious.

"Oh I get tired, but," she patted her belly, "this part doesn't hurt. Not until this little one seems to think it's time to run around, anyway."

"Huh?" Cherilyn's brow furrowed.

"She means the baby is kicking," Agnes chimed in. She and Andrew Marton had been married all of six months and, though not pregnant yet, she spoke with authority.

"Oh!" Cherilyn replied with awe. She opened another pod of peas, scooped the orbs into her bowl and dropped the empty pod into the bucket between her and Elaina, her cheeks tinged with pink.

"Like right now," Elaina said. "Do you want to feel?"

"I can feel?" the younger girl asked.

"Sure. Give me your hand."

Cherilyn wiped her hand on the dish towel lying on the table then reached out to her sister, who placed her hand low on her pregnant belly. At just that moment the baby inside moved, and Cherilyn jumped and squealed.

Freda laughed out loud as her granddaughters marveled at this miracle of new life. "All right, all right. Let's get these peas shelled so we can get them ready for the jars!"

Summer ended and fall began. Elaina had called Doreen's school and explained that she was in Arkansas and would be until the baby was born. She told the school secretary she would enroll her daughter in Hilltop School until they returned home. Arrangements were made and Doreen started second grade at the school her mother and aunts had attended.

Elaina had tried to write Grant letters, to let him know about his children, but she couldn't bring herself to put the words on paper. She told her grandmother, who told her not to worry about it. She was certain Louise was giving Alec reports, and knew that Alec would tell Grant.

Several times Grandma had had family over for dinner. Aunt Harriet and part of her crew had come. They nearly filled up the yard, much less the house. It was fun for the children because they had other children to play with. At other times, Aunt Claudia had brought most of her children and grandchildren over.

Elaina enjoyed reconnecting with her cousins, meeting their spouses and children. She laughed and cried at the many stories of life, good and bad. Her cousin Caleb shared with her his desire to go to Florida to find work. He had read about the building boom going on there since the war had ended.

"I ain't much for a factory, 'Laina. It'd flat-out kill me, I think. If I could work outside and make good money, that would suit me jus' fine."

While Elaina listened, the tiniest seed of a possibility was planted.

The weather was still warm when October arrived, a fact that both pleased and frustrated Elaina. She felt like a balloon about to pop, and the Arkansas heat and humidity made her feel sticky and dirty. She was glad, though, that the children could still enjoy playtime outside, knowing that back in Detroit sweaters and jackets were already being pulled out.

She felt the first twinge of labor on Wednesday night. She had just gotten the children laid down for the night. She sank onto the couch and breathed deeply, wondering if this was the real thing. She leaned back and very soon felt the next contraction start.

"Grandma, I think I might need to go to the hospital."

"Is it time, Sis?" Her grandmother was so calm and reassuring. All her years as a country midwife still kicked in when labor began.

Elaina answered, her face crinkled in a mask of pain. "Yes, ma'am," she gasped.

"All righty, then. I'll call Clement and get him over here. You just relax and let that baby start workin' its way into this world."

All Elaina could do was nod as she listened to her grandmother summon her brother with instructions to hurry but be careful. Once he arrived, she told him what he needed to do and helped him get Elaina in the car. She still knew how to deliver babies, but age had wreaked havoc on her body, preventing her from serving the women of her family and community.

"I'll stay here with the babies, Sis. You go on and trust that I'll take good care of them. Do you want me to call your mama?"

"I wish she would be there for me, Grandma, but I can't imagine she would come to the birth of her daughter's illegitimate baby—even if it's not illegitimate." She balled her hands into her cotton shift and groaned. Then she looked at her grandmother. "No, Grandma, don't call her." She didn't want to feel rejected again.

Clement spun left and right in the loose gravel on the road and Elaina was certain he was enjoying this speedy drive through the countryside. They arrived at the county hospital, and shortly before daybreak Abigail Jeanette entered the world, her thick crown of hair black as night. Elaina noted sardonically that her daughter's nose and mouth looked just like Grant's.

Clem called their grandmother from the hospital room, made sure Elaina was set for the time being, and left to go to work. Elaina lay back and drifted to sleep, wondering what she would do now that her baby was here.

Elaina stayed with her grandmother another month, wishing she could just stay forever. Cherilyn was at the house almost daily, caring for the baby. She was completely enamored of the child and begged her sister to let her keep her.

"I can adopt her, 'Laina. I just know I can. Or you can just leave her here with me and I'll keep her and raise her like my own."

"Oh Cherilyn, I love you so much, but you aren't married yet. And you know Mama wouldn't let you keep her at her house."

"I'll make her let me. Or I'll move out. Maybe Grandma would let me live here." Her cheeks flushed with her desire to have Abigail as her own.

Brushing a tendril of black hair back from her forehead, Elaina said, "Cherilyn, if Mama would let you, I would sign whatever papers are necessary. I don't think Grant wants her. He's only trying to get Doreen and Seth in the divorce. I don't know what to do. I won't even have a place to live when this is over. I'll have to get a job…" Her voice trailed off. Having her life fall apart at twenty-two was incomprehensible, and thinking about it was agony.

Louise had seen her carrying her beautiful Abigail when they were at church, but never came close enough to hold her. Elaina's heart broke for the rejection the little girl was receiving from her own grandmother.

November's winds started blowing colder and she knew it was time to return to Michigan, to the city where she would have to go to court to defend herself. Alec had called Grandma Freda's house and told her that the court date was set for November 20th. She had no money, so she couldn't hire a lawyer to protect her, but she would go to court to do what she could.

Clement drove Elaina and the children to the bus station. She rode in the passenger seat, her baby daughter on her lap. She still had some of the money she had brought from Michigan, but her brother had to help finish paying for the bus tickets to get her and her brood home.

"I'll send that back to you once I get to workin'," she promised.

"I'm not worried about it. I'm happy to help you. You're my sister."

"Yeah well, I'm Alec's sister, too, but he don' see it that way," Elaina retorted.

"His loss, Elaina. He'll be sorry for that one day."

"I wish I could believe that like you do, Clem."

"Well, I'll believe it for both of us. The Good Book says God takes care of us, and He don't like folks lyin' about His children. It'll come around. You'll see."

Chapter 30

November 21st found Elaina packing up her belongings in the little house. The judge had taken everything and given it to Grant after he had told the judge that she had left the children alone many times to have her affairs. He painted her as a despicable mother and a horribly unfaithful wife.

The judge believed what he was told because Grant used statements from her own brother and mother declaring her unfit as a mother. He gave Grant full custody of the children, except Abigail. He didn't want to raise some other man's child, he had said. The judge declared Elaina's only visitation of Doreen and Seth would be when Grant approved it. She knew he never would.

She had tried to tell her side of the story, but in the face of Grant's confidence and witnesses she had little chance of making a difference. It was a done deal when she walked into the courtroom.

Now she was leaving their home. She could only pray that Grant would allow her to see the children every so often.

As they left the courthouse Grant had said to her, "The children and I will be at Alec's house until Sunday evening. That will give you the rest of today and almost three more. Get all your stuff out; you won't be comin' back." With that he turned and walked away.

Elaina had suspected she would be kicked out, and had spent the past two weeks scouring the newspaper for work. She wasn't trained in anything except being a housewife and mother.

Just this past Monday morning she had left Seth and Abigail with the next door neighbor, walked Doreen to school, and headed out on the bus to look for a job. She had seen several waitress positions in Greektown, located just outside the area of downtown Detroit where they had lived upon their arrival in the city. She walked into Miki's Restaurant and Lounge on Beaubien. There was a bar along one wall, but most of the space was taken with tables. The walls were covered with old family portraits showing the Greek countryside. The place appeared clean, and Elaina stepped up to the bar where a middle-aged man was wiping glasses.

"May I help you?" he queried, his Greek accent heavy.

Elaina lay the newspaper ad section on the bar and said shyly, "Yes sir, I'm looking for a job." She tried hard to keep her Arkansas accent from coming through.

The man continued wiping the glasses and looked her up and down. "What do you do?" he asked.

"Right now, sir, nothing. I mean, I've been raising my children and being a wife."

"You don't have children anymore?"

Tears glistened as Elaina said, "That's sort of the case, sir. My husband is divorcing me. He's trying to get the children, and since I don't have a lawyer, I think he'll get them. Except for the baby. She's just a month old now. He doesn't want her."

The man's eyebrows lifted and he set down the glass he was wiping. He moved closer to Elaina and motioned for her to sit down. "He don't want your baby? Why not?" he asked.

Sighing deeply, Elaina said, "He says she's not his."

"Is she?" the man asked bluntly.

"Yes sir, she is. Anyone who looks at her can see she's the spittin' image of her daddy and that her daddy is Grant."

"Ahh. I see. He's got a little missus on the side and he's taken you for everything, huh?" He lifted his rag and wiped across the richly shining wood of the bar.

Elaina's eyes widened. "I don't-I—" she stammered. "I don't know if he has someone else." Gathering her confidence, she said, "I just know he doesn't want me, and I have to find a job and a place to live."

"What's your name? I'm Mikolas Gournaris. I'm the owner of this place." He spread his arms to encompass the bar and the restaurant. "Have you ever been a waitress before?"

"Not unless you count taking the children's plates to the table," she replied honestly.

He clicked his tongue against his teeth and shook his head. He walked to the other end of the bar and lifted a small section of it, creating an opening he walked through. "You wait here," he called back over his shoulder.

Elaina sat nervously, hearing the man's yell in the back of the restaurant answered by a woman's voice. Soon Mikolas returned, trailed by a beautiful dark-haired beauty who was speaking to him in hushed tones, using a language Elaina had never heard.

"What is your name?" Mikolas asked as he returned to his place behind the bar. The woman walked to where Elaina sat.

"Elaina Kerr," she answered.

"Here, Leona. This is Elaina. She is a mama being kicked out of her home with a little baby. She needs a job and she's never been a waitress."

Mrs. Gounaris' ebony eyes were set in a near-perfect face. Elaina did a double take, looking at the picture of a Greek goddess behind the bar, then back to the woman beside her. She extended her hand to the woman.

"You almost look Greek," the woman said, reaching past the outstretched hand to turn Elaina's face side to side. "Are you Greek?"

"No, ma'am. I'm from Arkansas."

Both the man and woman laughed merrily. She sat on the stool next to Elaina and asked her to tell her the story she'd told Mikolas.

When Elaina finished Leona looked at Mikolas and said, "You know what we must do, do you not, Mikolas?"

"I think I do, Leona," he said. He walked to the old cash register and opened the drawer of it, using a knob near the back of the antique machine. He reached into the drawer, then walked back to his wife and handed the thing he'd picked up to her.

"My name is Leona Gounaris, Elaina." She grinned at her husband. "He doesn't always remember to introduce me. He is a good husband, though. I forgive him for that." She held up a key. "This is the key to your rooms." She waved to the back of the restaurant, where Elaina saw a staircase she had previously missed. "They are up there. You will move in there and we will teach you to be a Greek waitress. Is that good?"

Elaina blinked back tears. "How much will the rooms cost?" She was trying to manage the little money she would earn.

"Cost? They are part of the job!"

"Will I be able to have someone come in and stay with Abigail when I'm working?" She wanted to be sure to not offend her new landlords.

"I think we can work that out. When do you think you will move in?"

"It will probably be this weekend" she replied. "The trial is Thursday and I'm sure I won't win."

Leona patted the younger woman's hand. "That will be fine. You will bring your things here and get moved in, and we will become your family for now."

Mikolas mentioned that Leona might want to show Elaina the small apartment over the restaurant so she could decide if she really wanted to live there. She threw up her hands and laughed, then escorted Elaina up the stairs and back toward the front of the building. She unlocked the door and handed Elaina the key.

"This is your new home, Elaina. What do you think?"

Elaina walked into the apartment to find a beautiful living room with a comfortable sofa and two soft chairs. The walls were a soft beige with a hint of green. They almost looked soft. She walked to the sofa and rubbed her hand across the fabric. She didn't want to stop touching it, it was the most luxurious thing she had ever touched.

To her right she saw a little kitchenette.

"You and your baby will eat with us in the restaurant," Leona noted. "Every day we have something special that is not on the menu. I make a little extra for our favorite customers, but mostly it's for me and Mikolas, and now for you."

Elaina could barely contain her excitement as Leona showed her the two bedrooms and the most modern bathroom she had seen. They were all small rooms, just right for her and Abigail.

As the two women stepped from the apartment, Elaina gushed, "Oh, Mrs. Gounaris! This is so beautiful! It's just right. Oh, I love it! I promise I will do my very best to learn to be a good Greek waitress for you!"

"Ha! I know you will. You will make our customers feel right at home. They will love you! Now, see here?" She pointed to the other end of the hallway. "There is the Gounaris apartment. That is where Mikolas and I live. We will be neighbors."

Elaina had talked with the couple for almost an hour before shaking their hands to seal the deal. She would live in the apartment and work for them. They would pay her $4.00 per day until she learned the job. They would increase that as she learned.

As she rode the city bus back to her neighborhood, Elaina couldn't keep from smiling. How had this happened? She had only checked on a couple of jobs, and now she had not only a job but a place to live as well. Once home, she changed out of her Sunday dress into a cotton shift and went next door. Her son had just had lunch and was ready for his nap.

"I know it's time for a nap." He groaned before she went on, "I'm thinking we need to go down the street to the park. I think the merry-go-round is calling your name." She continued to work on speaking better, believing that the folks she served would rather not hear her Arkansas hillbilly accent.

Seth looked at his mother quizzically, cupping his hand to his ear. "Mama, I don't hear anyone calling our names."

Elaina giggled. "It's not really, sweetie. I just think that we need to go play a little bit."

Seth started dancing and clapping.

Elaina gathered up Abigail, thanked her neighbor, and told her she would tell her about the trip later. She winked before turning, to let her friend know the news was good.

Seth played on the slide and swings. He rode the merry-go-round so much he said his tummy started to hurt.

"That's enough, little man," his mother said. "Let's go home and rest before it's time to get your sister."

By the time they got home his tummy had settled down, and he lay down and fell right to sleep. Elaina watched him closely, hoping and wishing that she would be able to keep on doing this every day. In the deepest recesses of her heart, she knew she wouldn't.

Now she packed up her few clothes and shoes into the suitcases she had carried to Arkansas. She gathered up the dishes that had been given her when she and Grant had married.

She thought, *I'll break them before I leave them for him to use.* She took the silverware, too. She wasn't sure if there was any at the apartment, but she felt the same about that as she did the plates and bowls. They were hers and she wasn't leaving them for Grant's other woman to have.

She pulled the embroidered pillowcases from the pillows, recalling how her mother had sat long hours with needle and thread to make them so pretty.

Two suitcases, two boxes, and a baby. She would have to make several trips on the bus to get everything moved. If Grant wasn't being so hard-hearted, she could call him and borrow the truck, but that was out of the question. She had an idea and brushed it away, then decided to check it out.

She lifted the telephone receiver and called Miki's Restaurant. She heard Leona's lovely accented voice answer.

"Mrs. Gounaris, this is Elaina."

"Oh, my girl! How are you? Did you go to the trial yet? Are you okay?" The questions came fast.

"Yes, ma'am. It was yesterday. Everything happened just like I thought." Her voice broke. "I've lost everything. Everything. My babies…" She couldn't go on.

"Oh, my poor girl. This is so wrong! Are you ready to come here?" Leona asked.

"That's why I called. I don't have much, but it's going to be hard to carry it all on the bus. Do you know a good cab that won't cost me a lot?"

"No!" Her explosive response shocked Elaina, who began apologizing.

"No, no. I don't mean to scare you. Mikolas and I will come to get you. Give me your address."

Elaina considered protesting, then realized it would do little good. Besides, it would be nice to not have to make several trips. She told Leona how to get there and set about doing the final cleaning of the house. Just as she finished the last swipe of the kitchen counter, she remembered her good cast iron skillet and pulled it from the oven. She added it to the box with the dishes and heard a car pull into the driveway.

She walked to the front door and opened it to find Mr. and Mrs. Gounaris getting out of their brand new Cadillac. They walked to her and gathered her up into a hug. Mikolas saw the boxes and suitcases just inside the door, and after making sure they were what she was taking began moving them to the trunk of the big car.

While the Greek man moved her belongings, Elaina introduced Leona to Abigail. The light in the woman's eyes was so kind and joyous when she saw the baby. She asked to hold the tiny girl, and Elaina lifted her from the sofa.

She cuddled the baby close to her, then said softly, "We cannot have little ones, Mikolas and I. God has decided I am not to be a mama." She breathed in the sweet scent of the baby.

"Oh, Mrs.—"

"Stop. You call me Leona, you hear?"

"Yes, ma'am. Leona." Elaina stumbled over the words.

"And you call him Mikolas," she said, jerking her head toward the door.

"I shall love your little girl! I can be her *theía*, her auntie." She looked at Elaina. "If that is all right with you."

"That would make me very happy, Leona. Her grandmother wouldn't even look at her after she was born. I would love for you to be her auntie."

"Then this is a wonderful day for us both! You now have a job, and a home where you don't have to deal with this husband of yours. It is sad that he is taking your other children, but this one, Abigail Jeanette, shall know the love of her mother and her new Greek family."

"Why don't you sit down, Leona, and I'll help Mikolas finish loading the car."

The older woman smiled and took a seat on the sofa, talking and cooing to the dark-haired baby. Abigail's eyes were riveted on Leona's.

Mikolas closed the trunk of the big car and walked back into the house. Elaina saw him as he took in the view of his wife holding the baby. His brusque features became soft, and she was pretty sure she saw a tear hastily wiped away.

"Mikolas, Leona, would you mind if I called my grandmother to let her know I'm moving and that I'm all right?"

Leona waved absently. "No, no, dear one, go ahead."

Once the operator connected the lines to Grandma Freda's home, Elaina made fast work of telling her about the job and the apartment. She told of Leona's becoming Abigail's *theía* and how she was already in love with the tiny bundle. Once she had given her grandmother the new address, she hung up the phone and looked around the house.

"I think that's all. I would like to leave a note for Doreen, but I know Grant won't let her have it."

Mikolas thought aloud, "Maybe if you put it where only she will be?"

Elaina thought about where that might be, and came to the conclusion that her daughter's school book might be the place. She hastily wrote a note.

> *My sweet Doreen, I love you so much. I love your brother so much, too. Your daddy and I can't live together anymore and I'm not allowed to have you live with me. I'm so sorry. Take good care of Seth. I will try to see you every week, I promise. That will be up to your daddy.*
>
> *Love, Mommy*

She walked into Doreen's bedroom and sat on her bed. She hugged the pillow her daughter slept on, breathing in the special scent that was all Doreen. Wiping away the unbidden tears, she found the girl's spelling book. She slipped the note deep into the book, hoping it wouldn't fall out and be discovered by Grant. She wiped her eyes and returned to the living room. She pulled the key from her pocket and lay it on the kitchen table. While she made sure the back door was locked, the older couple took her baby to the car and got settled. Elaina whisked up the baby blankets and walked to the front door. She locked the door and pulled it shut, her heart broken.

Chapter 31

Elaina worked hard learning how to be a top-notch waitress at Miki's Restaurant and Lounge. She earned the love and respect of the regulars, who asked for her tables and paid her with excellent tips.

Once she dumped a full glass of water on a lady. She had been utterly embarrassed. The woman was with some of her regular customers, and had bumped Elaina's arm as she was serving their table. She rushed to the ladies room while Elaina went to the kitchen to grab towels. When she delivered them to the restroom, she and her victim talked.

"I'm so sorry!" Elaina said, helping to sop the water from the lovely pantsuit.

"Oh pishposh, Elaina! It was my own fault! Don't be so upset. It's just water, and this pantsuit will dry nicely. It's washable anyway." Smoothing over the damp areas, she said, "See there? It's barely even visible. I'll be just fine."

"Thank you," Elaina said. "Your dessert is on me tonight. Leona made baklava this morning. It smells heavenly!"

"Now *that* I will take you up on!"

The two laughed together as they returned to the table, where Mikolas stood talking to the others there.

"Miki," the woman said, "do you realize what a gem you have in this little lady?"

"Indeed we do, Mrs. Moran. She's not just our employee, she's part of our family. Matter of fact, Leona is upstairs with her beautiful baby girl right now!"

Lorene Moran smiled broadly, "Oh, I know Leona is loving that! Please tell her I said hello. I wouldn't want to interrupt her special time."

Mikolas assured her he would. When he made sure the socialite and her party were settled and happy, he walked to the kitchen.

"Elaina!" he shouted over the din of dinner preparations.

"Yes, sir?" she timidly answered.

"Do you know who that was? That was Lorene and Charles Moran. They're in town from California for his parents' big anniversary party. You've heard of John Bell and Serena Moran?"

Elaina felt her face grow hot. She was sure it was bright red. She had just dumped water on one of the richest people in the city!

"I have a message for you from Mr. Moran," Mikolas continued.

"Yes, sir?"

"He said to tell you that Lorene had already been baptized once, but he didn't think it would hurt her to have it done again." Mikolas laughed heartily.

"They're not mad?" Elaina questioned.

"Not at all, my dear. Even as I came in here, they were all laughing about it." Turning serious, he turned her to face him. "There is nothing to fear in this place, Elaina. No one will hurt you for making a mistake." He lightly touched her cheek. "Do you understand this?"

Elaina nodded, unable to speak, wondering how Mikolas had figured out what she had been thinking, how she had felt.

"Thank you, Mikolas. I didn't realize I was so scared." She kissed him quickly on the cheek and drew plates from their resting place to deliver to customers.

Elaina called Grant every weekend to talk to the children. Every time he told her they were out or playing or busy. He had a million excuses for why she couldn't talk to them. She had tried complaining to Alec, but he told her she'd gotten what she deserved.

In a flash her Drew temper had risen to the surface, and she spat, "Well, fine. It will be a cold day in hell before you see my face or that of your niece again. You'll never be my brother again!" And she had hung up when he had begun to speak.

She was finished, she thought. Her mother didn't want her anymore, her brother didn't want her anymore. Well, fine. Let them both have Grant and his new woman. She had learned from her former neighbor that within a week of her moving out, Grant had a new woman over at the house almost every night. She wondered how long before he made an honest woman out of her.

Her only regret was the children. She would walk away from the others, but her babies didn't deserve this. They deserved to know that their mother loved them deeply. Mikolas had spoken to his attorney about Elaina's case, asking him if there was anything she could do to see her children. He had gotten a copy of the divorce decree from the courthouse and read it. He had been shaking his head when he talked to Mikolas and Elaina.

"This is a *fait accompli*," he had said. "The judge decreed that you are an unfit mother to—" He looked at the paperwork in his hand. "—Doreen and Seth. Your ex-husband can allow you to visit the children, but only with an approved supervisor present. Mind you, he doesn't have to let you see them at all."

"Not at all?" Elaina had asked sadly.

"I'm sorry, Elaina. This was a dirty deal," the attorney said as tears filled the young woman's eyes.

"I understand. Thank you for looking at it and telling me. Thank you, Mikolas, for asking."

That had been a month ago, almost eighteen months after the divorce, and still, every week when she called, she was denied the chance to talk to her children. She had ridden the bus to the park near their house, hoping to catch sight of them, but it seemed they were never there anymore.

"I have to do *something*," Elaina said aloud as she walked up the stairs to her apartment. Leona had Abigail in their apartment, where she had set up a bedroom just for the baby, furnished with all the best furniture and toys a baby could ever want.

Elaina entered her apartment, recalling when she had stayed with Grandma Freda that Caleb had talked about going to Florida to work and live. She wondered if he had done that. She sat down on the sofa and lifted the receiver of the telephone.

"Caleb Keys, Stafford, Arkansas, please," she told the operator. She was somewhat surprised to hear the phone ringing. He must still live back home.

"Hello?" he answered.

"Caleb! It's me, Elaina! How are you?"

"Well, I'll be. How's life in the big city? Grandma told me about your divorce, Elaina. Are you okay?"

"I'm gettin' by, Caleb," Elaina replied. "I've got a good job and I have a place to live. Abigail's doin' great!" She slipped easily into the lazy Southern tongue of her childhood.

"How 'bout your other two?"

"I haven't seen 'em or heard from 'em since the divorce, right at eighteen months ago," she said flatly.

"That's not right, 'Laina. That's just not right. How can he do that?"

"'Cause he convinced Mama and Alec that I was a whore, and they helped him convince the judge that I'm an unfit mama. So he said I can only see my children when there's a supervisor watchin' and only if Grant says I can."

"That's just wrong. No wonder Grandma was so mad! She flat out shunned your mama. I seen it! She walked right past her on the square and never said nothin' and never looked at her. Your mama looked like she'd been slapped."

Elaina shook her head, thinking about that. She didn't like to think of her mama being hurt by *her* mama, but she didn't know what to do about it. It was a bed of Mama's own making.

"So, what are you up to these days?" she asked. "Still thinkin' about Florida?"

"I'm just workin' at the shoe factory every day. Yeah, I've thought about Florida a lot. I'd love to see the beach and work outside all the time. No more snow!" His voice, which had started off weary, picked up life as he went on.

"I was thinkin' about Florida, too," Elaina said softly.

"You was?" Caleb sounded excited. "Do you want to go, too?"

"I'm thinkin' that might be what I need, Caleb. It's killin' me to be a short bus ride from my babies and I can't see 'em. Grant just won't let me, and the judge says that's the way it is. Maybe if I go to Florida, I can make a life there." Her voice trailed off.

"I'm game, 'Laina. Want me to come pick you up?" he asked.

"That would be kinda silly, wouldn't it? How about I'll come home for a quick visit with Grandma and let her know what's goin' on and we'll leave from there."

And just like that the plans were made. Elaina slipped down the hall and knocked on the Gounaris' door. Leona answered her knock and invited her in.

"Abigail is taking a nap, the precious girl," Leona informed her.

"I figured she might be. I'll look in on her before I go down to work. Leona, I have a big, big favor. I think you and Mikolas might need to talk this over before you answer."

"Oh, dear! What is so big that would need both of us thinking about it?"

Elaina related to the woman what the attorney had said and how she felt about it. Her voice broke several times as she shared about Grant having another woman now, and how he never let her talk to her children much less see them.

"I just don't know what else to do, Leona. It breaks my heart to be so close and so far away."

"Your old husband is a bad man, Elaina. I am so sorry you did not get a Mikolas."

"Me too," she agreed. "My cousin Caleb is going to Florida to find work in construction. I was thinking I could go down there with him and get settled, then send for Abigail. That is, if you'll keep her while I'm gone." Tears filled her eyes at the thought of leaving her daughter.

A light shone in Leona's eyes as she replied, "Of course we will keep this beautiful *moró korítsi!* We will treat her as our very own, if that is all right with you."

"I love how you take care of her, Leona. You love her like I do." The twenty-four-year-old mother sniffled.

Leona clasped the younger woman's hand. "I know this hurts your heart so bad. I am so sorry to be so happy when you are so sad."

Elaina wiped her eyes. "It's okay, Leona. It's just—" She covered her mouth as a sob stole her breath. "My Seth and Doreen were stolen from me and now I'm choosing to leave Abigail behind. Maybe I *am* a horrible mother."

"Nonsense, Elaina! You are a fine mother. I see how you steal away every chance you get to spend time with our girl. When others are going out back to smoke or talk you are up here, playing with this precious one. She knows her mama, and she knows her mama is good."

"She won't know me long if I'm not here, though," the young mother sobbed.

"She will know her mama as long as I have breath."

"How can that be?"

"We will take pictures before you leave and Mikolas and I will hang them in her room and tell her stories of her beautiful mother, and when you write letters we will read them to her. She will know you, Elaina."

"You would do that?"

"Of course I will do that! You are her mama." Leona released Elaina's hand then asked, "When do you think you will be leaving?"

"I have to make the arrangements to go home to see Grandma first, then we'll leave from there. So, probably the day after tomorrow—if that won't cause trouble for you in the restaurant."

"Perhaps you can stay through the weekend?" the woman asked cautiously. "It would be very hard without you over the weekend."

Nodding, Elaina said, "Of course. I'll get a ticket for Monday. It might even be cheaper that way. I'll call Grandma and tell her I'm coming."

"That's fine. I will tell Mikolas and we will put an ad in the paper today to seek someone to fill in for you. It will be difficult." The woman's eyes suddenly filled with tears. "I feel like my sister is moving away!" she cried.

Elaina hugged her closely. "I will stay in touch. You will always have my heart, Leona. Perhaps you and Mikolas can come to visit me."

"We will see, my dear. We will see. Come, let us look in on our girl. She should be waking soon."

Chapter 32

Elaina stayed and played with her daughter over an hour before returning to her apartment to make the phone calls. She first called the bus station and got the schedule for Monday, then she called her grandmother and told her when she would be arriving in Stafford. Grandma seemed happy to hear from her and offered to make the arrangements for getting her from the station to the house. Elaina was glad to let her.

Once the phone calls were made, she still had an hour before her shift started, so she walked the few blocks to the bus station and bought her ticket for early Monday morning. As she walked back to the restaurant, there was a new spring in her step and she walked along with a new confidence.

When she arrived home, she quickly deposited her pocketbook upstairs. As she raced toward the stairs to start her shift, she ran into Mikolas.

"I hear that you are leaving us," he said.

"At least for a time, Mikolas," she replied. She hated hurting him this way after he had taken such a chance on her.

His smile lit his face. "I am proud of you, little mama. You have learned so much here, you can wait tables in the finest of places. You will always find work. Matter of fact, I have cousins in Tomoka. If you want to stay there, I am sure they can give you work."

"Oh, Mikolas! You are such a doll!" She hugged him fiercely. "You remind me of my daddy. He was a wonderful man."

He nodded. "Ahh, to be reminded of a daddy's girl's daddy, that is a great honor. Now, let us go down and enjoy this night of serving the best customers in Detroit." Winking at her, he continued, "without pouring water on any of them."

They laughed as they walked down the stairs, Elaina feeling as though a giant weight had been lifted from her shoulders and her heart. She had high hopes for this new adventure.

The visit with Grandma Freda was all too short, but it was good to be able to sit across the table from her and talk about all that had happened in the past year and a half. Elaina's eyes misted as she talked about how kind and loving Leona and Mikolas had been to her, then brightened as she talked about how Abigail and Leona had bonded so well. A twinge went through her as she spoke of this relationship. She loved that Leona loved her daughter, but she often felt like Abigail loved Leona over her. She mentioned it to her grandmother.

"I mean, I realize I don't spend as much time with Abigail as Leona does, but I'm still her mama. It kinda makes me sad, Grandma."

"I understand, child. I do. And while that hurts, it's been such a blessing to have Leona there for you when your own mama was working against you. I'd love to meet this Leona and Mikolas. They've treated my girl right, and I appreciate them a lot."

"You're right, Grandma. And I'm really thankful for them. I have their address if you might want to write a letter to them. I'm sure they'd love to hear from you. I talked about you all the time."

"You did, huh?"

"Yes, ma'am. They knew how Mama had done, and I wanted them to know that it wasn't all my family who thought that way. She loved the notion that Cherilyn wanted to adopt Abigail even though she was single and only seventeen."

"Cherilyn wanted to adopt? I didn' know that." Freda dipped the end of her birch stick into the snuff jar and placed it in her mouth. "Huh. I'm right proud of that girl. She was willin' to take on all the ridicule and anger of your mama in order to have your little one stay in the family. What a good heart that one has."

"Yes'm. She begged and begged, but I took the baby on home to Michigan with me."

"And that might be best for everyone, Sis. Your little girl is well loved by a couple who couldn't bear a baby of their own. You've been as much a blessing to them as they have to you."

Elaina pondered those words. "I never thought about that, Grandma. I mean, Leona said it was good for her, too, but I only thought that it was so kind of them to help me. I guess they see it as kind for me to share Abigail with them."

"I think they do, child." Freda leaned back in her chair and closed her eyes, a smile on her face as she dozed off.

The sight of palm trees was a strange one to Elaina. She looked at them much as she had looked at the tall buildings in Detroit.

"Caleb! Can you believe this sunshine? It's hot as a pistol here!" She wiped her forehead and leaned her head nearer the window of her cousin's car to let the breeze blow over her. She was driving as he directed each turn by looking over a map they had picked up at a gas station just before the state line.

"It sure is hot, 'Laina. I'm not so sure about this workin' outside thing anymore."

She laughed. "We've come an awful long way for you to back out now! It will be fine. You'll see. It's extra hot because we're cooped up in this car."

They were now crossing the lower part of the state, headed for the ocean. Their plan was to go to the Palm Beach area, where Elaina would get a job waitressing at a fancy restaurant. They had read that Palm Beach was the high society vacation place and decided that would be a good place to get a good paying job. Once they were there, Caleb would check with the construction crews they knew would be everywhere building roads and bridges and hotels.

Now, as they cruised along the two-lane highway, both windows down, Caleb looked up from the map and said, "Okay, 'Laina, when we get up here to Highway 1 you wanna turn right. That should take us right into Palm Beach. I think we should see the turn in just a few minutes."

Elaina stopped at White City Gulf where the serviceman filled up the gas tank, checked the oil, and washed the windshield. Elaina and Caleb visited the restrooms and switched seats. Elaina was happy about this move because it would allow her to look around more than when she was driving. She thought the air felt electric, like something amazing was about to happen.

As they drove down US Highway 1, often viewing the ocean on their left and a river to their right, the cousins were enthralled with the new world they were entering. They had no idea where they were going to live or work, but on this great adventure neither thing mattered.

Chapter 33

As often happens plans change, and they did for Caleb and Elaina. They had stayed in a rooming house in West Palm Beach for almost a month, but neither was able to get a job. Caleb decided to make his way back to Arkansas, but Elaina was determined to stay in Florida. She simply had to make a life for herself so she could get her daughter here with her.

Mikolas and Leona had told her to call them collect to stay in touch, and so she talked to them at least once a week. She heard how Abigail was growing. She loved hearing how her daughter mastered each new skill. Each time she called Elaina worked hard to sound excited for the couple, but once she hung up the phone she cried great gulping tears that took her breath.

"Abigail Jeanette, one day I'll be back to get you. Your mama loves you so much!" she said to the air.

Elaina had made her way inland to Mayaca. She worked in several little restaurants along the eastern side of the big lake, serving fishermen and construction workers. She landed in a little town near the Everglades called Muckland. She worked as a waitress in a bar restaurant where she became familiar with the fishermen, farmers, and the men building roads and buildings. She had found a little trailer for rent near the lake, under the big live oak trees dripping with Spanish moss.

One Thursday night Elaina was flirting with the guys in her section of the restaurant, knowing that doing so would net her better tips. She tried to make each man feel like he was at home, being served by someone who cared about him. She would banter back and forth with all of them, and everyone enjoyed the fun. Back at Table 5, the one nearest the back of the dining room, was a group of guys who were working on the bridge just outside town. She had seen the barge tied to the bank of the canal where the boats would take the sugar cane and other crops out to sell.

Elaina had never seen that one fellow before. He had sun-darkened skin topped with dark, loose curls on his head. His laugh was easy as he drank and ate with his buddies. They were telling jokes and stories. She had overheard that he'd recently gotten out of the Navy. As she went about taking orders and bringing salad and slaw and more beer, she felt his gaze on her. Every time she looked at him he was looking right back at her, and every time her cheeks grew pinker.

Friday night found the same group back at the same table at suppertime, and he was with them. Elaina had thought about him a lot overnight and throughout the day. He was muscular from his hard work, and looked a lot like the movie star Montgomery Clift. She delivered glasses of water to the table, wondering how she would be able to introduce herself to him.

Her regular guys handled that chore for her.

"'Laina, this is Vince," said Dave, one of the first customers she had ever served here.

"Hey, Vince. Are you drinking draft again tonight?"

"Did Dave say 'Laina'?" Vince asked.

"That's me. Elaina Kerr."

"Hello, Elaina. Yeah, I want a draft. I might have two or three," he declared.

She took the bar orders for the rest of the table and walked away.

During that hot summer in the bar just outside the Everglades, romance blossomed. Vince kept coming back for supper night after night, whether the other guys came in or not, and Elaina began to come in on her evenings off to spend time with him.

August's Saturday nights were spent at the Prince Theater, watching the epic romance *From Here to Eternity,* followed by the antics of Jerry Lewis and Dean Martin in *The Caddy,* and the fun of *Roman Holiday.* Elaina felt so happy and carefree she began to forget about her life in Michigan, though her family's betrayal and having to leave her children behind remained heavy in the part of her heart she hid from everyone, even herself.

"I like living here," Elaina said, leaning against the bar and sipping a cold beer in a frosty mug. "I used to love fishing with Daddy and the family. I miss having seasons, though."

"Yeah, but you can't beat the weather. I had enough of rain and cold in the North Atlantic. I'm happy here with the sunshine," Vince said. He toasted her with his mug, then walked to the jukebox. Dropping a couple quarters in the slot, he entered the numbers for several songs. Returning to the bar, he asked the brunette, "You like fishing, huh? What kind of fishing have you done?"

"Mostly catfish, crappie, and bream. We fished in the Dermot River back home." She told him of knocking the catalpa worms from the trees to use for bait. "Those catfish couldn't resist those worms!"

"I was thinking I might rent a boat and we could go out on the lake and fish a while. How about Sunday? Are you off?"

"I am, and I'd love that!" She clapped her hands like a child, then giggled. "It's been a long time since I got to do that. Grant wasn't much for fishing."

"Then Sunday it is. I'll come by to get you about six in the morning, and we'll get on the lake just at daybreak."

Elaina's eyebrows lifted as she thought about having to work the night before, but figured she might snooze a little on the boat. "All right. I'll be ready."

And ready she was. She had on a wide-brimmed hat like her mother and aunts had worn to the river and wore a pair of pedal pushers and a sleeveless blouse, her feet clad in plain sneakers.

"Well, aren't you just dolled up?" Vince asked as he grabbed her up and hugged her, kissing her lightly on the cheek.

"Do you have any poles or tackle?" she asked.

"I do not. Not yet. We'll see what they've got at the fish camp." He opened the door and settled her into his old Chevy.

The young couple had an enjoyable day on the lake, catching several speckled perch, what Elaina had called crappie, and bream. Back at the fish camp, they used the area set aside for cleaning the fish and worked side by side. Once back at Elaina's trailer, she rolled the fish in cornmeal and fried them while frying potatoes and heating up a can of pork and beans.

Later, pushing back from the table, Vince said, "Oh my goodness. You are one fine cook, Elaina Kerr. I might have to marry you just to have you as a cook."

"No, I don't think so," she said seriously as she collected the plates from the table. "I don't think I want to go through that again."

"I understand that. I don't ever want to have to deal with that again either. That woman took me for everything I had. It wasn't much, but it was all I had. Every penny I'd saved while in the Navy was gone, and I spent time in jail for it."

Recalling the story he'd told, Elaina said, "I'm sure! That was just so—so—" Words failed her and she simply shook her head. Thinking that the woman he loved and trusted started seeing another man when he was at sea made Elaina see red. Then, when Vince had returned home, she had emptied their bank account knowing he was buying things to fix their house. He had been court martialed for theft and more. Her heart ached for what Vince had been through.

Vince walked up behind her as she washed the dishes and slid his arms around her waist. "We could just live in sin," he whispered against her neck.

"We *what?*" she squawked.

"You know, a common law marriage. If we live together, after a year or so it's as if we're married, so it's not like it's illegal or even wrong."

"I don't know," Elaina mused. He had told her of being a Baptist, but with all the drinking he did and hearing these words she didn't think he held much store in his faith.

He kissed her neck, then returned to the table. "Think about it, 'Laina. I care for you and you care for me. We'd be able to spend more time together. No more me having to leave to go home, since I'd *be* home."

She thought about it as she slowly swirled the rag across each plate. She thought about it as she drew each piece of silverware through the rag, making sure to get every bit of food off. She thought about it as she wrapped the leftover fish in tin foil and placed it in the refrigerator. She thought about it as she wiped the skillets clean and wiped the counters and stove top. Making this choice couldn't be any worse than not keeping her daughter. She figured God was mad at her anyway. This wouldn't make it much worse.

Elaina walked to the refrigerator and pulled out two beers. She opened both and handed one to Vince, then walked outside to sit in one of the metal chairs in her front yard overlooking

Lake Mayaca. The breeze from the lake was refreshing as she sat there, quietly contemplating.

"What happens if we decide we don't really like each other much?" she asked.

"Then I'll leave and we'll both be just fine."

"What do we tell everyone?"

"Oh, we'll come up with a story. As far as anyone will know, we ran off and tied the knot."

Elaina lifted the bottle to her lips and drew deeply of the liquid inside.

"What do you think?" Vince asked after several minutes.

"I think I'm tired of being alone," she replied. "I think we're a pretty good match. And if we're not, like you said, we can just go our own way and be done with it."

"Yeah," Vince said softly.

"Okay. Let's do it. Let's come up with a story."

"Well, everyone will know we didn't get married around here; it wouldn't be in the papers, and everyone knows everyone."

"Yeah, we'd have to have gone clear to Georgia for an overnight wedding."

"Well, there we go! That's our answer. We went to—" He broke off and stood. "Be right back," he said, walking around to the driveway. She heard his car door slam and in a moment he returned with a road map of Florida. Using the light from the kitchen window, he looked at it. A few towns just across the state line in Georgia were displayed.

"Look here. If we traveled up US 1, this is where we'd cross over, and here's the town. Kingsland. We can get married in Kingsland, Georgia."

Elaina laughed. "Here we are planning a wedding as though we're really going to have one."

They acted normal the next week, Vince bunking with his buddy like usual and Elaina going home each night. She asked her boss for the weekend off, including Friday. Vince told his boss on Thursday that he needed Friday off. And that day they moved Vince's things from his little apartment near the coast to her trailer near the big lake, where they enjoyed a honeymoon without the complications of a ceremony. Late that afternoon they made a trip across the state to a jeweler in Fort Myers to buy a simple wedding band for the bride.

Saturday morning, Vince looked at Elaina as she fished in the bow of the rented boat. "How's it going up there, Mrs. Koebner?"

She smiled broadly at him. "Just fine, Mr. Koebner."

The two laughed. Once docked Vince and Elaina carried their gear to the car, discussing the possibility of making an appearance at the bar that evening.

"I feel sort of like a schoolgirl again," Elaina shared.

"You look much better than any schoolgirl, honey," Vince replied.

"I just feel all excited, all tingly inside."

"Yeah. I feel kinda excited, too. I know all those other guys are going to be disappointed."

"Disappointed?" She frowned. "Why would they be disappointed? Won't they be happy we got married?"

"They'll be disappointed that you married me instead of them!" Vince grabbed her up and swung her around, then set her on her feet and kissed her soundly. "Now, let's go show everyone my new bride."

The couple sprang their surprise on their friends and bar family that evening and many rounds were bought. They couldn't have asked for a better reception for the wedding they hadn't really had. Now, though, they were seen as a married couple. And a whole new adventure began for Elaina.

Chapter 34

Sitting at the bar, Elaina began to write,

Dearest Leona,

I love the picture you sent. Abigail is growing so beautiful! I miss her horribly. I can't believe she's almost four years old, but that's just four months away. I'll send a birthday gift in time. I was thinking about one of the dolls from the Seminole reservation. Do you think she would like that?

I wanted to tell you that I just got married. I'm sure you remember me writing to you about Vince. He is so handsome, Leona! Much better looking than you-know-who.

Have you seen him or the children? I miss my babies. Doreen is almost eleven! I bet she looks so grown up! I know I did by that time. And Seth is just turned seven. I would so love to see them.

Anyway, just a quick note to let you know I'm okay. We're probably moving soon, Vince's job will be changing. Did I tell you he works construction? He's helping build the bridges for the highways down here. Did I tell you he was in the Navy before? A man's man!

Take care, dear. Hug Mikolas for me and give him a peck on the cheek. I love you both. Spoil my girl for me, I know you're doing a great job with her. I owe you so much for that.

Yours,
Elaina

She smiled, thinking of Mikolas' reaction to the news of her remarriage. He would want to know if he was a good man, if he was treating her right. All the things that a good big brother or father might say. She adored the Greek couple, and was so grateful that they were providing such a good life for her Abigail Jeanette.

She folded the letter and sealed it in the envelope addressed for Detroit. Licking the stamp, she pressed it on the corner, then walked the several blocks to the post office.

As she strolled back to the restaurant Elaina thought about Doreen with her dark hair, so thick and wavy. She wondered how her eyes were doing, if she was healthy. She wondered if she laughed and played at school, and if Grant's new wife was taking her to the park and the library. That girl loved to read.

She remembered her imp, Seth, and how he would call his sister out to play, teasing her into chasing him. She loved his throaty laugh. His eyes and hair were as dark as his father's, but she thought he would be much more handsome than his daddy.

Elaina stopped at a bench and sat, looking out at the lake, unable to see the other side from here. It seemed almost as vast as the ocean.

She wondered about her mother, if she was well. Clement had snuck a couple of letters to her to let her know Agnes had had a little boy, and Cherilyn had gotten married to Agnes' husband's brother. She chuckled thinking how that double family tie was going to be fun to keep up with. She knew the Martons and had always thought them a good family. She believed her sisters had married well. She had wanted to write back but, knowing how small Stafford was, knew the mailman would let it slip that Clement had gotten a letter from Florida, and she didn't want to cause him trouble with Mama.

She grinned, thinking how she was able to write to Grandma anytime she wanted to, because Grandma Freda didn't care if Louise got mad. She'd tell her that who she gets letters from is none of her business, and Mama would take it.

In those letters she had lamented to Grandma about not seeing the children, how she missed them and Abigail. She would pass along all Leona said about her baby daughter, knowing that Grandma loved that little mite of a girl as much as she did. She had written to Grandma yesterday, telling her much the same as she had just written to Leona.

Elaina knew the fact of her marriage to Vince was a lie, but she *felt* like she was married to him. They were living together, she cooked for him, did his laundry, while he brought home good money, paid the rent and groceries, and she was sure she loved him. His devil-may-care attitude was refreshing to a young woman who had grown up worried about what everyone thought of her. Now, with these letters, the deal was sealed. As far as anyone was concerned she was now Mrs. Elaina Koebner, and she loved signing her new checks with that name.

Standing from the bench she finished the walk to the restaurant, where she set about her day. Vince had told her she didn't have to work, but she wasn't ready to quit yet. What would she do with herself all day? She would just brood over her children and mother, so she continued to work. She enjoyed laughing with the customers, and flirted with the construction crews that came in. They all knew she was married to Vince, but they loved having the attention of a pretty young woman.

Soon Vince's job in Muckland was finished, and the construction company sent him to a job in Avilés. It was a pretty city in north Florida that was very old. Their little trailer home on a two-lane highway was small, but cozy.

They both loved seafood and soon found their favorite place, Poppy's. It looked like a shack about to fall down and the sign was a beached boat near the road. Inside, the atmosphere was bright and the aroma of the day's fresh catch cooking filled the air. They would sit at the board tables covered with red and white checkered tablecloths every Friday night and enjoy the latest catch off the boats with a couple bottles of beer. Sometimes they were joined by some of the men Vince worked with, other times it was just the two of them. On those occasions when they entered as a party of two, it didn't take long before Vince had included other people in their Friday merriment.

He doesn't know a stranger! Elaina thought more than once.

As December neared Elaina shopped at the Sears store in town, buying toys and dresses for her daughter, all the while wishing she could send her older two the things she longed to give. She knew that if she did, Grant would just throw them in the trash and never let the children know she had sent anything. How she wished she had known the woman he had had the affair with and then married. Maybe she would be willing to pass on her love and gifts to the children.

Chapter 35

It was almost eleven o'clock on Monday morning, the sun shining brightly, but the temperature hovering near zero. Elaina shook her head, looking at the basket of damp-from-the-washer clothes needing to be hung to dry.

She went to the bedroom and knelt down to pull out the suitcases she had kept from her days in Michigan. She kept her warm winter coat in the largest one with a couple mothballs to keep it safe. She wrinkled her nose as the chemical odor assailed her. Standing, she shook the coat like she shook freshly cleaned sheets, hearing the hem snap. Again and again Elaina shook the coat, hoping to wave some of the moth ball aroma out of it.

Well, that's about all I can do, she thought as she swung the coat around her shoulders and slid her arms into the sleeves.

She carried the laundry basket outside to the clothesline and quickly lifted each item to the line and secured it in place with a clothespin. By the time she finished, her fingers were numb from the combination of dampness from the clothing and very cold air.

I haven't felt cold like this since I left Michigan, she thought. *Or Arkansas.* As she walked past the clothes she had hung, she noticed Vince's pants felt stiff. They had frozen before the sun could dry them. Elaina hoped the sun would soon win the battle against the cold and dry the clothes.

Early in the summer of 1958, Elaina received a letter from Leona.

> *Dearest Elaina,*
>
> *I hope this letter finds you happy and healthy. I am enclosing a photograph of our precious Abigail. Isn't she just beautiful? I hope you don't mind, I've been teaching her some Greek. She thinks she's as Greek as we are and we don't correct her. Please forgive us for this bit of selfishness.*
>
> *As you know, our girl is set to start school this fall. She will begin in kindergarten in September. The problem is, I don't have the authority to sign the papers to register her in the school system.*
>
> *I can send you the documents our lawyer says are needed, but I was wondering about something else. Mikolas tells me I am out of line for asking this, but I simply must.*

Elaina lifted her eyes, fearful of reading the rest. She took a deep breath and began again.

> *As you know, dear Elaina, Mikolas and I will never have children of our own. I believe God put you and our sweet Abigail here in our lives to ease the pain of not having a baby of our own. Then when you decided to allow us to*

*keep her while you make a life for yourself, it was like a
dream come true.*

*Now you've been gone over four years and she is ready
to start school, I wonder if it might be okay with you if
Mikolas and I adopt Abigail Jeanette. I know this is a shock
to you! Please don't fret, dear one. If you decide the answer
is no, we will continue to love and care for this beautiful
girl until you're able to come and get her.*

*I'm just hoping to go from being her sometime mama
to being her real mama.*

Blessings to you and your Vince,
Leona

Elaina sat in stunned silence. She stood and walked the
length of the trailer, then back again. She fumed and ranted
to the air, then sat again to reread the letter.

When Vince arrived home that evening, he found her still
seated at the table. The usual aromas of her preparing supper
were absent and he could tell she was distressed.

"'Laina, what is it? What's wrong?"

"I got a letter from Leona today" she stated flatly.

"Is everyone okay? Is Abigail sick? Is Leona or Mikolas
sick?" He had learned all the names from her stories about
them all. She had delighted in sharing with him how they had
rescued her from despair after her divorce.

"No, no. Everything is fine. They're fine, Abigail is fine.
She'll start school in September."

Vince took a deep breath and sat down opposite his wife.
"Then what's wrong?" he asked.

"They want to adopt Abigail."

"Oh," Vince said quietly.

"They're excellent parents to her. They're really all the
parents she's ever known, I guess. She started staying with
Leona when she was just a tiny little thing, and I haven't been

in her life for four years. I can't believe it's been that long, but it really has." Elaina began to weep.

"Oh, honey!" Vince moved around the table and knelt beside her chair.

"I can't, Vince. I can't say no. I want to. I want to bring her down here right now and never let her go, but I can't. I just can't. That would be like ripping my little girl's heart right out of her chest. Leona is her mommy now." She smiled weakly at him.

"Do you want to call her to talk?" Vince asked.

Elaina nodded and he stretched the phone the short distance across the trailer to set it before her. He lifted the receiver and dialed zero, handed it to her, then sat down in the chair nearest her.

After giving the operator the number, it was several moments before Leona was on the line.

"Leona?" Elaina said.

"Elaina? Is that you?" she heard the older woman say.

"Yes, ma'am. It's me."

Leona cried out, calling for Mikolas to come to the phone. She babbled on about how things were going until he arrived at her side.

"Is this Elaina?" she heard Mikolas say.

"It's me, Mikolas. I'm here," she said, tears brimming in her eyes.

"It's so good to hear your voice! It's good to get letters from you, but to hear you is much more wonderful!" Elaina could hear the warmth in his voice.

"It's good to hear you, too. I called because I got Leona's letter today."

The silence on the line was palpable. Elaina went on quickly, "I'm so grateful for all you have done for me and for Abigail Jeanette. You are the best people I met in Michigan."

She heard Leona sniffle and speak softly in Greek to Mikolas before she said, "What do you think, dear? About what I asked?"

Elaina swallowed hard and said, "I don't want to do that, Leona." She heard the woman cry out, though it sounded like she had covered the phone. She raced to finish her words, "I don't want to, Leona, but I know it's the best decision for my daughter."

Elaina heard a clatter through the receiver and thought Leona must have dropped the phone. She called into the instrument, "Leona? Leona? Mikolas! Is she all right? Somebody talk to me!" She looked at Vince, feeling frightened.

The rustling of the phone being picked up was loud in Elaina's ear, then she heard the soft voice of her friend, "You are giving me the best gift I have ever received. I could not ask for more."

Leona and Elaina cried as they made the arrangements to accomplish the legal matter of adoption. When Mikolas spoke into the phone Elaina thought she heard tears in his voice, too. He kept clearing his voice as he spoke.

"You ladies make the plans. I have a restaurant to run, especially now that I have a little girl to raise."

"That silly man!" Leona said. "There's no need for you to come all the way up here, dear. We have relatives in Tomoka Beach. Let us come there. Is that too far a drive for you?"

"No, ma'am. Tomoka is just fine. When should we meet?"

The plans were made to meet at an attorney's office in two weeks, when Elaina would sign the papers to turn all her rights as mother of Abigail over to Leona and Mikolas. She knew that she'd be much better off with them. They finally finished talking and she hung up the phone.

Vince pulled her up to stand and wrapped his arms around her. "I know that was hard," he said simply.

She nodded against his chest, her tears flowing freely.

Chapter 36

Two weeks passed and Elaina drove to Tomoka, with Vince riding along. She introduced him to the Gounarises, and Leona whispered to Elaina that he was indeed better looking than you-know-who. Both ladies giggled.

Elaina looked at the pretty little girl holding Leona's hand. She squatted down to talk to her.

"Hello, I'm Elaina. Your mommy and daddy and I have known each other for some time."

"Hello, Mrs. Elaina," the youngster said primly. "Mommy has told me who you are."

Elaina looked up at Leona.

"We could not lie to the child, Elaina. We told her that her mommy had had to go away and could not take her along. We explained that you left her with us because you knew she would be loved and cared for as if we were you, that you trusted us to take good care of her. Just like we talked about, your pictures hang in her room and we always share your letters with her."

"Ahh, I see. And tell me, Miss Abigail, have you been happy living with the Gounarises?"

"Oh, yes, ma'am!" the child declared with excitement.

"I see." Elaina's voice broke as she said, "I wish I had been able to bring you with me." She looked away, her eyes brimming with tears.

"Mommy," the little girl placed her hand on Elaina's shoulder, "I know you love me. Mrs. Leona and Mr. Mikolas have told me every day that you say it. I get to read your letters... well, Mrs. Leona reads them to me."

Elaina had gasped when she heard the word "Mommy". Her tears overflowed as she looked at the little girl.

"You are such a lovely young lady! How old are you now, twenty-two?"

Abigail giggled. "No, Mommy. I'm only five."

"Well, you sure sound much older. What would you say, Miss Abigail, if we made it so Mrs. Leona and Mr. Mikolas became your real mommy and daddy?"

Brown eyes grew wide with surprise. "You can do that?" she asked Elaina.

"Uh-huh. I can. I really, really want to have you come live with me, but I think that would make Mrs. Leona and Mr. Mikolas very sad, don't you?"

Unsure what to answer, the little girl looked from one adult face to the other.

"I will always be your mommy, too, Abigail. Just that I'll be living down here and you'll be growing up with a mommy and daddy in Michigan."

The little girl motioned for Leona to lean down, then whispered in her ear, "Is it all right for me to be happy now?"

Leona nodded to the little girl, her smile bright as the sun.

"I'm happy, Abigail, so it's okay for you to be happy." Elaina stood and said to the couple, "Shall we go sign some papers to make you a mommy and daddy?"

The papers were signed and the Gounarises invited the Koebners out for lunch at their relative's Greek restaurant. They talked and enjoyed the meal, listening to Abigail tell stories about her preschool and her toys. She reached into the bag she had been carrying and lifted out the Seminole doll Elaina had sent to her for her birthday.

"Isn't she beautiful?" she asked everyone at the table.

Once the lunch was over, the families parted company with promises to call and write. Elaina asked Vince to drive. She was having a hard time seeing through the tears.

They drove in silence for an hour headed north to Avilés when Elaina realized they were gliding along beside the ocean. It was more familiar now than when she first rode along with Caleb, but it still had the power to soothe her mind.

"She's awful pretty, 'Laina," Vince said after a while. "She looks just like you."

"She favors her daddy some, too," she replied absently.

"Do you think you'd like to have another one?" he asked hesitantly.

"Another one what?"

"Another baby."

She shook her head and said, "I don't know, Vince. This right here is the hardest thing I have ever in my life done. That little girl will never know her father or her sister and brother. She won't know me. She'll forget me in a few months. I have three children I will never see again."

"I won't do that to you, 'Laina. I would never do that to you. I was just asking. I thought maybe one day you and me might…" His voice trailed off.

"We'll see," she said, her tear-filled eyes turned toward the Atlantic's crashing waves.

The weather was warm but not hot, a nice February day as Elaina sat in a chair outside their little house just outside Johnsville. It had been two years since she had given her daughter up and her heart still ached for Abigail. She patted her belly, knowing there was new life there. She had known before the nurse had called her. She hadn't planned this, but she wasn't unhappy about it. A little fearful perhaps, but not unhappy. She and Vince had been together almost four years now, and they were happy enough. She believed he wanted a child, but she still wasn't sure yet that this common law marriage would last.

Their life together had been anything but boring. Vince's work had moved them from Muckland to Avilés, to the north side of Lake Mayaca, and now to Johnsville. Each place they moved, they found a new family in a local bar. It didn't matter the location, the people were pretty much the same, she thought. Troubles and woes abounded, but together at the bar everyone dropped those and enjoyed one another. She considered telling Vince while they were at the bar tonight. It would give him the chance to brag about becoming a father to all their friends.

Nodding her approval of her plan, she rose and went into the house to wash the dishes. She had left last night's dishes and added this morning's, so she had a sink full.

As she wiped each dish with the cloth then rinsed and set it in the drainer, she thought about her other three pregnancies. With Doreen she had been just a child. She had just turned fifteen when she became pregnant. Everything was exciting and frightening as she went through the growth of her baby, believing her marriage was forever and that her mother would always be there for her.

Elaina grunted as she thought about that. Forever didn't mean much anymore. Not when a man could lie and have everyone believe him, take away her children, and make them not even want to write to her. And her mother?

"I won't be like that," she swore. "I will love my babies and stand by them no matter what."

As the afternoon wore on, she prepared a hearty meal of steak and gravy, mashed potatoes and green beans. She was just finishing up when Vince walked through the door.

"What smells so good?" he asked.

Elaina told him, lifting the covers from the pans as she did so, allowing the aroma to fill the air. "If you'll wash up, it's ready to eat," she said.

"I'll be right back!" he said over his shoulder, already walking to the bathroom to clean up.

When he returned, he found the table set and Elaina seated, waiting for him. "What's the occasion?" he asked, spooning potatoes onto his plate.

"Oh, nothing. I got the meat on sale and thought I'd fix something good with it. I know you like my gravy."

"I like your everything, Mrs. Koebner." He grinned impishly.

Elaina blushed as she watched him add a piece of chopped steak to the plate, then pour gravy over it and the potatoes. She lifted a spoonful of beans from the pan and he held his plate near to receive them. He began eating, and she added food to her plate and joined him.

After supper Vince took a shower while Elaina cleaned up, putting leftovers in bowls to serve tomorrow and sliding them into the refrigerator. She smiled as her plan kept working its way out.

Once Vince came back to the living room, she smiled and asked him if he wanted to go out for a beer and maybe a little dancing. She knew his weakness. He loved to dance. It was embarrassing sometimes, especially when he had had too much to drink. He would take her to the dancefloor during a slow dance, a love song playing, and about halfway through he'd lead her into a jitterbug, and she could only hang on to keep up. She would never forget the way people laughed at them.

Vince loved that. She would have preferred just finishing the slow dance, but she had endured much worse.

They arrived at the bar and were seated on their usual stools, talking with the bartender and the others around them.

As their second beer arrived, the foam standing above the rim of the tall frosty glasses, and Elaina leaned over to speak softly to Vince.

"I have something important I need to tell you," she said.

"What's that?" He took a sip of beer.

"Your wish is going to come true," she declared seemingly nonchalantly, taking a sip of her beer.

"My wish? What wish?"

She ducked her head, her cheeks reddening before she faced him and said quietly, "Your wish to be a daddy."

Vince's eyes flew open and his mouth dropped open. He leaned close to his wife and whispered, "A baby?"

Elaina nodded.

Vince let out a war whoop that startled everyone in the bar. "Next round's on me! I'm going to be a daddy!"

The shouts of congratulations and pats on the back came quickly and earnestly. Seeing the look on Vince's face as each person came and spoke to him, she knew she'd made the right choice to tell him here.

She enjoyed the evening, and when they returned home and were snuggled together in bed she whispered, "Are you really happy about this?"

"Oh God, Elaina. Yes, I'm happy! I couldn't be happier about anything in my life."

She tucked herself under his chin, his arm draped over her, and drifted off to dream of what would come.

Chapter 37

Elaina was folding laundry in the cozy block house in the little town of Lake Mayaca. It had been their home for almost a year. Beth was sitting on the floor playing with her wooden blocks. Her hair had the prettiest little strawberry-blond curls. She was just starting to get talkative. Elaina was listening to her telling her doll a story in toddler language, recalling how Doreen had read stories to her dolls when the phone rang.

"Hello?" she said.

"Elaina?" She recognized the voice but couldn't believe it.

"Mama? Is that you?" she asked incredulously.

"It's me, Elaina. Please don't hang up."

"I'm not going to hang up on you, Mama."

"Okay, good. I would like to see you, if that would be all right," her mother said. It sounded like she was really afraid she would hear a negative answer.

"You're not going to remind me how horrible I am, are you, Mama? Because I won't stand for that." Now thirty-one,

Elaina had gained confidence and strength she hadn't possessed at twenty-two.

"No, child; I will tell you how horrible I've been."

Elaina gasped softly. Her mother's voice sounded so soft and loving. It was nothing like she had been the last time they had talked, how long ago was it? Ten years?

"Mama, I live in Florida now. I'm married again. We have enough room if you want to come and stay."

"Could you come and pick me up, Elaina? I'm at the Fort Pierce bus station."

"You're what?" the young woman exclaimed.

"I'm at the Fort Pierce bus station. I've been on the road for a day and a half and I'm tired. Can you come get me?"

"I'll be right there, Mama." She started to hang up, then said, "It will take me about an hour, Mama, but I'll be right there."

"I'll be waiting," her mother said simply.

Elaina grabbed up her daughter, quickly changed her diaper, then pulled a summer dress over her head and picked up the diaper bag. She jotted a quick note for Vince in case he came home early, then practically ran to the car.

She talked to Beth about taking a little trip as she slid the child's chubby legs into place in the little chair that hooked over the back of the car's front seat. She dropped the diaper bag in the passenger seat and placed her pocketbook on the seat beside it.

Once on the highway Elaina made good time, covering the miles in less than an hour. She parked in the lot at the bus station and took a deep breath. She lifted her daughter from the car seat and settled the child on her hip, grabbed her pocketbook, and slammed the car door.

I never knew it would be so hard to walk into a bus station! she thought to herself.

Once inside the station, she looked for her mother and finally spotted her in the coffee shop. Her hair was a lot whiter, but otherwise it was her beautiful Mama.

Elaina walked up to the booth where her mother sat and said softly, "Mama?"

Louise turned and stood quickly, wrapping her daughter and granddaughter in a hug, kissing Elaina on the cheek.

"Oh, my. Oh Elaina, will you forgive me? I'm so sorry. I was so wrong to doubt you. Please, please forgive me."

"Mama, I love you!"

They sat down in the booth. "Mama, this is Elaina Beth. She's my daughter. Mama? How did you know I was here?"

Louise laughed. "Your husband."

Confused, Elaina said, "Vince? I don't understand."

"Your Vince sent me a letter asking me about our, uh, problem. He wanted to know if I wanted to try to make up with you. I've only wanted to do that for the last nine years, but I had no way to get in touch with you."

"Nobody asked the Gounarises, Mama. They've known."

"You're right, honey. I didn't. I didn't know for sure which restaurant you were at and I didn't know what to do. I'm sure I could have done a better job of trying to find you, but this is where I am now."

"Okay, Mama," Elaina said, thinking she could have asked Grandma Freda, because she had the address and the phone number. Apparently they didn't talk about this situation much.

"I found out that the one cheating in your marriage was Grant. He married the woman even before you had Abigail. I didn't know it when you were last at home, and Alec only found out about it from one of his Masonic buddies. Anyway, when Vince wrote to me, I was afraid you didn't really want to see me. He seemed pretty sure it was the right thing to do, because he's the one who sent me the money for the bus ticket."

Elaina smiled, thinking how she loved that man for doing this. She had wanted to talk to her mother, but was too afraid to write to her. How on earth did he get Mama's address? She laughed.

"I guess he knows my heart better than I do, Mama."

"Maybe so. When he sent the money, he told me to write and let him know when I was coming, but I just got on the next bus headed this way. He's going to be surprised, too."

"I'm sure he'll be happy to meet you, Mama."

About that time Elaina's cheery toddler banged the spoon on the table, ready to be included in the conversation. Both women laughed and Elaina introduced her daughter to her mother again.

"Beth, this is your Grandma Drew."

"Oh, little one," Louise whispered. "You have brought these two stubborn Drew women back together. You're a special one, you are."

Beth gurgled happily.

On the drive home, Louise and Beth got to know one another as only a grandma and granddaughter can. By the time they reached the driveway, it was as though the ten years of separation had never happened. Elaina could see that Vince was already home, and honked the horn as she turned off the car.

"Where are my beautiful ladies?" Vince boomed as he neared the car. Noticing Louise he said, "You must be Mrs. Drew."

"No, sir. I must be Louise." She stuck out her hand and shook his. "Thank you, son, for writing to me. You have made this old woman's heart very happy." Tears filled her eyes as she spoke, and she leaned into the car to get her granddaughter.

"Well now, Miz Louise, what do you think of this little stinker?" he said as he tickled his daughter.

"She is so pretty!" Louise said, looking at Beth. "And she's smart, too, I can tell."

"Ha! That's Grandma for you!" Vince laughed and, taking the keys from Elaina, opened the trunk to retrieve Louise's suitcase.

The family enjoyed supper together and talked long into the night. They spent the weekend showing Louise all around the area.

Sunday afternoon, while Beth was napping, the trio talked. Elaina asked about each member of the family. When she asked about Clement, her mother got quiet.

"What's wrong with Clem, Mama?" she asked.

"Oh, they say he's better now, but he's had tuberculosis."

Elaina gasped. "Oh no! Mama! Is he okay? Where is he?"

"They say he's fine now, 'Laina. He spent two years at the Arkansas Sanatorium, you know the one down by Fort Smith? He's back in Stafford now. He stays a time with each of the girls. He's not very strong, but the doctors say he's cured of the TB."

"Oh my goodness, Mama! I had no idea!" Elaina cried, tears running down her cheeks. Clement was the only one, other than Grandma Freda, who had stood by her when Grant was doing his deeds.

Vince said, "I wonder if a trip to Florida would help his breathing."

Both women looked at him.

"What? He might have to sleep on the couch, but we could house him. Why don't we get him on a bus down here?"

Within a week Clement joined the family and became instant friends with Vince. They cut up and picked on each other then worked together to pick on the women. Elaina saw how taken he was with Beth, and how she loved him instantly.

Clement and Louise stayed with the Koebners for a month. Elaina and her mother became friends and Clement's health improved. He shamelessly spoiled Beth every chance he got. Every weekend brought a new adventure. They went to the Seminole Indian Reservation in the Everglades and to the beach near Tequesta. They drove up to Fort King, where they went on a boat ride and had fun at an amusement park. While at the western-themed park, they were excited to meet Irene Ryan and Dan Blocker, well known as Granny Clampett and Hoss Cartwright.

Chapter 38

During their stay, Louise, and Clement talked at length with Elaina about the things that had happened.

"I don't know if I can really forgive Alec, Mama," the young woman said. "He was mighty ugly, and he's the one who convinced you I was doing wrong."

"He's really sorry, honey. He feels pretty betrayed by Grant, too," her mother said.

"I understand her, Mama. Alec was downright mean to her, and he riled up others to be mean to her. Especially Jodie, and she's got a vile tongue. It's not right," Clem pronounced.

"Well," their mother said, "I'll leave that up to you. I just know he'll contact you to talk about it. I bet I could call him and he'd say it over the phone, if you wanted to."

Elaina started shaking her head. "I don't know, Mama."

"How about this, daughter. I'll call Alec and tell him Clement and I are here. I won't stay on the line long, but I'll give him your number and let him know he can call and maybe talk to you. Will that be okay?"

Elaina sighed heavily. "I reckon, Mama. I bet he don't call back, though."

Late that afternoon, Elaina listened as Louise made the call and found Alec at home. She talked momentarily with him, informing him that she and Clement were staying with Vince and Elaina. She then gave him their phone number and told him when he was ready to do right by his sister, he should call her back.

Elaina was in the midst of frying fish when the phone rang.

"Hello?" she said into the receiver.

"'Laina?" Her mouth dropped as she heard her brother's voice.

"Alec, is that you?" she inquired as she slid down into a chair at the table.

"It is, 'Laina." She heard the tears in his voice. "Oh 'Laina, will you ever be able to forgive me? I was so wrong to believe that liar when he said those things about you."

Elaina's ire rose. "Yes, you were, Alec. I can't believe you, my very own brother, would not only believe those lies but tell them to others!"

He was quiet for a moment then said, "You're right. I let him convince me. I was stupid, 'Laina. I was just plain stupid. Listen, you know my number. If you get to a place where you can forgive me, please give me a call."

"Alec! Don't hang up!" she cried into the phone. "I'm going to forgive you, but I've gotta yell at you some first. Do you understand that?"

He chuckled, remembering a little raven-haired girl who had to yell at whoever angered her before she could be their friend again. "I understand, Sis. I'm so sorry. I listened to Grant and somehow forgot that I've known you from birth. I think I knew in my heart that you weren't the girl he was describing, but you never let on that he was doing things to you. Mama and I have talked and I think now I see that you were scared of him."

Elaina nodded. "I was some, I guess. He was always right. He never made a mistake, but I made plenty. He always talked about my weight. If I gained an ounce, he started talking about how I'd gotten too fat. I believed him, too, Alec. When he said he was at a meeting or working late, I believed him. I guess I was wrong, too. I'm sad and mad that you and Jodie and Mama didn't believe me, but I guess that's gone now. I miss my other big brother."

Elaina looked up and winked at Clement, who had taken over frying the fish. His nod and wink gave her strength and confidence.

The brother and sister talked on for some time, comparing notes about her ex-husband and her children. Alec and Jodie had continued the weekly dinners with Grant and the children for about two months, he told her. Then Grant came up with a reason every week for not getting together. It wasn't long until Alec had heard of Grant's marrying Claudia. They had gotten married the week after the judge declared the divorce final.

Elaina was stunned. She had been trying and trying to see her children during that time! She pressed her lips together, trying not to say things about the man she had once loved. Mostly, she didn't want her mother to hear her cuss like a construction worker.

Their call ended with promises to stay in touch. Elaina had given her brother her current address and promised to let him know when it changed, knowing that when Vince's job changed they would move.

Far too soon Louise and Clement were making their plans to return to Stafford, calling the bus station for schedules and prices. Louise kept trying to convince her daughter to bring her little family home for the Rafferty family reunion.

"Oh honey, you know it would be so good to see you there. Mother won't always be with us, and your Aunt Harriet is getting up there in years, too."

Laughing, Elaina said, "Mama, you're only eight years younger than Aunt Harriet!"

"Well, that may be the case, but you know I'm right. Besides, you haven't seen your sisters in a coon's age. They all have children now and you just need to be there."

"Oh, Mama. I don't know. I'll talk to Vince about it. It'll be a mighty long drive for just a couple days. I don't know if he can get off long enough for us to drive up there. We wouldn't have much time to visit."

Louise patted Elaina's hand. "Whatever you can do, Sis. I don't have room at my house, with only the one bedroom, but Kate's got space. Or Cherilyn might be able to put you up. Just come. We'll figure that all out when you get there."

"We'll see, Mama." Elaina recalled the reunions of her past, back when Grandpa was still alive, riding herd on everyone.

He was a hard man, she thought, *but he was so gentle, too. Maybe now it's time to go back.*

Chapter 39

The Koebners made the July trip to Stafford. Vince had wrangled a few days off. Though he wouldn't be getting any pay, he would have a job when he got back. That was important in the construction trade.

They left when Vince got home on Thursday afternoon, driving into the night. They had found an attachment for Beth's car seat that looked like a steering wheel, so she could "help" drive most of the way. They found a travel court where they spent the night, and ate breakfast next door in the little diner.

Back on the road, Elaina's mind went back to the trip she and Caleb had made going to Florida on these same roads. Back then she was angry and hurt, leaving all of her family behind. Now she was returning to that family. She still felt hurt, and wondered when that would go away.

They arrived in Stafford on Friday afternoon and drove to Louise's house. It wasn't the one Elaina had grown up in; her mother now lived in town, just off the main street. The house was a little frame one with lap siding and a nice porch on the front. Vince pulled the car in the driveway and got out. He helped Elaina get Beth and the diaper bag out and walked with his wife to the front door.

The screen door was latched, but the couple could see inside and could tell that Louise was in the kitchen.

Vince coaxed Beth to holler for her grandma.

"Grandma! Grandma!" the little girl called.

Louise rushed from the kitchen, wiping her hands on the patterned apron around her waist.

"There's my girl!" she cried, quickly unlatching the screen door and grabbing her daughter and granddaughter into a hug. She smiled at Vince, who winked at her.

"Whatcha got cookin', Miz Drew?" he drawled, teasing her.

She swatted his shoulder and ushered the family in. "It's so good to see you-all! I'm so glad you decided to come, Elaina. And Vince, I'm working on some pies for tomorrow's reunion, and I'll thank you to stay out of them." She nodded at him. "At least until they cool."

Elaina changed Beth's diaper, then let her roam the house while she helped her mother with dishes for the potluck dinner the next day.

"What's in this pot?" Vince asked, lifting the lid.

"It's your supper, young man." the older woman said, swatting him with the dish towel she'd been using. "A nice roast with potatoes and carrots." Vince smacked his lips as he hugged his mother-in-law.

Louise called her other daughters to tell them their sister was there, and before long Beth was joined by other children, and the house took on a party atmosphere.

As evening drew near, Cherilyn and Agnes went home to finish their own preparations for the reunion and dinner for their husbands. Kate helped Elaina finish up the dumplings, then gathered up her two children and led the way to her house.

Vince and Douglas, Kate's husband, hit it off famously. They kept an eye on the children playing in the back yard while the women worked in the kitchen.

The next day dawned cloudless and hot.

Elaina thought, *This is how I remember it. This makes me feel like I'm gettin' ready to go to the fields!*

She got Beth up and dressed her in a pretty dress, lacy socks and shoes, talking to her as she worked.

"There's my pretty girl. You are going to meet so many people today! You met cousins yesterday, but there are even more!"

The little girl tried repeating some of her mother's words, and Elaina chuckled.

Final preparations were made for the lunchtime reunion. Everything was loaded into the cars and then driven to the Stafford picnic grounds. The times of holding this gathering in the front yard of the home place had gone long ago when Louise's brothers' and sisters' families had grown so large then began having their own children. The final decision was based on the picnic grounds having the shelter they could all gather under in the shade. July in Stafford is always hot.

Once at the picnic shelter, Elaina was grabbed up in numerous hugs and conversations. The first was by her Aunt Harriet.

"Girl! I haven't seen you in a coon's age! Where have you been? Oh! Is this your baby? She's such a doll! Just look at those curls! And is that handsome fella over there your husband? My, he looks like a television star!" she gushed excitedly. "I've got my grandbabies running around here somewhere. You'll see them all soon enough." Leaning in to her niece, she spoke softer, "'Laina, baby, your mama's been pining over you something powerful. She's been seeing your other babies sometimes, but she knows you was done wrong and that you should have them babies, too. We all know you was done wrong."

With tears welling in her eyes, Elaina replied, "Thank you, Aunt Harriet. Me and Mama have talked a lot. Did you know she came to Florida to see me? And Clem did, too. We've done a lot of talking."

Nodding her understanding and seeing others coming to visit with Elaina, she hugged her again and said, "Just give folks time, honey. Some of 'em haven't heard the truth yet. They'll come around."

Enveloped by two sisters reintroducing her to their children and introducing her to their husbands, Elaina's head was spinning, but she felt incredibly happy. In a flash, her daughter was herded off to play with her cousins, toddling away holding the hand of Cherilyn's oldest, Lissa. Elaina smiled, thinking, *This is how it's s'posed to be.*

Elaina was lifting the covers from the various pots and pans before the lines started, when she heard the nasal tones of her sister-in-law.

"Well, if it' ain't really and truly our Elaina! Alec, c'mon and see! Elaina made it." Jodie loudly announced. She set a large pot of green beans on the table then turned to whisk Elaina into a hug.

Elaina had given forgiveness, but she tensed in this moment. It was hard not to hear the names Jodie had called her, the things she said about her as a mother. She drew back from the woman and looked her in the eyes.

"Jodie. It's good to see you. I hope Adele is doing well."

"Oh 'Laina," Jodie spoke softly, drawing her sister-in-law from the others, "I was so horrible to you, I wouldn't blame you if you never talked to me again. I know you and Alec have talked on the phone, but I just haven't been brave enough to do that yet. I wanted to see you so you could see how sorry I am."

Elaina shook her head. "I still can't understand how you of all people would believe the lies Grant told about me," she said, keeping her voice low. "You were with me on some of those trips downtown. You sat on the bench with me in the park. You *knew*, Jodie!"

"You're right, I did. And I'm so ashamed of myself, I can't begin to tell you. I was wrong, Elaina. I was stupid, and I was wrong to let that hateful man turn my head from family. Can you ever truly forgive me?"

Elaina took a deep breath and held out her hands. "Oh, you nut. I have to forgive you. I love you like a sister and I've missed you. Your words hurt me, but I understand that you were as deceived by Grant as anyone. Even I didn't see what was happening and I was living right in the middle of it. How could I have missed that he was having an affair?"

"I don't know, honey. We all did." Jodie slid her hands into Elaina's and they talked quietly until Alec walked up.

"Sis!" was all he could say before breaking down in tears. Elaina walked into her brother's arms and wrapped hers around his waist. She buried her face in his shoulder and they wept together.

Elaina had been dreading this moment when she would be faced with talking to these two, but now she realized that God had done some powerful work in her heart. She had thought she would hate even seeing them, but she didn't. She saw two people heartbroken at being duped into hurting her.

Standing up straight, she wiped her eyes and motioned with her head. "It's almost time, y'all. We can talk over the meal or at Mama's house later. Right now, I'd better get Miss Beth a plate ready."

The day was hot, the food delicious, and the talk interesting. Elaina learned the courting stories of her three sisters and what it was like for the two to be married to brothers, while hearing from her brothers-in-law how hard it was to live with Drew women.

After the meal, as folks sat around talking, Aunt Harriet held court beside Grandma Freda, explaining to those gathered that the stories told about their own Elaina were completely untrue and that she had never done the things her former husband had accused her of. There were those who murmured, questioning this story, until Freda told what Alec had told her about what happened after the divorce. Elaina wanted to run away but Grandma reached over and took her hand as she sat there, her cheeks ablaze while her grandmother spoke.

"Yes, we've seen him and those babies here a couple times since he divorced Elaina, but that man denied his own daughter, Abigail! And she was a most beautiful little girl. I held her in my own two arms. Alexander told me and Louise how he found out Grant was lying to everyone. The man had that new floozy moved into his house before Elaina's scent was even gone!

"So, now, we've got it all set to rights. Our girl is here and she's got a good man taking care of her now. And have you seen little Elaina Beth? She's just a darling! I won't say that this fella, Vince, is handsome, that would go to his head, but I've talked to him and I like him. He's the one who brought Elaina back to us."

A cheer went up among the tables. The children playing under the shady oak trees, though not knowing why, joined in with the cheers.

Grandma Freda continued, "I wish we would still be able to see our Doreen and Seth, but I don't know that their daddy will ever bring them back here. We can always hope. As for the baby he denied, she's now the daughter of a nice Greek couple in Detroit. Elaina tells me they love her so much it's crazy. She's in good hands. Elaina had no choice but to let them adopt sweet Abigail Jeanette. It was the best thing for the child.

"Now, I've said enough. Y'all enjoy your dessert and stuff. I'm gon' sit down."

That night, Louise's children and their children came to her house. It was snug, yet enough room for everyone to sit and talk. Stories were told, and laughter wafted through the open windows and filled the evening air. The children played outside, catching lightning bugs until the darkness was too deep. Vince and Elaina drove back to Kate's house to sleep, with a promise to stop by Louise's before leaving town the next morning.

As they made their way through Alabama back toward home, Vince asked, "Was it as bad as you thought it would be?"

"Oh, no. Not at all," Elaina said with a smile.

"Was it as good as you hoped?" he asked.

"Every bit, maybe more."

"Was anyone unkind? I tried to keep an eye out for that, but something might have got past me."

"I got a couple cold shoulders until Grandma gave her speech. I've never seen or heard her do anything like that, Vince. That was so strange, but it was so sweet!"

"I'm glad you had a good time. It's good to be part of your family. It's important."

He tickled his daughter's bare toes in the seat next to him, her car seat holding her several inches above it. She squealed, drawing her legs up and away from him.

"Daddy!" she cried out.

"What?" he cried back.

"'Top!" she said simply.

Vince laughed heartily as they continued the trip home.

Chapter 40

Elaina bent over and picked up another shirt and lifted it to the clothesline. The morning was warm and she suspected it was going to get hot. She was glad for the big oak trees that sheltered the house they were renting.

As she hung up rest of the clothes from the wicker laundry basket, she thought about the past years since that first reunion back home. They had moved around some more, finally settling in Bostrom Beach.

That was a nice house, she thought. *It was nice to have enough room to let Clement come to stay with us some.*

She remembered the times he would come and stay with them for five or six months of the year. He was a great help to her, helping to take care of Beth.

She reminisced, *I'll never forget that time Skippy growled and barked and wouldn't let him take Beth out of the yard for a walk because he thought Clem was a stranger.* She laughed aloud at the memory. Clem's eyes had been wide as saucers when she had to go out in the yard to rescue him.

Now Mama and Clem were both gone. She had only had her mother for seven years after they'd made up. When Agnes had called and said how sick Mama was, Vince had driven her straight up there. He returned home, but she and Beth had stayed. She had even enrolled Beth in school so she wouldn't lose any learning while her beloved grandma was sick. Elaina had known this would be her only time to say goodbye and did so when she left her mother's side, but learning of her death was devastating. She went alone to the funeral. She didn't think taking Beth a good thing. She was only eight and needed to stay in school. Besides, she wanted to be alone with her thoughts and her family.

The funeral had been lovely, with so many people from the community sharing how much they had loved Louise. She was a strong woman, they had all said, raising up her family after losing her husband so early on. It was good to hear the memories.

Less than three years later, Clem left them. He had struggled with Parkinson's Disease for so many years. Elaina could still see how his left hand was drawn up from the disease, forming a triangle. He had never let it get him down, but his body, having survived the tuberculosis, then being overtaken by the Parkinson's, finally gave up. Neither of them had gotten to see this new place here in Allendale.

Mama would have loved this place, and I think we would have had to force Clem to come inside, she thought, blinking back tears. *I wish they both could have come here.*

Twice while they were living in Bostrom she had miscarried, both of them boys. She and Vince had dearly wanted more children, but she just couldn't carry them to term. It broke her heart that she couldn't give Vince more children. He said he loved the family just as they were, but still she worried.

Elaina clipped the last clothespin on the line then placed her hands on her hips, looking at their house. She loved this place. It was a very old house, one of the old-timey Florida homes. A frame house facing the lake with a porch all the way across the front of the house. Every room had a door that led onto that porch, and part of it was screened in. The exterior of the house was painted white with black shutters. The kitchen reminded her so much of her mother's, with its tall cabinets and metal walls and ceiling.

Elaina bent over to pick up the empty laundry basket and chuckled, thinking about the first time they had experienced a thunderstorm in this old house. It was nice to not have to close the windows on the front side of the house. Having to do that made it stifling in the heat. But it was pretty scary to see lightning run around the walls of the kitchen. Beth had noticed it first, screaming there was fire in the kitchen.

"Mama! Look! There's fire on the wall! No. It's not there now. What's going on?"

She and her daughter had stood in the living room near the doorway into the kitchen to see if it would happen again. Just as lightning flashed brightly outside, they saw a fire bolt trace all the way around the kitchen walls. After that, whenever a thunderstorm approached, they stayed out of the kitchen.

The house was part of an old truck farm where pineapples and other produce were grown and taken to market. In the yard around the house there were eighteen huge live oak trees, along with some other trees she didn't know. There was room for a garden, and she enjoyed having the fresh vegetables Vince grew. She learned how to can again, something she hadn't done since she was a child at her mother's knee.

Vince had moved them here to Allendale when he went to work building the huge amusement park. Such was the life of a construction man. Just when you thought you were settled, it was time to move again. He had been on a crew setting the uprights for the train in the sky called a monorail. Now the multi-themed park was open and it was a big deal. Even Alec and her sisters were going to come visit them to go there.

She walked back into the house, planning to get the dishes done up before the next load of laundry was ready to hang. Instead, she sat down in the living room. With all the windows up, it was the coolest room in the house.

Beth was at school, now in seventh grade. That girl was starting to be a handful. She was smart, brought home honor roll grades, but with that smartness came a smart mouth. Sometimes she just couldn't stand the way the girl talked to her. Other times they were like really good friends. Mostly, anymore, they didn't talk a whole lot. During vacation from school, she spent most of her time over at a friend's house. That was okay, Elaina thought. At least when she was over there, they weren't arguing. She did wish her daughter wanted to spend time with her, though.

Her mind returned to the retracing of their past. Elaina could envision the little bar in Bostrom that she and Vince had enjoyed. It was just up the road from the grocery store where she was a cashier. They could meet there for a cold one before picking Beth up from her day school. Weekends were spent at Bennett's Bar in Tomoka. The bar had a great little booth near the back door where Beth could sit and read. Boy, that girl loved to read! It was a homey place. Sometimes the owner would give Beth the marked quarters to play the jukebox. That tickled the girl no end. Elaina missed that place that had been like home for almost ten years.

Since they had moved to Allendale, they hadn't really found a bar family like they'd known back in Bostrom, or even Mayaca. Not too long ago they met some of Vince's friends at a place called the White Rabbit. They had a lot of laughs and danced a little, but it just didn't feel like home. Vince had started going to a bar in one of the local hotels. It didn't suit her, but he really liked it. There were times she and Beth would go there, but it just wasn't like Bennett's.

Elaina heard the washing machine finish and rose to hang up the last load of the day. She wanted to get them on the line before it got really hot. Once all the clothes were hanging on the line, lightly lifted by the gentle breeze, she went inside and ran the hot water, making a soapy bath to wash dishes. She hated doing these chores. Sometimes she would make Beth do them, but she hated doing them, too.

"Ah well," she said to herself, "if they're going to get done, I'm going to have to do them."

At least it was Friday, which meant they would be going out to eat. She wondered where they would go this time. It really didn't matter as long as she wasn't cooking and cleaning up afterward.

She was looking forward to tomorrow, too. Their friends Kevin and Gina had invited them over for a pool party. Beth was all excited, too. She didn't swim well, but she enjoyed getting in the pool and having fun.

Chapter 41

Saturday arrived and the family loaded up in their new used car. Having a second car had made it much easier for Elaina to get errands done and take Beth to the library and such.

Vince handed Elaina the torn piece of paper on which Keith had written the directions to his house. She read off each turn as he came to it.

"My goodness!" she declared. "This is farther out in the country than we are!"

In truth the drive had only taken them twenty minutes, but they had passed very few houses.

Gina met them as they arrived at the house. She was wearing a bathing suit with a long shirt over it. Elaina felt self-conscious; she had gained so much weight that she really didn't like even wearing shorts now.

"It's great to see you both—" Gina's voice dropped when she saw Beth get out of the back seat. "Oh. You brought Beth."

"Yes," Elaina said. "She's so excited to get to swim in your pool."

Gina drew Elaina and Vince away from Beth. "I guess Kevin didn't make it clear to Vince. This is a grown-up party. We didn't expect any children."

"Oh." Elaina choked the word out. "Oh, dear. Well, I guess we'll just have to go back home."

Gina said quietly, "She's a good girl, though. We could let her just hang out here in the garage. It's cool enough and we have a little TV here. She can watch that. No need to go home."

Vince clapped his hands and turned to his daughter. "Buckshot, I'm sorry. Your gray-haired old daddy messed up. The party at the pool is just for the grown-ups. But Gina said there's a TV right here in the garage. See? There's a couch there, too. You can watch TV and drink some sodas and hang out. Is that all right?"

"Sure, Dad." Beth shrugged, her disappointment barely masked.

"There. We're all set," Vince said. He made sure Beth got the TV on and the antenna adjusted. The picture was a little fuzzy, but you could mostly see what was going on. "There you go, Buckshot. Got your own little place all set up here. We'll come back in and check on you all afternoon."

Elaina and Vince followed Gina through the door to the pool area, where the fun was already in full swing. Everyone had a beer. Kevin greeted them with a great booming voice and handed each of them a beer.

"This will get you started. We've got the stuff to make daiquiris and other drinks, too. Now, you need to meet everyone." He walked them around the pool, introducing them to the other three couples and a single fellow named Eddie. "Now, I'll be grilling in a little bit. Make yourselves at home. If you need the powder room, just go right through that door," he told them.

Elaina wandered back to where Gina was talking with another woman. Each woman's husband worked on the same construction crew. As she sat down on the chaise lounge, she lowered the black sunglasses over her eyes and listened to the other two talking. One of the women was drinking a fruity-looking frozen concoction and she asked about it. Gina explained that it was a frozen daiquiri and that they had the fixings in the little kitchen just off the garage.

"Sounds good," Elaina said.

"Come on, I need another one. I'll show you how to make them," Gina replied.

The two walked the path through the garage, where Elaina noticed Beth watching the Saturday afternoon horror film. That child loved to be scared by those things. She ruffled her daughter's hair as she passed and asked if she was doing okay.

"I'm all right," Beth mumbled.

In just a few moments they passed back through, and Elaina told her daughter she would bring her something to eat once it was ready. Beth nodded, her eyes never leaving the television.

Elaina settled back onto the chaise and sipped her drink, loving the taste of the strawberries and the chill of the ice. The zing of the rum didn't hurt, either. The group around the pool talked and laughed, some swam and splashed. Soon Kevin called out that food was ready. Gina had slipped into the house to bring out potato salad and coleslaw to go along with the ribs, burgers, and hot dogs from the grill. Elaina fixed a plate with a hamburger and the different salads on it and delivered it to Beth, who then joined her in the drink kitchen and watched her make another daiquiri. She kissed her daughter on the cheek then headed back out to the pool.

After devouring the ribs and burgers, the group settled back and talked. The beer and rum flowed. The laughter rang out loud and often. Elaina was happy when the single guy, she thought he was a cousin to Kevin, offered to refill her daiquiri. What a nice man he was, and handsome, too. She asked him to check on Beth as he went through the garage.

Elaina's opinion of Eddie rose as he made more trips back and forth to the kitchen. He had taken on the role of bartender for the frozen drinks. She tried to remember how many of those darned strawberry things she had drunk. It wouldn't come to her.

Around six in the evening those around the pool picked at the leftovers from the grill, had a couple more drinks each, then parted ways. Elaina and Vince roused Beth from her place on the couch in the garage and left for home.

"Well, did you have fun today, Buckshot?" Vince said.

"Yeah, lots of fun, Dad, sitting in a stinky garage watching TV," the twelve-year-old replied.

"Don't sass your father," Elaina intoned.

"Yeah, okay," Beth said.

"What was wrong with the day?" Vince asked, seemingly surprised.

"Nothing, Dad. You had tons of fun. I sat in a hot garage listening to all you 'grown-ups' having fun," their daughter stated flatly. "I'm fine."

Elaina looked across the seat at Vince and shrugged. They drove home in silence. Vince and Elaina had entered the house when they heard the car door slam. Beth walked in through the back door and directly to her bedroom.

"I guess she's mad about something," Vince said.

"I guess so. She seems to be mad a lot lately. I guess it's being a teenager." Elaina yawned. "I think I'm going on to bed."

Chapter 42

Beth had just started high school and was in the marching band. Even though she was a freshman, she had been nominated for the senior band by her middle school band teacher. Elaina was proud of her accomplishment. Tonight she had watched as Mrs. Boyett picked Beth up and drove her to band practice. They carpooled every week so that neither of them had to go out twice for these Thursday night practices. Their daughters were great friends and it was always fun for them to be together.

Elaina and Vince were sitting in the living room, watching television while she kept an eye on the clock. She would have to leave at quarter till eight to pick the girls up. Suddenly Vince rose and almost ran to the bathroom, holding his stomach and groaning. Elaina ran after him.

"What's wrong, Vince?" she cried, seeing him bent over the toilet.

His only reply was a groan. She peered around him and saw the water in the bowl had turned red. Bright red. Like when her daddy was sick. Elaina felt faint.

"Oh my God, Vince. You've got to go to the hospital!"

He nodded as he moved to the sink to wash his face.

"I'm going to call Mrs. Boyett and let her know what's happening. Hopefully she can get the girls tonight."

"Call my brother, too," she heard him say weakly.

"Your what?"

"My brother Walter. He lives in Jacksonville."

"Vince, what are you talking about? You don't have a brother!" Elaina's eyes filled with tears, thinking her husband was losing his mind and dying right before her eyes.

She quickly called Mrs. Boyett and told her what was going on, asking her to drop Beth off at the emergency room to meet with them. Then she helped Vince into the car. He had said he was cold, so she had helped him into his jacket and covered him with a blanket once he was in the car.

On the thirty-minute drive to the hospital, she asked again about this brother she had never heard about.

"I have a brother who lives in Jacksonville. I think my mother lives with him, at least part of the time. I have three brothers who live in Iowa and a sister who lives outside Chicago," he told her.

"You told me your parents were dead and you have no other family. You said you were an only child," Elaina said, her words dripping with accusation.

"I know what I've told you. Will you please try to get hold of Wally when we get to the hospital? I don't think there are any other Koebners in the city." He lay his head back on the seat. "Tell him it's about Curly."

Elaina's mind was reeling. She drove like a madwoman, praying she wouldn't get them in a wreck and thanking God that Allendale now had a hospital of their own instead of having to go to Jernigan. She had heard many horror stories about the hospital up there.

She pulled into the drop-off area at the emergency room and helped Vince into the building. She told the nurse at the desk what had happened at home, and the nurse immediately drew Vince through the doors to the examination rooms. She called back to Elaina that she would be allowed to see him soon.

Elaina walked outside to move the car, finding a place to park in the parking lot closest to the emergency room. After shutting off the car, she tried to fit the puzzle pieces together.

"Vince's mother is alive? He has four brothers and a sister?" Everything he had told her about his family was a lie. She shook her head and walked back into the waiting area. She walked to the pay phone on the far wall and lifted the receiver. Dialing the number for information, she asked for a Walter Koebner in Jacksonville. Writing the number down, she wondered how she would make this call. What would she say?

"Hi, I'm Curly's wife. He's in the emergency room, bleeding from inside. He wants you to know." Oh, there had to be a better way. She drew all the coins she had from her purse and lay them on the shelf of the phone booth. She turned the dial ten times, hoping this was the right person and that he wouldn't hang up on her.

"Hello?" a gravelly voice answered.

"Hello. Is this Walter Koebner?" Elaina asked politely.

"Yes, this is Walter."

She took a deep breath and said, "Do you have a brother you call Curly?" She heard him gasp.

"Yes!" he almost shouted. "Do you know him?"

"I do," she replied. "I'm his wife."

"His wife? Okay. Okay. So, where's he living now?" This man seemed really concerned for his brother, Elaina thought.

"We live in Allendale now. I have some bad news, though."

"Bad news? What bad news? What's wrong?" he asked.

"Vince— Curly started throwing up blood tonight. Bright red blood. I just got him to the emergency room. I don't know what's happening, but he asked me to call you. I didn't even know you existed until just now," Elaina explained.

"Makes sense. He's been out of touch with us since he got out of the Navy. Listen, tell me where you are and I'll come right down."

Elaina explained where the hospital was, and had just hung up when the nurse opened the doors to the examination rooms and called her name.

"Mrs. Koebner?"

"That's me!" She rose and walked quickly to the doors.

"Come this way, please," the nurse said efficiently as she turned and walked away.

Elaina followed quickly behind the nurse into a room, where she saw Vince hooked up to machines and tubes running from bottles to his arm. She saw a small bottle hanging on another pole with a dark liquid flowing into his arm. Her mind flashed back to that time she had seen her father in the hospital and tears filled her eyes. At forty-six, she was older than her mother was when her father died. She remembered all that her mother had gone through in the aftermath of Daddy's death, and it scared her to think it was happening to her.

Vince waved her over. "There, there. What're those tears for?" he asked gently.

"Nothing." She wiped them away. "What's wrong?" she asked both Vince and the nurse, who was there adjusting the knobs on the tubes.

"The doctor says he has internal bleeding. He believes it's coming from his stomach. We have some more tests to run, though, to be sure what's going on."

"Oh," Elaina replied without emotion.

"Did you get hold of Wally?" Vince asked her.

"Yeah. He's on his way."

"How did he sound?" he asked.

"I don't know. He sounded really surprised to hear a stranger say your nickname then tell him you might be dying." Elaina saw the nurse's brows go up. She was impressed that the woman kept an otherwise blank expression.

"What did he say?"

"He's on his way. He's coming to be here with you." She repeated, slipping her hand into his. He nodded then closed his eyes.

"He probably needs to rest as much as possible," the nurse told Elaina.

"Okay. Can I stay with him?"

"I think that will be okay."

"Our daughter will be getting here soon. She's fifteen. I didn't want to take the time to go to band practice to get her, so a friend is dropping her off. She volunteers here, so she knows her way around."

"I'll have the gals out front keep an eye out for her," the nurse replied, and left the room.

By the time Beth arrived, Vince and Elaina had been given the news. Vince had a perforated ulcer and it had to be repaired right away. The plans were made for his surgery very early the next morning.

The receptionist let Elaina know her daughter was in the waiting room, and she went out to talk to her. The Boyetts were still there, Mr. Boyett having joined his wife for this task. Both listened with concern as she outlined what was going on. They promised they would check back in with her, then left.

Beth sat in the chair, looking shell-shocked. "Is he going to die, Mom?" she asked.

"I don't think so. The doctor seems to know what he's talking about. He said that they can do an operation that will not only stop the bleeding but will take out the rest of the ulcer so that it won't happen again."

"Okay. Mom, I don't want to go in there," Beth said. "I can just go down the hall here to the cafeteria and wait, if that's all right with you." She knew the hospital like home, having been a volunteer there for the last year, working there most Saturdays.

"I guess that's all right. Your daddy is sleeping; they gave him some medicine to make him rest. I'll come get you when we get a room."

"Okay, Mom. I love you," Beth replied, giving her mother a fierce hug.

Elaina remembered the feelings when her own father had been in such dire circumstances. She watched her daughter walk up the hallway with purpose. She knew this place and felt comfortable here. She liked that her daughter had this confidence. She went back to the examination room, where she sat holding Vince's hand.

Chapter 43

Close to midnight, a man and woman entered the examination room. "Elaina?" the woman asked quietly.

"Yes, I'm Elaina."

"I'm Mary, this is Wally," the woman introduced, walking to where Elaina sat.

"Oh! You really did come right down," Elaina replied in surprise.

"Yeah, we did. I haven't seen my brother in almost twenty years, then you call and say he may die? Damn right I came right down," Walter replied, looking at his brother. "I'm glad you called, Elaina. Really glad."

Elaina noticed Vince's eyes open slightly. "Vince? Your brother is here."

His eyes opened wider, finally focusing on the man at the foot of the bed.

"Wally," he murmured.

"I'm here, Curly. You rest now. The doctors are going to take care of you. I'll see you afterwards and we'll talk then."

Mary chimed in, "For once in your life do what the doctors say, Curly."

Vince's eyes closed, but there was a smile on his face as he drifted back to sleep.

Elaina motioned for the couple to join her in the waiting room. She thought about going to the cafeteria where Beth was, but decided to keep her out of this until she knew better what was going on.

The three sat down, pulling the chairs close, though the waiting room was empty.

Elaina said to them, "Why have I never heard about you? Did something happen in your family? Vince has always said that his parents were gone and he had no brothers or sisters."

Walter shook his head. "I guess he really wanted to cut ties," he said. "I don't know all of what went on, but there was stuff that Curly and Mom didn't agree on and they were at odds. Then, when he had that trouble at the end of his career in the Navy, he just shut us all out."

"So he didn't grow up in North Florida?" Elaina asked.

Walter laughed. "No, we grew up in a tiny town in Iowa."

"He said he has brothers in Iowa," she replied. "And a sister?"

"Yeah, there's six of us altogether."

"All of you still living?"

"That's right."

"And your parents?"

"Well, Dad died right after Christmas in '46. I was just sixteen; Curly was twenty-three and in the Navy. Mom spends time living with us and with the others. She's about to turn 80."

"Wow," Elaina said dully. "I never knew."

"Really?" Walter asked. "You asked about North Florida. Is that what he told you?"

After Elaina shared the stories Vince had told her about his family situation, they all sat shaking their heads in wonder.

"Okay, so tell me about you. Y'all live in Jacksonville?" Elaina inquired.

Mary took over the telling. "Yes, we do. Wally works for the phone company. Has since he got out of the Navy. I'm a nurse in one of the big hospitals there. We have two boys. The oldest is almost seventeen, the youngest is just about fourteen."

"That puts our Beth right in the middle," Elaina replied. "What about the others?"

The couple told her about the brothers and their wives, their children, and the one sister and her family. Elaina's head swam as she learned of Vince's large family. She wondered idly what else he had kept from her.

A blond nurse in dark green scrubs stepped into the waiting room. She carried a clipboard that she handed to Elaina.

"We need permission to operate on Mr. Koebner. If you'll just sign here and here," she indicated. "And if you want to see him before we take him back, you'll have about ten minutes."

Elaina's eyes went wide. She had thought they had until later in morning. Something must be really bad. She looked up the hall where she could see the dark rectangle windows of the cafeteria. She wondered if she should run and get Beth or just let her be. She seemed worried, and unwilling to see her father. She decided to spend the time with Vince and talk to Beth after they took him back.

Once Vince was out of surgery and in a room, Elaina found her daughter asleep on a couch in the lobby. That girl could sleep anywhere! The two went home to get cleaned up and get some rest. Beth asked if she could go to school the next day. Elaina thought that was a good idea, since the girl wouldn't come in her father's room anyway.

Early the next afternoon, Elaina walked into the room where her sleeping husband lay. She walked to the side of the bed and leaned over to kiss his forehead, careful not to disturb the tube that came from his nose. Some sort of fluid drained from it almost constantly. She noticed his color seemed better. She slipped her hand into his.

"Good afternoon, Sleeping Beauty. How are you feeling?"

She watched his eyes flutter open. He seemed to be searching for her, so she moved closer. The way his eyes lit up when he recognized her made her heart skip a beat.

He motioned for something to drink and she poured a bit of water into the small plastic cup sitting on the table beside the bed. He managed to get a sip then smiled a goofy, half-drunk smile up at her.

They talked quietly for almost half an hour before they heard a knock at the door.

"Hey! What's going on in here?" Elaina heard her new brother-in-law's jovial voice as he walked into the room. He seemed so opposite Vince physically, with a rounder body and reddish hair. She wasn't sure where that had come in if the family was German, but his mannerisms were so like her husband's it amazed her.

She squeezed Vince's hand and asked him, "Do you know who this is?" pointing to Walter and Mary.

Vince nodded. "Wally and Mary."

"At least he knows us today," Walter said wryly.

"How is he doing today?" Mary asked.

Elaina shrugged. "I haven't talked to anyone yet. I suppose he's doing okay."

"Maybe I can get the nurses to talk to me," Mary said, walking back out the door and disappearing down the hallway to the nurse's station.

The news was mixed. The surgeon had had to remove almost two-thirds of Vince's stomach in order to save his life. He had been bleeding pretty badly. He would have to make some changes as far as the foods he could eat for a time. Once he was healed up, he would be able to return to normal except for the amount.

Thankful that the other bed in the semi-private room was empty, Elaina pulled an extra chair from beside that bed over near Vince's. Walter sat near to the head of the bed so he and his brother could catch up. They talked on and on. Elaina enjoyed talking with Mary and learned more about the family. The trio walked down the hall to the cafeteria for lunch, where Walter and Mary questioned Elaina about her family and how she and Vince had met. The story about their trip to Kingsland, Georgia where they got married brought great laughter.

It was almost four o'clock when Beth walked into her father's room. She had ridden the bus to school. Elaina had arranged for a friend to drop her off at the hospital. Elaina watched her hesitate as she walked into the room. The look on her face showed wonder at who the people visiting her dad were.

"Hey, Beth. Dad's all right. He's taking another nap right now, but this is your Uncle Walter and Aunt Mary," Elaina said, walking to her daughter.

Looking at her mother, Beth said, "My aunt and uncle? Dad's—"

"Dad's brother and his wife," her mother explained.

"Mom, I thought Dad was an only child like me," Beth stated flatly.

"Me too, but it seems that he's not. I just learned last night that your dad has four brothers and one sister. Oh, and his mother's still alive."

"No, Mom. Dad said his mom and dad died a long time ago."

Elaina tried to smile. "I know, honey. I know. The truth is, you have a bunch of aunts and uncles and cousins you've never met, and a grandma, too." She recalled her daughter's broken heart when her own mother passed away.

"Hey, Buckshot," the raspy voice from the bed called.

Beth turned around and walked to her father. "Hey, Dad. You scared us."

"I know I did. I'm sorry. I sure didn't mean to. This snuck up on me." He tried to smile. "Did you meet Wally and Mary?"

"Mom was just telling me about them." She turned back to her aunt and uncle. "I'm Beth. I'm the daughter." She offered her hand to both, then turned to her mother. "I've got homework. Can I go to the lobby or the cafeteria to do it?"

Elaina nodded. "I guess so. Either one. I'll know where to come find you when I need you." She sighed when the teen walked out of the room. She stepped to look out the door and saw her turn left down the next hallway and knew she was headed to the lobby.

The doctor came in again and examined Vince. He told him and the family that everything was looking good and in a few days he would be able to go home. Elaina, Walter, and Mary said their good-byes with promises to be there in the morning, then walked out to the lobby. There they found Beth talking with the receptionist.

"I was thinking we might go get something to eat," Walter said, walking up to her.

"Sure, okay."

Elaina took her daughter's arm and they walked to the car together. The other two followed them to the local barbecue joint where they had ribs and pork slices, coleslaw, fries, and plenty of iced tea. Away from the hospital Beth began to warm up to her aunt and uncle, joining in the same teasing banter with Walter that she enjoyed with her father. Elaina smiled to herself, watching them.

She thought to herself, *This might be a good thing, having family this close.*

The next summer, most of the Koebners came down to visit. It was somewhat overwhelming to meet two of the other three brothers, their wives, and one child. They had already visited back and forth with Wally and Mary and their two boys, Jon and Vincent. Elaina had heard Vince and Wally talk about Berrin and Ronnie, so she felt like she knew them.

Their wives were so nice, they all seemed to have missed their brother-in-law as much as their husbands had.

Over the next several years they hosted her mother-in-law, Maddalene Koebner at their home, taking turns with the other children. She was a tiny but very independent woman. Her beautifully thick white hair flowed in waves around her face. When Vince or Beth weren't around, Maddie refused to call her Elaina or 'Laina. She called her Linda. Most of the time she just chuckled about it, but at times she wondered why she knew her name well when the others were around, but not when they were alone.

For Maddie's 80th birthday, they met the Jacksonville family at the home of their friends in Fort King. Vince grilled ribs and the women put together potato salad and coleslaw and other side dishes. A big watermelon was iced down and everyone ate plenty. Then the time came for the birthday girl to have her cake. Wally went to their van to retrieve it and, after unboxing it, set it on the table in front of her.

She clapped her hands and squealed like a little girl, then stopped and shook her head.

"What's wrong, Mom?" Vince said, holding back laughter.

"Maddie? What's wrong?" Mary asked.

"This cake is wrong! I will not eat it," Maddalene declared.

Elaina slipped beside her and recognized what had angered her mother-in-law. The lettering on the cake spelled out, "Happy 81st Birthday!" Fiercely proud, the elderly German woman would have nothing to do with the cake until Mary wisely scooped the numeral from the icing. Meanwhile the mischievous culprits of the prank laughed long and hard while being drilled with stares from their mother. Every time they looked at her and saw her spite, they howled again.

Elaina could easily see where her husband had gotten his humor. His brother was so like him. And even in her supposedly hurt feelings, they were much like their mother.

Chapter 44

Grandma Koebner adored Beth and spoiled her with abandon.

"Mom, I have to be so careful when I'm out with Grandma!" Beth said one afternoon as the older woman napped.

"What do you mean? Does she stumble? Do we need to get her a cane?"

"No, not like that. If I lift my eyebrows at a shirt or dress or anything at all, she stops to buy it for me!"

Elaina loved this, knowing that her mother would have done much the same thing had she been given the chance.

It was a great gathering at the house, and one day they all went to the world-renowned theme park. Everyone laughed at Grandma, because they had insisted that she get a wheelchair to use if she got tired. She pushed it around most of the day, refusing to be an invalid.

In that third year after Vince's surgery, his construction work started to dry up. The union had no jobs to send him out on. He kept checking in, but the unemployment checks didn't go nearly as far as his regular pay.

"I don't know, 'Laina. I've been talking to Tony," he said, speaking of a longtime friend of theirs. "He's worked overseas a couple times and made really good money. He says if you stay over there long enough, you don't have to pay taxes. It sounds like a good deal."

"It sounds good to leave your wife and daughter for that long?" she retorted.

"It sounds good to keep a roof over the heads of my wife and daughter," he returned hotly.

"You do realize that Tony and Ann are getting a divorce, don't you?" she asked.

"I think he said something about that."

"Do you realize that's because he went over there and stayed so much?"

"I think there's a lot more to it," Vince said.

"Maybe so, but his running away to the tropics didn't help," Elaina declared.

"He didn't run away!" Vince yelled.

"Then why isn't he at home taking care of *his* wife and daughter?" Elaina yelled back.

"Oh hell, Elaina. There's no talking to you. I'm going to the bar. I'll be back later."

"Yeah, go ahead and run away. I'll be here, taking care of our daughter."

Every time Vince brought up the topic of going overseas to work, an argument ensued. Elaina feared that if he left he would never return.

One evening over supper, he said softly, "What if I went to work over there and it allowed us to buy our own place?"

"What?" Elaina returned. "Buy our own place? Like a house?"

"Maybe not a house, but a mobile home on our own property. A place all our own."

Elaina's eyebrows lifted. "Do you really think you could make that much money?" Her heart pounded. It had been their dream for the longest time to have a place all their own. They loved this old house on the lake, but it wasn't theirs and it never would be. The owners would never sell it.

"Think about it, 'Laina. If I'm making three thousand a month and we don't have to pay taxes on it, that's $36,000! That's more than double what I've been making! It would be like using one year's pay to buy the house and land and still have the pay to live on."

Elaina lay her fork on her plate and looked at her husband. She looked at her daughter, who was paying attention but saying nothing, probably because she had heard and hated all the arguing.

Slowly she nodded her head. "That would be a wonderful thing, Vince, to have our own place."

Vince stood from the table, his plate still half filled. "It's only four o'clock in Idaho; I'll call the contractor company and tell them I want to go." He leaned down and kissed his wife on the cheek then walked to the living room.

That call led to Vince's being flown to Idaho for the application process and discussions and some training. When he returned, he told Elaina about the trip and all he had gotten done in preparation for going to Indonesia.

"And I got Wally to set up a bank account so that they can deposit my money straight into it. That will make everything much easier."

Elaina's jaw dropped. "What did you say?"

Vince repeated the news that he had had his brother open a bank account that his pay would go into.

"So, I won't be getting your pay?" she asked incredulously.

"No, you'll still get my pay," he cajoled. "It's just that Wally can manage it for us so that we'll have plenty of money when I get back. All you'll have to do is call him to get a check, no problem."

Elaina fumed. "And why wasn't I the one you called to set up an account with? I'm your wife!"

"Well, I want to be sure that the money I send home is spent how I want it spent," he stated flatly.

"Like you want it spent? You mean, like for the electric and rent and clothes for your daughter and food on the table? You don't want it spent that way?"

"That's not what I mean, Elaina. I mean that sometimes…" He stammered over his words. "Sometimes you go a little overboard and spend money like it's water. I don't want that to happen. Wally said he would help me. I just want to take care of you."

"Huh. Take care of me? Take care of *me*? Good thing I've got the job at the gift shop so I can take care of me. I don't want to spend any of your precious money." She walked from the kitchen to their bedroom, crying.

"'Laina" he whined. "Come on. That's not what I said. That's not what I meant."

She refused to hear him. He was leaving her, she just knew it. He was going to leave her and Beth and never come back. They had been together almost twenty years, with her paying their bills, and now he didn't trust her to handle his money. Her thoughts went back to Grant and how he had set things up for the divorce.

"Vince?" she said, walking to the kitchen doorway. "Are you leaving me? Are you planning a divorce?"

His anger flared. "I just might, 'Laina. Here I am trying to make a way for us and all you do is try to block it. I'm going to go talk to Joanne. Maybe she'll be happy for me getting a job making double what I am now." He stomped from the house, letting the screen door slam behind him as he opened the car door to drive to the hotel bar where Joanne was the bartender.

Elaina walked to the living room and sat in her chair. Beth peeked out of her bedroom.

"Mom? Are you okay?" she asked, seeing the tears.

"I'm okay, honey," she replied, not really meaning it. "Your dad and I just had an argument."

"Is he leaving us?" Beth asked bluntly.

"No, no. He's not leaving us." She smiled at her daughter. "He's trying to make some good money for us and get us our own property and house."

"What's wrong with this house, Mom?"

"Nothing at all, honey. I love this house. But it's important to your dad and me to have our very own place. We would love to buy this one, but it would be so expensive, and we're certain the Starrs won't sell it to us. Your daddy is trying to take care of us," she explained.

"Then why are y'all arguing so much?" Beth asked.

"Oh, it's nothing. He said something that bothered me and I blew up. It's okay, sweetheart. Do you have your homework done?"

"Almost. I'm working on my algebra."

"All right. Go finish that up. I'll be right here when you get done."

Beth turned and went back to her room, and Elaina rose and went to hers. She needed to let these tears flow, but she didn't want Beth to see or hear them. She was so afraid.

Chapter 45

Vince was finally home! Elaina watched the airplane taxi into the gate where her husband would disembark. She was like a schoolgirl watching for her beau, patiently impatient. She searched every face exiting into the airport until she saw his. He noticed her at the same time and he beamed. He rushed over to her and swallowed her up in his arms.

"Oh, Elaina, this feels so good! I'm so happy to be home!"

"Mmm, I'm happy to have you home, even though you don't know your home right now." She giggled softly. She had sent him a few pictures of the mobile home she and Beth had found, but he had never seen the house or the land.

The couple walked to the luggage carousel to retrieve Vince's bags, then walked to where Elaina had parked the car.

"You probably ought to drive. I don't even know where I'm going," Vince stated.

"That's okay, things have changed a lot around here in the past two years. Sit back and enjoy the scenery."

"Is Beth at home?"

"No. She's at work today, selling ice cream to all the tourists at the theme park."

"Well, I guess I'll have to wait till she gets off to give her a hug."

"She'll be home this evening. She knows you're coming in."

Elaina drove carefully through the streets of Jernigan, minding the traffic and filling Vince in on the things of life that had been happening.

She drove down the two-lane highway that served as a back road from the airport to Mt. Peace. In her dealings of buying the mobile home, she had learned how to get around the city much better.

"So, you said the place is in Mt. Peace?" Vince asked, thinking about the quaint little town.

"Yes, but not up in the city area. Do you remember where we went to Kevin and Gina's for that pool party?"

"Yeah, that's way out in the boonies."

Elaina laughed. "Well, it's not that far out. Same direction, but we'll turn off earlier."

"All right, Mrs. Koebner, lead on!" His interest turned as he noticed the train cars on a railroad siding. They were gaily painted and looked like a circus train he'd seen as a child. "What's this?" he asked.

"This area is the winter home of the circus. Not the big one, but we see their signs around all the time. They travel all over the nation, you know." Elaina followed the sharp curve that took them across the tracks and back south again.

As they drove through the town of Mt. Peace, Vince's head was on a swivel. Elaina recalled how she had done the same when she and Grant had first arrived in Detroit, and a smile crossed her face.

They had driven out of town and into a more rural setting, with cattle in pastures on both sides of the roads. The next road boasted several homes on both sides of the roads.

"This is Mt. Peace Manor. We're part of it."

"That's nice. It's not a real subdivision, is it?"

"No. Well, I guess it is, but it's not. Like I told you, we have one whole acre of land."

Vince smiled. He had never owned property of his own and now he owned a whole acre. A man could do a lot with an acre of ground.

They passed two little stores on the road and Elaina pointed out which one she preferred. It had a few groceries, the necessities you might need like eggs, bread, and milk, plus they sold bait and gasoline. They were less than three miles from the lake.

Elaina slowed the car. "All right. We're almost there. Once we pass this piece with the trees and palmettos, our property will begin."

Vince sat up in the seat, almost holding his breath in anticipation. When he saw the cleared land with the single-wide, white with brown trim, mobile home on it he sighed. Elaina had even bought a metal shed and had it installed to hold his tools and the lawn mower, and other items that wouldn't fit in the house. He reached over and grabbed his wife's hand.

"It's all ours, honey," she said. "Well, once we pay off all the notes." She had set up payments under Wally's instruction so that they didn't drain the bank accounts completely.

She turned into the driveway and parked at the end of the trailer and pointed up. "That's our bedroom window right there."

"Isn't it noisy being so close to the road?" They were situated on a corner lot. One of the roads was the paved road and the other was a dirt road.

"Not at all. Everything slows down out here after about eight o'clock. On the weekend you might hear some fellas driving by revving their motors and cutting up, but for the most part it's almost as quiet as living on the lake."

"All right. Well give me the tour, then we'll come back out and get my stuff." He seemed excited to see their new home. Elaina smiled broadly and led him to the back door.

"I couldn't set it much anywhere else. The old trailer that was here already had plumbing and electric and stuff. Wally told me that if we set it here we'd save money, so I did. Besides, this concrete pad was already here and it didn't make sense not to use it."

Vince nodded. Elaina handed him the key she had had made for him. She stepped out of the way and waved him to the door.

"Your castle awaits, sir."

"You nut!" He laughed.

The door opened into a hallway, with a door to his right and one almost directly in front of him. He turned to look in each, finding their bedroom and the bathroom.

"Beth has a half bath in her room, Vince. Tickled her to death to get that."

"I bet that helps a lot since Miss Priss takes a while to get ready now with her makeup and all."

"You have no idea!" She sighed.

They stopped in the hall as Elaina opened the folding doors to reveal their washer and dryer. The space came complete with a rod to hang clothes on. She beamed as she showed off this treasure. Vince patted her softly on the back.

They turned the corner into the kitchen. It wasn't huge, but it was big enough. "Is this big enough, 'Laina?" he asked.

"It sure is. And I don't feel like I'm shut off from everything since it's open into the living room."

"I like that, too," he said, looking at the little partition near the dining table. It was solid about four feet up, then spindles like on stairs to the ceiling. Even though it was a wall of sorts, it was open.

He continued through the living room to the door on the other side.

"That's Beth's room. I have no idea what it looks like right now," Elaina called.

Chuckling, he opened the door and walked in, inspecting the closet and the bathroom. When he emerged into the living room again, Elaina stood waiting.

"It's very nice. Very nice. You did a good job, Elaina." He pulled her close and kissed her tenderly. "I knew we could do this. Now we have a home that's ours, not one that someone else makes decisions for." She looked adoringly at her husband, glowing under his praise. "What do you say we go get my suitcases in? I have some things for you and Beth."

The couple unloaded the car together, and Elaina set to preparing a late lunch for them while Vince unpacked his bags. She hummed a happy tune as she shuffled around the kitchen. Her kitchen. Her world was right again—her husband had come home. Her fears were put to rest.

Chapter 46

When Beth got home, she rocketed through the door into her father's arms. "Dad! You made it! It's so good you're home! What do you think of the house? Mom and I picked it out. It was so hot! Holy cow, you're home!" Her words tumbled over each other in her joy and Vince laughed aloud.

"Whoa there, young lady. Hello. It's good to see you, too." He hugged her again.

Giggling, Beth started telling him about the days on end she and Mom had searched through every mobile home sales lot in the area to find the perfect trailer for them.

"Dad, it was so hot! And none of these things had the windows open or air conditioning in them. It was like walking from one oven to another. I was so tired of doing that."

"I'm glad you helped your mom, Beth."

"Me too," Elaina replied. "She's been a big help to me."

Elaina's mind wandered to the days of their searching for the trailer after she had bought the land. It had been so annoying then, having to call Walter to get the money for the down payment and to get the money for the permits to put the trailer on the land. She had even had to wait for him to approve the purchase of the land before she could buy it! She had felt like a child having to go to her father for her allowance, and she hadn't even know the man for five years yet.

She and Vince hadn't talked about it anymore, but she still didn't understand why he had done that. She still felt so belittled by it. That time, though, drew her and her in-laws closer. She and Beth had made several trips to the younger Koebner's house. She could tell Beth enjoyed having cousins close at hand. She and the two boys became as close as siblings.

She was so happy that Beth had wanted a pickup truck for her first vehicle, even though she was having to make about as many payments for it as the child was. It came in very handy when they moved from the lake house to the new one. It kept them from having to rent a truck for moving.

Beth had been so proud of that truck, even though it was the most basic. She had picked it out, gotten the color she wanted, and had payments she thought she could afford. She had traded in the old blue car her daddy had left her when he went overseas. She had wanted a truck ever since her driver's education teacher had said it was a safer choice for young drivers. Her mama liked that idea, too.

Elaina listened to father and daughter talk as she remembered Beth's telling of the salesman taking her down the street to a park to help her brush up on driving a stick shift. The idea of the truck bucking and jumping like a kangaroo was ludicrous until you watched her daughter tell the tale.

The move hadn't taken long, as most of the furniture in the house had belonged to the house. The trailer came with two beds and some living room furniture, along with a table and chairs for the kitchen. Fortunately, Walter and his boys came down to help move the washer and dryer, television, and to help carry the boxes she and Beth had packed. She remembered this living room with boxes stacked up against the walls. What a time that had been. She wished even now that she had gotten central air conditioning to go with the heat, but she had opted to buy a window unit big enough to freeze them out of the room.

Vince's voice brought her back to the present. "Well, I miss all those big old oak trees, and we'll have to drive a bit to go fishin', but I think we'll just call this home."

Over the next several months, Elaina noticed a change in her husband. He seemed more settled, more something she couldn't put her finger on. They didn't fight so much now. He didn't even seem so bothered that Beth was going to the church school. He was too proud that her graduation was still two months away but she had already finished all her courses. The self-paced studies had allowed her to finish early and she was now working at the theme park five days a week as a full-time employee.

The time flew until Beth's graduation night. They dressed up in their finest, and Beth wore the pretty blue dress she had found. It was a dream on her and she looked beautiful in it, her reddish brown waves falling to her shoulders. Seated near the front, Elaina and Vince were looking at the program. As one they looked at each other when they saw their daughter's name listed as valedictorian.

"Our girl is truly a smart one," Vince said. Elaina could only nod, her breath stolen in pride and joy, and when the principal announced her speech she hung on every word.

After the graduation ceremony, Vince and Elaina took Beth and her boyfriend to the local ice cream parlor. They had offered a nice dinner, but Beth chose the place. Several of her friends joined them there, and the party was on. Elaina enjoyed seeing her daughter so happy.

Chapter 47

Elaina heard Beth's truck pull up into the yard. Vince was in the shower so she went into the bathroom and told him the kids were home, closing the door as she exited. She didn't want him walking out half naked when they had a guest.

When Beth came in, her latest boyfriend was with her—a very polite young man named Timothy Wolf. Though he had all the right words and mannerisms, she just didn't feel right about this boy. Maybe it was because Beth was growing more and more independent and spending less time with her parents, but she just didn't really like this guy.

Once everyone was gathered in the living room, Beth started, "Mom, Dad, Tim and I have something to tell you."

Oh no, Elaina thought.

"Tim asked me to marry him tonight!" Beth gushed. "We were on the observation deck of the big hotel at the Park and he proposed! It was so romantic!" Her smile was soft as she lay her head on Tim's shoulder."

Oh no! Elaina thought again.

Vince harrumphed. "This changes everything, Beth. Tim, I don't know you or your family. We need to change that before I agree to this."

"Of course, Mr. Koebner. What do you want to know?"

Vince sighed visibly. "I don't know. It just bothers me that we don't know anything about you. You've only been dating Beth what, three months? How can two young people know that they want to make a lifelong commitment after only three months?"

Tim took Beth's hand in his and said to her parents, "It's not hard to love Beth. She's so kind and considerate. She's patient and fun. She laughs at my jokes and I laugh at hers. I want to snatch her up before someone else does."

Elaina wanted to roll her eyes but closed them instead, listening.

"I was born on the west coast of the state. My dad is Henry Wolf. He was born in Indiana. My mother is Mary Wolf. She was born in Kentucky. They owned a small grocery store near Tampa and now Mom works at the theme park and Dad sells stuff at the flea market. They're living in the big campground on the way to the Park until they find a house to buy down here. Anything else?"

"Do you go to church?" Elaina asked softly.

"Not right now, ma'am. I haven't found one yet since we moved down here."

Elaina nodded.

"What do you plan to do with your life, son?" Vince asked. "I want to know you'll be able to support my girl well."

"I'm full time at the Park as you know, and I plan to become an EMT as soon as classes start again."

Elaina listed to the conversation as it went on, but she couldn't engage. She felt this wasn't right for her daughter, but she could tell by the look on Beth's face that there would be no talking her out of it tonight. She was glowing with the thought of becoming a wife.

Just two months later, Vince walked their daughter down the aisle. She had walked through all the preparations for the wedding with Beth to plan and pay for the wedding. They managed to keep the costs down by getting the invitations done at the local newspaper office and she had asked the pastor if the church could get their Christmas poinsettias a week early so they could be decorations for the wedding. She was so happy that he had agreed. That had saved a bundle! And the dress that Beth had chosen was exactly what she had dreamed of, and had only cost a hundred and fifty dollars! She had been so proud of her daughter for being careful with their money.

As she watched her husband in his tuxedo walking their girl in her beautiful white wedding gown down the aisle, tears came to her eyes. She knew the photographers were there capturing every moment, but she just knew she would remember each one.

"Just look at her bouquet!" she heard someone whisper.

"Oh! It's not really a bouquet!" came the reply.

Elaina thought, *No, that's a Bible with a lacy cover and a rose arc on it. My poor girl was too short for the cascading bouquet she wanted. She cried the day the florist had told her that… until she saw this in the book on the florist's counter. Nothing else would do.*

The reception was simple, just the cake and some nuts and mints. It was, after all, a wedding after dinner.

Elaina was thrilled when people told her how beautiful Beth was and how handsome her new son-in-law was. Henry and Mary were there, beaming at their son, excited for him to be marrying Beth. She noticed when the flash lit up a moment when Mary had her arm around her son, looking so lovingly into his face.

Tim and Beth rented a little duplex near downtown Allendale and came to dinner at their house often. Vince said it was because they never had any money. Elaina knew it was because, even though their daughter had fled their home, she missed it terribly. It was exactly how she had felt in those first months after she married Grant.

"I can't believe we're doing this again," Elaina whined as they loaded the car with Vince's suitcases.

"I know, honey, but if I don't we won't have the money to live on. There's just no work up here. Unless you want to move to Tequesta. They're booming down there, but we'd have to sell this place to get one down there to live in."

Elaina pouted as she got behind the wheel. "I know, I know. But I wish I could at least go with you. I'll be here in this house all alone."

"You've got your church ladies, and Beth isn't far away. You wouldn't like where I'm going either. There's nothing out there. Desert and mountains. The only interesting thing is Mount Ararat where they say Noah's Ark is, but you can't go up there; the government won't let you. You'd have to stay in the construction camp all the time unless I have R & R. At least here you'll have people around you that you know."

"I understand, but I'm just going to be so lonely." She wiped a tear from her cheek, reminding herself that at least this time he trusted her to receive his pay in their account and she didn't have to get Wally's permission to spend it.

Vince was headed to Turkey to help build a coal-fired electric plant. His work in Indonesia had caught the eye of this company and they hired him as a superintendent. She was proud of that. Still, so much all at once had her reeling.

She stayed with him at the airport gate, waiting for the plane that would carry him to New York, then Germany, then on to Turkey. He had signed another two-year contract. As the passengers were called to board the plane she hugged her husband tightly, silently willing him to stay, knowing he could not.

"I love you," she whispered.

"I love you, my beautiful girl. I'll write to you as often as I can and you better write me back!" She smiled. She cherished each letter, and knew that he had kept every one she had written to him in Indonesia.

"I will for sure," she replied, tears in her eyes.

"There now, let's stop that," he said, his voice gruff with his own tears. "Let's be happy; let's think about what we'll do with the money we'll make this time. Maybe you should go to Stafford for the reunion this year. Get out and about some, my girl. I'll be dreaming of you!" He called the last words as he made his way to the door that led to the airplane.

Chapter 48

It was April Fool's day and Elaina had already been caught in some pretty sneaky jokes, always laughing them off. That evening, Tim and Beth were coming to have dinner with her so she steeled herself for whatever trickery they would come up with. It was so good to laugh with the young people.

When they'd finished eating, Beth turned to her and said, "Mom, we have some news for you."

Aha, here it comes. It's their April Fool's joke on me, Elaina thought before saying, "What news, sweetie?"

Her daughter looked at her husband, who said, "We're having a baby!"

Before she let the thought rest in her mind, Elaina cried, "April Fool's!"

Beth laughed and shook her head. "No, Mom. No April Fool. It's real. The doctor confirmed it. I'm about two months pregnant."

Elaina's mouth fell open as she tried to catch her breath. "You're having a baby?" she asked, incredulous.

"Yes, Mom. We're having a baby."

"Oh my goodness! Oh, I need to let your daddy know. Oh, I can't just call him. Oh. Oh, my! My baby is having a baby!" She moved from her chair and wrapped her arms around her daughter. "I'm so happy for you, Beth! So very happy!"

That night Elaina wrote Vince a letter, telling him he was about to be a grandpa. She wished she could be there to see his face when he read that. She had thought about placing a call through the corporate office, but that was for emergencies not good news. She mailed the letter off the first thing the next morning and waited to hear from him.

Almost two weeks to the day, at ten o'clock in the morning, the phone rang in the Koebner home. Elaina answered, thinking it was her friend Cindy from church.

"'Laina?" Vince's voice said across the miles.

"Vince! It's you?" He had called her a couple times while overseas, but it was usually a collect call from a pay phone.

"It's me. I got your letter today. We're really going to be grandparents?" She could hear the excitement bubbling in his voice.

"We're going to be grandparents!" she exclaimed joyfully.

"Well, hell," he growled. "Our little girl is going to have a baby."

"She sure is. Do you think you'll be able to be home for that?"

"Oh, I doubt it. You know I have to stay out of the country a certain amount of time or we'll have to pay the taxes. I'll be home as soon as I can afterwards, though, you can bet your bottom dollar on that."

They talked for several minutes, trying to be mindful of the expense of the overseas phone call, unsure if the company would make Vince pay for it or not.

"Goodnight, Elaina. I love you. Take good care of our girl," he finally said.

"Love you, too, Vince. I'll keep you updated. Be careful out there."

Elaina floated through the day, feeling truly happy. She was about to be a grandmother, and her true love now knew he was going to be a grandfather.

Halfway through May, Elaina made the decision to go to her reunion, like Vince had suggested. She decided, though, to make it a big trip; not just there and back like they had done so many times. She made the plans to start that way in June and go on to Iowa to visit her in-laws for a bit before heading to Stafford. She called her sister-in-law Ilsa to make arrangements for a place to stay.

Next she called her sister Kate to make arrangements to stay with her while in Stafford.

"Oh Sis, you know you can stay here with me and Douglas. We've got a room that's just right for you."

"Thank you, Kate. That's so nice."

"Aw shoot, Sis, I love you. Hey, did you know Doreen is coming this year with her brood?"

Elaina was speechless for a moment. "Doreen? My Doreen?"

"Yep. Her and her new husband and their six kids are all comin' to town for the picnic and the reunion."

"New husband? So she's not married to her son's father anymore?"

"No, no. He got put out. I don't know what happened but she's married to a fine fella now, so we've been told."

"I'm so glad she has kept in touch with all of you even though I couldn't be in touch with her." Elaina stopped for a moment. "Six kids? Has Doreen had more children?"

"No, Sis. Three of them are his from his previous marriage."

Elaina pressed her hand to her chest. She was going to get to see her daughter after how many years? Twenty-seven?

"'Laina? Are you still there?" Kate asked.

"Oh! I'm sorry… I was thinking." Her voice fell away.

"I understand. You're thinking about how long it's been since you've seen and talked to your girl."

"I am. It's been twenty-seven years since I saw her or heard her voice. What if she doesn't want to meet me? No, I'll just stay away this time. Don't worry about putting me up."

"Oh, hush that stuff!" her little sister stated. "It's high time there was some healin' and talkin' goin' on, and you have the chance for that next month. You just get yourself up here to do that. Last I heard they'll be staying with Agnes and Andrew."

The sisters talked on, making the arrangements they could, then Elaina hung up the phone. She pulled out the old photo album she had kept over the years. As she turned the black pages, the old photos spoke to her. After she and her mother had reconciled their differences, Louise had sent her pictures of her children. She was thankful that Grant allowed them to visit their grandmother and family in Stafford. After her mother passed away, the visits came less frequently and her sisters weren't as faithful to send her pictures, but they would pass on the information they got from Doreen and Seth.

"Oh, God! I will get to see my daughter again. She's almost thirty-five now. Will she want to see me? What has Grant told her all these years? I don't know if I can face her, Lord. Will she think I abandoned her and Seth?" Elaina's tears fell freely, a mixture of fear and happiness.

The next morning brought new determination, and Elaina made a list of everything she needed to get done before heading off on her grand adventure. She now had Beth's truck, and since it was much newer than the car she decided to drive it on her journey. It didn't have an air conditioner, though, and it was going to be hot up there in Iowa and certainly in Arkansas. She wiped her brow just thinking about those summers picking cotton.

She decided that top of her list would be to get a fan for the truck. She thought that having one like the school bus drivers had would be just right. With both windows down and the wing vents turned right, that fan could keep her cool as a cucumber. The auto parts store had just what she needed and Mr. Prince at church installed it for her.

She purchased an atlas and marked out her trip to take her from Central Florida to Iowa, then down to Arkansas. There were highways most of the way and some interstates, too. She liked the speed of the interstates, but she missed the friendliness of little towns where she could stop and stretch her legs, so she mapped out a combination of both.

All this planning reminded her of the trip home after that time of taking care of her mother. She would show Beth the sign they were looking for and the little girl would help her search it out. They worked together to get home. It was a grand memory.

Chapter 49

Elaina's visit in Iowa was so pleasant she almost didn't want to leave. She had taken three whole days to get there. Had she gone the whole way on the interstate it would have only taken two, but she was sightseeing some as she went. Now she was giving herself two days to get to Stafford, even though it was barely over eight hours on the big interstates. She wanted a night on the road to think about the upcoming visit with Doreen and her grandchildren. Grandchildren she had never met. What would that be like? They knew Claudia as their grandmother, not her. Had Doreen told them about her?

She hugged Ilsa and Marlis and Rose before she got into the truck. Ilsa handed her a bag with snacks in it, saying, "Here, you might want something along the way. There's a couple apples in there and some snack mix, too. You'll have to get you something to drink, but here you've got some goodies from us. There might be a ham sandwich in there, too."

"Oh, Ilsa! Some of that ham from last night?"

Her sister-in-law nodded. "The very same."

"I might eat that before I get to the highway!" Elaina laughed. She loved this family and was thankful again that she had gotten to know them.

Backing out of the driveway, she waved out the window and headed toward her first highway to her own family home place.

It was nearly four o'clock in the afternoon when Elaina pulled into the driveway above Kate's house. She saw her sister through the kitchen window, waving at her to come on in.

Once she had her luggage in her temporary bedroom, Elaina joined her sister in the kitchen.

"How was your trip? Tell me all about it!" Kate insisted. She and Douglas didn't travel much, so she loved to hear from her sisters about theirs.

Elaina told about the drive to Iowa and the stay there. They discussed family and friends and covered all sorts of subjects, never resting on one for long.

Suddenly Kate said, "Oh my goodness! I almost forgot! Here I am fixing stuff for dinner tonight and didn't even tell you that dinner is at Agnes'. We're taking a couple dishes to feed everyone."

Elaina looked confused and Kate answered the unasked question, "Doreen and her family are there. Agnes called to have a potluck so we could all get to know each other. It's been a while since Doreen has been home."

"Do you think she'll want to see me?" Elaina asked timidly.

"Pishposh! Of course she will. And your grand-youngins will, too." Looking her older sister over, she said, "You kinda look road weary, though, Sis. You might want to freshen up. It will take me a little bit to get this casserole and pots of vegetables all ready. You go on and clean up. You know where everything is."

Elaina kissed her sister on the cheek and rushed to the bedroom. She pulled clean clothes and her bathroom bag from the suitcase and went into the bathroom. Elaina made fast work of the shower despite taking the time to wash her hair. She was so glad now that she had the permanent in it. Fixing her hair after a shower was as simple as rubbing it with a towel and fluffing it with her fingers. When she returned to the kitchen, Kate was boxing up the dishes filled with food ready to feed the families gathering at their sister's house.

On the drive to the country, Kate said, "I'll bet Agnes and Andrew have their camper set up, otherwise where would they put all those kids? They'll be fine out there as long as the mosquitoes don't carry them away." The women laughed, knowing that the Arkansas mosquitoes were vicious and huge.

As the two sisters entered the house, carrying the boxes with the food in them, Agnes cleared off a place on her counter to set each one out. Elaina felt an arm go around her shoulder and looked into a face that looked so like hers it brought a gasp.

"Hello, Mom," Doreen said quietly.

Turning, Elaina took her daughter's face in her hands and looked at her for what seemed like minutes. "Oh, my sweet girl. My sweet, sweet girl." Tears fell from the eyes of both women.

"Doreen, I have never stopped loving you. I never wanted to leave you. Never."

"I know, Mom. I found the note you left me." She smiled wistfully. "I know that wasn't you. Claudia told me a while back that it was Dad. He had decided he didn't want you around us at all. He told her that you didn't want anything to do with us. That's what he told me and Seth, too. I think I knew then that you would never have left us. I just knew it." The swarm of people around them didn't matter. They only saw and heard each other in this beautiful moment.

"I hate to say it, but Seth still believes Dad. He was so little when everything happened and he doesn't remember you like I do. He believes all the stuff Dad has told him. I try to convince him that it's not true. I tell him I remember what you were like, that you didn't hurt us. That you took great care of us, making sure we were fed so well even when Dad didn't come home until so late at night."

"You remember that?" Elaina asked softly.

"Yeah, I do. I used to hear you crying in the living room all alone on the nights he was working late. Claudia said he wasn't working late. He was with her."

"I figured that out, Doreen. Thank you for trying with Seth. Maybe someday he'll come around."

"Maybe. But I think he's got some of that famous Drew stubbornness in him."

"Oh goodness, we're doomed!" Elaina laughed aloud.

"Here, Mom. Meet my husband, Glenn."

A large dark-haired man stepped close and wrapped his arms around his mother-in-law and said, "Hey there, Mom! Good to finally meet you!"

In moments Elaina was surrounded by six young people, from the second grader to her eldest granddaughter who was now sixteen. She was overwhelmed, hearing them already calling her Grandma. She couldn't keep the tears from falling and had to explain several times they were happy tears, not sad ones.

"Dinner's on!" Agnes called out. "Who's prayin'? Andrew?"

Andrew led the family in saying grace, then the chaos began.

"Now, the table is for the adults; you children find you some places on the floor or in the living room to eat. If you drop somethin', pick it up or wipe it up."

Elaina's face shone as she ate supper next to her first daughter. Her sisters kept whispering as they watched, seeing a joy on her face that had been missing for far too long. The family talked and laughed long into the night and made the arrangements to meet at the parade the next day.

"Well, was that as good as you expected, 'Laina?" Kate asked on the way home.

"Oh, Kate. It was so much more than I could have expected. She had already told the children about me. They were already calling me Grandma without any hesitation. I can't believe that!"

"She never forgot her mama, Sis. When she's been here in the past, she's spent time in all of our photo albums looking at pictures of you. She even knows Vince and Beth."

"Oh my." Elaina couldn't speak, her heart was in her throat.

Kate patted her hand and smiled. "You've got several days to spend here loving on her and y'all gettin' to know each other. Several days you can spoil those grandbabies that aren't babies."

"Thank you, Kate."

"What for?"

"Just for being you and for loving me through everything."

"Aw phew, girl! You're my big sister."

Elaina collapsed in bed that night, so tired, her heart so full. Before turning out the light she wrote a post card to Vince, planning to post it the next day. It would take slightly less time to get to Turkey, and she wanted to let him know how this meeting had gone.

The rest of the week went by like a whirlwind, the days spent with Independence Day activities and sightseeing with the family. Elaina showed Doreen and Glenn where Doreen had lived when she was born. She pointed out where she had grown up and where the grape arbor stood that she and Grant had married under. She drove around another curve and pointed out where her grandparents had lived.

"I remember staying there, Mom!" Doreen cried. "Grandpa Rafferty used to brag about being able to pee off the porch of the house and hit the roof of the barn. Seth used to try so hard to do that, but he never could!" Her laughter quickly had everyone joining in.

One afternoon, they drove out to the camping spot on the Dermot River where the family campouts had been. Elaina smiled as she recalled how they would set up the wagons and catch the worms and cook the fish. Her grandchildren were entranced as they listened to the stories, sitting by the river where it all happened.

"Mom?"

"Yes, dear?"

"Tell me about my sister. Beth, right?"

Elaina smiled. "Yes, her name is Beth. She's almost nineteen now, expecting her first baby."

"Oh! She's pregnant? Is she married to a good man?"

"I think so. They seem to get along really well. He's pretty excited about becoming a daddy. He's taking classes to become an EMT so he can take better care of them."

"That's good. What's she like?"

Elaina retrieved her wallet to show Doreen pictures of Beth. She had some from her childhood and her wedding. She even had one from when she was in the high school band, wearing braces and all smiles. She shared stories about her and couldn't help but believe that, given the chance, the two women would be fast friends.

Far too soon, her time in Stafford was over. Doreen and Glenn had to head back home to Michigan where they lived. Glenn had to get back to work at the gas company and Doreen had to get back to her job, too.

They all met at the buffet restaurant in town that last night so all the family could visit instead of cooking. It was like a big party, laughter ringing out often. As they parted that evening, Elaina hugged her daughter extra tight and thanked her for accepting her.

"I just wish we'd done it sooner, Mom. We've missed out on so much."

"No more though, right?"

"No more. And I'll keep after Seth, too. He needs to get his head on straight. Maybe Claudia will talk to him like she did me. Meanwhile, I'll talk to his wife, too."

Elaina patted Doreen's arm. "When it's time, it will be time. If you have the chance to let him know I love him, just tell him that."

The two women hugged again, then headed for their lodgings. Both were leaving early the next morning.

Elaina took the time to do some exploring on her way home, driving down the Mississippi River to see some of the antebellum homes along the way. Those beautiful mansions always fascinated her. She loved to dream about being the mistress of such a house, wearing the big hoop skirts and having all her needs met before she even said a word. She explored Louisiana, Mississippi, and Alabama before she headed back into Florida, enjoying every moment. If Vince had been there, she wouldn't have been able to ooh and ahh as much. He would have teased her incessantly, or he would have found someone else to chat with and ignore all the things to see.

Chapter 50

The end of October arrived and about eight o'clock in the morning, the phone rang.

"Mom?" Beth said when she answered.

"Yes? Beth, are you okay?" She heard pain in her daughter's voice.

"My back is killing me, Mom. I can't even get out of bed. I don't think I can go shopping with you today."

"Oh I'm so sorry, honey. Well, we'll go another time. You're not in labor, are you? It's getting about time."

"I don't feel anything down there, Mom, just in my back."

Elaina nodded, thinking it could still be labor, but held her tongue. Sometimes that girl thought she knew everything about everything.

"Well, you take some Tylenol and get some rest. Let me know if I can do anything for you."

"Thanks, Mom. I love you."

Once she'd hung up the phone, Elaina set about getting the house cleaned and laundry done. She suspected her grandchild was on its way.

She was sitting in the comfortable chair in the living room, having just had a bedtime snack, when the phone rang.

"Hello?" she answered.

"'Laina? It's Tim. I just talked to the hospital."

"Is Beth all right?"

"Yeah, she's okay. We're pretty sure that these back pains are actually labor. When I talked to them at the hospital, they said unless she really goes into hard labor not to get there before 11:30. They said that would keep the costs from being so much."

"Okay. So, you're going to get there at 11:30?"

"Yeah. I imagine they'll take her on back to labor and delivery right away."

"Okay. I'll be down there."

Well, she thought, *my baby is about to have her baby. I'll just wash up a little and get ready to go. It's going to be a long night!*

"Hey baby, how are you doing?" Elaina asked as she walked into the labor room.

"Fine Mom, just my back hurts like crazy."

"Well, I guess you're going to be one of those who has her labor pains in her back."

"Great. Aren't I the lucky one?" Beth said snidely.

"You'll be just fine. I heard that your doctor is already here. Seems he lined up several of you to have babies tonight."

Beth laughed. "Not sure how he managed that. I just wish he'd do something to make me stop hurting."

Elaina patted her daughter's hand. "I know, honey, but soon enough you'll be holding your precious baby and all this will be a memory soon forgotten."

Beth yawned and closed her eyes. "I hope so, Mom."

Elaina walked back to the waiting room where five families waited for childbirth to happen. Tim and his parents sat with her and they chatted throughout the night. Mary tried to nap a little, because she would have to leave to go to work around four o'clock. Working in the big kitchen of the theme park didn't leave her much room for calling in to take off for her grandchild to be born.

"They told me I can get a phone call from Tim when the baby is born, so I can know what they have," she told the group. "Then I'll just finish out my shift and come on home."

"At least you can get that call, Mary," Elaina said. "I'd hate for you to have to go all day without knowing!"

"Ha! She'd be on the phone on her break if she couldn't," Tim laughed.

"Darn right I would!" Mary replied. "I've got my grand-daughter from your half-sister, but you're our only one. I want to know right away."

Elaina nodded understanding. She had just met the grand-children of her oldest daughter, but that was different. This was the grandchild of her and Vince together. This was extra special and she would be anxious to get word of the child, too.

"Mr. Wolf?" the doctor's Filipino-accented voice filled the room.

"That's me!" Tim stood. He, Henry, and Elaina were the only ones left in the room. All the other babies had been born and their families had left. Mary had gone on to work, saddened that their baby hadn't made his or her appearance yet.

Elaina watched as Tim talked to the doctor. He seemed ecstatic hearing the news of his child. She nodded, thinking that's how a daddy should behave. The doctor left the room and Tim walked over to them.

"We have a daughter!" He was beaming.

"Oh, Tim! That's so wonderful! Girls are such joy! When will we get to see her and Beth?"

"In a few minutes. I've got to call Mom." He walked to the pay phone down the hall and made the call, then returned to sit with his father. The three talked quietly awaiting their chance to see the new Wolf baby.

"Mr. Wolf?" a petite nurse said from the door.

Tim's eyes went wide. "That's me," he said.

"Oh, there's no problem, I just need to clear something up."

"Okay." Tim dragged the word out.

"Did the doctor just tell you that your wife gave birth to a girl?"

Tim said proudly, "He sure did!"

"That's what I thought. I'm not sure how to tell you this, but she didn't have a girl. She had a boy. You have a fine new son, Mr. Wolf. He weighs in at six pounds, seven ounces and is eighteen inches long. He's very nearly perfect in my opinion."

Elaina, Henry, and Tim sat dumbfounded. How on earth had the doctor made that mistake? They asked the nurse.

"He's been up since yesterday. Even though all we had were boys delivered tonight, I think he just wished for a girl. I really can't say. I hope it's not a problem."

"No problem at all. Just wondering why he didn't notice the stem," Henry said, laughing.

The nurse joined the laughter and told them they would be allowed back soon.

"Well, I can't call Mom back," Tim said. "She's going to have two days of congratulations from her coworkers. One for thinking she has a granddaughter and the other for knowing she has a grandson."

Elaina laughed with them and sighed with relief. Her girl was okay, she had a brand new grandson, and soon she'd hear Vince's voice. They had also made arrangements for a phone call. She would call the special number the corporate office had given them and they would get a message to her husband. He would then be allowed to call her back, using the office phone at no charge.

She woke when the nurse returned and told them they could go back to the nursery area. She hadn't realized she was that tired. Walking with her son-in-law and his father, they reached the window through which they could see five fine baby boys. In just a moment they saw the tag on the incubator that said "Wolf."

"Oh, look at him!" Elaina cried softly. "He's just perfect!" The little round face peeked out of the blankets and she could see him squirm.

Tim moved up and put his arm around her. "I counted, Granny. He's got all ten fingers and all ten toes." He had gotten to see and hold the baby as he visited Beth.

"Well, I said he's perfect, didn't I? And don't call me Granny. I'll be Grandma, but don't call me Granny." She had a vision of Granny Clampett on the popular television show from the sixties and didn't want to be bundled with her. She might be a country girl, but that was just ridiculous.

Once at home, Elaina placed the call. It took about thirty minutes, but soon her phone rang and she snapped up the receiver.

"Hello?" she said.

"So, we have a baby?" Vince's voice boomed loudly from over six thousand miles away.

"We sure do! He's just beautiful, Vince. Almost as beautiful as his mama was when she was born."

"So, it's a boy?" Her husband's voice was filled with wonder.

"Yes! Oh, I didn't tell you that!" She giggled. "He was born at 5:35 this morning and weighed six pounds, seven ounces, and is eighteen inches long."

"How's our girl? Did she do okay? Is she all right?" His voice was now filled with concern.

"Oh, she came through like a champ, honey. She's just fine. When I left the hospital, she was sleeping soundly."

Elaina went on to describe all that had happened since the phone call yesterday morning, including the doctor's mistake. They laughed heartily over that one.

"Well, send me some pictures as soon as you can! I need to get off here," Vince said, obviously not wanting to do so.

"I will. I'm going to catch a nap then go back down there in a few hours. I'll take my camera then and get them right to the Eckerd's to be developed. As soon as I pick them up, they'll be on their way to you. I love you, Vince."

"Love you, too, 'Laina. You take care."

In mere moments Elaina was snuggled happily in her bed, sound asleep.

Chapter 51

"Okay, Wally. As soon as Beth can get here, we'll be on our way. That will be a couple hours." Elaina heard Vince hang up the phone.

"What's wrong?" she asked him quietly, though she suspected she knew.

"Mom's gone," he said, quietly weeping. "She passed away early this morning."

Elaina walked to him and wrapped her arms around him. After being estranged for so long, he had only had his mother back for seven years. The last time they were in Iowa, they had visited her in the nursing home. Oh, how she had fussed about having to be there, and in the next breath talked lovingly about all her friends there.

"What's the plan?" she asked.

"We're going to go to Jacksonville to join Mary and Wally, then we'll drive on to Iowa. Probably all night so we can be there with Wilfred and Berrin and Ronnie."

"Okay, let me get some things put in the suitcase. You call Beth and let her know."

In less than two hours, Beth arrived with two-year-old Timothy. They had been living in Southwest Florida for almost two years where Tim was working as an EMT. He was currently working a 48-hour shift and couldn't leave, but Beth had said she absolutely had to go. Once in Jacksonville, they had supper and climbed into the Koebner van for the long trip to the Midwest. Wally's oldest son was in the Navy, but their youngest rode along.

"It hasn't been too bad a trip," Elaina said to Mary as they walked together to the restroom at the truck stop.

"No, I've been real proud of the way Timothy has behaved. Not bad for a little boy who likes to move. He sure loves throwing his 'two rocks'!" Both women laughed. Every time they stopped to stretch their legs, if there were rocks around, the child would pick up a handful, but show them to everyone and declare they were his 'two rocks'.

Breakfast the next morning was in Peoria, Illinois. Everyone had their noses scrunched up, trying to not smell the sulfurous odor of the water. They quickly learned that it was unavoidable. If they ordered coffee, the smell became the taste there. Beth and Vincent ordered soft drinks, but the ice carried the odor and taste. It was a memorable breakfast.

They arrived in the little town where Vince and Wally had grown up and drove to the motel just off the highway. The Florida crew had lunch together with the Iowa crew that afternoon, meeting them at a local restaurant. The Iowa brothers had made the arrangements to have the wake that evening and the mass the morning after.

Beth had just finished getting Timothy dressed when Vince gathered her and Elaina close.

"I have to tell you both something."

Elaina looked worried. "What is it, honey?"

"You might see a man there tonight who looks a lot like me. He's my son, Jeremy."

"Your *what*?" Beth cried.

"My son. From my first marriage."

Beth was incredulous and didn't want to hear more. She stepped into the bathroom and closed the door. Elaina just looked at him.

"Why haven't you told us this before now? I thought all the secrets were finished."

"I don't know, 'Laina. I guess I thought I had more time. I didn't expect to lose Mom after only seven years."

"Didn't you think when she was in the nursing home her end might be near?" she hissed. "What other lies are you hiding?"

"None. That's it."

"That's what you said last time, when I found out you had family. What am I going to do with you?"

"I really don't care, Elaina. My mother just died. I'm about to face my son who I haven't seen since he was Timothy's age. He knew my family all these years. Of course he's going to be there. I just don't know how he's going to act."

Elaina folded her arms across her chest and sat on the bed. "The one you're really going to have to apologize to is your daughter."

"Why is that?"

"Because you've lied to her again."

"Oh hell, Elaina. I'm going on out to meet Mary and Wally."

Elaina watched him walk out the door to the warm evening, then heard the bathroom door open. Beth looked at her quizzically.

"Did you know about this, Mom?" she asked.

"No, I did not. Your grandma said something once about a Jeremy, but I didn't know he was your father's son."

The young woman nodded and walked to her son. She took the little boy by the hand and walked with him out the door.

The evening went off well enough. Her Beth was a polite woman and met her half-brother with courtesy, then left him to visit with her aunts, uncles, and cousins she had known for several years.

Elaina stood with Vince most of the evening, listening to him talk to others he hadn't seen in decades who were there in memory of Maddie. She laughed at some of the stories, recalling how she had seen her stomping her foot when she didn't get her way. She learned more about the life the Koebners had lived as her husband was growing up, but there was no talk about that first marriage or the son. She met Jeremy and his wife. They had adopted two children, a boy and a girl. Both were very polite. Elaina wondered what they had been told, if anything, about her and Vince.

The next day was a whirlwind. Elaina had never been to a funeral mass before, having grown up in a Baptist home. She hadn't realized Vince was Catholic until she had met his family. Once the mass was over, the family followed the hearse up the big hill at the edge of town to the cemetery where most of the Koebner family was buried. Vince paid a somber homage to his father. Elaina could tell he didn't want anyone noticing, but she saw his damp cheeks as he looked up from the headstone bearing his father's name.

Once the priest had spoken the final words over his former parishioner, the family returned to the church fellowship hall for a meal provided by those in the church who cared for the grieving.

They're not so different from us Baptists, Elaina thought. *We bring food to the family, too. And here they are just serving us like we're somebody.*

Beth seemed more at ease today, taking care of Timothy and enjoying her cousins. They were laughing now that the services were over. Those who had known Grandma Koebner the longest were sharing stories with her about growing up with the feisty woman as their grandmother. It was good to see Beth's head thrown back and hear her laughter.

"Let's go get changed," Vince said, "then we can go out and visit the Klach farm. I haven't seen Franz in years."

"What's that, Dad?" Beth asked.

"It's the dairy farm I worked on when I was a kid. I'd like to show it to you."

"Cool."

The group went back to the motel and changed clothes. They headed out to the country where farms dotted the land as far as the eye could see. Wally turned up a gravel driveway that boasted three silos and a huge barn, along with a beautiful white farmhouse surrounded by gigantic oak trees. Elaina looked at Mary knowingly. They both dreamed of having a house like that.

"Oh mein Gott!" Elaina heard as the man strolled from the barn toward the van. "Is that you, Curly?" His German accent was as pronounced as a recent immigrant's.

"Franz! It's good to see you," Vince said happily.

"I'm sorry to hear about your mother. She was a good woman."

"Thanks, Franz. Hey, you remember my baby brother Wally, right?"

"Ja, I remember. How are you, Wally?" He offered his hand to shake.

"Doing okay, Franz. How's your family?"

The conversation went on, covering years and miles and back again. Franz explained that the cattle were out in the pasture and wouldn't be back until later in the day for the evening milking, but he had some other animals that little Timothy might enjoy.

Beth sat her son in the cargo area of the van with both the back doors wide open to the breeze. As he sat there, his legs spread out in front of him, their host brought two tiny baby rabbits and placed them on the floor of the van in front of him. Elaina laughed as the boy's eyes grew wide with wonder. The bunnies made tiny hops around the enclosure of his legs, sniffing. He giggled when their whiskers brushed his bare skin, and Elaina's heart sang with the joy of it.

Soon they made their way back to Florida and life as they had known it.

Chapter 52

Elaina loved the Wednesday night services at church. The preacher would speak a bit, but it was mainly about prayer. They would write down or call out names of folks who need prayer. Tonight, her heart was heavy with a heartbreaking need.

She wrote Mary's name on the prayer list, asking the people to pray. About three months ago, her son-in-law's mother had gone to the dentist and had a root canal done. Soon after that, she had had swelling all along her jaw and down into her neck. That was when she had been diagnosed with lymphoma cancer. They said it was all throughout her system and there was no cure.

It was so hard to watch the woman who was just a few months ago so energetic now so wracked with pain she could hardly move. Elaina thought of her weekends before this happened. She and Henry would be up early on Friday and Saturday mornings, going to yard sales all around the county, shopping for items to sell at the flea market on Monday. Once home, she would research what the prices should be and get them marked and packed into boxes for Henry to take to market. All while she did laundry, cleaned house, and cooked meals. But now, the doctors held out little hope for her survival. Already she had been through weeks of chemotherapy. Henry had taken her home to Kentucky to visit with her family there. She hadn't seen them in many years, and wanted to be able to say good-bye.

Beth had said it was a long, rough trip, with Mary having to stop quite often, the chemo making her sick that first day on the road.

Now she was back and forth to the university hospital to have radiation. The doctors told Mary that if the radiation didn't work, they could try to get her in the trial for the experimental drugs they were testing. Her daughter's mother-in-law had agreed to that plan. Beth had told her that Mary had said, if she was going to die maybe her death would mean something for someone else.

She prayed for her often now, despite the fact that from the moment they had learned Timothy was coming, both of them had entered into an unspoken and crazy competition, seeing which of them could find the right furniture or the right outfit or the right toy for the coming grandchild.

"That was such a stupid way to behave on both our parts," Elaina muttered softly. "He loves us both and always will. I just hate that he might lose his Granny so early on." She wiped a tear and passed on the prayer list.

The next day as she and her husband were having lunch, Elaina said, "Vince?"

"Uh-huh?"

"You know what's going on with Mary, right?"

"I know Beth said she's got cancer. It's not looking good, is it?"

"Not at all. I don't know how many of the radiation treatments she's had, but if that doesn't work they're going to try that experimental stuff."

"That is bad. I wonder how Henry's holding up."

"About as well as can be expected, I suppose." Elaina paused. "Vince, I want to get married."

"We are married, 'Laina. You know common-law is real in Florida."

"I know, but I've been thinking about Mary and Henry and all the things that come with—" she hesitated, "you know, when she passes. I want to have all our papers right, just in case. Can we do that?"

"Well, I guess we can. Where do you want to do it?" Vince asked.

"I don't want it to be in the Allendale papers; I'd hate for Beth to find out that way."

"If we do it right, she won't ever have to know."

"That's what I'm talking about. What about over in Crane Creek?" Elaina mentioned the city on the coast in the next county. "We don't hardly hear anything from over there, so it's not likely that the news would be published here. And I don't think Beth has friends in the courthouse there like she does here."

Vince chuckled. "Sounds like the same problem we had back in '56."

"Stop it, Vince! This is important. We don't want everyone knowing. Someone might tell Beth." Her greatest fear was that her daughter would find out they weren't actually married. She understood that they were married as common-law, but Vince always made such a big deal of other people shacking up that she felt ashamed of what they were doing.

"Okay, okay. Let's do it in Crane Creek. We can go over there, get the license, get hitched, have lunch, and come home all in one afternoon."

"Are you sure? There's no waiting period?"

"I forgot about that. I guess you'll get two lunches instead of one. Do you want to head over this afternoon and get the license?"

"That would be good, then we can get married," she counted on her fingers, "Friday. That would work out perfectly."

"Well get your drawers on, woman! Let's do this!"

They drove the hour to the coast and visited the courthouse to get all signed up for their license, then went out for an early supper at a seafood restaurant. On Friday, they made the trip again and stood in the clerk's office to be married.

As they left the courthouse, Vince took her hand and asked, "Does that make you feel better?"

"It does, Vince. I feel like we're both protected a little more. Like there won't be any problems if one of us goes on."

"And we did it without anyone finding out. Now, where do you want to have dinner, Mrs. Koebner?"

When they arrived home they found a note from Beth, telling them she and Tim and the baby had stopped by and found them gone. They were at Henry and Mary's and would spend the night there.

"Oh, I hate we missed them," Elaina said.

"Me, too. Do you want me to call over there and get them to come back out?"

"No. Let them stay there and spend time with his mom. I don't think she's long for this world."

Chapter 53

"Mom?"

Elaina heard the tears in her daughter's voice on the phone. "Yes, baby? What's wrong?"

"Can I come and stay with you for a few days?"

"Well, of course you can. Beth, what's going on?"

"Oh, Mom. It's so horrible."

Elaina sat in her chair, waiting for Beth to be able to speak.

"Tim is having an affair, Mom. I've known about it since March. I thought he would change, but he hasn't. I just need to get away so I can think some things through."

"Then get yourself down here. Do you need me to send some money?" Elaina's heart was breaking and angry all at the same time. All the emotions she'd felt when Grant had fooled her came rushing to the forefront.

"No. Henry is giving me the money to make the trip down. I'll be careful with it, and if I need some to get home on I might borrow it from you. I'll be headed down on Saturday, so Timothy can finish the week at school."

The arrangements were made and Elaina's mind turned to how she would tell Vince. Why hadn't Beth thought she could share that hurt with her? She had wanted her daughter to trust her, but it just never seemed to happen.

Predictably, Vince blew up. "What the hell is that boy thinking?" he yelled.

"I don't know, Vince. I just know Beth has caught him at it and she's hurting and needs us." She returned to preparing supper.

"I should go up there and wring his ever-lovin' neck!" Vince growled.

"And what good would that do?" Elaina placed her hands on her hips. "Our daughter needs us now like never before. She needs both of us to be thinking about her. And our grandson needs us, too. I can't imagine his little heart breaking."

"Okay, fine. I'll wait until they've come and gone before I do anything."

Elaina sighed. Her husband had some big righteous anger, but it didn't usually make good sense. "Go on and get your shower. I should have supper ready when you finish."

Beth and Timothy arrived Saturday evening. When Beth first got out of the car, Elaina gasped. She was so thin! She did a double take, thinking maybe the girl was sick, but no. She had been working out.

"Beth! I like to not have known you! What's all this about?"

"Oh, I just started working out, Mom. Help me get our stuff inside?"

Elaina was already wrapped up in the hugs of her grandson. "I missed you, Grandma!" he said over and over.

"I've missed you, too! Say, aren't you supposed to be in school?"

He grinned happily. "Next week, Grandma, but Mommy got my teacher to give her my work for the week and I can keep up with it here."

"What a smart mommy!" Elaina said. The two pals grabbed items from the car and walked into the house together.

The family babbled and chatted through supper and the cleanup afterwards. Before long, Vince was snoozing in his chair and Timothy was watching television. Elaina spirited Beth to her bedroom to talk.

"I thought if I lost weight and got skinny, he would still love me," Beth cried. "I was so wrong. It didn't do a thing. He says I'm doing it to cheat on him!"

Nodding, Elaina chided, "Oh honey, he's got something else on his mind, and it isn't you or Timothy."

"I guess so, Mom," Beth agreed, then told her mother all the things she had been living with since early spring.

Wiping her tears again, Beth took a deep breath and said, "I've been reading a book about how to handle this. It says to tell him that this behavior is not acceptable to me, and if he wants to keep it up, he can, but he won't be around me or his son. I think I'm going to do that. Tell him that, I mean."

Elaina said, "I wish I'd been as strong as you when all this happened to me."

"I'm not strong, Mom. I even had to run home to you. It's killing me, because I know he'll be with her this whole week."

"I know honey, but you have to take care of you and you have to take care of our boy. How is he handling this? Does he know what's going on?"

"He knows we're arguing every time Tim is home. I don't think he understands that his daddy has a girlfriend."

Elaina nodded. The two women cried and talked a little longer, then freshened up and went back to the living room.

"So, Mr. Timothy, don't you think it's ice cream time?" Elaina asked her grandson.

"I think so, Grandma. I still have a spot right here that needs filling up." He pointed to his tummy and grinned.

The week was fun and fast-paced. She watched her daughter help her son with his schoolwork. That boy was so smart that it only took one afternoon for him to finish all the work for the week! A few days they acted like tourists and visited sites that were fun. Then, it was Saturday again. Vince and Elaina had to send Beth and Timothy off to make the long drive back home. As they stood in the driveway, watching their daughter make the turn onto the road, Vince growled, "I still think I should go…"

"Hush, Vince! Smile and wave."

Beth called a couple days later and told her mother that she had indeed told Tim he had to make a decision. She gave him a deadline of five days.

Beth told her that when she gave Tim that choice, he blew up and chose to leave his family. He had said he would just go stay with his father. Elaina chuckled, thinking, *Henry would have told him to get his butt back into his marriage and do the right thing.*

Saturday morning, the phone rang. It was Beth. Tim had decided to stay with her and to stop the affair. He even asked to have his workplace transferred back to Pallville, away from the woman he had been seeing. She heard real hope in her daughter's voice, and hoped along with her that this was all over.

She would get reports from Beth about Tim's new job, that he had a great partner, a single mom who was working as an EMT to take care of herself and her daughter. Beth talked about the numerous times they would all get together to have dinner or go out on the town or just hang out. It sounded so good for them to have solid friends, and Elaina sighed with relief for her family's happiness.

Another phone call came two years later, retelling the same story. It had been almost two years since Beth and Timothy made that trip to stay with them, and now it seemed that Tim and the woman he was partnered with were having an affair.

Vince was so angry when he heard the news. That man was hurting his little girl, never mind that she was almost thirty!

They were sitting in the funeral home, the service for Tim's dad just finished. There were several folks from the church Henry and Mary had been members of who stopped to talk with Tim and Beth. Timothy sat next to her, sometimes crying, sometimes just watching the people.

"What do you say we stop at Denny's on the way home to get a bite to eat?" Vince said. "I'll buy."

"Thanks, Dad. That sounds good," Beth replied. Tim seemed to not be completely there, but nodded his head.

They were seated in the big booth at the restaurant and had just ordered. Suddenly, Tim looked at his pager and said, "I have to make a call." He stood and walked to the pay phone in the foyer of the restaurant.

"He's calling Jenny," Beth said flatly.

"He's *what?*" Vince asked, his anger instantly hot as he started to rise.

"No, Dad, don't. Just stay here and spend the time with me and Timothy," Beth pleaded.

Elaina was livid. That man had walked away from his wife and son to call that girlfriend and stayed on the phone with her almost an hour! Beth went to him when the food was delivered to the table. He told her to go back to the table. The nerve of that man!

"What do you want me to do with his food?" Beth asked her parents.

"Let's get a box. Maybe you and Timothy can have it later for a snack," her father replied.

When they walked out of the restaurant, Beth and Timothy got into their car and left Tim sitting there. She heard her daughter say "We're leaving!" as she walked by. Her son-in-law didn't acknowledge his wife.

The announcement of the divorce wasn't news, only that it took another nine months for Beth to file. Of course, in that time she had changed jobs and was trying to set herself up to take care of herself and Timothy as a single mother.

Chapter 54

She and Vince talked late into the night on the phone with Beth, planning her next move. She would stay in Tennessee until Timothy's Christmas vacation from school, then move to live with them. They had learned of a program that would help her get a job and also go to school to get a better career. Beth wanted to become a paralegal, and that was one of the programs. It sounded perfect!

Early in November, Beth called. "Mom, the divorce is filed, Tim has been served the papers, and I've met a man."

"Sounds good, honey— Wait, what? You met a man? I thought you didn't want anything to do with men anymore."

"I know, but he's so different, Mom."

"I hear you. Until he's not so different."

"I know, I know. I'm scared, too. I mean, I still have to wait until the end of January for this divorce to be final. This is too soon, right?"

"It sounds like it to me, Beth, but I'm not you."

"Thanks, Mom. Right now, Ean has insisted that Timothy and I come and stay at his house."

"He *what?*" Elaina cried out.

"He saw the condition of the house, Mom. He saw that we're living there alone, no kitchen sink, barely any food, and the only heat we have is those two stack heaters. He wants us to come live at his house so we wouldn't be living like that."

"He's not taking advantage of your broken heart, is he?"

"No, ma'am. He's a perfect gentleman. He's got two sons, Tim and Larry. They're bookends around Timothy."

"Huh," Elaina grunted skeptically.

"Seriously, Mom. He got custody of his boys in his divorce. The judge gave them to him. He wouldn't have taken them from their mother if he wasn't a good man, would he?"

Elaina's mind flashed back almost forty years to her own divorce. "Maybe not, Beth, but be careful. Your heart is so tender right now."

"I know, Mom. I know. Actually, he already asked me to marry him."

"*What?*" she exploded.

"Easy, Mom. He asked. I kinda said yes, but we've only been dating about two weeks, so it's not a full yes." Elaina sputtered as her daughter went on quickly, "I told him about our plans to move me to Florida and we talked about that. We know we're both newly divorced and that we might make a bad choice at this time, so I'm going to come down to Florida to stay with you while Timothy is out of school. If that time doesn't cool our love, then I'll come back up and marry him. If it does, then he'll help us get my stuff moved."

"Oh Beth, your daddy's not going to be happy about this."

"I know, but maybe you can explain to him that I'm happy and at peace?"

"I see, you want me to have to face his anger."

"Well, yeah, since you're there and married to him and all." Elaina could hear the smile in her daughter's voice.

"Okay, fine. I'll tell your daddy, but we're still coming up to get you and Timothy in December. And I want to meet this man, Ean. I want to look him in the eyes and decide if I think he's a good man or not. I had a feeling about Tim and I never said anything back then. I wish I had. It might have hurt you for a bit, but it would have saved you all this pain."

"And I wouldn't have Timothy," the younger woman said softly.

"And you wouldn't have Timothy," Elaina agreed. "Okay. But I want the chance to meet him, anyway."

"Yes, ma'am. We'll meet you guys for lunch on neutral ground, maybe at a restaurant. Then you and Dad can grill him and watch his eyes and decide for yourselves if he's good enough for me."

"Here, Vince. It's right there on the left. See? China Town," Elaina directed her husband into the parking lot of the restaurant where they would meet Beth's new man friend.

"I just can't believe she's shacking up with this guy," Vince growled.

"You mean like we did for twenty-seven years?"

"That's different!" he retorted.

"How is it different? We lived together as man and wife without the benefit of a marriage ceremony or license. Oh, don't worry about it now, there they are! My, he's a handsome fellow."

They parked and joined Beth and Ean at the door to the restaurant. Once seated, they talked about Ean's upbringing and his family. Vince asked some very pointed questions, even mentioning how Tim had treated Beth.

"Mr. Koebner, I don't lie, I don't cheat. I wouldn't want those done to me, so I don't do them to others. Every time Beth has told me about things her ex has done to her, I want to go wring his neck, but that wouldn't get us anywhere. I just want to spend the rest of my life making her happy and helping her raise Timothy."

Elaina watched as her husband sat back in the chair, arms folded on his chest, but noticed his clenched jaw wasn't as tight as it was moments ago. Before long, the two men were bantering back and forth, telling farm stories and tales of ages past. She rolled her eyes when Vince headed off on the subject of the difference between "Yankees" and "Damn Yankees".

She tried to redirect the conversation, but Vince kept on. Finally, after about ten minutes of listening, Ean said, "So, Vince, where were you born?"

"Iowa."

"I see," Ean went on. "And where do you live now?"

"Florida," Vince declared.

Ean lifted a bite of food from his plate and held it just in front of his mouth. "So, what does that make you?" he asked quietly before putting the bite in his mouth.

Elaina and Beth waited breathlessly for the explosion. No one ever got the best of Vince. He always had a comeback. This time, though, he sat there, eyes wide and his face growing redder with each moment.

"Oh, Dad!" Beth tried to speak, but her laughter bubbled over too much.

Elaina tried, her own laughter taking her breath. "You really kinda asked for that, Vince."

And soon, all four were laughing heartily. Elaina had fallen in love with this new man, too. She could see the way Beth looked at him, and was happy to see Ean look at her daughter with such love and kindness. His boys were so polite. Boys for sure, but they listened when they were told something.

The next March Beth and Ean married. She and Vince hadn't been there, because they just weren't able to travel, but she heard all about it. They included all three boys in the ceremony, along with their best friends. They were already attending a church regularly and had the boys involved there, too.

Chapter 55

Here she was, sixty-three years old and they were moving again, this time to Tennessee. Partly to be near their daughter and partly to get out of this place. It was so different now, a horrid rat race. They were both tired of it. The Allendale they had moved to had quite a bit of rural area and little traffic except out by the theme park, but now traffic had taken over the entire county. She was ready to leave. She loved the area where Beth and Ean lived and hoped they could find a nice house to rent.

"Ho, ho!" She heard his voice as he came in the back door.

"Hey, I'm in the kitchen," she called.

"Wow, you've got a lot done today," Vince declared, leaning down to kiss her on the cheek. "Do you think we'll get it all done by next weekend? The kids are flying down to help us get moved."

"I think so, if you'll help me this weekend. We have to decide what we're taking out of the sheds."

"Are you ready to get out of here, Mama?" Vince asked, sliding his arms around her.

Looking up at him she said, "I sure am. I'll miss Wally's family, but I'm not going to miss this place. I mean, I'm going to miss our house here. It's been our home for a good long time. Our first real home. But I'm not going to miss all the traffic and crowds. It's gotten crazy over the last twenty-something years!"

"You've done so much today, do you want to go to town and get some supper?" he asked.

"Oh, yes! I sure do!" she replied happily. "Let me wash my hands and I'll be ready to go in a flash."

"Well, I'd really like to get a shower before we go," Vince chuckled.

"Well, okay. You go shower and I'll work a little longer in here. Then when you get done, I'll wash up and we'll get going." Did she sound as eager as she felt? She had been wrapped up in memories all day long and she was tired, ready to move to real life again.

They chose to go to the local fish joint where they enjoyed all-you-can-eat catfish, hush puppies, fries, and slaw. It was almost as good as they had had living near the Everglades.

"I might miss this place," she told Vince.

"Yeah, me too. We might have to come back sometime this next week since we won't have it for a while."

"Oh, that would be nice." She smiled at him across the table before drinking more of her sweet tea. "I wish we had a place to move into when we get up there."

"That would be nice, but Ean and Beth have invited us to stay with them until we find a place. Hopefully it won't take too long and we can get out of their hair."

"What do you say we go see Wally and Mary this weekend? We could have a good visit and swing by to see the younger Koebners on the way back home. Kind of a good-bye trip," Vince suggested.

Elaina thought a moment and answered, "We've got so much to pack up yet, Vince. I guess we could, I just want to be sure we have everything done when the kids get here next Friday. Ean won't have more than the weekend to help us before he has to get to work, and it will take a whole day to drive up there."

On the way home from supper they discussed the logistics of a trip to see family before their leaving, and decided instead to invite them to join them at their house. Once home they placed the phone calls, asking the family to come and visit. All were happy to do just that, but not over the weekend. Plans were made for them to gather the next Thursday night to load the truck they were going to rent. Vince seemed relieved to know he would have the men to help him load the furniture, and Elaina was excited to have the women and the little girl just to be there. They both agreed that this would be the hardest part of moving away.

As Vince talked to his nephew, the boy who was 16 when she found out Vince had a family, Elaina thought about how they loved his little girl so much. Jon had married a lovely woman named Linda and their daughter was like her own granddaughter. Linda's mother had gotten angry over some sleight and walked away from her daughter and her family, so Elaina and Vince had stepped in. They had spent a lot of time loving on that family. It was good they only lived a little over an hour from them. She and Vince missed Beth and her family, so this helped them, too. It was nothing for her to talk with Linda once a week and visit them in person at least once a month.

"I probably know Linda better than I know my own daughter," Elaina thought out loud. "We'll still be able to talk on the phone, and maybe they'll come up for a visit to the mountains. I hope so."

While Vince talked, she turned on the television and sat back in her rocker, mapping out in her mind the packing to be accomplished in the coming days.

"What flight are they on?" Vince asked again as they entered the airport terminal.

Elaina told him again, and they looked on the arrivals board to determine if Ean and Beth's flight was on time. It was and the arrival time was only about fifteen minutes away.

"They weren't going to check any suitcases, were they?" Vince asked.

"No, they weren't. We should just find a place along this hallway where they'll come in." Elaina pointed to a row of chairs that were empty and faced the direction of the gates where passengers were hurrying from airplanes.

They sat, though Vince jumped up every few minutes to check the board again. Finally, almost fifteen minutes later, he returned from the board and said, "The plane has landed. It's here."

Elaina looked at her watch and laughed. "Just like it said, huh?" Vince was just so excited.

"There they are!" he fairly shouted as the two walked toward them.

"There's my girl!" Elaina said as she hugged Beth while Vince shook Ean's hand.

They went to a fast food restaurant for a quick supper, then bedded down on pallets at the house. Elaina had laid them out, as Vince and Wally were loading the last bit of furniture in the truck. In the morning, they would roll up these two beds and throw them into the car's back seat. Everything was coming together for this move to actually happen. They had signed the papers on the house. It was sold and now they would receive payments each month for the next twenty years.

The next day their little caravan wound its way to Tennessee, finally arriving at Ean and Beth's house late in the evening. Everyone was tired and bedtime was immediate, once Elaina got to hug Timothy and his stepbrothers.

The first week, they looked at the ads in the newspaper for houses to rent. Nothing seemed right. Almost every house they looked at had brown paneling and Vince nixed it flatly. It even became a point of laughter. Beth would walk into a house and see something brown and turn around as if to leave, saying, "Nope, it's too brown," and they would all laugh.

The second week they were living with Ean and Beth, Vince woke up in the middle of the night. He called to her from the bathroom.

"Elaina, come help!" Instant fear washed over her as she stumbled down the hallway to the bathroom.

"What's going on?" she asked.

"I'm passing blood." He pointed to the toilet, where she saw dark blood mixed into the water.

"Oh, Vince! Let's get you to the hospital!" she cried softly, so as not to wake their two grandsons right behind the door next to them.

"I'm not going to the hospital. I'll be fine. I just want you to get me back to the bed."

"Mom? Dad? What's going on?" Beth stood in the hallway.

"Your daddy is passing blood and he won't go to the emergency room."

Rubbing her eyes, Beth asked her father, "Why not, Dad?"

"Oh, it's nothing. Probably a hemorrhoid or something. I just feel weak and want your mama to help me back to bed."

"Was it bright or dark?" she asked like a nurse.

"Dark," Elaina replied.

"Dad, get dressed. You're going to the emergency room."

"I am not. I'm going back to bed." Vince turned toward their bedroom.

Beth stepped back to her bedroom and Elaina could hear voices. In just a moment, Ean walked up to them.

"Vince, you're going to the emergency room," he declared.

"No, I'm not. I am not!" Vince stated forcefully. Elaina worried that he simply wouldn't listen and something worse would happen.

"Vince, this is how it's going to be. I'm going back in my room to get dressed. When I'm dressed, you're going to the car if I have to carry you. You just have to decide if you're going to be dressed when you go or go in your boxers." Ean and Beth turned back toward their room.

"I reckon he means that, doesn't he?" Vince said. Ean usually called him and Elaina 'Grandma' and 'Grandpa'. Since he didn't this time, he must really be serious.

"I'm getting dressed," Elaina said as she walked into their bedroom, and Vince followed her and pulled on a pair of dungarees.

The diagnosis was that he had been bleeding internally, but it wasn't so severe as to require surgery of any kind. He was told to not take aspirin or ibuprofen again, as it thinned his blood too much.

While he rested the next day, Elaina took on the job of doing all the laundry for the household. She rather enjoyed this task. She could quickly see the value of her labor. The boys were having fun in the back yard. They had a trampoline that all three boys loved. The youngest, Larry, popped through the door. The eight-year-old breathlessly told her he was going to the bathroom. He slid through the kitchen wearing his socks. As he rushed back toward the back door, Elaina stopped him. She had just folded up a load of boys' socks and underwear.

"Larry, you need to take off your socks before you walk through the grass."

"But Grandma, I need them on to jump on the trampoline."

"But Larry, you're turning your socks green from walking through the yard in them. I'm not doing another load of laundry because you choose to destroy your socks. Take them off."

As she spoke, his eyes grew wide and he finally bent over and removed his socks. "There you go! You can put them back on when you get on the trampoline. Thank you," she said soothingly.

"Yes, Grandma," the boy said as he sprang through the back door.

Elaina knew that having two extra people living in her home was wearing on Beth. She remembered when her own mother and brother had stayed with her and Vince, and when Maddie had stayed with them for several months. It was never actually bad, but it was different, so she was glad when after almost six weeks of looking they found a nice rental house near town yet in a rural setting. It was a nice brick ranch with a carport. The only thing wrong with it was the residue of cigarette smokers on the walls. Some deep cleaning would take care of that. The rent was at the high end of their budget, but Vince planned to pick up some jobs here and there so they figured they would make it fine. At least there was no brown paneling.

Chapter 56

Early the next spring, Wally called and talked with Vince. He and Mary were planning a trip to California for his Navy reunion. The plan was to take their time getting to San Francisco for the reunion, then take their time getting home, and they wanted Vince and Elaina to go with them. It didn't take them long to agree to the trip. Elaina loved to travel, and loved traveling with Mary and Wally. She was so excited she started planning that night, looking through her atlas at the possible places they would go and the stops they could make.

"I'll have to get another camera" she murmured. "My old one doesn't take good pictures at all."

Vince laughed as he watched her mapping out their journey. "You're going to know every road between here and California, aren't you?"

"Maybe. Vince, do you realize we might get to see the Grand Canyon?" she asked, her eyes bright with excitement.

"It's just a big hole in the ground" he said, teasing her.

Ignoring her husband she went on, "And once we leave San Francisco, do you think we'll get to see the Redwoods? Maybe go up into Washington? Oregon is supposed to be so pretty and so is Washington."

"You never know," Vince said as he walked to the kitchen to get a bowl of ice cream. "If it's anything like their other trips, we'll just go till we decide to stop and then go some more."

And that's what they did. Once they left Tennessee the foursome traveled through Arkansas, Oklahoma, Texas, New Mexico, and into Arizona. Along the way, they traveled easy. The only schedule they had to keep was reaching San Francisco for the reunion, and it was over two weeks away. They watched the billboards, and if they saw someplace they wanted to visit the driver turned off and visit they did.

At every hotel they stayed at, Mary and Elaina donned their swimsuits and did exercises in the pool.

"I'll never have the thin body I had when Wally and I married," Mary said, "but I feel better. I feel more limber."

"I like it," Elaina said. "As long as I can stay in the shallow end of the pool, I'm okay."

"I'm not advanced enough to do the treading water version of these, either," Mary agreed.

They were nearing Santa Fe when Elaina said, "Vince, do you remember that show we watched about that mysterious carpenter building the staircase for the nuns?"

"Yeah, I remember that. It was in Santa Fe or near it, right?"

"I think so. Let's watch for signs. That would be something to see."

All four adults were like children watching for the signs. Finally, Mary called out from the back seat, "There's one! It's Loretto Chapel and it's five miles ahead."

"All right!" Wally called out from the driver's seat, and the plan to visit was put in place.

Touring the museum and hearing the legend of the carpenter mesmerized everyone, especially Vince. Being a carpenter, he walked all around the famous staircase, examining the pegs closely and trying to work out how the staircase could have been built with no supports.

"He was a much better carpenter than me," Vince declared as they were leaving. "Where are we going to eat?"

Laughing at Vince's fast turn to food, the four got into the van and headed for the Bull Ring Restaurant they'd seen signs for. After hearty steaks, the group drove on down the highway and found a place to stop for the night. The next morning found them on the road to the Grand Canyon. Though none of them wanted to go rafting or ride the burros down the narrow paths in the canyon, they oohed and aahed over the vast beauty, and of course took plenty of pictures.

Despite their stops and starts, they made it to the reunion in plenty of time and enjoyed a wonderful dinner and party. Vince was able to reminisce with the other sailors, though most of them were several years younger than him. Elaina watched him talking first with this group then that. He was treated almost like royalty, having the distinction of being at Omaha Beach on D-Day. She and Mary visited with some of the other wives there. Mary knew quite a few from previous reunions, and they enjoyed catching up.

When she crawled into bed that night, Elaina said, "That was a nice gathering, don't you think?"

"It was a nice dinner," Vince replied. "Wally sure is well-respected among these fellows."

"Mary, too. I mean, among the wives. She seems to know everyone and is loved by most all of them."

"I'm proud of my little brother. He's done real well for himself."

Patting his hand, Elaina said, "You've got reason to be proud of yourself, too. Don't forget that. We may not have all the money that Mary and Wally have, but we have our daughter and each other, and money can't buy that."

Rolling over, Vince wrapped his wife up in his arms. "You're right, 'Laina. I'm the richest man in the world."

The rest of the journey included Oregon and Washington, Idaho, and a jaunt into Montana. Vince had been to every state except that one, so Wally made sure to route them through it.

They were astounded that in June they were warned that they might need snow chains in Yosemite, but they ventured on and thankfully didn't need them. They managed to drive up the mountains and back down without a problem. They saw snow, but the roads were in good shape.

They had just left South Dakota and were spending the night in a little family motel. Elaina decided she would call Beth to check in with her. When Ean answered the phone, he told her that Beth had had emergency gall bladder surgery earlier in the week. He assured her that everything was fine and that Beth was going back to work on Monday.

"Less than a week after surgery? Is she crazy?" Elaina asked her son-in-law, recalling her own gall bladder surgery almost thirty years ago.

"I think she'll be okay. She came home from the hospital the day after the surgery. She's getting around here pretty good."

"I'm not sure, Ean..." Her voice trailed off.

"I talked to the doctor, Grandma. He said that since she works in an office, she can go back. She just can't lift or anything. The moving around should actually do her some good."

"Well, okay. Do I need to get on home?" she asked.

"I don't think so. We're doing okay. You and the old folks have a good time and we'll see you when you get back. I hope you're taking lots of pictures!"

Elaina laughed. "You know I am!"

Once they were back home Elaina took her film to be processed, dreading the cost, but excited to see the photographic memories of this trip. She and Vince relived the vacation as they put the pictures in albums.

Chapter 57

Several weeks later after church on a Sunday, Elaina and Vince sat at the table with Beth and her family at a local restaurant. The boys were shooting straw papers at one another and trying to top each other's stories about who knew what. She could never keep up.

Ean and Vince were talking and Beth was laughing.

"Did I miss something?" she asked.

Ean said, "Oh, I was just reminding Grandpa what he said that day we left your house in Florida."

"What did he say?" She looked at her husband. "I must have been in the car already, I missed it."

"Do you want to tell her or shall I?" Ean's grin was broad and he barely held back his laughter.

"Oh, just tell her," Vince growled.

"That morning when we left your place in Florida, Grandpa came up to the big truck. I was ready to pull out when he grabbed the door of the truck open. Like to have scared me to death!"

Elaina looked at Beth, who sat with her chin on her hand as though hearing the story for the first time, but her eyes dancing with the merriment of memory.

"I looked down at him, 'cause I was sitting up in the truck." Elaina nodded.

"And he says to me, 'I'm going to Tennessee, but I'm not going to be at church all the time like you are.'" Ean imitated his father-in-law's gruff voice.

"Oh!" Elaina laughed, "and now we're there all the time, and he's the one pushing me to get ready to get there!"

By now the boys had joined in picking on Grandpa, and the object of the teasing beamed. He enjoyed his family and loved being the center of attention.

Once their meal was over and they headed to their vehicles, Vince called out to Ean, "So, are you going to be there tonight?" Everyone laughed exuberantly.

Elaina thought about this as they drove home. Vince never had wanted to go to church. He had balked and fought her when Beth got saved and wanted to attend church as a teen. Some of their biggest arguments had come when Beth had wanted to attend the Christian school. Now it didn't matter what was going on at the church, Vince was there. He came down and helped with maintenance projects around the building and he visited with the pastor at least once a month, taking him to lunch for a chat.

Her son-in-law was right. A change had occurred, but she didn't think it was funny. She thought it was a miracle. She knew that the church school of his youth was hard and the church of his youth was unrelenting. She knew that the pastor of the big church he had been attending when he and his second wife divorced had recommended that he find another church since Ellen was still attending there. She knew the scars of his heart, though they had never really discussed them. It had taken a long time for Vince to let go of those hurts and return to church for the right reasons.

Come to think of it, it took a while for me to get back on the right track with church and church people, she thought.

She had made sure that Beth attended summer church events when they lived in Tomoka, and they had attended Sunday School there for a brief time, especially on Easter. But she never really got into the church, just went and sat in the pew and then left. It was their daughter who drew her back.

A friend of Beth's had invited her to a youth rally on a Saturday night and they had agreed to let her go. She spent the night with that friend and went to church with her family the next day. After the second or third youth rally, she started wanting to go to church every week. With them living almost thirty minutes from the church she grudgingly decided to stay and attend, too. She was surprised that day when the pastor had those wanting salvation to come to the front and Beth made that walk. She saw the youth director's wife sit down beside her daughter and talk with her.

"I never could have done that," Elaina thought out loud. "I could have told her everything about God and Jesus and she never would have listened."

That night Vince went to church with them, choosing not to miss his daughter's baptism. Elaina noticed that in even that short time, there was a change in the girl. She still had a strong will, but the nervousness seemed gone. She didn't seem to cower when a storm came along or in situations where she didn't really know what to do.

Now, as a woman, her daughter was a force to be reckoned with. She was leading a group of teen girls in a missions group, teaching them about God and serving others. She was involved in the women's group at the church, too, even leading the Wednesday night service sometimes. Elaina felt overwhelmed, realizing how this had worked out.

I ran away from God when my family chose Grant over me, and I never really wanted to go back, not like every Sunday back, but now, I love God. And I love going to church and I love seeing my husband and my daughter involved in church.

"Thank you, God," she murmured.

"What?" Vince asked.

"Just thinking, honey. Did you really say that to Ean? That you weren't going to be at church?"

"Yeah, maybe," he replied.

She giggled softly. "God kinda changed that, didn't He?"

"Yeah. I guess He did."

Later that week, Elaina met up with her best friend Janice at the church. They had a special room in the basement of the multipurpose building where they created ceramic items. There were others who joined them at times, but usually it was just the two of them. Working with her hands helped the arthritis pain seem less, and she liked painting the little characters as gifts for people. Most of all, though, she enjoyed that time alone with Janice when they could talk about everything. They held nothing back, they both knew the other's secrets, and they were both fine with that. They trusted each other immensely.

"Do you think you'd like to make a little side money?" Janice asked her, painting the angel candle holder.

"Doing what?" Elaina asked.

"Working with me."

"Doing what?" Elaina drew out the same words.

"Down at the bank. You know," Janice replied, holding her paint brush up in the air and pointing it toward the bank's main office just up the road.

"What would I be doing?"

"We sort through the checks that go into the bank statements and make sure that the right checks go with the right statements. Can't be letting John Doe's checks go out in Joe Smith's statement, you know."

"I might like to give it a try. Is it hard? How often do you do it? How long does it take?"

"Whoa, girl! One at a time. I can't think that far and fast."

"Ha! You're one of the smartest women I know!" Elaina intoned.

"Well, maybe. Anyway, no. It's not hard. You look at the name on the statement, you see what the check number range is supposed to be, and you make sure that's all that's going in that envelope. There's about half a dozen of us doing this."

Nodding, Elaina asked, "How often?"

"Well, bank statements only go out once a month."

"Oh, yeah. Right. How long does it take? I mean, like, how many hours a day and how many days?"

"Right now, it takes us about six hours a day for a week. If you come in, it will take fewer hours a day. We've got plenty of work, though."

Elaina chose to join the team of women working one week a month to sort out bank statements. She knew she wasn't going to get rich doing it, but it enabled her to have some running around money that she didn't have to ask Vince for. The sting of his first trip overseas lingered unbidden in the back of her mind.

Chapter 58

Vince and Elaina's grandson Timothy was away at the Air Force boot camp in San Antonio, Texas. They had learned that his graduation would be the first Friday in September, just five weeks away. When Beth told her about it, she was so excited to go see her boy grown into a man in his shining moment.

Beth had tried repeatedly to get her daddy to go with them to see Timothy graduate, but the thought that his daughter's ex-husband might be there led him to refuse. The reason he gave everyone was that they couldn't afford it, though she knew the truth. He had asked Beth if Tim would be there and she had told him she didn't know, but since he was the boy's father he very well could be.

"That settles it," Vince declared.

"Settles what?" Elaina looked up from her word search puzzle.

"We're not going to San Antonio."

"We're not?" She tried to keep her voice pleasant, but she wasn't giving in on this one.

"It's pretty likely that man will be there and I'm not going to grace him with my presence. I'm just not," he said gruffly.

"Well, aren't you all high and mighty? You'll run from him instead of standing for your grandson? You know that Air Force base is a big one. You don't have to be with him."

"Elaina, we're not going and that's that."

Elaina threw her puzzle book down and stood. Her face was flushed as she faced her husband. "Well Mr. Koebner, *you* may not be going, but *I* will be. There is nothing that is going to stop me from supporting our grandson. You and I have missed out on *everything* in our other kids' lives and in all our grandchildren's lives. I am *not* missing this one. I *will* be going to San Antonio to support my daughter and my grandson. If you want to sit here and be sour, that's *your* choice. Don't expect me to support you in it. I won't."

She walked into their bedroom and slammed the door. Elaina's heart was broken. Vince didn't want anything to do with their grandson's big accomplishment because of the young man's father. She couldn't understand that. Thankfully, she had enough of her own money saved up that he couldn't tell her that she couldn't go.

The next day Beth called. She had found an inexpensive flight for the three of them, Beth, Ean and her mother, as well as a rental car and a fancy hotel for pennies. The cost wasn't bad, but it didn't matter. She was going to be there for her grandson.

The trip was a dream, except that the airline lost their luggage. Fortunately, Beth had told her to pack her medicines and night clothes in her carry-on bag. They stopped at a store after supper and picked up some underthings and clothing to wear to the graduation. She washed out her unmentionables in the sink and hung them to dry before bed, evoking memories of being a child at home.

Elaina clapped as her grandson paraded by with his unit, marching along so proud. After the graduation, they had met up with Timothy's wife and father. Elaina thought that maybe it was a good thing Vince hadn't come. He would have made a fool of himself and embarrassed his family. She wasn't surprised that Beth and Ean invited Tim to ride with them to the Base Exchange for lunch. It was almost 100 degrees in San Antonio, even though it was barely eleven o'clock. With the BX about a mile away, her daughter insisted that her ex-husband ride with them. Beth knew Tim had had heart surgery, and didn't need to be walking in that heat. Elaina's heart swelled with pride, knowing her daughter was past the things that Tim had done. Or if not past it, she was coping and treating him as a friend, not a foe.

They spent the afternoon walking around downtown San Antonio. They walked to the Alamo. She was surprised that it was actually pretty small, and the city had grown up all around it. Even so, she could still see John Wayne fighting the battle. They rode the boat on the Riverwalk and shopped. Beth kept asking her if she wanted to sit down a while. Of course not! She wanted to spend every moment she could with Timothy and her family. She wasn't about to miss out on anything.

In the weeks following the trip, problems had risen over the fact that Vince had bought a new truck just before the trip. It was a used one, but it cost him almost ten thousand dollars. When Beth heard that, she was livid. When Vince said he couldn't understand why she was so angry, why she wouldn't even talk to him, Elaina would just shake her head.

"It sounds like you had a great trip, Mom," Doreen said.

"It was good. It was hotter than Arkansas down there," Elaina replied.

Hearing her daughter laugh was such a gift. "That's mighty hot!" she said.

Elaina went on to describe what they had seen and what the graduation had been like. When she grew quiet, Doreen posed a question.

"Mom, do you think you could send letters and cards to Seth's wife?"

"What?"

"I've talked to Kate. She and I think that maybe if you send letters and cards to her and the kids, she can read them to him and you can prove to him that you're still here, and that you love him."

"Of course I can send letters and cards! Do you have their address?"

"I do." She read the address off and Elaina carefully wrote it down. "Oh, and Mom?"

"Yes, dear?"

"He doesn't go by Seth anymore. He goes by Aaron."

"Thank you, Doreen. You don't know how much I appreciate this."

"I think I do, Mom. I can't imagine what it would have been like to lose two of my kids like you did."

Once she had hung up the phone, Elaina grabbed a tablet and started writing her first letter, thanking God for Kate and her willingness to help her get to know her son.

About two months after the San Antonio trip, Elaina was folding clothes from the dryer when she heard Vince talking and realized he was on the phone. She stepped into the hallway to hear his words.

"I want to see you, Beth," she heard him say. "Come here during your lunch hour."

Oh dear, Elaina thought. *He has commanded Beth to come here during her lunch hour. What on earth is he thinking?* She finished folding the clothes, put them in their respective places, then joined her husband in the living room.

"I called Beth," he said without preamble.

"Oh?" Elaina replied, not wanting him to know she had heard him on the phone.

"I told her to get herself here while she's at lunch."

"Should I fix something for us to have?" Elaina asked.

"I don't care. I'm going to get to the bottom of this mess."

"What mess are you talking about, Vince?"

"Why she won't talk to me or have anything to do with me. What have I done that's so wrong? I'm going to get her to tell me what's eating her."

"I see," she replied simply.

"Do you know what's going on?" he growled.

"I have a good idea."

"Well, what the hell is it?"

"Your daughter is as stubborn as you, honey, and she's mad that you didn't go to Timothy's boot camp graduation. You said you didn't have the money to go, then you went out and spent ten grand on a truck. She's hurt and angry."

"Well, what's to be hurt about?" He shook his head. "Never mind. I'll ask her when she gets here. You just let me handle it."

"Oh, don't worry. I'm not getting in between you two Koebners."

Elaina was watching for Beth's arrival and greeted her on the front porch with a hug. She told her quietly that she loved her, then motioned her into the house. Beth sat down on the sofa after declining the offer of a glass of water.

"I'm here, Dad. What do you want to say to me?"

There would be no mincing of words today, Elaina realized. She sat down and lifted a crossword puzzle book to her lap, needing something to focus on as the storm raged.

"I want to know what the hell is going on," Vince stated flatly.

"What do you mean?" Beth sounded determined, but respectful. Elaina smiled slightly, figuring that her daughter had gotten advice from her husband about how to handle her daddy.

"I want to know why you won't talk to me. I try to call your house and everyone but you will get on the phone, and no one will get you to come to the phone."

"That's because I have told them I do not want to talk to you right now, Dad."

"Well, why is that?" he bellowed.

Elaina watched her daughter take a deep breath, close her eyes briefly, then begin to speak. "I'm angry with you, Dad. I don't want to talk to you. I don't believe that I can talk to you until I've gotten this anger under control."

"What the hell do you have to be so angry about?"

Another deep breath. "I'm angry that you lied to me, Dad," she said simply.

Vince sputtered, "I lied to you? What makes you think I lied to you?"

Visibly working to keep her tone respectful, she replied, "You told me that you didn't have enough money to go to San Antonio, a mere two hundred dollars, then you went out and spent ten thousand dollars on a truck."

"Oh, hell!" He drew the words out. "I didn't have the money for that trip. I needed the truck. It's just that simple."

"Okay. May I leave now?" his daughter asked.

"Are you talking to me again?" Vince retorted.

"Not yet. I'm still angry."

Vince sighed heavily. "I don't understand why you can't see this, Beth. I didn't lie to you. I told you I didn't want to go to San Antonio."

"I know that, Dad, then you said it was because you didn't have the money. Right after you asked if Tim would be there.

I never cared if you didn't want to go because of him. I just want you to admit that you ducked out on your grandson because of it."

Elaina tried to keep her eyes on the puzzle, tried to read the clues, but could only manage to doodle to make it look like she was busily filling in blanks. She admired her daughter's resolve today. They had talked while on the trip and she knew the hurt she bore.

"I didn't go because we didn't have the money for me to go," he reiterated.

"Dad, it was going to cost you less than two hundred dollars. That's all. One-fifty for the flight and the rest for meals."

"Well, I didn't have it."

"Yet you were able to go out and spend ten thousand for a truck."

"I need the truck."

"I understand, Dad. You're not ready to say why you didn't go, not even to yourself. I get that. May I go now?"

"No, you may not go!" he hollered, his face reddening. "I told you I didn't have the money. Why won't you believe that?"

"Because you spent ten thousand when you said you didn't have two hundred. That's a significant difference, Dad."

"Well, I didn't have to pay the whole ten thousand!" he declared.

"I understand that, but you had to borrow that, and you chose to not add two hundred dollars to the loan so that you could go and see your only grandson graduate from the hardest thing he's ever done. You lied to me, Dad. You lied to Mom. You lied to Ean and you lied to Timothy. The worst thing is that you're lying to yourself and you don't even know it."

Vince sat back as he threw up his hands. "You just won't listen."

"I guess not, Dad. Now, I have to leave. I have to get my lunch and take it back to my desk and I have to get myself together before I go and do that." Rising, she walked to her mother and kissed her on the cheek. "I still love you, Dad. That's not changed. I'm very angry, though, and it's best if I don't talk with you and visit with you right now. Once I get calmed down, you'll see me like before."

With that Beth turned and walked out the door.

Once the door closed, Elaina looked at him, "Well, do you feel better now?"

"She's such a stubborn, hard-headed woman. I don't get it. I didn't do anything."

"Exactly."

"What does that mean?" he asked.

"It means that you didn't do anything. You didn't go and support your daughter. You didn't support your grandson. You had the chance to be there for him, but you chose to stay home and not do anything. I think you're not going to be seeing your daughter until you figure that out, dear."

Vince rose and walked to the kitchen, then stuck his head back into the living room. "I'm going to the store. I'll be back in a while."

"Yes, dear," she replied, shaking her head. She hoped he would one day apologize to Beth but, knowing his record, she doubted that would ever happen.

Chapter 59

Elaina was excited. Timothy was getting married to his high school sweetheart in April. She and Beth didn't have much to do for the wedding, but it was exciting anyway. Timothy was in Mississippi getting more training for his career in the Air Force and would come in just in time to get married, then move to his regular duty station. He thought that was going to be in Arizona.

I wonder if I can get Vince to take a trip to Arizona once they're settled there, she thought.

She had just started supper when the phone rang. Answering it she said, "Hello?"

"Mom? It's me," her daughter say haltingly.

"Beth, what's wrong?" Her heart was in her throat. She knew this was dire news, and was scared to death.

"I just found out this afternoon that I have…" Beth took a deep breath. "Mom, I have melanoma cancer. It's stage three. There's only five stages. Mom, I'm so scared."

Elaina covered her mouth with her hand. "Oh, my," she said softly. "Are they sure?"

"Yes, ma'am. Remember that place on my ear? The one the hair stylist fussed at me about?"

"I do. I thought you had that cut off."

"I did, but the doctor sent it for testing, even though he thought it was nothing. The lab sent back that it's Stage three melanoma."

Tears rolled down her face. Hadn't Beth just been telling her the story of President Reagan's daughter having died of that cancer? Now to find out her daughter had it was too much.

"Okay Beth, what are we going to do?"

"Well, my dermatologist is sending me to a doctor who specializes in this. He actually is the best in the area on tumors of the face and neck. I'll see him early next week."

"I'm going to put you on the prayer list at church."

"That's fine, Mom. I'm sure I can use all the prayers I can get."

"How's Ean?" Elaina asked, certain he would be devastated by the news.

"He met me up at the doctor's office. He's shaken, Mom, but he's my rock. He's in there cooking supper for us and talking to the boys about it."

The two women talked a few more minutes and made plans to get together over the weekend. Nothing like a dire diagnosis to make you realize you need to spend more time together.

Finally she said, "All right, honey. I'll see you Saturday."

"See who Saturday?" Vince said from the kitchen door, kicking his muddy garden shoes off on the back porch.

"That was Beth. We're going to get together this weekend and do something."

"Is it a holiday or someone's birthday?" He looked at his wife and noticed the tears on her face. "Whoa, now! What's going on? What's wrong?"

Elaina sighed heavily. "Our girl has cancer, Vince."

"*What?*" he said, incredulous.

Elaina turned off the stove and they walked into the living room to sit down to talk. Vince turned down the television as she wiped her eyes. She explained what Beth had told her, and included that this was the same cancer that had killed the president's daughter.

Vince sat there in stunned silence for so long, then said softly, "What do we do, Mama? What do we do to fight this?"

"She's seeing a specialist next week, a guy who's the best at face and neck tumors." Her voice shook just saying the word. "He'll help her decide what to do. If it's bad enough, I guess she'll have to have chemo or radiation or whatever else they do."

"She won't like losing her hair!" Vince laughed.

"No, she sure wouldn't like that," she agreed.

"Have you called the prayer chain?" he asked.

"No, you came in and I've been talking to you."

Vince nodded. "How about I call and get that done and you finish up supper so we can eat before it's too late." How he knew her. Getting her to working with her hands would help ease her mind. She just loved this man she was growing old with.

They went into the mountains on Saturday, something everyone enjoyed. The boys, being mostly grown with things of their own to do, declined, but the adults enjoyed the crisp air and relaxing atmosphere. They cooked lunch and supper there, then drove around the loop road looking for animals.

Beth's appointment was Tuesday and Elaina was on pins and needles all day. Ean was going with her so he could learn everything at the same time and support Beth. When the phone finally rang that evening, Elaina snatched it up.

"Beth? Is that you?"

She heard giggles as her daughter answered, "Yes, Mom, it's me. Are you okay?"

"I might be a mite nervous. Did you go to the doctor?"

"Yes, ma'am. I did."

"What did he say?"

"He said it's best if I have surgery."

"Okay, what kind of surgery?"

"Well, they like to remove a certain amount of flesh according to the size of the tumor. For me that means they want to take about a third of my ear."

"Oh," Elaina said softly.

"He said they could just take the whole ear off and put in these pins and I could use a prosthetic ear."

"Like a wooden leg, except for your ear?"

"Exactly. I told him no on that, Mom. I said, 'I can't even remember to put earrings in, how would I remember to put my ear on?'" Elaina joined her daughter in her peals of laughter.

"Did he think you'll need chemo?"

"He's not sure. They won't know for sure until they know if it's gone inside to my lymph nodes. He can do a test while he's working on my ear. They'll inject a radioactive dye in the place of the tumor and follow where it goes. They'll take that lymph node while I'm still in surgery and test it. If there's no cancer cells, they stop right there. If there are cancer cells, they go to the next node and so on until they find one free of cancer. That way they only take out the lymph nodes that are necessary instead of all of them across my face and down my neck."

"Oh, my. I didn't realize that was a possibility."

"Me neither. But I did do some research since I found out last week. I wanted to know the latest treatments, so I asked him about it today. He seemed impressed that I knew about that, and really willing to do it that way. I really like this doctor, Mom. When we were talking about all this, he lifted his shirt up and showed us his scar where he had melanoma removed."

"Wow! So he really knows how you're feeling and what's coming up for you."

"Yeah, that made a big difference for me. I don't feel as nervous now."

"That's good. So, when's your surgery?"

"I talked to him about that. We've got two weeks before Timothy's wedding. I'm not going to be wearing bandages for that." Elaina started to interrupt, but Beth stopped her. "No, Mom. I asked him. The cancer is basically removed. The dermatologist took it off. Since it's not there, he doesn't see major risk in waiting for the wedding. So, I'll have surgery the following Tuesday."

"Are you sure?"

"Yes, Mom. You know Ean would have me in there tomorrow if the doctor thought it was risky."

"Okay, okay. Then we'll worry about celebrating Timothy getting married and then about you getting well."

"That's about it. Do you want me to tell Dad or are you okay to do it?"

"I'll take care of it. He'll be happy to hear the doctor isn't really worried about it."

"Love you, Mom. Talk later!" Beth hung up and Elaina breathed a sigh of relief. She really believed her daughter would be okay, that they had gotten all of the tumor the first time. They just needed to go through this part to be sure. Nodding, she scooted to the edge of her chair and slipped her shoes on to walk outside where Vince was busy tilling the garden. As soon as he saw her, he turned off the machine and came over. In a few moments, she shared all Beth had said and they both cried a few tears of relief.

"I think that news calls for supper out," he declared. "Let me finish up here and we'll go get a bite."

"I'm not going to argue with that."

Chapter 60

It was a pretty Saturday afternoon and the church was decorated simply. Timothy looked spectacular in his tuxedo and his bride wore the prettiest princess dress. It wasn't a typical wedding dress, but it was beautiful. Beth looked beautiful in her sunny yellow skirt and blouse. Vince wore his best brown suit and she wore one of her navy blue church dresses. She felt a little frumpy, as she had put on quite a bit of weight, but she was so happy for her grandson that it didn't matter.

With all the ruckus over the trip to San Antonio last year, Elaina was a little leery about today. She assumed that Tim would be there. It wasn't every day that one's son got married.

It wasn't until after the wedding that she saw him, sitting in the pew behind her and Vince, though at the other end. He was wearing a pair of old blue jeans and a faded button-down shirt.

Did he not realize this was a wedding? she thought. *What kind of memory is that for his son and new daughter-in-law?*

She felt a hand on her arm and turned to see her own daughter. "He came in just before the bride," she whispered. "He said he didn't even know what time it was supposed to be. What a lie! I called and left a message for him last week so he would know to be here for the rehearsal and the wedding pictures!" Beth hissed, her anger apparent.

Elaina set aside her own anger and patted Beth's hand. Smiling brightly, she said, "Focus on Timothy. Only him. Don't let his father sidetrack you."

Vince bumped her with his elbow and grunted. She nodded to him. They would talk about this later in the car. For now, she would smile her prettiest and work to make her grandson's day the best ever.

Within the week, the newlyweds were gone. They had left on their way to Phoenix, Arizona where Timothy would be a meteorologist. She was so proud of that boy. He could do anything he set his mind to. She remembered telling him that all through the years. He would sit on her lap as a toddler and she would ruffle the hair on his neck and tell him how smart and how kind he was. When he got too big to sit on her lap he would sit in the floor in front of her chair, just to have Grandma play with his hair.

"Sweet, sweet memories," she murmured.

Two years later, Elaina's day was interrupted with good news.

"Well, Mom, you're going to be a great-grandmother." Beth stated matter-of-factly.

"Oh! Timothy and his wife are pregnant?"

"Nope. Ean's Tim and his girlfriend are expecting. It was so funny, Mom. Ean and I were thinking there was something up, but they never told us anything. Then, while we were in Florida last week, Tim called us to tell us." She laughed. "Ean said he was afraid to tell us when we were in the same county."

Elaina chuckled. "Well, I wish they had gotten married first, but I can't wait to meet this baby and call you Grandma!"

"Ha! I know. As smart as Tim is and as pretty as Tabitha is, this little one will be amazing. I can't wait!"

The next June, both women got their wish. Tabitha had a beautiful baby boy with huge eyes surrounded by long lashes like his daddy. And Tim was so proud they could hardly stand him.

Vince said after the new family had left the house, "That boy's head barely fit through the front door, he's so proud of that baby."

"He's got a right to be proud! Do you remember how he used to be? This girl has made such a turnaround in him. She's helped him get his head straight, and now that he's a dad I think it will do him even more good."

"Yeah, I thought he wasn't going to make it back then. I tried telling him some things when he lived here with us those few months, but he knew it all and didn't want to listen. I guess now he might remember some of what I told him. He seems to be doing really good as a block mason. That should take care of them pretty good. Probably better than we had it when Beth was born."

The new great-grandparents talked on into the evening, admiring the Polaroid photos Tabitha had left them.

"That dementia stuff is horrible!" Elaina complained to Vince, angrily swiping a wisp of hair from her face.

"What are you talking about?" he asked.

"Janice. You know she has dementia. She's had it for a while, but now she doesn't even know me. Some days when I go to see her she doesn't even know how to use a fork or spoon." She flopped down on the sofa with an exasperated sigh. "It started out with simple things like not remembering where her car was or thinking that her portable phone was supposed to have a cord. Now she's over in that nursing home and can't take care of herself. I hate it!"

Vince nodded. "I hate it for her, too, 'Laina. Janice was always such a feisty woman. No one could get the best of her. Smart and strong. I'm sure it hurts you a lot to see her this way now."

"It does. It really, really does. I'm not sure I can go back there, Vince. I just don't know."

"You don't have to, 'Laina. Maybe go back once to say goodbye. You might let her daughter know you can't do it anymore. Isn't Beth friends with her son?"

"Yeah, I know I don't have to, but she's my friend, Vince. I can't just abandon her. I'm a big girl. I can handle the hurt."

Elaina continued her biweekly visits, sitting and chatting with Janice as best she could. She didn't try to bring up things they had shared, as it seemed to distress her friend. Instead, they would watch television together and sometimes she would read a book to Janice. Many times, if she was there at lunchtime she was able to help her friend eat. If she helped, more of the food went inside her.

Then, the sad day came. Elaina got the phone call that her partner in crime had passed away.

"It's really for the best," she told her husband. "Now she won't be fretting and furious all at once. She's at peace now, finally back with her husband." Even so, Elaina's heart was breaking. She had never had such a close friend and now she had lost her. She walked to the bedroom. She needed a good old-fashioned cry right now.

Chapter 61

"Oh my goodness!" Elaina squealed.

"What?" Vince asked, waking from a nap. Watching baseball games seemed to always set him to snoozing.

"We just got an invitation to Suzanne's wedding."

"Suzanne? Who's Suzanne?"

"Aaron's daughter. You know, my son Seth?"

"That's nice. When is she getting married?"

"In January. That's just a couple months away. Oh, I'd love to go. That might be the only chance I have to talk with Seth I just can't get used to calling him Aaron."

"Well, where is it? Don't they live in Dallas?"

"They live in Dallas, but the wedding is in Tahoe."

"Oh. I'm not sure we can do that. We could drive to Dallas, but that's a mighty long trip."

"I know. I'm just dreaming. It would be nice to see him face to face and tell him I've always loved him."

That afternoon, Elaina called Beth and told her about the invitation. Then a few hours later Beth called back with flight reservation numbers, a rental car reservation, and suggestions on a hotel.

"Wait, Beth. I can't afford to pay this!" she cried.

"That's the good thing about it, Mom. You don't have to." Elaina felt tears begin to roll down her cheeks.

"You can't afford it, either," she scolded softly.

"Ean said we could. I'm sorry I can't afford to pay for the hotel, too, but you guys will have to take care of that. I've got you landing in Reno. That means you'll have a drive of about an hour to get to the wedding."

"That shouldn't be too bad. Oh Beth, this is so amazing! I just hope that Seth isn't mad and will let me talk to him. I mean, I know we can't talk about the past a lot, but I hope I can get him to hear me that I've never stopped loving him and Doreen. She said that Claudia told him the truth, but he still didn't really believe it. What his father said to him as a little boy seems to have really stuck."

"We'll just be praying for that, Mom. That he'll let you love on him and hear the truth."

"Thank you, baby." Elaina hung up the phone and told Vince they were going to a wedding.

"We're what?"

"Ean and Beth have paid for our flight and rental car to Reno. All we'll have to pay is our hotel and food, and she said she can get a hotel pretty cheap. It's only an hour drive from there to where the wedding is."

"Huh. Well, you women have this all worked out."

"We sure do. Are you about ready for some pizza?"

Elaina sat next to a snoozing Vince on their flight home, having enjoyed their trip to see her granddaughter get married.

Elaina thought it had been a beautiful wedding, right on the shore of the lake. She had never seen mountains so high, snow so deep, or water so blue. And her son. She had known him immediately when he walked into the room before the wedding, even after fifty years. Her heart almost broke just seeing him, the emotions of all those wasted years overwhelming her. Vince had kept his hand on her back, his touch reminding her he was right there with her. She closed her eyes as she recalled their meeting.

"Hello, Aaron," she said, mindful to use his first name.

"Hello, Mother."

"It's so good to see you. Everything looks so beautiful."

"That's all Kate and Suzanne. They had pictures in their minds of what they wanted. All I had to do was pay for it," he chuckled.

Elaina and Vince laughed with him, then she said, "This is Vince, Aaron."

"Good to meet you," the younger man said as they shook hands.

Elaina took a deep breath and, before she lost her courage, said, "Do you think we might have a few minutes to talk, Aaron?"

"I'm not sure, Mother. I have to be wherever they tell me, but I suppose we could talk some right now. Let's sit down."

Vince held the chair for his wife to sit down in, then stepped away from the two so they could speak privately.

Elaina's eyes were teary as she started, "I just wanted to—I want to" She sighed deeply. "I want to apologize to you."

"What for? You didn't do anything, did you? Mom told me all about the divorce and stuff."

"I didn't fight for you and your sister like I should have. I don't know what I could have done, but even when your father wouldn't let me talk to you on the phone I could have come to the house and stood on the sidewalk until you and Doreen saw me. At least you would have known that I wanted to be near you."

"I don't know. I think Dad would have told us that as you were crazy or had you arrested or something."

"He might have, but…"

"Besides, didn't you have a baby to take care of?"

"I did. Your sister, Abigail Jeanette."

"I was so little, I don't really remember. Just what Dad said about why you weren't there anymore. Uh-oh. There's the wedding boss. I bet I'm supposed to be somewhere right now. It really is good to see you, Mother. I'd like to talk more, but it's going to get hectic pretty quickly here and I really don't want it to take away from Suzanne's wedding."

"Absolutely not. Would you let her know I'm here and that I love her so much?"

"I will." He rose and started to turn away.

"And Aaron?" Elaina said softly, causing him to stop and turn back to her. "I love you so much, too. I always have." He nodded then walked through the door, leaving her sitting there wiping her eyes.

Elaina smiled, recalling those moments, thinking how wonderful it had been to talk with him. Maybe now she could send him letters directly. Maybe.

Chapter 62

"Hey, 'Laina!" Vince called out as he walked through the back door.

"I'm hanging clothes!" she called back to him.

Elaina heard his footsteps come through the house hurriedly and wondered what had him all upset.

"I was just talking to the landlady."

"That's nice. How is she?"

"She's fine, except her nephew has convinced her to sell everything and move into an assisted living place."

"Assisted living? She's far too independent for that, and she doesn't have any physical issues."

"I know, I know, but he's got her convinced that's the best, so she's going along with it. That means she's selling this place."

Elaina carried their clothes to the bedroom closet and hung them there. Turning to her husband she asked quietly, "What does that mean for us?"

"It means we need to find a place. She's selling all her rentals. All of them."

"Can we just buy this one?" After living in the little bungalow-style house for almost seventeen years, she didn't relish leaving it. At eighty-one, she didn't relish moving again at all.

"That would be nice, not having to leave our home. We've lived here longer than just about anywhere."

"Maybe Ean and Beth can give us some advice. Remember how when Beth first started working up here, she learned how to trace down deeds and such?" Elaina mentioned.

Vince moved to the living room to place the call as Elaina put up the rest of the clean laundry. This was still her favorite chore and she loved seeing it completed.

"Well," Beth began, "the first thing the current owner needs to do is provide you with a survey of the property they're selling. As far as I can tell, there's no deed for this place."

"No deed?" Vince asked.

"It's what they call an orphan property, Dad," she explained. "They had a big piece of property and they cut this piece off and that piece off and another over here, leaving this one. Best I can tell, though, there's nothing that tells exactly what this piece of property is or where the lines for it lay."

"Huh. Well, why don't you call the real estate guy and talk to him about it. You've got our power of attorney. You can do all that, right?"

"I can. I'll call him first thing in the morning."

The next afternoon, the real estate agent met them at the house. Beth had brought along her good friend who had a lot of experience in deeds and properties, having worked a number of years for a manufactured housing conglomerate.

Elaina marveled at the way Beth handled herself talking with the man, speaking his language and drawing out truth that he didn't really want to tell. That afternoon, walking along the fence between them and their neighbors, it was easy to see that a sliver of the land that belonged to the property they were looking to buy was built on by their neighbors.

"That will have to be rectified in the legal description before anything can be done with this property," Beth stated.

"I don't know," the agent drawled. "I'm not sure the owner wants to pay for a survey or new deed."

"There isn't an old deed," Beth declared.

"There's no deed?"

"Not one. This is an orphan."

"An orphan?" the agent asked.

Beth's friend explained to the man about the term and how this property fit it. She showed him the property pin they had found and pointed out the way the line should go, which was right through the neighbor's carport.

He said again, "Well, I don't know if the owner will do the survey."

Beth replied, "That's fine, that means this property has a cloud on it and we won't be able to make an offer." Then she shook the man's hand and walked toward the house. Elaina and Vince stood and talked to their neighbors as the agent walked away, looking confused.

The next week a survey crew was on the scene, taking measurements, and doing all the things they do. Elaina laughed when she saw them pull into the driveway.

"Look, Vince! Our girl got her way."

Vince looked through the window, watching the crew unload their equipment and laughed. "She's something, isn't she?"

Once the survey was in, they made an offer on the house. Their landlady's nephew was doing the negotiations as her power of attorney and returned a counteroffer of double what they had offered.

Elaina wept when she saw the paper. "There's no way we can do that."

"There's no way you *would* do that, Mom. You guys know this house. You know about the sagging foundations, the floors propped up by an iron pole and wood blocks. There's $50,000-worth of repairs that need to be made!"

"I know, but I really wanted to stay here."

"What if we could find you a nice little house that would be all yours without the expense?"

"You could do that?"

"Of course we could! I know a Realtor and will get him to show me some houses. When I find a couple that I think would work for you, I'll grab you guys and take you to see them."

Though eighty-one years old, Elaina clapped her hands like a child. "That will be fun! Do you remember when we went looking at all those mobile homes to find the right one?"

"I sure do. Now we'll find the right place for you."

"Hey, 'Laina! Beth's coming over in a little bit to pick us up."

"What? I was about to start supper, and I'm not dressed for going out."

"Get your drawers on, Granny—we're going house hunting."

"Oh!" she cried, dropping the potatoes back into the bin and sliding the still-wrapped chicken back into the refrigerator. "I'll be ready in ten minutes!"

Vince laughed. He knew she was always ready to go and do no matter what. That was one thing she and his mother had in common. All anyone had to do was say, 'Do you want to go...' and they were ready.

Beth talked about the first house they were headed to. She said it was a foreclosure and had some work that needed to be done. She said it was pretty yucky inside, but it would be a good starting point. When she turned down the driveway, Elaina could feel her heart pounding. This was so beautiful with huge oak and maple trees, and they were only five minutes from downtown. When Beth turned off the car, Elaina stared at the little white frame house with a covered porch across the front.

When she stepped out of the car, she said simply, "This is it."

"Well, Mom, you haven't seen the inside yet. It's pretty rough," Beth reminded her.

"That doesn't matter," she said. "This is it. This is my house. It's mine."

Chapter 63

Entering the house, they walked into a little living room with plenty of windows. There was a bedroom just off that room, another down the hall, and a third off the kitchen. They could tell that carpet had been on the floors in the bedrooms, but was now gone. The kitchen was big enough to put a table in to eat there, and there was a utility room or mud room where the back door was. In the back of the house was a nice deck, and an above ground pool that looked more like a frog pond.

"How much of this land goes with the house?" Vince asked Beth.

"Everything from this fence to that one, to the trees in the front and the fence at the back. There's just over three-quarters of an acre."

"Really? That much?" Vince commented.

As they walked the length of the deck, Elaina looked at Vince. She hoped he could see in her eyes her excitement about this house. Yes, that utility room stank. It seemed to have been used as a kennel and was pretty nasty, but that could all be cleaned up. They could put down some flooring and paint here and there, and this house would be perfect for them.

"Okay, I have two more for y'all to see this evening," Beth said, guiding them back out to the car. While she locked the door, Elaina told Vince, "This is it, honey. This is our house."

"I don't know, 'Laina. It's small and I'm not sure we can get that floor in the first bedroom leveled up. And that back room. What on earth were those people thinking to let their animals live in that mess?"

Elaina nodded, riding quietly to the other two houses. The first was in an older subdivision where the neighbors were quite close. She didn't like that. The price was right and there wasn't as much work to be done, but it didn't feel right. The last house had a bit of a yard, but just didn't feel cozy enough. Her mind was made up.

Within a month they closed the deal on the little house she loved, and the family went to work getting it ready. They had been able to get a loan through the electric company to replace the HVAC unit. Ean and Tim and a friend leveled up the floor in the first bedroom that they were going to use as a fun room, where they could play cards or dominoes when friends would come over. They put down all new laminate flooring throughout the bedrooms, kitchen, and utility room.

"Come on, Grandma!" Tabitha said, and they whisked her off to the home improvement store to choose the colors for her new home. It was a bit overwhelming, but she and Beth helped her choose colors that were soft and pretty and made her feel happy.

Then, Tabitha enlisted her mother and sister and some friends to help get the painting done. Beth spent hours getting the utility room ready to paint. She'd had to clean up a lot of pet waste and seal the floors and part of the walls with something that would finally kill that smell.

Outside the back door, they stood on an open deck that surrounded the aboveground pool. It was obvious the pool hadn't been used in a long time. Elaina wasn't sure there weren't trout swimming in that water.

Once the closing was complete, everyone set to work getting it ready to move in to. New flooring, a new heat and air unit, lots of cleaning, new paint, and it was soon all theirs.

The new house was almost ready, so Beth and Tabitha met at their old house to get stuff packed up. Elaina wasn't sure how she felt about that. She had always handled that, but she had to admit it was nice to have someone else do all that sorting and lifting and moving.

The hard part was when they would bring something to her to ask her if she wanted to keep it or give it away or throw it away. All this was her stuff. She and Vince had gathered all this over their fifty-five years together. Why, some of those knick-knacks were older than Beth!

"Grandma, I think you have enough of these old address labels!" Tabitha said, walking into the living room with a stack of them in her hands.

"Don't throw those away. I might need those," Elaina said quickly.

"Grandma, you're moving," Tabitha said wryly.

"I know that, but I'll need these when I send in the bills."

"Grandma, this won't be your address after next week."

Elaina shook her head. She should have realized that. What was wrong with her thinking?

"I guess you're right, Miss Priss." she called her daughter by a favorite nickname.

She stopped in her tracks then said, "I'll be right back," and walked into the bathroom.

She had been talking to Tabitha, not Beth. But in her mind she was talking to her daughter, not her granddaughter. She knew which was which, but sometimes it got mixed up on her tongue. After splashing some water on her face, she lifted the fluffy towel to her face and patted it dry. "Get it together, old girl," she murmured to herself.

The next weekend was the big move. Ean and Beth showed up with a bunch of folks from their church, along with Tim and Tabitha. In a matter of minutes, they had the old house emptied and were driving to the new house. Once there, Ean had her and Vince sit down on the front porch to keep from being run over. Two old folks might get hurt that way. Elaina watched in wonder as the people worked together to move their bed and furniture off the trailers and into the house. It was amazing to see the teamwork and hear the laughter. She could hear Beth and Tabitha directing where everything would go inside the house.

She took her husband's hand. "I think we'll be sleeping here tonight."

"I think you're right. I might need a nap before then, though. All this moving is wearing me out!" They laughed easily together.

Before long, everyone but family stopped by to tell them goodbye and headed out to spend their Saturday enjoying themselves. Elaina told every one of them how much she appreciated their help, that they couldn't have done it without them.

Chapter 64

The summer of 2011, just six months after moving into their new home, Elaina was driving to the doctor's office. As she pulled onto the main road from the side road, she heard a car horn blast behind her. Startled, she pulled over into the left lane so the other driver could go on by. Suddenly, she was hearing a car horn in front of her so she moved back into the right lane. That guy behind her never came up past her. What on earth was going on with these people? She shook her head.

The doctor did some tests on her and told her to return the next week. She liked Dr. Potter. He was the only general practitioner she had seen up here. He was so kind and conscientious. She drove to the grocery store to pick up a few items, then drove home.

That evening, the phone rang.

"Hello?" she answered.

"Mom?" Beth's voice.

"Hey! How are you?"

"I'm good. Mom, are you okay?"

She heard concern in her daughter's voice. "Yeah, I'm okay. I saw Dr. Potter today and he did some blood work. I have to go back next week. He's always got to check something, you know."

"Yeah, he's funny like that, Mom. When is your appointment next week?"

"Oh, it's sometime on Thursday, no. It's Tuesday. Oh, hold on. I've got the card in my purse. Hold on." She lifted her purse from its resting place and burrowed into the pocket where she always kept appointment cards and retrieved the one she had gotten that afternoon.

"Here we go. It's Thursday at one o'clock. Right after lunch. I like to get him then so it doesn't take so long to see him," Elaina said.

"Great! How about I come and take you out to lunch then go with you to the doctor?" Beth offered.

"That would be nice, sweetheart, but you don't have to do that. I know you're busy."

"Not too busy to take my mom out for lunch, I'm not. Let's see, I should probably pick you up about eleven-thirty to give us an hour to eat."

"That sounds good, Beth. I'm looking forward to it."

"Me too, Mom. I love you. Can I talk to Dad?"

"Sure, honey. I love you, too."

Elaina handed the phone to Vince and listened for a moment as he talked to their daughter. She listened as he began some story she'd heard a million times, then left the room to clean up the kitchen. It was good that father and daughter were talking now.

Their lunch was fun. They went to McAllister's Deli. After eating their fill, they headed to the doctor's office.

Elaina liked this doctor's office. She had been a patient with them for so long, everyone knew her and treated her well. She enjoyed the attention heaped on her from the front door to the examination room. On this day she went along like usual, but with Beth in tow. She introduced her daughter to those who didn't already know her. Once they were seated in the examination room, Beth went across the hall to the restroom. She considered doing the same once Beth returned.

The nurse had already been in and taken her temperature and blood pressure. It was pretty good this time. Elaina had been taking medicine for it for as long as she could remember. Beth went over all her medicines with the nurse while she listened. She couldn't remember what she was taking half the time. She just knew to take one of these round ones in the morning, one of these pink ones in the evening, and so on. Beth would ask her what each one was for, and she knew sort of what they were for, but couldn't really explain it.

When the doctor came in, he shook Beth's hand. She had been his patient long ago and they caught up for a moment. The doctor looked at Elaina's blood work results and declared that she was in good shape. Then he did a strange thing. He asked her about her memory. She told him that she would forget some things but that she was doing okay, nothing unusual.

"Would you mind if we did a few tests to just check you out?" Dr. Potter asked. "I just want to get a gauge of how you're doing."

"I guess that would be okay," Elaina replied, looking to her daughter for confirmation.

When Beth nodded with her bright smile, she felt better. She knew Dr. Potter wouldn't hurt her, but she trusted Beth to be sure she was taken care of.

The nurse came back in and ran her through different tests that were unlike any medical testing she had ever had.

"Okay Mrs. Koebner, can you tell me what year this is?" the pretty nurse asked.

"It's 1975," Elaina replied.

"And what season are we in?"

"Oh, it's hot as a pistol outside. It's summertime."

The nurse laughed. "Which month of the summer is it?"

Elaina thought for a moment. "I think it's August. Is it August?" She looked to Beth for the answer.

"No cheating on your test, young lady!" the nurse chided.

"Well, she's not telling me anyway," Elaina returned. "August."

"Great. Now, can you tell me where we are?"

"Oh, well, we're at Dr. Potter's office."

"We sure are, Mrs. Koebner. You're doing great. Now, I'm going to name three objects and I want you to remember them for me, okay?"

Elaina nodded and paid close attention.

"Here are your words: pen, orange, shoe."

Elaina repeated the three words back to the nurse.

"Okay, now you remember those three for me while we count backwards from 100 by sevens."

"By sevens? I wasn't good with math when I was a schoolgirl! Let's see, one hundred," she counted back on her fingers, "ninety-three, eighty-six, ninety..." she shook her head. "I can't do that."

"Can you spell 'world' backwards?"

"Backwards? Why do you want everything backwards? Huh, well, the world is a little backwards sometimes." She grinned at Beth, who grinned back at her. "That would be D-L-R-O-W."

"Very good, Mrs. Koebner. Can you remember those three objects I asked you to remember?"

Elaina looked at Beth, who just raised her eyebrows. Then she looked at the nurse and recalled how she had held up her pen when she said the word.

"Pen and..." She shook her head, and kept trying to draw up the other two words. She looked down at the floor and saw her feet, "shoe!"

The nurse nodded, wrote on the piece of paper, then asked, "Can you name these two things?" She held up a pencil and her wristwatch.

Elaina rolled her eyes, "That's a pencil," she pointed to it, "and that's a wristwatch."

"I know some of these questions seem downright ridiculous, but these are what we have to go through," the nurse commiserated. "Can you say, 'no ifs, ands, or buts'?"

Elaina repeated those easily enough and listened for her next instruction.

"Okay, Mrs. Koebner, I'm going to hand you this paper. I need for you to take it in your right hand, fold it in half, and with your left hand lay it on the floor."

Elaina frowned and asked the nurse to repeat all that. When she had, Elaina held out her right hand and took the piece of paper. She folded it over, making sure the corners were lined up, then she folded it over again. Then she held the paper in her right hand, looked at it and leaned over to lay it on the floor.

"There. All done," she declared.

"Yes, ma'am. Thank you." The nurse picked up the paper, wrote on it, then asked Elaina to do what the words said.

Elaina looked at the paper and read the words, 'Close your eyes' and closed her eyes. Then she opened one and said, "If I close them for too long, it will become a nap."

When the three of them finished laughing, the nurse handed her a pen and asked her to write a sentence. Any sentence.

"Just make something up?" she asked.

"Yes, ma'am."

Elaina closed her eyes for a brief moment then wrote "I love you" and handed the paper back.

"Aw, thank you, Mrs. Koebner. Okay, one last thing. If you would, please look at this drawing and then draw it on your paper. Can you do that?" The drawing showed two interlocked pentagons.

"I don't know," Elaina answered hesitantly. "This is like math. I'm not too good at drawing."

"It's okay. It doesn't have to be perfect, just give it your best."

Elaina placed the pen on the paper and slowly drew a square and about an inch away from it drew a lopsided rectangle. She looked at them, looked at the example, then pushed the paper to the nurse.

"That's the best I can do," she stated.

"That's exactly what we wanted, Mrs. Koebner." The nurse patted her hand. "I'll give these to Dr. Potter and he'll be back in shortly."

"Hurry up and wait, huh?" Elaina said to her daughter. "I hate that this is taking up your whole day."

"I planned for it, Mom. My afternoon is all yours."

She smiled hearing that. She hated to be an imposition, knowing that Beth had her own life and business. That she had cleared up her schedule just for her mom was really nice.

Dr. Potter came back in and sat down. He looked at the paper in his hands and at his computer, then at Elaina.

"Well, Mrs. Koebner, we did the mental status test and what we're seeing is that there might be some short term memory issues going on here as well as some other issues. It looks like we might be looking at some mild to moderate Alzheimer's or dementia."

Elaina gasped. Looking quickly at Beth she thought she saw tears welling up in her eyes. She swallowed hard. Could this be why she was having such a hard time finding things at home, or why she kept missing appointments?

"Oh, my. Well, what does that mean?" she asked the doctor, remembering her dear friend Janice dying in the nursing home after so long with the disease.

"We can put you on some medication that sometimes helps in this situation. It doesn't cure it, but it tends to slow down the progression. If you want, I can refer you to the university neuroscience department where they can give a more conclusive diagnosis." He glanced at Beth. "They have other tests and doctors who only deal with these sorts of issues. They're the ones who diagnosed that famous women's basketball coach."

"Okay." Elaina was feeling overwhelmed.

"It's all right, Mom. I'm getting all this down. We'll get it figured out."

"Sure, Mrs. Koebner. It just means there're some things we have to be more careful about. Tell me, have you noticed any problems recently when you're driving?"

Elaina remembered that guy honking his horn at her then never passing her, and recalled that trip to church a few weeks ago when she felt completely lost on the way home, even driving around downtown twice before recognizing the right road home.

"I might have some trouble, yes," she admitted, casting a glance at Beth.

"I thought you might. Listen, we don't want you to be scared or feel overwhelmed. Maybe it's time to let Beth do more of the driving for you. You took care of her all those years, now you can let her return the favor."

"Do you think so?" she asked the doctor, feeling like a burden was being lifted from her shoulders.

"I think it would be a good thing for you to give Beth your car keys, and when you need to go somewhere you just call her up. There's also friends and there are senior services that can help. I think you'll feel less stressed about driving if you don't have to do it."

Tears stung her eyes as she looked at him gratefully. "I'm so glad you said so. I got scared when I was driving just last week, and I didn't know how to get myself out of it."

Reaching out to hold her hand, Dr. Potter said, "See there? Now you won't have to be scared. I am certain that Beth will be sure that you can get where you need to be without being scared about it."

Elaina looked at her daughter, who nodded determinedly, then handed over her keys on the metal and leather keyring.

Once in the car, Elaina told her daughter, "I feel so much better now. I really did scare myself driving the other day."

"You didn't tell me about that, Mom," Beth replied.

"I didn't want to worry you!"

"It's okay. How about from now on, if something scares you you let me know?"

"I will."

"Great. Now, let's go get this prescription filled and we'll get you all settled back at home. Did you like your lunch today?"

"It was so good! I love their salads there. They're always so different."

Chapter 65

When mother and daughter arrived home Vince was sitting in his chair, asleep. He sat up in that chair almost all the time nowadays, Elaina mused. She walked over and swatted his foot propped up on the footrest of the recliner.

"Huh? What?" he called gruffly.

"Turn that blasted television down!" she said. "We need to tell you something."

Vince groggily reached for the television remote resting on the table beside his chair and began pushing the volume button. He was still recovering from his last fall. He had slipped on the sidewalk at church and broken his arm at the elbow. He had been home from the rehab at the nursing home about a week and still grumbled about having to use the walker with the unusual arm addition that kept pressure off his broken place. Elaina was glad she had the television in the bedroom. Sometimes all Vince wanted to watch was baseball and she just didn't like that. Ean and Beth had brought her a chair she could use in there and she enjoyed not having to watch hours on end of baseball.

"Well, did you two enjoy your lunch?" Vince asked the two women.

"Sure did, we used your credit card and went whole hog!" Beth retorted.

"Oh. Well, as long as you enjoyed it," Vince whined.

"We ate at that deli you and I go to on Sundays," Elaina replied. "It was really good."

"Did you bring me anything?" he inquired.

"Not a thing!" Beth said, rubbing her tummy, which caused her father to laugh aloud.

Turning serious, Vince asked, "What did the doctor say?"

Beth sat on the love seat and motioned for her mother to share.

"You tell him, Beth."

"Yes, ma'am. Mom has mild to moderate Alzheimer's dementia, Dad. She's having some trouble with remembering things and with the way she sees things. The doctor recommended that she not drive anymore. She handed me her keys before we left his office."

Vince nodded, thinking. "So, I'll have to take over the driving now. I can do that."

Beth shook her head. "Not yet you won't. The doctor and the physical therapist specifically said no driving because of that elbow. So, until you're cleared I'm your ride."

"I can drive!" Vince bellowed.

"I'm sure you know how!" Beth bellowed back. "It's just that while you're still recovering from that fall, you're not allowed to. If you drive now and have an accident, your insurance won't pay anything for it. Can you afford that?"

Elaina listened to the two bat the subject back and forth until she grew tired of the conversation. She wasn't sure the insurance would do that, but it sounded good. She had told

Beth that Vince's driving had scared her on numerous occasions, so she wasn't going to get in the middle of this.

"I'm going to lie down for a little bit before we have supper," she stated, rising from her plush rocking chair.

Beth jumped up and walked to her. "I love you, Mom. We'll get through this thing, don't worry. Don't forget to add these new pills to your medicine box." She pressed the bottle of tablets into Elaina's hand.

"All right. I won't forget. Be careful going home, honey. I love you."

She went into her room and set the bottle of pills on top of her medicine box and slipped off her shoes. She turned the covers back on the bed and slipped under them. This felt so good. She lifted the remote control for the television and turned it on, thinking she should be able to catch the last episode of Law & Order for the day, and then she dozed off.

How long had it been since she had given up driving? Nowadays she had a hard time remembering how old she was.

"Let's see." She thought hard for a moment. "I was born in nineteen…" Elaina squeezed her eyes shut, trying to bring the date to her mind. It was harder and harder to do. "Thirty!" she said suddenly. "And today it's nineteen… no. It's two-thousand…" She squeezed her eyes closed again, then looked at the date on the day's newspaper. "Twelve!" That was it. She quickly scribbled the two dates on the edge of her word search puzzle and subtracted to determine her age. "I'm eighty-two years old?" she queried her empty bedroom. "Huh. I'm eighty-two. I'm an old lady now." She lay the puzzle down and finished dressing.

Not driving wasn't really too bad. The couple who lived down the road a bit would stop by and pick them up on their way to the senior center to play dominoes on Friday mornings. That was actually nice, to have that time to visit with them.

"I really like the—oh, what is their name? It was just on the tip of my tongue," Elaina mused.

Beth had called last night and told her to be ready for a doctor's visit. What doctor would this be? It didn't matter. They weren't going to be able to fix what ailed her. She chuckled as she fluffed her freshly washed hair. Now she would just put on her shoes and be ready to go.

"Good morning, Mom!" she heard Beth's voice in the hallway.

"Morning!" She finished tying her shoe and stood up.

"Not going to wear your new shoes?" her daughter asked.

"They hurt my toe. It just kills me."

"Which toe does it hurt, Mom?" A note of concern in Beth's voice.

"That second one. The way my big toe leans over those shoes are just too tight, and they hurt my toe."

Beth sighed. "Mom, we just got you those new shoes and had the perfect fitting done."

Elaina thought for a moment. She didn't remember having any shoe fitting done. She waved her hand in the air with exasperation. "Well, it hurts my toe."

"The toe we had surgery on a few months ago?"

"That surgery was ages ago. They removed that toe, and now it still hurts."

"Not that surgery, Mom. The one where they fixed the bunion and— you know what? Never mind. We'll just go with these. Don't forget your purse."

Beth walked into the living room and spoke with Vince. "Sure you don't want to go with us?" she asked.

"Nah, I'll stay here and hold down the fort."

"Are we afraid the fort is going to try to go somewhere?" Their joking never ended.

Elaina stepped into the living room, her lipstick freshly applied, holding her purse and a light jacket. She knew she would get cold in the doctor's office. She always did.

Vince got up from his chair, pushed his walker out of the way, and hugged her close. "You girls go out and have a good time."

"We will. We'll think about you when we have lunch."

They drove to the university hospital and found a parking place. It seemed like they had to walk miles, and she had to sit down for a moment to catch her breath, but then they got seated in a lovely waiting room. There was a big aquarium and a television she could watch. Beth filled out the paperwork. She had all the information down and Elaina didn't even have to think about it.

At first, Elaina thought the doctor was another nurse, then she realized the doctor was wearing the prettiest bright red high heels. She smiled, remembering that once upon a time she could wear shoes like that.

The doctor went over all the questions the nurse had asked, then had her to go into the hallway and walk down it.

"I believe, based on the answers you gave and the gait test we did, taking into account the tests your primary doctor did, that Mrs. Koebner has mid-stage Alzheimer's Disease and vascular dementia." She went on to explain that to Beth, but Elaina's mind went to her brother, Alec. He had had hardening of the arteries for several years before he died. Was this the same thing?

"Mrs. Koebner?" the doctor inquired.

"Yes?" she replied.

"I want to change the medicines Dr. Potter has you on. This new one should help you not have such a hard time with your memory. And the crying you told me about, I have some medicine that will help with that. I'm giving you a sample of it. If that helps, you'll be able to get the prescription filled. Does that sound good to you?"

"I guess, so. I like your shoes, Doctor."

"Thank you so much! I try to wear something bright and happy in the office. Now, I've given your daughter the samples and the paperwork. You should be good to go until we see you again in three months." Elaina felt so confused, but tried to listen as the doctor took her hand. "You're fine, Mrs. Koebner, just a few little wiring mishaps here and there. We're going to do all we can to take great care of you. If you need me, Beth has my phone number. You just call me and we'll get you in here to take care of you."

"Okay," she replied, returning the squeeze the doctor gave her hand.

Elaina followed Beth back to the car, and they drove to Olive Garden. Once they had ordered and had begun eating their salad and bread sticks, Elaina asked, "What did that pretty doctor think is wrong with me? She didn't even look at my toes."

Beth smiled. "It's okay, Mom. She's not going to work on your toes. She's the doctor to help with your memory."

"Oh." Elaina took a bite of salad.

"Mom, I'm going to be right here with you. I'm not going anywhere."

"I don't want to go to a home somewhere, Beth. I want to be at my house." She felt the tears run down her cheeks.

"No way, Mom!" her daughter exclaimed. "You've got to stay there and keep Dad in line!"

"Somebody has to," she agreed.

Chapter 66

It was her third visit to the pretty memory doctor and the first one since she fell in the middle of the night. That was a rough few days! She had bonked her head on the floor and her rings had caught on something and almost took her finger off. And goodness, the bruises! She had looked like she had been in a boxing match. Now she was healed up from all that, but she felt bad. She couldn't explain it. The only place she felt completely safe was in her room in their house, and even there some man kept sneaking in and lying down in the bed with her. When she would wake up in the middle of the night and he was there, she would beat him and kick him until he ran out of her room.

Elaina enjoyed going out on the deck at the back of their house. The sun would be so warm and inviting and she could look over her roses. They had grown so big and were so pretty. Someone had planted those for her there, but she couldn't remember who. Must have been Vince. He was always such a gardener.

Now she sat in the examination room again, listening as the doctor and Beth discussed the fall and the dizzy spell and her stays in the hospital.

"So, Mrs. Koebner, tell me how you're feeling now."

Elaina shrugged, and muttered, "Okay, I guess."

The doctor made a note, nodding her head, and said, "You don't sound too happy about something. Is there something wrong?"

"I fell. Did Beth tell you about that? I had to stay in the hospital."

"She did tell me. She also told me that you don't like to come out of your room much anymore."

Elaina lifted a shoulder, a half-shrug as though she didn't care enough to fully shrug.

"Can you answer a question for me, Mrs. Koebner?" the doctor asked.

Elaina nodded.

"Do you want to keep going? Do you want to live?"

Shaking her head slowly, Elaina answered, "Not really."

"I understand. It's been rough lately, hasn't it?"

"Yes, it has," Elaina replied.

She heard the doctor talking to Beth about some medicine she could consider. She said something about side effects, that it could cause some kind of problems, but that it should make her feel better about life and living.

She lifted her eyes to see her daughter taking a bag of samples from the doctor.

"Mrs. Koebner, I think this will help you feel better. We want you to be able to go outside and enjoy those roses, and maybe even go play dominoes some. Would that be good to you?"

"Yeah, it would be nice," Elaina replied absently.

Once they were home and Beth had made her go ahead and take one of the new pills, Elaina lay down. She felt like her whole body and head were too heavy to hold up. She felt the bed shift and looked up to see her daughter sitting there.

"I love you, Mom. You just rest this afternoon. It was a big day! Dad will call you when he gets supper ready; will you promise me you'll eat some?"

What was it with these two always fussing at her to eat? She ate all the time! Just because they didn't see her eat didn't mean it wasn't happening.

"Yes, dear. I'll eat something later on. You go on home and get your work done. Thank you for taking such good care of me."

"You're welcome! Thank you for going with me today."

The bedroom door closed, leaving her alone in the darkness. She liked it like this. She lifted the remote to turn on the television, switching to the channel that showed old western shows, and promptly fell asleep.

It was a lovely Tuesday morning. Elaina dressed and went into the kitchen to fix herself a cup of coffee and a slice of toast. She swiped some peanut butter onto the toasted bread, then carried her breakfast into the living room where Vince sat reading the paper and napping. She felt good today. She had been feeling a lot better the past few months. More like living. She still didn't want to leave the house. It was her safe place. But now she spent time working on the jigsaw puzzles Beth kept her supplied with, along with the word search puzzles she had handy. She had helped do the laundry yesterday. She was trying to teach Vince how to do it right, and most of the time now he did pretty good.

Vince asked her how she was feeling and checked to see if she had taken her medicine that morning. She told him she had and asked if he had taken his. This was their ritual to keep each other on their toes.

About ten o'clock, Ean and Beth's pastor dropped by. She liked this guy. He was so unlike any pastors she had ever known. He asked how she was feeling and she told him of the fall a few months ago.

"I heard about that. We were praying for you the whole time, Mrs. Elaina."

"But I'm doing pretty good today. I've been working on a puzzle. Do you want to see it?"

"I sure would!" he said.

The preacher followed her into the spare room they used to show off their accomplishments and enjoy games. They had a drop-leaf table that she was currently using to put together the puzzle bright with cardinals and gold finches.

"That's going to be real pretty, Mrs. Elaina," he told her.

"I think so," she said, nimbly dropping a piece into place. "See there? I found a piece just now. That's how I always do it. I find a piece or two, then I go do something else."

They returned to the living room where they talked on about different things, then Vince brought up their youngest grandson and the trouble he was in. Currently in jail, Vince kept trying to think of ways to fix the boy.

Elaina shook her head. "I figured out all I can do is pray for him, so I do."

"I think you're right, Mrs. Elaina. We can't do anything, but God can do everything," the pastor stated.

He had said his goodbyes, then she and Vince had their lunch. Some lovely folks came by every day and brought packages of hot meals to them. She didn't always like what they brought, but they were so kind to bring them something she couldn't refuse it.

Elaina finished brushing her teeth after lunch and walked into the living room again. She heard Vince saying, "Here she is, I'll let you talk to her."

"Hello?" she said into the telephone.

"'Laina?" she heard the voice of her sister-in-law, Mary.

"Oh, it's so good to hear from you!" she said.

The two talked nearly an hour, sharing what was going on in their lives. Elaina told her about the preacher having just left and how she liked that one. When they finished talking, she went into her bedroom for a brief nap while her stories were on. Vince didn't like watching those, so she left him with college basketball and went to rest and enjoy her shows.

She got up around four o'clock and was sitting in her chair when she heard Vince starting supper. She had seen some pork chops by the sink earlier. She liked those. Maybe he would make gravy tonight. She was feeling a little hungry.

An hour later, Elaina pushed back from the table. "That was so good," she told her husband.

"I did do pretty good, didn't I?" He tucked his thumbs into his shirt, pretending to brag.

She laughed. It had been a good dinner. Not only was the food good, but they had talked and talked. It had been forever since they'd talked like that. They remembered living near the Glades, some of the jobs he had worked on, some of the friends they had seen come and go over the years. They had laughed a lot. She carried their plates to the sink.

"I'll take care of those in a little bit," Vince said, following her with the rest of the dishes to be washed. He reached around her to place them in the sink, successfully giving her a hug, too.

"I love you, Grandma," he whispered in her ear.

"I love you, too" she replied softly. And she did. He was a good husband, had always made sure they had enough to eat and a place to live. They were never rich, but they were comfortable. Even now, living on retirement benefits, they had this beautiful place to live.

They walked to the living room together where they both sat down. They watched the news, each giving commentary on the various stories. When the news went off, Elaina stood up.

"I'm going to get washed up and get ready for bed," she stated as she walked to the bedroom to get her nightgown and slippers.

She walked into the bathroom and turned on the hot water to let it run and get warm. She slipped her shoes off and had just dropped her socks into the hamper, when she felt herself falling. She didn't reach out to stop herself and she wasn't afraid.

She saw her daddy there, just beyond her reach. He was beckoning her to come on, like he did when they were headed to the fields.

She dropped everything and ran to him.

Acknowledgments

MY REASON
First to my Lord and Savior, Jesus Christ who is my
strength, my comfort, my shield and my safety.
Mom felt the same way.

THE WOMEN
who have loved me and poured into me and helped me
grow into the survivor I am today.
Lula Hayes Dover, Roberta Dover Stoeffler
Una Pollard, Betty Pollard, Sue Benson,
Elizabeth Stoeffler, Rhonda Wigington, Jan McCoy,
Ellie Mann, and Kay Dillard

THE ENCOURAGERS
who constantly remind me that I can do all things through Christ.
Parker Benson, Darren Wigington
Brenda Haire, Nicole Smith, Norma Johnson
Erik & Jamie Swanson, Chris & LaDonna Taylor,
and Kary Oberbrunner

MY BEST FRIEND and CHIEF SUPPORTER
Jack Bryant

MY FAMILY
who love and support me always.
Chris W. Love, Chris Bryant, Travis Bryant
Nicholas Bryant, Dylan Bryant, Shaylie Bryant
Angela McNeese, and Tanisha Bryant

THE HELPERS WITHOUT WHOM THIS BOOK WOULDN'T BE
My Amazing Beta Readers
who endured the reading of the raw material so you
wouldn't have to.
Beth Huneycutt, Lorie Gurnett,
Ginger Holloway, and Laurie Head

My Most Excellent Editor
who dug in to all the material, questioned me about
phrasing and why is this happening here until the finished
product you hold in your hands was a reality.
Kim Huther

My Amazing Cover Designer
(Isn't it beautiful?)
He listened to my every request and turned my thoughts
into reality.
Bien Swinton

Book Trailer
View at bit.ly/Book2Elaina
Marco del Rio for producing the beautiful trailer
and
Teri Austin for giving Elaina a voice.

About the Author

Faye Bryant grew up hearing the stories of her family and has used those stories of life and death, betrayal and reconciliation, faith and family to create the **Grandma, Mom, and Me Saga.** First in the series was *Louise,* and the final installment will be *Beth,* due out in early fall of 2020.

She is also the author of *Ramblings from the Shower | Integrity, Faith, and Other Simple Yet Slippery Issues* as well as *Coffee, Bible, Journal: Musings from the Comfy Chair with a View.*

Faye struggled under the weight of many layers of a past that kept her hidden and helpless. All that has changed. Through an ongoing process of recovery, she has discovered who she was created to be. Now she is the founder of Build a Better Legacy, dedicated to helping those held captive by past family trauma or choices to grow past surviving to thriving.

Faye and her husband, Jack, live in a beautiful valley in the Smoky Mountains.

Connect at: FayeBryant.com

Explore the Build A Better Legacy Experience.

It's time to move past your past into a life well-lived and a history well-preserved.

Learn how to examine your past and your family's past without getting lost in it.

Determine what it means to really be you.

Imagine author Faye Bryant leading you through a life-changing process where you move past your past and grow into the person you were meant to be, and leave a healthy and happy inheritance for those who will follow you.

Get started today at FAYEBRYANT.COM

What's the cost of not intentionally changing YOUR LEGACY?

"The most damaging thing in the life of a child is the unlived life of the parent." Carl Jung

"The two most important days of your life are the day you were born and the day you discover why." Mark Twain

Let Faye Bryant help you discover *your* why and write *your* OPUS to help you say yes to the people and events that matter most and no to those that don't; take control of your calendar and experience margin once again; and create a life worth living defined by purpose and passion.

Visit FayeBryant.com/Coach to start your journey today.

CPSIA information can be obtained
at www.ICGtesting.com
Printed in the USA
BVHW071047121219
566475BV00001B/182/P

9 781640 857490